...NG

'Stands with Alan Furst for authentic detail and atmosphere'
Donald James, author of *Monstrum,* on *Zoo Station*

'Think Robert Harris and *Fatherland* mixed
with a dash of Le Carré'
Sue Baker, *Publishing News,* on *Zoo Station*

'A wonderfully d............................spicious début,

'Excellent an............................ength is his
fleshing out o............................us nature of
eve...e'

'An extra...............................ermany'

'Exciting and frightening all at once . . . It's got everything
going for it'
Julie Walters

'One of the brightest lights in the shadowy world of historical
spy fiction'
Birmingham Post

ALSO BY DAVID DOWNING

Silesian Station
Stettin Station
Potsdam Station

David Downing is the author of numerous works of fiction and non-fiction. His first 'John Russell and Effi Koenen' novel, *Zoo Station*, was published by Old Street in 2007, and became a word-of-mouth bestseller. It was followed by *Silesian Station* in 2008, *Stettin Station* in 2009 and *Potsdam Station* in 2010. He lives in Surrey with his wife and two cats.

ZOO STATION

DAVID DOWNING

First published in 2007 by Old Street Publishing Ltd.

This edition published in 2011 by Old Street Publishing Ltd.
Yowlestone House, Tiverton, Devon EX16 8LN

www.oldstreetpublishing.co.uk

ISBN 978-1-906964-58-0

Copyright © David Downing 2007

In memory of

Martha Pappenheim (1900-2001)
who escaped from Germany in 1939
and went on to help the children of
those who did not, and

Yvonne Pappenheim (1912-2005)
who married Martha's brother Fritz,
and spent a lifetime fighting injustice

AUTHOR'S NOTE

This is a work of fiction, but every attempt has been made to keep within the bounds of historical possibility. References to the Nazis' planned murder of the mentally handicapped are mostly taken from Michael Burleigh's exhaustive history *Death and Deliverance*, and even the more ludicrous of the news stories mentioned in passing are depressingly authentic.

Into the blue

There were two hours left of 1938. In Danzig it had been snowing on and off all day, and a gang of children were enjoying a snowball fight in front of the grain warehouses which lined the old waterfront. John Russell paused to watch them for a few moments, then walked on up the cobbled street towards the blue and yellow lights.

The Sweden Bar was far from crowded, and those few faces that turned his way weren't exactly brimming over with festive spirit. In fact, most of them looked like they'd rather be somewhere else.

It was an easy thing to want. The Christmas decorations hadn't been removed, just allowed to drop, and now formed part of the flooring, along with patches of melting slush, floating cigarette ends and the odd broken bottle. The bar was famous for the savagery of its international brawls, but on this particular night the various groups of Swedes, Finns and Letts seemed devoid of the energy needed to get one started. Usually a table or two of German naval ratings could be relied upon to provide the necessary spark, but the only Germans present were a couple of ageing prostitutes, and they were getting ready to leave.

Russell took a stool at the bar, bought himself a *Goldwasser* and glanced through the month-old copy of the *New York Herald Tribune* which, for some inexplicable reason, was lying there. One of his own articles was in it, a piece on German attitudes to their pets. It was accompanied by a cute-looking photograph of a Schnauzer.

Seeing him reading, a solitary Swede two stools down asked

him, in perfect English, if he spoke that language. Russell admitted that he did.

'You are English!' the Swede exclaimed, and shifted his considerable bulk to the stool adjoining Russell's.

Their conversation went from friendly to sentimental, and sentimental to maudlin, at what seemed like breakneck pace. Three *Goldwassers* later, the Swede was telling him that he, Lars, was not the true father of his children. Vibeke had never admitted it, but he knew it to be true.

Russell gave him an encouraging pat on the shoulder, and Lars sunk forward, his head making a dull clunk as it made contact with the polished surface of the bar. 'Happy New Year,' Russell murmured. He shifted the Swede's head slightly to ease his breathing, and got up to leave.

Outside, the sky was beginning to clear, the air almost cold enough to sober him up. An organ was playing in the Protestant Seamen's church, nothing hymnal, just a slow lament, as if the organist was saying a personal farewell to the year gone by. It was a quarter to midnight.

Russell walked back across the city, conscious of the moisture seeping in through the holes in his shoes. The Langermarkt was full of couples, laughing and squealing as they clutched each other for balance on the slippery pavements.

He cut over the Breite Gasse and reached the Holzmarkt just as the bells began pealing in the New Year. The square was full of celebrating people, and an insistent hand pulled him into a circle of revellers dancing and singing in the snow. When the song ended and the circle broke up, the Polish girl on his left reached up and brushed her lips against his, eyes shining with happiness. It was, he thought, a better than expected opening to 1939.

* * *

His hotel's reception area was deserted, and the sounds of celebration emanating from the kitchen at the back suggested the night staff were enjoying their own private party. Russell thought about making himself a hot chocolate and drying his shoes in one of the ovens, but decided against. He took his key, clambered up the stairs to the third floor, and trundled down the corridor to his room. Closing the door behind him, he became painfully aware that the occupants of the neighbouring rooms were still welcoming in the new year, a singsong on one side, floor-shaking sex on the other. He took off his sodden shoes and socks, dried his wet feet with a towel and sank back onto the vibrating bed.

There was a discreet, barely audible tap on his door.

Cursing, he levered himself off the bed and prised the door open. A man in a crumpled suit and open shirt stared back at him.

'Mr John Russell,' the man said in English, as if he was introducing Russell to himself. The Russian accent was slight, but unmistakable. 'Could I talk with you for a few minutes?'

'It's a bit late …' Russell began. The man's face was vaguely familiar. 'But why not?' he continued, as the singers next door reached for a new and louder chorus. 'A journalist should never turn down a conversation,' he murmured, mostly to himself, as he let the man in. 'Take the chair,' he suggested.

His visitor sat back and crossed one leg over the other, hitching up his trouser leg as he did so. 'We have met before,' he said. 'A long time ago. My name is Shchepkin. Yevgeny Grigorovich Shchepkin. We …'

'Yes,' Russell interrupted, as the memory clicked into place. 'The discussion group on journalism at the fifth Congress. The summer of '24.'

Shchepkin nodded his acknowledgement. 'I remember your contributions,' he said. 'Full of passion,' he added, his eyes circling the room and resting, for a few seconds, on his host's dilapidated shoes.

Russell perched himself on the edge of the bed. 'As you said – a long time ago.' He and Ilse had met at that conference, and set in motion their ten-year cycle of marriage, parenthood, separation and divorce. Shchepkin's hair had been black and wavy in 1924; now it was a close-cropped grey. They were both a little older than the century, Russell guessed, and Shchepkin was wearing pretty well, considering what he'd probably been through the last fifteen years. He had a handsome face of indeterminate nationality, with deep brown eyes above prominent slanting cheekbones, an aquiline nose and lips just the full side of perfect. He could have passed for a citizen of most European countries, and probably had.

The Russian completed his survey of the room. 'This is a dreadful hotel,' he said.

Russell laughed. 'Is that what you wanted to talk about?'

'No. Of course not.'

'So what are you here for?'

'Ah.' Shchepkin hitched his trouser leg again. 'I am here to offer you work.'

Russell raised an eyebrow. 'You? Who exactly do you represent?'

The Russian shrugged. 'My country. The Writers' Union. It doesn't matter. You will be working for us. You know who we are.'

'No,' Russell said. 'I mean, no I'm not interested. I ...'

'Don't be so hasty,' Shchepkin said. 'Hear me out. We aren't asking you to do anything which your German hosts could object to.' The Russian allowed himself a smile. 'Let me tell you exactly what we have in mind. We want a series of articles about positive aspects of the Nazi regime.' He paused for a few seconds, waiting in vain for Russell to demand an explanation. 'You are not German but you live in Berlin,' he went on. 'You once had a reputation as a journalist of the left, and though that reputation has, shall we say, faded, no one could accuse you of being an apologist for the Nazis ...'

'But you want me to be just that.'

'No, no. We want positive aspects, not a positive picture overall. That would not be believable.'

Russell was curious in spite of himself. Or because of the *Goldwassers*. 'Do you just need my name on these articles?' he asked. 'Or do you want me to write them as well?'

'Oh, we want you to write them. We like your style – all that irony.'

Russell shook his head – Stalin and irony didn't seem like much of a match.

Shchepkin misread the gesture. 'Look,' he said, 'let me put all my cards on the table.'

Russell grinned.

Shchepkin offered a wry smile in return. 'Well, most of them anyway. Look, we are aware of your situation. You have a German son and a German lady-friend, and you want to stay in Germany if you possibly can. Of course if a war breaks out you will have to leave, or else they will intern you. But until that moment comes – and maybe it won't, miracles do happen – until it does you want to earn your living as a journalist without upsetting your hosts. What better way than this? You write nice things about the Nazis – not too nice, of course, the articles have to be credible – but you stress their good side.'

'Does shit have a good side?' Russell wondered out loud.

'Come, come,' Shchepkin insisted, 'you know better than that. Unemployment eliminated, a renewed sense of community, healthy children, cruises for workers, cars for the people ...'

'You should work for Joe Goebbels.'

Shchepkin gave him a mock-reproachful look.

'OK,' Russell said, 'I take your point. Let me ask you a question. There's only one reason you'd want that sort of article – you're softening up your own people for some sort of deal with the devil. Right?'

Shchepkin flexed his shoulders in an eloquent shrug.

'Why?'

The Russian grunted. 'Why deal with the devil? I don't know what the leadership is thinking. But I could make an educated guess, and so could you.'

Russell could. 'The western powers are trying to push Hitler east, so Stalin has to push him west? Are we talking about a non-aggression pact, or something more?'

Shchepkin looked almost affronted. 'What more could there be? Any deal with that man can only be temporary. We know what he is.'

Russell nodded. It made sense. He closed his eyes, as if it were possible to blank out the approaching calamity. On the other side of the opposite wall, his musical neighbours were intoning one of those Polish river songs which could reduce a statue to tears. Through the wall behind him silence had fallen, but his bed was still quivering like a tuning fork.

'We'd also like some information,' Shchepkin was saying, almost apologetically. 'Nothing military,' he added quickly, seeing the look on Russell's face. 'No armament statistics or those naval plans that Sherlock Holmes is always being asked to recover. Nothing of that sort. We just want a better idea of what ordinary Germans are thinking. How they are taking the changes in working conditions, how they are likely to react if war comes – that sort of thing. We don't want any secrets, just your opinions. And nothing on paper. You can deliver them in person, on a monthly basis.'

Russell looked sceptical.

Shchepkin ploughed on. 'You will be well paid – very well. In any currency, any bank, any country, that you choose. You can move into a better rooming house …'

'I like my rooming house.'

'You can buy things for your son, your girlfriend. You can have your shoes mended.'

'I don't …'

'The money is only an extra. You were with us once …'

'A long, long time ago.'

'Yes, I know. But you cared about your fellow human beings. I heard you talk. That doesn't change. And if we go under there will be nothing left.'

'A cynic might say there's not much to choose between you.'

'The cynic would be wrong,' Shchepkin replied, exasperated and perhaps a little angry. 'We have spilt blood, yes. But reluctantly, and in faith of a better future. *They* enjoy it. Their idea of progress is a European slave-state.'

'I know.'

'One more thing. If money and politics don't persuade you, think of this. We will be grateful, and we have influence almost everywhere. And a man like you, in a situation like yours, is going to need influential friends.'

'No doubt about that.'

Shchepkin was on his feet. 'Think about it, Mr Russell,' he said, drawing an envelope from the inside pocket of his jacket and placing it on the nightstand. 'All the details are in here – how many words, delivery dates, fees, and so on. If you decide to do the articles, write to our press attaché in Berlin, telling him who you are, and that you've had the idea for them yourself. He will ask you to send him one in the post. The Gestapo will read it, and pass it on. You will then receive your first fee and suggestions for future stories. The last-but-one letters of the words in the opening sentence will spell out the name of a city outside Germany which you can reach fairly easily. Prague, perhaps, or Cracow. You will spend the last weekend of the month in that city. And be sure to make your hotel reservation at least a week in advance. Once you are there, someone will contact you.'

'I'll think about it,' Russell said, mostly to avoid further argu-ment. He wanted to spend his weekends with his son Paul and his girlfriend Effi, not the Shchepkins of this world.

The Russian nodded and let himself out. As if on cue, the Polish choir lapsed into silence.

Russell was woken by the scream of a locomotive whistle. Or at least, that was his first impression. Lying there awake all he could hear was a gathering swell of high-pitched voices. It sounded like a school playground full of terrified children.

He threw on some clothes and made his way downstairs. It was still dark, the street deserted, the tramlines hidden beneath a virginal sheet of snow. In the Hauptbahnhof booking hall a couple of would-be travellers were hunched in their seats, eyes averted, praying that they hadn't strayed into dangerous territory. Russell strode through the unmanned ticket barrier. There were trucks in the goods yard beyond the far platform, and a train which stretched out beyond the station throat. People were gathered under the yellow lights, mostly families by the look of them, because there were lots of children. And there were men in uniform. Brownshirts.

A sudden shrill whistle from the distant locomotive produced an eerie echo from the milling crowd, as if all the children had shrieked at once.

Russell took the subway steps two at a time, half-expecting to find that the tunnel had been blocked off. It hadn't. On the far side, he emerged into a milling crowd of shouting, screaming people. He had already guessed what was happening – this was a *Kindertransport*, one of the trains hired to transport the ten thousand Jewish children that Britain had agreed to accept after *Kristallnacht*. The shriek had risen at the moment the guards started separating the children from their parents, and the two groups were now being shoved apart by snarling Brownshirts. Parents were backing away, tears running down their cheeks, as their children were herded onto the train, some waving frantically, some almost reluctantly, as if they feared to recognise the separation.

Further up the platform a violent dispute was underway between an SA Truppführer and a woman with a red cross on her sleeve. Both were screaming at the other, he in German, she in northern-accented English. The woman was beside herself with anger, almost spitting in the Brownshirt's eye, and it was obviously taking all the control he had not to smash his fist in her face. A few feet away one of the mothers was being helped to her feet by another woman. Blood was streaming from her nose.

Russell strode up to them and flashed his Foreign Ministry press accreditation, which at least gave the man a new outlet for his anger.

'What the fuck are you doing here?' the Truppführer shouted. He had a depressingly porcine face, and the bulk to go with it.

'Trying to help,' Russell said calmly. 'I speak English.'

'Well then tell this English bitch to get back on the train with the kike brats where she belongs.'

Russell turned to the woman, a petite brunette who couldn't have been much more than twenty-five. 'He's not worth screaming at,' he told her in English. 'And it won't do you any good. In fact, you'll only make matters worse.'

'I …' She seemed lost for words.

'I know,' Russell said. 'You can't believe people could behave like this. But this lot do. All the time.'

As if to emphasise the point, the Truppführer man started shouting again. When she shouted back he seized her arm, and she kicked him in the shin. He backhanded her across the face with what seemed enormous force, spinning her round and dumping her face-first on the snowy platform. She groaned and shook her head.

Russell put himself between them. 'Look,' he said to the man, 'this will get you court-martialled if you're not careful. The Führer doesn't want you giving the English this sort of a propaganda victory. I know they're only kikes, and I'm sure you feel like I do – that we should put all the adults on the damn train with them, and get rid of the vermin once and for all – but that's for the Führer to decide, not us.'

The British woman was groggily raising herself onto all fours. The storm-trooper took one last look at his victim, made a 'pah!' noise that any pantomime villain would have been proud of and strode away down the platform.

Russell helped her to her feet.

'What did you say to him?' she asked, gingerly feeling an already swelling cheek.

'I appealed to his better nature.'

'There must be someone …' she began.

'There isn't,' he assured her. 'The laws don't apply to Jews, or anyone who acts on their behalf. Just look after the children. They look like they need it.'

'I don't need you to tell me …'

'I know you don't. I'm just trying …'

She was looking past his shoulder. 'He's coming back.'

The Truppführer had a Sturmführer with him, a smaller man

with round glasses and a chubby face. Out of uniform – assuming they ever took them off – he put them down as a shopkeeper and minor civil servant. Danzig's finest.

'Your papers,' the Sturmführer demanded.

'They're in my hotel room.'

'What is your name?'

'John Russell.'

'You are English?'

'I'm an English journalist. I live in the Reich, and I have full accreditation from the Ministry of Propaganda in Berlin.'

'We shall check that.'

'Of course.'

'And what are you doing here?'

'I came to see what was happening. As journalists do. I intervened in the argument between your colleague and this Red Cross worker because I thought his behaviour was damaging the reputation of the Reich.'

The Sturmführer paused for thought, then turned to his subordinate. 'I'm sure my colleague regrets any misunderstanding,' he said meaningfully.

The Truppführer looked at the woman. 'I apologise,' he said woodenly.

'He apologises,' Russell told her.

'Tell him to go to hell,' she said.

'She accepts your apology,' Russell told the two Brownshirts.

'Good. Now she must get back on the train, and you must come with us.'

Russell sighed. 'You should get on the train,' he told her. 'You won't get anywhere by protesting.'

She took a deep breath. 'All right,' she said, as if it was anything but. 'Thank you,' she added, offering her hand.

Russell took it. 'Tell the press when you get back to civilization,' he said. 'And good luck.'

He watched her mount the steps and disappear into the train. The children were all aboard now; most had their faces pressed against the windows, and were frantically wiping their breath from the glass to get a last clear look at their parents. A few had managed to force back the sliding ventilators and wedge their faces in the narrow gap. Some were shouting, some pleading. Most were crying.

Russell tore his gaze from the windows just in time to see a small girl leap nimbly down from the train and race across the platform. The storm-trooper by the door spun to catch her, but slipped in the slush as he did so, and fell face-first onto the platform. As he struggled to his feet a boy of around ten rushed past him.

The little girl's arms were tightly wrapped around her kneeling mother's neck. 'Esther, we have to get on the train,' the boy said angrily, but daughter and mother were both crying too hard to notice him. The father's anguished appeals to reason – 'Ruth, we have to let her go; Esther, you must go with your brother' – fell on equally deaf ears.

The storm-trooper, red-faced with anger, took a fistful of the girl's long black hair and yanked. The shock tore her arms from her mother's neck, and he started dragging the girl across the slush-strewn platform to the train. The mother shrieked and went after them. The man let go of the girl and crashed his rubber cosh across one side of the mother's face. She sank back, a rivulet of blood running onto her coat collar. As the storm-trooper went to hit the woman again, her husband grabbed for the cosh, but two other Brownshirts wrestled him to the ground, and started raining down blows on his head. The boy picked up his whimpering sister and shepherded her back onto the train.

More storm-troopers came racing up, but they needn't have

bothered. Like Russell, the watching parents were too stunned to protest, let alone intervene.

'I don't want to go,' a small voice said behind him.

He turned to find its owner. She was standing on a seatback in the train, her face twisted sideways in an open ventilator window, brown eyes brimming with tears. She couldn't have been more than five.

'Please, can you tell the policemen that I don't want to go? My name is Fräulein Gisela Kluger.'

Russell walked across to the train, wondering what on earth he could say. 'I'm afraid you have to make this trip,' he said. 'Your mother and father think you'll be safer in England.'

'But I don't want to,' she said, a large tear sliding down either cheek.

'I know, but ...' Another whistle shrilled down the platform; a spasm of steam escaped from the locomotive. 'I'm sorry,' he said helplessly.

The train jerked into motion. A momentary panic flitted across her face, followed by a look that Russell would long remember – one that blended accusation, incomprehension and the sort of grief that no five-year-old should have to bear.

As the train pulled away a tiny hand poked out through the window and waved.

'I'm sorry,' Russell murmured.

A hand grasped his arm. The Truppführer's. 'You, English. Come with us.'

He was ushered down the platform in the Sturmführer's wake. Most of the mothers and fathers were still focussed on the disappearing train, their eyes clinging to the red tail-light, the last flicker of family. They had sent their children away. To save their lives, they had turned them into orphans.

One woman, her eyes closed, was kneeling in the snow, a low keening noise rising up from inside her. The sound stayed with Russell as he was led out of the station. The sound of a heart caving in.

In the goods yard the Truppführer pushed him towards a car. 'My hotel's just across the road,' Russell protested.

'We will collect your papers,' the Sturmführer said.

As they bundled him into the car, it occurred to Russell that Shchepkin's envelope was still sitting on his nightstand.

Danzig was waking up as they drove back towards the city centre, shopkeepers clearing the night's snow off their patches of pavement. Russell kept his eyes on where they were going, hoping to God it wasn't some SA barracks out of humanity's hearing range. As they pulled up outside an official police station on Hundegasse he managed to suppress a sigh of relief.

The Truppführer pulled him out of the car and pushed him violently towards the entrance doors. Russell slipped in the snow, and fell onto the steps, catching a shin on one of the hard edges. He had no time to check the wound, though – the Truppführer was already propelling him forward.

Inside, a uniformed police officer was cradling a steaming cup of coffee. He looked up without much interest, sighed, and reached for the duty book. 'Name?'

Russell told him. 'I'm English,' he added.

The man was not impressed. 'We all have to come from somewhere. Now empty your pockets.'

Russell did as he was told. 'Who's in charge here?' he asked. 'The police or the SA?'

The policeman gave him a contemptuous look. 'Take a guess,' he suggested.

Russell felt a sinking sensation in his stomach. 'I want to speak to the British Consulate,' he said.

'No need for that,' the Truppführer said behind him. 'What's your hotel name and room number?' Armed with this information, he went back out through the doors. Russell had a glimpse of grey light in the eastern sky.

He tried pleading with the duty officer, and received a shrug for his pains. A younger policeman was summoned to take him downstairs, where two rows of cells lay either side of a dimly lit corridor. They had tiled floors and brick walls, black up to waist level, white above. It only needed a splash of blood to exhaust the Nazi palette.

Russell slumped to the floor, his back against the far wall. No need to feel frightened, he told himself. They wouldn't do any permanent damage to a foreign journalist.

They would if they thought he was a spy. What had Shchepkin put in the damn envelope? If Russell's past experience of Stalin's NKVD security police was anything to go by, there was an institutional reluctance to spell anything out which verged on paranoia. And they wouldn't want to leave him with anything he might conceivably use against them.

All of which was good news.

But what language was the damn letter written in? If it was in Russian, or if roubles were mentioned, that would be enough for goons like the Truppführer.

He told himself to calm down. He had talked himself out of worse situations than this.

His shin was oozing blood, but didn't look too bad. His stomach felt queasy, though whether from hunger or fear was hard to tell. Both, probably.

It felt like more than an hour had passed when he heard feet on the stairs. Booted feet, and several of them.

The sliding panel on his door clanged open and clanged shut again. The boots moved on. Another clang, but this time a door swung open. A voice protested – a voice Russell thought he recognised – the Jew who'd tried to protect his wife. The voice rose, and was cut off, leaving echoes inside Russell's head. What had cut it off? A fist? A knee? A cosh? A door slammed shut.

Silence reasserted itself, a heavy silence which offered no reassurance. Eventually a door scraped open, a remark drew laughter, and the boots were back in the corridor. Russell felt his breath catch as they headed his way, but they clattered on past and up the stairs, leaving him staring at his shaking hands. Pressing his ear to the door he could hear no groans of pain, only the stillness of unconsciousness or death.

Time went by. He'd rushed out of the hotel without his watch, and when a tray of food was eventually shoved through his hatch he wondered if it was lunch or supper. The boots never came back, and with each hour that passed he found himself feeling a little more optimistic. When the door finally opened, his stomach lurched, but it was only the policeman who'd brought him down.

'This way, Herr Russell,' the man said, nodding him towards the stairs.

They beat people up in the cells, Russell told himself. Upstairs had to be better.

Two corridors and two flights of stairs later, he was ushered through a door labelled Kriminalinspektor Tesmer. The man himself had greased black hair, blue eyes, thin lips, and a bad case of five o'clock shadow. 'Please sit,' he told Russell.

He took one last look at the Englishman's passport, and then passed it across the desk along with the journalist's accreditation. There was no sign of Shchepkin's envelope.

'Everything is satisfactory,' Tesmer said with a sudden,

unconvincing smile. 'And I'm sorry this has taken so long.'

Russell reached for his documents. 'I can go?' he asked, trying not to sound too relieved.

'Just one question.'

'Yes?' There was no life behind the eyes, Russell thought. This was a man to be careful with.

'Why did you come to Danzig, Herr Russell? To write a story about the Jewish children?'

'No. I had no idea a *Kindertransport* was leaving from here. I'm staying at the hotel opposite the station, and the noise woke me up. I just walked across to see what was going on.'

'Then why did you come?'

Why indeed? Because he'd felt drawn to the place, the way a good journalist was always drawn to a story that mattered. A city in thrall to thugs and fools, and doomed for precisely that reason. Danzig was Europe writ small. It was a story for everyone.

Almost everyone.

'Stamps,' he said, suddenly remembering a conversation he'd overhead in the Café Weitzke. The city's German and Polish post offices were both putting out stamps to commemorate centuries-old victories over each other. 'I do occasional pieces for philately journals, and the two post offices here are bringing out some interesting new issues. I'm hoping to interview the postmasters tomorrow.'

Tesmer looked disappointed, like a fisherman realising that this catch was too small to eat. 'Enjoy your stay,' he said curtly.

Once outside, Russell discovered it was almost ten o'clock. A bar supplied him with a sandwich and a much-needed drink, and he trudged back to his hotel through mostly empty streets. Shchepkin's envelope was still lying where he'd left it.

It had been opened, though. Russell took out the single sheet and read it. They wanted four articles of between 1,200 and 1,500 words, delivered at fortnightly intervals, beginning in mid-January. The money was more generous than he'd expected – as much as an ordinary Soviet worker earned over a Five Year Plan. The thought crossed his mind that a car would transform his Saturdays with his son Paul.

The letter was in German, the promised fee in Reichsmarks. There was nothing to say where the offer came from or what the articles would be about. 'God bless the NKVD,' Russell murmured to himself.

He woke around ten. Thick snow was cascading past his window, almost obscuring the station opposite. He used the lobby phone to call the two post offices, and was granted audiences with their Postmasters late that afternoon. When he emerged from the Café Weitzke on Langgasse, replete with scrambled eggs, Kashubian mushrooms and a mocha, it was still only midday. He had five hours to kill.

It had almost stopped snowing, but the sky was still heavy with cloud. As he stood there wondering what to do, there was a sudden swell of music from the loudspeakers which peppered the city. Hitler's New Year speech to the nation, Russell remembered. Danzig wasn't yet part of the German Reich, but try telling the Nazis that.

Russell sometimes enjoyed listening to Hitler. The man's sheer effrontery was entertaining, and knowing that millions were being taken in by his ludicrous bloodlust gave the whole experience a deplorably thrilling edge. If the Führer told them that gravity was a Jewish trick then millions of Germans would be practising levitation before the sun set.

Russell wasn't in the mood. A couple of hours by the sea, he thought. There wouldn't be any loudspeakers on the beach.

Hitler was just being introduced when a tram with a Brosen destination board burrowed out of the Langgasse Gate. Russell took a seat on the right and watched through the window as the tram skirted the Holzmarkt, swung right into Elisabethwall, and passed his hotel at the bottom of the Stadtgraben.

It was about six kilometres to Brosen. Russell had taken the same ride back in 1935, during his last visit to Danzig. He'd been doing a series of articles on Germans at play, and it had been the middle of summer. The resort had been awash with holiday-makers, and he had gone for a paddle.

Not today. It was as dark as it had been all morning, and the sparks from the overhead wires lit up the housefronts on either side of the street as the tram clanged and squealed its way out of the city. The loudspeakers were still audible, though. As they passed through the outlying suburbs of Langfuhr and Saspe, Russell caught snatches of the familiar voice, and one short passage in which the Führer offered the German people his fulsome congratulations for their 'wonderful behaviour' in 1938. He was probably talking about *Kristallnacht*.

By the time the tram reached Brosen the sky had visibly lightened. Russell got off outside the closed casino, where a single loudspeaker was doing its manful best to distort the Führer's message. Russell listened to the crackle for a few seconds, struck by the notion that he and Hitler were sharing a private moment together. The latter was promising help with the 'general pacification of the world'. Russell wondered how much irony one nation could eat.

He walked down past the boarded-up refreshment stands and padlocked beach huts to the snow-strewn beach. The previous season's final water temperature was still legible on the lifeguard hut blackboard, alongside a poster explaining the mysteries of artificial respiration. The men in the poster all wore striped bathing suits and moustaches, like a posse of cartoon Führers.

The sea was gunmetal grey, the sky almost as dark, slate grey with a yellowish tinge. There was no one in sight.

A couple of kilometres to the east, two beacon lights marked the end of Danzig's channel to the sea, and Russell started walking towards them. Out to the left the lighthouse at the end of the dredged channel flickered into life with each revolution. To the north, a darker line marked the outflung arm of the Hela peninsular. Between the two a smudge of a freighter was inching out across the bay.

The stamp story was made for him, he thought. A story that amused, and didn't condemn. A story of stupidity, and rather lovable stupidity at that. He could implant a few ironies just beneath the skin of the text for those who wanted to pick at it, leave enough clues to the real situation for those who already understood it. They would congratulate themselves on reading between the lines, and him for writing between them. And he could sit on his necessary fence for a few more months, until Hitler drove something through it.

Too many metaphors, he told himself. And not nearly enough satisfaction.

He thought about the real Danzig story. Ten years ago he'd have written it, and written it well. But not now. Step out of line that far, and the toadies at the Propaganda Ministry would have him deported before he could say 'Heil Hitler'. He'd be saying goodbye to his son, probably for the duration of a war. And probably to Effi as well. She'd told him often enough that she'd go to England, or better still America, with him, but he had his doubts whether she meant it, whether she'd ever willingly leave her sister, parents, agent and vast array of friends for life in a new country where no one knew who she was.

He left the path and walked down to the edge of the water, searching for pebbles to skim. He wanted to take Shchepkin's offer, he realised, but he wasn't sure why. He only half-bought the argument that by helping the Soviets he'd be hurting the Nazis. If he really wanted to take Hitler on there were more effective ways, most of them depressingly self-sacrificial. The money would be nice, but the risks would be high. The Nazis still beheaded spies.

He skimmed a flat pebble between two waves. Could he trust Shchepkin? Of course he couldn't. The Soviets might want what they said they wanted – no more, no less – but even if they did, that wouldn't be the end of it. You didn't do a few articles for Stalin, bank the cheques and move on. You would be on a list, one of their people, someone to call up when something else was needed. And once you were on the list, they took refusals badly.

And then there was the attitude of his own country to worry about. He didn't need England now, but the way things were going he soon might, and writing for Stalin would hardly endear him to the Foreign Office. He could end up *persona non grata* with just about everyone. Why was he even thinking about it?

He knew why. A couple of weeks before Christmas Paul had told him about an exercise that new recruits into the *Jungvolk* were forced to undergo. They were taken out into the countryside without maps and invited to find their way back home the best they could. It was called a *Fahrt ins Blau*, a journey into the blue.

The idea had appealed to Paul, as it probably did to most boys of eleven. It appealed to Russell too. If he took this journey into the blue he might, conceivably, find his way home again.

He skimmed his last stone, a large one that took a single bounce and sank. The sparse daylight was receding. The freighter and the

Hela peninsula had both been sucked into the surrounding grey, and the beam from the lighthouse was sending shivers of reflection back off the darkening sea. He was in the middle of nowhere, lost in space. With ice for feet.

The two postmasters were both short-sighted men in sober suits with small moustaches. The Polish one could hardly wait for the honour of distributing his new stamps. A minion was sent for samples, and came back with King Jagiello and Queen Hedwig. The Polish queen, the postmaster explained, had spurned a German prince in favour of marrying the Lithuanian Jagiello. Their joint kingdom had forced the Prussians to accept the first Polish Corridor and bi-national status for Danzig. Admittedly this had all happened in the early fifteenth century but – and here the postmaster leaned back in his chair with a self-satisfied smile – the contemporary relevance should be obvious. Even to a German.

The German postmaster had his own sample. His stamp featured a beautiful miniature of stout Danzigers routing the Polish forces of King Stephan Batory in 1577. 'A German city defended by German arms,' he announced smugly. Russell repeated the question he had put to the Polish postmaster – weren't these stamps a little provocative? Shouldn't the civil authorities be trying to reduce the tension between their two countries, rather than using their stamps to stoke up old quarrels?

The German postmaster gave the same reply as his Polish opposite number. How, he asked, could anyone take postage stamps that seriously?

Russell's train left the Hauptbahnhof at ten o'clock. After paying for a sleeping berth he could barely afford, he sat in the restaurant car for the better part of two hours, nursing a single gold-flecked schnapps, feeling restless and uncertain. The Polish customs checked his visa just before Dirschau and the German authorities examined his passport at Flatow, on the far side of the Polish Corridor. He had no trouble with the latter – if the Danzig SA were submitting a report on his visit they were probably still struggling with their spelling.

He thought about the *Kindertransport*, and wondered where it was at that moment. Still chugging west across Germany, most likely. The Englishwoman's cheek would be purple by now – he hoped she would go to the press when she got back and make a real stink. Not that it would do any good. It had taken her five minutes to learn what Nazism was all about, but there was no substitute for first-hand experience. If you told people, they didn't believe you. No one, their eyes always said, could be as bad as that.

He walked back down the train to his sleeping compartment. The two lower berths were empty, one of the upper pair occupied by a gently snoring German youth. Russell sat on the berth beneath him, pulled back the edge of the curtain, and stared out at the frozen fields of Pomerania.

He lay back and shut his eyes. Fräulein Gisela Kluger looked back at him.

He would write Shchepkin's articles. See where the journey took him. Into the blue. Or into the black.

Ha! Ho! He!

Russell's train steamed across the bridge over Friedrichstrasse and into the station of the same name just before eight in the morning. An eastbound Stadtbahn train was disgorging its morning load on the other side of the island platform, and he stood behind the stairwell waiting for the crowd to clear. On the other side of the tracks an angry local was shaking a burnt almond machine in the vain hope that his coin would be returned.

A railway official intervened and the two men stood there shouting at each other.

Welcome to Berlin, Russell thought.

He took the steps down to the underground concourse, bought a newspaper at the waiting room kiosk, and found himself a seat in the station buffet. The sight of his neighbour, a stout man in an Orpo uniform, cramming his mouth with large slices of blood sausage did nothing for Russell's appetite, and he settled for a buttered roll and four-fruit jam with his large milky coffee.

His newspaper shielded him from the blood sausage eater, but not from Nazi reality. He dutifully read Goebbels' latest speech on the vibrancy of modern German culture, but there was nothing new in it. More anti-Jewish laws had come into force on January 1: driving automobiles, working in retail and making craft goods had all been added to the *verboten* list. What was left, Russell wondered. Emigration, he supposed. So why make it so hard for the poor bastards to leave?

He skimmed through the rest. More villages *judenfrei*, more kilometres of Autobahn, more indignation about Polish behaviour in the Corridor. A new U-boat epic at the cinema, children collecting old tin cans for Winter Relief, a new recipe for the monthly one-pot-stew. A Reich that will last a thousand years. Six down, nine hundred and ninety-four to go.

He thought about taking the U-bahn but decided he needed some exercise. Emerging onto Friedrichstrasse he found the remains of the last snowfall dribbling into the gutters. A ribbon of pale sunlight lit the upper walls on the eastern side of the street, but the street itself was still sunk in shadows. Little knots of people were gathered at the doors of about-to-open shops, many of them talking in that loud, insistent manner which non-Berliners found so annoying.

It was a three-kilometre walk to his rooms near Hallesches Tor. He crossed Unter den Linden by the Café Bauer, and strode south through the financial district, towards the bridge which carried the elevated U-bahn over Mohrenstrasse. Berlin was not a beautiful city, but the rows of grey stone had a solidity, a dependability, about them.

On one corner of Leipzigerstrasse a frankfurter stall was gushing steam into the air, on another the astrologer whom Effi sometimes consulted was busy erecting his canvas booth. The man claimed he'd prepared a chart for Hitler in pre-Führer days, but refused to divulge what was in it. Nothing good, Russell suspected.

Another kilometre and he was turning off Friedrichstrasse, cutting through the side streets to Neuenburgerstrasse and his apartment block. Walking south from Leipzigerstrasse was like walking down a ladder of social class, and the area in which he lived was still hoping for a visit from the twentieth century. Most of the apartment blocks were five storeys high, and each pair boasted a high brick archway leading into a dark well of a courtyard. A bedraggled birch tree stood in his, still clinging to its mantle of snow.

The concierge's door was open, light spilling into the dark lobby. Russell knocked, and Frau Heidegger emerged almost instantly, her frown turning to a smile when she saw who it was. 'Herr Russell! You said you would be back yesterday. We were beginning to worry.'

'I tried to telephone,' he lied, 'but …'

'Ah, the Poles,' Frau Heidegger said resignedly, as if nothing better could be expected from her neighbours to the east. She wiped her hands on her apron and ushered him in. 'Come, you must have a coffee.'

Accepting was easier than refusing. He took the proffered seat in her living room and gazed about him as she re-heated – for the last of heaven knows how many times – her eternal pot of coffee. Her Advent wreath was still hanging from the light fixture along with its four gutted candles. On the walnut chest of drawers two packs of cards stood beside her precious People's Radio. It was Tuesday, Russell realised, the day Frau Heidegger and three of her opposite numbers in the nearby blocks played skat.

She came back with the coffee and a small pile of post: a postcard from Paul, a probable Christmas card from his mother in the US, a letter from his American agent and a business letter with a Berlin postmark.

'You had two telephone messages,' the concierge said, looking down through her pince-nez at a small piece of paper. 'Your fiancée' – Frau Heidegger always referred to Effi in that way, despite the fact that no prospective marriage had ever been mentioned – 'says she will be back extremely late on Thursday night and will meet you at the Café Uhlandeck at noon on Friday. Does that sound right?'

'Yes.'

'And a Herr Conway – yes? – he would like you to call him as soon as possible.'

'I'll call him after I've had my coffee,' Russell said, taking a first exploratory sip. It was burnt, but so strong and sweet that you hardly noticed.

Frau Heidegger was telling him how she'd recently caught one of the tenants – the Sudeten German on the first floor who Russell hardly knew – opening a window. This was strictly forbidden when the heating was on, and the tenant had only been forgiven on the grounds that he came 'from the mountains' and could hardly be expected to know any better. He didn't know how lucky he was, Russell thought; his own rooms on the fourth floor sometimes resembled neighbouring ovens. During one warm week in December he had regularly set his alarm for 3 a.m., when the concierge was fairly certain to be asleep and he could throw open his windows for a life-saving blast of cool air.

He took another sip of coffee, idly wondering whether the War Ministry would be interested in developing it as a weapon. 'Thank you, Frau Heidegger,' he said, carefully replacing the half-full cup in its saucer and getting to his feet. 'I've had two cups already this morning,' he added by way of an excuse.

'It's good to have you back,' she said, following him to the door. She didn't close it though, presumably because she might miss something.

He walked over to the telephone at the foot of the stairs. It had been a source of great pride to Frau Heidegger when it was installed a couple of years earlier – her block was the first on Neuenburger-strasse to be connected. But it had soon turned into something of a mixed blessing. A popular propensity for ringing at all times of the day and night had necessitated the introduction of a curfew, and the phone was now off the hook from ten at night till eight in the morning. It could still be used for outgoing calls during that time, but heaven help anyone who forgot to take it off again. He

27

unhooked the earpiece and dialled the British Embassy's number. Doug Conway worked in the commercial department, or so he claimed. Russell had met him at the Blau-Weiss Club, where English-speaking expatriates played tennis, talked about how beastly their German hosts were, and lamented the lack of reliable domestic help. Russell hated the place, but time spent there was often good for business. As a journalist he had made a lot of useful contacts; as a part-time English tutor he had been pointed in the direction of several clients. He hoped Doug Conway had found him another.

'I'm rushed off my feet today,' Conway told him. 'But I can squeeze in an early lunch. Wertheim at 12.30?'

'Fine,' Russell agreed, and replaced the receiver. He started up the four flights of stairs which led to his rooms. At the top he paused for breath before unlocking the door, and wondered for the umpteenth time about moving to a block with a lift. His rooms were stuffy and hot, so he left the front door ajar and risked opening a window by a few millimetres.

Stretched out on the threadbare sofa, he went through his mail. Paul's postcard began 'Dear Dad', but seemed mostly concerned with the Christmas presents he'd received from his stepfather. The boy did say he was looking forward to the football on Saturday, though, and Russell took another look out of the window to convince himself that the weather was warming up and that the game would be played.

The American envelope did contain a Christmas card from his mother. Above the picture of a snowbound Times Square she had written one cryptic line: 'This might be a good year to visit me.' She was probably referring to the situation in Europe, although for all Russell knew she might have contracted an incurable disease. She certainly wouldn't tell him if she had.

He opened the business letters. The one from America contained a cheque for fifty-three dollars and twenty-seven cents, payment for an article on 'Strength Through Joy' cruises which a dozen US papers had taken. That was the good news. The Berlin letter was a final, rather abusively written demand for payment on a typewriter repair bill, which would account for more than half the dollar inflow.

Looking round the room at the all-too-familiar furniture and yellowing white walls, at the poster from Effi's first film, the tired collage of photographs and the dusty, overloaded bookshelves, he felt a wave of depression wash over him.

The city's largest Wertheim occupied a site twice the size of the late-lamented Reichstag, and a frontage running to 330 metres. Inside, it boasted 83 lifts, 100,000 light bulbs and 1,000 telephone extensions. Russell knew all this because he had written an article on the store a year or so earlier. More to the point, the restaurant offered good food and service at a very reasonable rate, and it was only a five minute walk from the British Embassy on Wilhelm-strasse.

Doug Conway had already secured a table, and was halfway through a gin and tonic. A tall man of around thirty-five with sleek blond hair and bright blue eyes, he looked custom-made for Nazi Berlin, but was in fact a fairly decent representative of the human race. State-educated and lowly born by Embassy standards – his father had been a parks superintendent in Leeds – he had arrived in Berlin just as the Nazis seized power. His pretty young wife Phyllis was probably brighter than he was, and had once jokingly told Russell that she intended to torch the Blau-Weiss Club before she left Berlin.

Conway's taste in food had not travelled far from his roots.

He looked pained when Russell ordered the pig's knuckle and sauerkraut, and plumped for the pot roast and mash for himself.

'I've got some teaching work for you if you want it,' he told Russell while they waited. 'It's a Jewish family called Wiesner. The father is – was – a doctor. His wife is ill most of the time, though I don't know what with – worry, most likely. Their son was taken off to Sachsenhausen after *Kristallnacht* and they haven't seen him since, though they have heard that he's still alive. And there are two daughters, Ruth and Marthe, who are both in their teens – thirteen and fifteen, or something like that. It's them you'd be teaching.'

Russell must have looked doubtful.

'You'd be doing me a real favour if you took them on,' Conway persisted. 'Dr Wiesner probably saved Phyllis's life – this was back in 1934 – there were complications with our daughter's birth and we couldn't have had a better doctor. He wasn't just efficient, he went out of his way to be helpful. And now he can't practise, of course. I don't know what he intends to do – I don't know what any of them can do – but he's obviously hoping to get his daughters to England or the States, and he probably thinks they'll have a better chance if they speak English. I have no idea what his money situation is, I'm afraid. If he can't earn, and with all the new taxes to pay … well … But if he can't pay your normal rate, then I'll top up whatever he can afford. Just don't tell him I'm doing it.'

'He might like the idea that somebody cares,' Russell said.

'I don't know about …'

'I'll go and see him.'

Conway smiled. 'I hoped you'd say that.' He pulled a folded piece of paper out of his inside pocket and passed it across the table. 'Here's his address.'

It was in Friedrichshain, hardly a normal stomping ground for high class Jewish doctors.

'He used to live in Lützow,' Conway explained. 'Now, of course, they're all hunkering down together in the poorest areas. Like medieval ghettos.'

The food arrived and they ate in silence for a couple of minutes, before exchanging news of their children and the German schools they were attending. Conway and his wife had also seen Effi's musical, and clearly wished they hadn't, though Conway was much too diplomatic actually to say so.

Over coffee Russell asked how the Embassy saw the next few months.

'Off the record?'

'Off the record.'

'We're on a knife-edge. If our moustachioed chum is happy with what he's got, then fine. The appeasers will say, "I told you so – he may be a nasty little shit, but he can be managed." But if he goes after more – Danzig or the Corridor or the rest of Czechoslovakia – then Churchill and his pals will be the ones saying, "I told you so." And there'll be a war.'

'Doug, how do you persuade the British people that the Czechs weren't worth fighting for, but the Poles are? The Czechs have a functioning democracy of sorts. The Poles would be just like this lot if they had any talent for organisation.'

Conway grimaced. 'That'll be up to the politicians. But I'll tell you what London's really worried about. If Hitler does behave for a few years, and if he keeps building tanks, U-boats and bombers at the current rate, then by '41 or '42 he'll be unstoppable. That's the real nightmare. As far as we're concerned – from a purely military point of view – the sooner the better.'

There was no telephone at the Wiesners' so Russell couldn't check on the convenience of his visit. But, as Conway had noted, the doctor didn't have much to go out for. No U-bahn had been built out into the working-class wastes of Friedrichshain, so Russell took a 13 tram from the Brandenburg Gate to Spittelmarkt and a 60 from there to Alexanderplatz and up Neue Königstrasse. The city deteriorated with each passing kilometre, and by the time he reached his destination most of it seemed to be for sale. The pavement was lined with makeshift tables, all piled high with belongings that would-be Jewish emigrants were trying to shift. The complete works of Dickens in German were on sale for a few Reichsmarks, a fine-looking violin for only a little more.

The Wiesners' block made his own seem middle class. The street was cobbled, the walls plastered with advertisements for auctions and lists of items for sale. On the pavement a group of painfully thin young girls were hopping their way through a game of 'Heaven and Earth' on a chalk-marked grid. In the courtyard of the Wiesners' building the far wall still bore the faintest outline of a large hammer and sickle and the much-faded slogan ERST ESSEN, DANN MIET – first food, then rent.

The Wiesners shared two over-crowded rooms on the second floor. Contrary to Conway's expectation, the doctor was out. He was only attending to a neighbour, however, and the older of the two daughters was sent to fetch him, leaving Russell to exchange small talk with his wife and their younger daughter Ruth. Frau Wiesner, a small woman with tied-back blonde hair and tired grey eyes, looked anything but Jewish, while Ruth bore a striking resemblance to Effi, both physically and, Russell judged, temperamentally. Effi had often been mistaken for a Jew, and various employers had insisted she always carry the *fragebogen* which testified to her aryan descent. She, of course, liked nothing better than shoving the mistake back in people's faces.

Dr Wiesner appeared after a few minutes looking decidedly

harassed. His wife and two daughters abruptly withdrew to the next room and closed the door behind them.

He was about fifty, Russell guessed, and ageing fast. He ran a hand through his thinning hair, and got straight down to business – as Conway had said, he hoped to send his daughters away to relations in England. He was working on getting them visas and exit permits, and in the meantime he wanted them to learn English.

'I speak a little,' he said in that language, 'and I will try and help them, but they need a proper teacher.'

'I've taught around twenty German children,' Russell said.

Wiesner grunted. 'German children,' he repeated. 'I'm afraid my children are no longer considered German.'

Russell said nothing.

'You are wondering why we stayed,' Wiesner said. 'I ask myself the same thing every day and I have many answers, but none of them is worth anything. My wife is not Jewish,' he added, 'so my children are only half-Jewish, or *mischlings* as the Nazis call them, and perhaps I thought … Well, I was a fool.' He reached behind himself and plucked a piece of paper from a shelf-full of music. It was, of all things, a page of *Der Stürmer*. 'Listen to this,' the doctor said, adjusting his glasses on his nose and holding the page almost at arm's length. '"Even if a Jew slept with an aryan woman once, the membranes of her vagina would be so impregnated with alien semen that the woman would never again be able to bear pure-blooded aryans."' He lowered the paper and looked at Russell. 'Who could believe such pre-scientific nonsense? It doesn't even make sense on their own illiterate terms – surely the master race would have the all-powerful blood, not the people they despise.' He saw something in Russell's face. 'I'm sorry. I don't know why I am telling you all this. It's just so hard to accept.'

'I understand,' Russell said.

'So why do you, an Englishman, stay in Germany?' Wiesner asked him.

Russell gave a short account of his situation.

'That is difficult,' the doctor agreed. 'But good news for my daughters if you agree to teach them.'

'How many lessons do you have in mind?'

'As many as you can manage. And as often.'

'Three times a week? Monday, Wednesday, Friday? It'll have to vary a bit, though. I can't do Friday this week, but I could do Thursday.'

'Whatever you say. Now for the difficult part. I have some money, but not very much. And – here I must trust you – I have some valuable stamps. I can show you the valuation in the current catalogue and add another ten per cent.'

It was a generous offer, but Russell couldn't accept it.

'The catalogue value will suit me fine.'

It was almost dark when he emerged from the Wiesners' block, and the tram rides home through the evening rush hour seemed endless. By the time he reached Hallesches Tor he was ready for supper, and his favourite beerhouse beneath the elevated U-bahn provided the necessary meatballs and potato pancakes. Over a second beer he decided not to sell any of Wiesner's stamps unless he really needed to. He would give them to Paul, whose collection could do with some rarities.

Always assuming his son would accept them. Paul was forever worrying about his father's financial state – an anxiety which Russell occasionally, and without much conviction, tried to blame on his ex-wife Ilse.

He looked at his watch. He needed to get home to ring Paul before his bedtime. A U-bahn rattled into the station above as he emerged from the beerhouse, and a stream of people was soon pouring down the iron staircase, exhaling puffs of yellow gas in the cold evening air. It was one of those Berlin days when the weather seemed uncertain what to do, one minute veering towards a western warmth, the next favouring an eastern chill.

As he turned into his street Russell noticed what looked like an empty car parked across from his apartment block. This was unusual – very few people in the area could afford one. He thought about crossing the street to take a look inside, and decided he was being paranoid. He hadn't done anything to upset the authorities. Not yet, anyway.

A blast of hot air greeted him as he opened the outside doors of the apartment block. Frau Heidegger's skat evening was in full swing, the volume of laughter suggesting a large consignment of empty bottles for the morning collection. Russell dialled the number of the house in Grunewald, then put the earpiece to one ear and a finger in the other. As he half-expected, Ilse picked up. They asked each other the usual questions, gave each other the usual answers, all with that faint awkwardness which they never seemed able to shake. The family had just got back from Hanover, and when Paul came on he was full of the wonders of the Autobahn and his stepfather's new Horch. As far as Saturday was concerned, his usual school lessons had been replaced by *Jungvolk* meetings, and these ran on until one o'clock. 'Mama says you can pick me up then.'

'Right.' Effi would be pleased, Russell thought. He wouldn't have to leave while she was still fast asleep.

'And we're still going to the Viktoria match?'

'Of course. I expect Uncle Thomas and Joachim will come as well.'

They chatted for another couple of minutes, before Ilse's voice in the background decreed that time was up. Feeling the usual mixture of elation and frustration, Russell started up the stairs.

He was waylaid on the third floor landing by the other resident journalist, a young American named Tyler McKinley. 'I thought I heard your weary tread,' the American said in English. 'Come in for a minute. I want to ask you something.'

It seemed simpler to say yes than no. McKinley's room wasn't particularly hot – like the other residents he took advantage of skat night to freshen the air – but it was full of pipe-smoke from the atrocious Balkan mixture he had adopted during a weekend trip to Trieste.

'How was Danzig?' his host asked, though Russell could see he was bursting with stuff of his own. There was something lovable about McKinley, but also something profoundly irritating. Russell hoped that this wasn't just because McKinley, with his quasi-religious belief in crusading journalism, reminded him of himself in long gone days. That was the trouble with the young – their stupidities brought back one's own.

'Interesting,' he answered, though it had been anything but in the way that McKinley meant. He considered telling him about the stamp wars, but could imagine the look of incomprehension and vague derision which that would elicit.

The younger man was already back in Berlin. 'I'm chasing a really interesting story,' he said. 'I don't want to say anything yet,' he added quickly, 'but … do you know anything about the KdF, the *Kanzlei des Führers*?'

'It's the great man's private chancellery.'

'Is it a government office?'

'No, it's a Party office, but an independent one. There's no connection to Bormann's bunch in Munich.'

McKinley was visibly excited. 'So who is it connected to?'

Russell shrugged. 'Nobody. It reports directly to Hitler as far as I know.'

'So if he wanted to do something on the quiet, it would be the ideal instrument.'

'Uh-huh.'

McKinley beamed, as if he'd just awarded himself a gold star.

'You want to tell me what you're talking about?' Russell asked, interested in spite of himself.

'Not yet,' the American said, but he couldn't resist one more question. 'Does the name Knauer mean anything to you?'

'A full back with Tennis Borussia a few years back?'

'What? Oh, a soccer player. No, I don't think so.' He reached for a lighter to re-start his pipe. 'But thanks for your help.'

'You're welcome,' Russell said, opening the door to leave. His room at the top of the building was sweltering, but mercifully smoke-free. Guessing that the skat game still had a couple of hours to run, he threw one window wide open and gazed out across the rooftops. In the far distance the red light atop the Funkturm winked above the roofscape.

He sat down at the typewriter, inserted a sheet of paper, and reminded himself that the letter he was about to write was – as far as the Soviets were concerned – just a long-winded way of saying yes. His real audience was the Gestapo.

Play the innocent, he thought. The Gestapo would think he was trying to fool the Soviets, and assume he was just being cynical.

He began by asserting the happy coincidence that National Socialism and the Union of Soviet Socialist Republics had one crucial word in common – socialism. That should give them both a laugh, he thought. They might seem like enemies, he continued, but clearly they had something important in common – socialism's determination to serve all the people. What could serve the people better than peace? And what served peace better than mutual understanding? If the Soviet people were offered, in a series of articles, a clearer idea of how much National Socialism had achieved for ordinary German people, then the chances of peace were bound to be enhanced. As an Englishman with a long experience of Germany, he was ideally placed to explain it to foreigners. And he had a strong personal reason for desiring peace – if war came, he added pathetically, he and his German-born son might be separated for years and years. 'Here I am,' he murmured to himself, 'a propaganda tool for the taking.' The Gestapo would lap it up.

He copied the address from Shchepkin's note onto an envelope, unearthed a stamp from the table drawer, and perched the completed missive on his typewriter. Hearing the sounds of departing concierges floating up from the courtyard he made a dive for the window and pulled it shut.

Bed, he thought. The bathroom on the floor below which he shared with McKinley and two other men – a stationery rep from Hamburg and a waiter from the Harz Mountains – was empty for once, though the lingering odour of McKinley's pipe smoke suggested a lengthy occupation earlier that evening. There was still a crack of light under the American's door, and Russell could hear the soft clicking of his typewriter – the newer machines were much quieter than his own antique.

In bed, he re-read Paul's postcard and resumed reading the detective novel he had forgotten to take to Danzig. Unable to remember who anyone was, he turned out the light and listened to the muffled hum of the traffic on nearby Lindenstrasse. The Führer was probably allowed to sleep with his windows open.

The next day was Wednesday, and he made the long trek out to Friedrichshain for his first session with the Wiesner girls. The elder daughter Marthe was a bit shy at first, but Ruth's enthusiasm proved infectious enough to bring her out. The two of them knew very little English, but they were a joy to teach, eager to learn and markedly more intelligent than the spoilt daughters of suburban Grunewald and Wilmersdorf whom Russell had taught in the past.

On Thursday, though, both girls looked as though they'd seen a ghost, and Russell wondered whether they'd had bad news about their brother in Sachsenhausen. When he asked if they were all right, he thought Marthe was going to cry, but she took a visible grip on herself and explained that her brother had come home the previous evening.

'But that's wonderful ...' Russell began.

'He doesn't seem like Albert,' Ruth broke in, looking over her shoulder at the door through to the other rooms. 'He has no hair, and he doesn't say anything,' she whispered.

'He will,' Marthe told her sister, putting an arm round her. 'He's just seen some terrible things, but he hasn't been hurt, not really. Now come on, we have to learn English. For everyone's sake.'

And they did, faster than any pupils Russell could remember. Neither mother nor brother emerged from the other rooms, and Doctor Wiesner was out on both days. On the Thursday he left Russell three stamps in an envelope on top of the latest Stanley Gibbons catalogue from England. Russell didn't bother to check the listings.

When he got back to Neuenburgerstrasse a telegram had arrived from his London agent, pointing out the need for exclusive photographs with his projected piece on Hitler's new Chancellery. After a quick lunch Russell dragged himself out to a photographic studio in the wilds of Neukölln, only to discover that the photographer in question, a Silesian named Zembski whom he'd used in the past, had just lost his official accreditation after starting a brawl at one of Goering's hunting parties. Zembski weighed over two hundred pounds, and could hardly be smuggled into the Führer's new insult to architecture, but he did prove willing to rent out one of his better cameras. After a short instruction course Russell carried the Leica back to Hallesches Tor.

Frau Heidegger was waiting for him – or anyone – in the lobby. Her husband had been killed in the last war – 'You might have been the one who shot him,' as she frequently told Russell – and his brother had just been round to see her, full of frightening information about the next one. She had assumed it would take place at some distance from her door, but this illusion had just been cruelly shattered. 'Cities will be bombed flat,' her brother-in-law had told her. 'Flat as ironing boards.'

Russell told her that, yes, English or French or Russian bombers could now reach Berlin, but that most of them would be shot down if they tried, because air defences were improving all the time. She didn't look convinced, but then neither was he. How many Europeans, he wondered, had any idea what kind of war they were headed for?

Friday morning was sunny and cold. After a late breakfast of rolls and coffee at a local café, Russell walked west along the Landwehrkanal. He wasn't due to meet Effi for a couple of hours, so he took his time, stopping to read his morning paper on a bench near the double-decker bridges which carried the U-bahn and Reichsbahn lines over the torpid brown water. Coal-laden barges chugged by, leaving thin trails of oil in their wake.

He walked along the footpath for another kilometre or so, leaving the canal where it passed under Potsdamerstrasse. Almost exactly twenty years earlier, the bodies of Rosa Luxemburg and Karl Liebknecht had been fished out of the waters close to this spot, and the empty site on the other side of the road had been home to a synagogue until the previous November. Rosa, of course, had been everything the Nazis despised – a Jew, a communist, a woman who refused to stay home and rear children. Russell was surprised that no official celebration had been decreed for the anniversary of her death.

Cutting through side streets, he eventually reached the domed U-bahn station at Nollerndorfplatz, and started walking up Kleist-strasse towards the distant spires of the Kaiser Memorial church.

As the U-bahn tracks beside him slid slowly underground, the shops grew progressively larger and richer, the awnings of the pavement cafés more decorative. Despite the cold, most of the outside seats were occupied; men and women sat in their overcoats, or tightly wrapped in large blankets, chewing their cream cakes and sipping at their steaming coffees.

Both pavements and road were crowded now. Shoppers streamed in and out of the Ka-De-We department store on Wittenbergplatz; cars and trams ran bumper to bumper along the narrower Tauenzienstrasse, jostling each other round the neo-Gothic pile of the Memorial Church, with its distressingly secular mosaics celebrating the highly dubious glories of past German emperors. Walking past it, and thinking about his conversation with Frau Heidegger, Russell had a sudden vision of jagged spires looming out of a broken roof, a future Berlin pre-figured in his memories of northern France.

He started up the busy Kurfürstendamm, or the Ku'damm, as everyone called it. The Café Uhlandeck, where he was due to meet Effi, was a ten minute stroll away, and he still had half an hour to spare. An African parrot in a pet shop caught his attention – it was the sort of birthday present Effi would love, but he doubted her ability to look after it properly. For one thing she was away too often; for another, she was Effi.

A woman in a fur coat emerged from the shop with two pedigree Schnauzers in tow. Both had enamel swastikas fastened to their collars, and Russell wondered whether they had pictures of the Führer pinned up inside their kennels. Would that be considered a sign of respect, or the lack of it? Political etiquette in the Third Reich was something of a minefield.

He passed the 'aryanised' Grünfeld factory, and the site of another destroyed synagogue. A photographic album of such sites could, he thought, be a best-seller in Nazi Germany. *Judenfrei: the photographic record.* Page after page of burnt synagogues, followed by 'then and now' pictures of aryanised firms. A foreword by the Führer, which would probably turn out to be longer than the book. The lucky author would probably get invitations to Goering's hunting weekends and Streicher's whipping orgies.

Russell stopped and watched a tram cross the intersection, bell clanging. Why was he feeling so angry this morning? Was it the *Kindertransport* and the Wiesner girls? Or just six years of accumulated disgust? Whatever it was, it served no purpose.

Reaching the Café Uhlandeck he sat at one of the outside tables and stared back down the Ku'damm in search of Effi's familiar silhouette. He had met her a few days before Christmas 1933, while researching a piece on Leni Riefenstahl for a Hollywood gossip magazine. At a studio party someone had pointed out a slim, black-haired woman in her late twenties, told Russell that her name was Effi Koenen, and that she had appeared alongside Riefenstahl before the actress had turned director.

Effi's part in that film, as she'd been only too happy to inform him, had consisted of 'five lines, two smiles, one pout and a dignified exit'. She had thought Riefenstahl a good actress, but had hated *Triumph of the Will* for its humourlessness. Russell had asked her out to dinner, and rather to his astonishment she had accepted. They had got on wonderfully – in the restaurant, on the half-drunken walk home to her flat, in her large soft bed. Five years later, they still did.

Effi's flat was a couple of blocks north of the Ku'damm, a three-room affair which her wealthy parents had bought in the early 1920s from a victim of the Great Inflation, and given to her as a twenty-fifth birthday present. Her acting career had been moderately successful – a film here, a play there, a musical if nothing else was on offer – without making her rich or particularly famous. She was occasionally recognised on the street when Russell was with her, and almost always for the part she had played in a 1934 film, the wife of a storm-trooper beaten to death by communists. That had been a 'seventeen-line, one-smile, one-scream, dignified-at-funeral' part.

She was currently appearing in *Barbarossa*, a musical biography of the twelfth-century Holy Roman Emperor, Frederick I. As one of his generals' wives, she sang part of the joyous send-off when they left for the Crusades, and part of the lament for those who failed to come home. Like most of the cast, she wasn't much of a singer, but no one had bothered to include musical ability, a decent script or memorable songs in the production. It was, as one of the early Berlin reviews put it, 'a hymn to national consciousness'.

Much to Effi's disgust it had pulled in large audiences, both in Berlin during the weeks leading up to Christmas and across the Reich during the holiday season itself. A second season in Berlin was beginning that night and Effi expected the seats to be full again – 'All those who couldn't believe how bad it was the first time will be coming back to make sure.'

Russell hadn't seen her for almost a fortnight, which seemed a long time. They generally spent as much of the weekend together as their – mostly her – work allowed, along with at least one night in midweek and an unpredictable number of lunches and afternoons. She was fond of saying that her three-year marriage to a now-famous actor had left her with a love of living alone, and had never suggested that Russell move in with her. He told himself and everyone else that he was happy, more than happy, with their days and nights together, and happy to spend the other days and nights without her. And most of the time he believed it. Just occasionally he found himself thinking that love was a full-time occupation, and that loving someone was resenting each hour apart. He did love Effi, from her long raven hair to her small brown toes. He loved everything about her, he thought, looking at his watch, except for her complete inability to arrive anywhere on time.

It was 12.25 when she finally appeared. She was wearing the black overcoat that almost reached her ankles, a new crimson scarf wrapped around her neck, chin and mouth, and the Russian fur hat she had bought in Moscow ten years before. Yet even trussed up like a mummy she turned the heads of male passers-by. 'I've got a cold,' was the first thing she said once they'd embraced. 'I need soup.'

Russell suggested going inside, but she refused. 'Fresh air's the best thing for colds,' she insisted.

He bought them bowls of soup and watched as she gulped hers down. 'We got in at four in the morning,' she said between spoonfuls, 'and we've got to be in early this evening to discuss some changes the musical director has in mind.'

'A new score?' Russell asked.

'If only. It'll be nothing. He just has to justify the fact that he's still being paid.' She started tearing up a roll and dropping it in the soup. 'You'll pick me up after the show?'

'Of course. I'll come and watch the last half hour if they'll let me in. Is it the same man on the door?'

'I don't know. But I'll make sure they know you're coming.' She spooned a chunk of sodden bread into her mouth. 'This is good. I feel better already. How have you been? How's Paul?'

'Haven't seen him yet. But he sounds all right.'

'Danzig?'

'Suitably gloomy,' he said. He told her about the stamp wars, which made her laugh, and the Soviet request for articles, which drew a raised eyebrow. 'It's just work,' he said. There didn't seem any point in mentioning the oral reports, or in spoiling their reunion with an account of the *Kindertransport* and his day in jail.

She stole the last of his roll to soak up the last of her soup. 'I feel much better,' she said again. 'And I've still got three hours before I have to be at the theatre,' she said, reaching out a slender hand for his. 'Shall we go back to the flat?'

Later that evening, Russell arrived backstage in time to hear the lament for the fallen heroes. It seemed more Wagnerian than ever, and he realised that the musical director had decided to apply the Third Reich's guiding principle – never speak when you can shout. The military widows now had an entire choir of breast-swelling Valkyries to augment their lamentations. The front rows of the audience looked suitably stunned.

After the show, Russell talked football with the stage-door-keeper while he waited for Effi. She emerged after half an hour or so, still snuffling, but full of post-performance energy. It was clear and cold outside, the pavements crowded with people. They walked arm in arm past the entrance to the aquarium, and along the southern side of the zoo towards the glowing glasshouse which straddled the elevated lines at Zoo station. The station buffet was packed, but they managed to find a couple of free stools and order a nightcap. This was the last place in Berlin where Jews could still buy a coffee, but there were no obvious Jewish faces. The city by night was an aryan preserve.

As they left the buffet an international express steamed out across Hardenbergstrasse, rumbling the girders of the bridge and pumping bursts of white smoke towards the stars. Russell found himself wishing, if only for a moment, that he and Effi were two of the silhouettes in the necklace of illuminated windows, headed for another life in Amsterdam or Paris or New York, anywhere, in fact, beyond Hitler's rancid realm.

It was almost one when they got back to the flat. Their lovemaking that afternoon had been almost frenzied, but now they took it slowly, luxuriously, taking each other to the brink again and again before finally, joyously, tumbling over it together. Wrapped in his arms, Effi went to sleep almost immediately, but Russell's brain refused to let him be. He had not been angry with the Nazis that morning, he realised. He had been angry with himself. Angry at his own helplessness. Angry that all he could manage were fantasies of escape.

It suddenly occurred to him that his imaginary book of photographs might make a real impact abroad. Especially in America, where the Jewish organisations had some political clout. He could get pictures of old Jewish businesses and synagogues from press libraries and shoot the ruins himself with Zembski's camera. Getting it out of the country would be a problem, but he'd worry about that – and ensuring his own anonymity – when the time came. And if anyone noticed him taking pictures of burnt-out synagogues he could say he was compiling the record of anti-Semitic triumphs he had originally envisaged. He smiled to himself in the dark.

Next morning they walked to their usual café in the Tiergarten for milky coffee and rolls. The winter sun was already high in the south-eastern sky, and as they strolled back along the northern bank of the Landwehrkanal it seemed as if most of Berlin had had the same idea. Effi had arranged to meet her older sister Zarah for lunch, something she often did when Russell was seeing his son. He had never really liked Zarah, who had none of Effi's fitful ability to look beyond herself, and had married an ambitious Nazi civil servant. Soon after Russell met Effi, she had asked for his help in arranging an abortion for Zarah in England. Zarah had travelled to London, decided at the last moment she couldn't go through with it, and had eventually given birth to a boy. Much to everyone's surprise, she had doted on the child from day one. Much to Russell's annoyance, she blamed him for the fact that she had nearly had an abortion.

After he and Effi parted, Russell caught a 76 tram outside the zoo for Grunewald, and watched the houses grow bigger as it worked its way past Halensee and into Berlin's prosperous south-western suburbs. Paul's school was a five-minute walk from the tram terminus, and just down the road from the large tree-shrouded villa which his stepfather Matthias Gehrts had inherited from his father. Both school and villa backed onto one of the small lakes which dotted the area, and sitting on the low wall beside the school gates Russell had occasional glimpses of sailboats between buildings.

A couple of women arrived on foot to pick up their sons, but his fellow dads all arrived in cars, and stood around discussing the reliability of their mechanics.

The *Jungvolk* appeared soon after one, buttoning their overcoats over their uniforms as they walked to the gate. Paul half-ran to greet him, a big smile on his face.

'So where shall we go today?' Russell asked.

'The Funkturm.'

'Again?' They had visited Berlin's radio tower at least half a dozen times in 1938.

'I like it there.'

'OK. Let's get a tram then. Do you want me to carry that?' he asked, indicating the large book his son was holding.

'We'll take turns,' Paul decided.

'What is it?' Russell asked.

'It's the yearbook,' Paul said, holding it out.

The *Hitler Youth Yearbook*, Russell realised, as he skimmed through the pages. There were five hundred of them. 'So what did you do today?'

'The same as usual to begin with. Roll-call and gymnastics and then the history lesson – that was all about Germania and the Romans and how most history people get it wrong about them. They think the Romans were civilised and the Germans were barbarians, but in fact it was the other way round – the Romans got mixed up with other races and got soft and lazy and forgot how to fight but the Germans stayed German and that made them strong.' They reached the tram stop just as a tram squealed to a halt. 'And after the history lesson,' Paul went on, once they were in their seats, 'we did some work on the map wall – remember? – we're doing a whole wall of maps of Germany from the beginning to now. It's beginning to look really good.' He looked out of the window. 'There's a shop down here that sells model soldiers, and they've got the new set of dead ones. Someone at school brought them in. They're really real.'

They would be, Russell thought. Death and toys, the German specialities.

'If they'd come out before Christmas, I'd have them now,' Paul said wistfully.

They reached Halensee Station and climbed down the steps

to the Ringbahn platform. 'And then we had a talk from this old man,' Paul said, as they watched an electric train pull away from the opposite platform and accelerate down the cutting. 'Quite old, anyway – he was much more than forty. He came to talk about the last war and what it was like. He said there weren't many aeroplanes or tanks, and there was lots of hand–to-hand fighting – is that true?'

'There was some. Depends what he meant by lots.'

'I think he meant it was happening all the time.' Paul looked up at Russell. 'I didn't believe a lot of the things he said. I mean, he said that the best thing a soldier could do was to die for his country. And one of the boys in the back asked him if he was sorry that he hadn't died, and the man didn't reply. The boy was told to report to the leader's room after the talk, and he looked pretty sick when he came out.'

'Did they give him a whacking?'

'No, I think they just shouted at him. He wasn't trying to be clever – he's just a bit stupid.'

Their train pulled in, and Paul spent the single stop ride staring out of the window at the skeletal Funkturm rising out of the tangle of railways. Erected in 1926, it looked like a smaller version of the Eiffel Tower, which probably galled the Nazis no end. 'The lift's going up,' Paul said, and they watched it climb towards the viewing platform 126 metres above the ground.

Fifteen minutes later they were waiting at the bottom for their own ride. One lift carried them to the restaurant level, fifty-five metres up, another to the circular walkway with its panoramic view of the city. The viewing platform was crowded, children queuing to use the coin-operated binoculars. Russell and his son worked their way slowly round, gazing out beyond the borders of the city at the forests and lakes in the south-west, the plains in the north and east.

The Olympic Stadium loomed close by to the west, and Berlin's two other high buildings – the office tower of the Borsig locomotive works and the futuristic Shellhaus – both seemed closer than usual in the clear air. As tradition demanded, once Paul got his hands on the binoculars he turned them towards the northern suburb of Gesundbrunnen, where Hertha's flag was fluttering above the roof of the Plumpe's solitary grandstand. 'Ha! Ho! He! Hertha BSC!' he chanted underneath his breath.

In the restaurant below they both ordered macaroni, ham and cheese, washed down, in Paul's case, with a bottle of Coca Cola.

'Would you like to see New York?' Russell asked, following a thread of thought that had begun on the viewing platform.

'Oh yes!' Paul exclaimed. 'It must be fantastic. The Empire State Building is more than three times as high as this, and it has a viewing platform right near the top.'

'We could stay with your grandmother.'

'When?'

'Not for a few years yet. When you finish school, maybe.'

Paul's face fell. 'There'll be a war before then.'

'Who says so?'

Paul looked at him with disbelief. 'Everybody does.'

'Sometimes everybody's wrong.'

'Yes, but ...' He blew into his straw, making the Coke bubble and fizz. 'Dad,' he began again, then stopped.

'What?'

'When you were in the war, did you want to die for England?'

'No, I didn't.' Russell was suddenly conscious of the people at the tables nearby. This was not a conversation to have in public.

'Did you want to fight at all?'

'Let's go back up top,' Russell suggested.

'OK,' Paul agreed, but only after he'd given Russell one of

those looks which suggested he should try harder at being a normal father.

They took the lift once more, and found an empty stretch of railing on the less popular side, facing away from the city. Down to their left an S-bahn train was pulling out of the Olympic Stadium station.

'I didn't want to fight,' Russell began, after pausing to marshal his thoughts. 'I didn't volunteer – I was conscripted. I could have refused, and probably gone to prison instead, but I wasn't certain enough about my feelings to do that. I thought maybe I was just afraid, and that I was hiding behind my opinions. But once I got to the trenches it was different. There were a few idiots who still believed in death and glory, but most of us knew that we'd been conned. All the governments were telling their soldiers that they had God and right on their side, and that dying for their country was the least they could do, but – well, think about it – what does it mean, dying for your country? What exactly is your country? The buildings and the grass and the trees? The people? The way of life? People say you should love your country, and be proud of it, and there are usually things to love and be proud of. But there are usually things to dislike as well, and every country has things to be ashamed of. So what does dying for your country achieve? Nothing, as far as I could see. Living for your country, you get the chance to make it better.' He looked at his son, whose expression was almost fierce.

'Our leader says that people who don't want to fight are cowards.'

'I expect some of them are. But … you remember the Boer War in South Africa, between the English and the Boers? Well, the Indian nationalist leader Gandhi, he was a leader of the Indians in South Africa then, and he refused to fight. Instead he organised

51

medical teams which helped the wounded on the battlefield. He and his people were always in the thick of the action, and lots of them were killed. They wouldn't fight, but they were about as far from cowards as you can get.'

Paul looked thoughtful.

'But I shouldn't say anything like that at a *Jungvolk* meeting,' Russell went on, suddenly conscious of the yearbook he was carrying. 'You'd just get yourself in trouble. Think about things, and decide what you think is right, but keep it to yourself, or the family at least. These are dangerous times we're living in, and a lot of people are frightened of people who don't think like they do. And frightened people tend to lash out.'

'But if you know something's wrong, isn't it cowardly to just keep quiet?'

This was what Russell was afraid of. How could you protect children from the general idiocy without putting them at risk? 'It can be,' he said carefully, 'but there's not much point picking a fight if you know you're bound to lose. Better to wait until you have some chance of winning. The important thing is not to lose sight of what is right and what is wrong. You may not be able to do anything about it at the time, but nothing lasts for ever. You'll get a chance eventually.'

Paul gave him a grown-up look, as if he knew full well that his father was talking as much about himself as his son.

After taking Paul home, Russell took the long tram ride back down Ku'damm, spent a couple of hours over dinner in a bar, and then went in search of a movie to watch. The new U-boat drama was showing at the Alhambra, a Zara Leander weepie at the Ufa Palast, and an American western at the Universum. He chose the last, and reached his seat just as the weekly newsreel was getting started. A rather beautiful piece on Christmas markets in the Rhineland was followed by lots of thunderous marching and a German volleyball triumph in Romania. Suitably lifted, the audience noisily enjoyed the western, which almost made up in spectacle what it lacked in every other department.

Effi's audience had gone home by the time he reached the theatre on Nurnbergstrasse, and he only had to wait a few minutes for her to emerge from the dressing rooms. She had forgotten to eat anything between the matinée and evening shows, and was starving. They walked to a new bar on the Ku'damm which one of the new Valkyries had told her served the most incredible omelettes.

They were indeed, but the male clientele, most of whom seemed to be in uniform, left a lot to be desired. Four SS men took a neighbouring table soon after their food arrived, and grew increasingly vocal with each round of schnapps. Russell could almost feel their need for a target take shape.

Effi was telling him about her sister Zarah's latest neurosis – she was increasingly worried that her infant son was a slow learner – when the first comments were directed at their table. One of the SS men had noticed Effi's Jewish looks, and loudly remarked on the fact to his companions. He was only about twenty, Russell thought, and when he succeeded in catching the young man's eye, had the brief satisfaction of seeing a hint of shame in the way he quickly looked away.

By this time Effi was rifling through her purse. Finding what she was looking for, she stood up, advanced on the SS table and held the *fragebogen* up to them, rather in the manner of a schoolteacher lecturing a bunch of particularly obtuse children. 'See this, you morons,' she said, loud enough for the whole bar to hear. 'Aryan descent, all the way back to Luther's time. Satisfied?'

The manager was already at her shoulder. 'Fräulein, please …' he began.

'I want these drunken pigs thrown out,' she told him.

The oldest of the SS men was also on his feet. 'I would advise you to be careful, Fräulein,' he said. 'You may not be a Jew, but that does not give you the right to insult members of the Führer's bodyguard.'

Effi ignored him. 'Are you going to throw these pigs out?' she asked the manager.

He looked mortified. 'I …'

'Very well. You won't get any more business from me. Or any of my friends. I hope,' she concluded with one last contemptuous glance at the SS, 'that you can make a living selling swill to these pigs.'

She headed for the door, as Russell, half-amused and half-fearful, counted out a few marks for their meal and listened to the SS men argue about whether to arrest her. When one of them took a step towards the door he blocked the way. 'You did call her a Jew,' he said mildly, looking straight at the oldest man. 'Surely you can understand how upsetting that might be. She meant no disrespect.'

The man gave him a slight bow of the head. 'She would do well to control her anger a little better,' he said coldly.

'She would,' Russell agreed. 'Have a good evening,' he added, and turned towards the door.

Outside he found Effi shaking with laughter, though whether from humour or hysteria he wasn't quite sure. He put an arm around her shoulder and waited for the shaking to stop. 'Let's go home.'

'Let's,' she agreed.

They crossed the busy avenue and headed up one of the side streets.

'Sometimes I wish I was a Jew,' she said. 'If the Nazis hate them that much, they must be real human beings.'

Russell grunted his agreement. 'I heard a joke the other day,' he said. 'Hitler goes rowing on the Wannsee, but he's not very good at it, and manages to overturn the boat. A boy in a passing boat manages to haul him out and save him from drowning. Hitler, as you can imagine, is overcome with gratitude and promises the boy whatever he wants. The boy thinks for a moment, and asks for a state funeral. Hitler says, "You're a bit young for that, aren't you?" The boy says, "Oh, *mein Führer*, when I tell my dad I've saved you from drowning he's going to kill me!"'

Effi started laughing again, and he did too. For what seemed like minutes they stood on the pavement, embracing like lovers, shaking with mirth.

Next afternoon Thomas and Joachim were waiting in the usual place, sitting on a low wall with cartons of half-consumed frankfurters and *kartoffelsalat* between them. Russell bought the same for himself and Paul.

Once inside the Plumpe they headed for their usual spot, opposite the edge of the penalty area, halfway up the terrace on the western side. As their two sons read each other's magazines, Russell and Thomas sat themselves down on the concrete step and chatted. 'How's business?' Russell asked.

'It's good,' Thomas said, unbuttoning his overcoat. He'd been running the family paper business since his and Ilse's father died a few years earlier. 'It's getting harder to find experienced staff, but other than that ...' He shrugged. 'There's no lack of orders. How about you?'

'Not too bad. I've got the opening of the new Chancellery tomorrow, and there should be a decent piece in that – the Americans like that sort of thing.'

'Well that's good. How about Danzig? Did you get anything there?'

'Not really.' Russell explained about the stamp wars.

Thomas rolled his eyes in frustration. 'Like children,' he muttered. 'Speaking of which, Joachim's been called up for his *arbeitsdienst.*'

'When?'

'The beginning of March.'

Russell looked up at Joachim, engrossed in his magazine. 'Ah,' he said, glad that Paul was still six years away from the year of drilling, draining swamps and digging roads which the Nazis imposed on all seventeen-year-old boys. 'How does he feel about it?'

'Oh, he can't wait,' Thomas said, glancing affectionately up at his son. 'I suppose it can't do him any harm. Unlike what'll probably follow.'

Russell knew what he meant. When they'd first become friends almost ten years ago, he and Thomas had talked a lot about their experiences in the war. Both had friends who'd survived the war in body, yet never recovered their peace of mind. And both knew that they themselves had been changed in ways that they would never fully understand. And that they had been the lucky ones.

'Happy days,' Russell murmured, and then laughed. 'We had a run-in with the SS last night,' he said, and told Thomas the story.

He wasn't as amused as Russell had expected. 'She'll go too far one of these days. The *fragebogen*'s just a piece of paper, after all. One day they'll take her in, tear it up, and the next thing you know her parents will be getting a bill for her burial.' He shook his head. 'Being right doesn't count any more.'

'I know,' Russell said. 'She knows. But she does it so well.'

A chorus of catcalls erupted around them – Viktoria Berlin were on their way out. As the two men got to their feet, Hertha emerged to a more affectionate welcome. Casting his eyes over the towering grandstand and the high, crowded terraces behind each goal, Russell felt the usual surge of excitement. Glancing to his left, he saw Paul's eyes mirror his own.

The first half was all Hertha, but Viktoria scored the only goal in a breakaway just before the interval. Joachim seethed with indignation, while Paul yo-yoed between hope and anxiety. Thomas smoked two cigarettes.

The second half followed the same pattern, and there were only ten minutes left when Hertha's inside-left was tripped in the penalty area. He took the penalty himself. The ball hit both posts before going in, leaving the crowd in hysterics. Then, a minute from time, with evening falling and the light swiftly fading, Hertha's centre-forward raced onto a long bouncing ball and volleyed it home from almost thirty yards. The Viktoria goalkeeper hadn't moved. As the stadium exploded with joy he just stood there, making angry gestures at his team-mates, the referee, the rest of the world.

Paul was ecstatic. Eyes shining, he joined in the chant now echoing round the ground – 'Ha! Ho! He! Hertha BSC! Ha! Ho! He! Hertha BSC!'

For an eleven-year-old, Russell thought fondly, this was as good as it gets.

It was dark by the time he dropped Paul off. He took a 76 back into town, ate supper at a beer restaurant just off the Potsdamerplatz, and walked the last kilometre home. Reaching his street, he noticed what looked like the same empty car parked across from his apartment block. He was on his way to investigate it when he heard the scream.

It was no ordinary scream. It was loud, lingering, and somehow managed to encompass surprise, terror and appalling pain. For a brief instant, Russell was back in the trenches, listening to someone who'd just lost a limb to a shell.

It came from further down the street.

He hesitated, but only long enough for his brain to register his hesitation as an essential corollary of living in Nazi Germany. All too often, screams meant officialdom, and experience suggested that officialdom was best avoided at such moments.

Still, investigating a scream of agony seemed legitimate behaviour, even in Nazi Germany. Not all crimes were committed by the state or its supporters. Russell walked resolutely on past the courtyard which his block shared with its neighbour, telling himself that valour was the better part of discretion.

The source of the disturbance was the further of the two blocks off the next courtyard. A couple of men were hovering in the entrance, obviously uncertain what to do. They eyed Russell nervously, and just looked at each other when he asked them what was going on. Both were in their forties, and an obvious facial similarity suggested brothers.

In the courtyard beyond, an open-backed lorry was parked with its engine running, and a single man in an SA uniform was walking towards them.

'Keep moving,' he told them, without any real conviction. His breath stank of beer.

'But we live here,' one of the two men said.

'Just wait there then,' the storm-trooper said, looking up at the illuminated windows on the third floor. 'You might get some free entertainment,' he added over his shoulder as he walked back towards the lorry.

Seconds later, another blood-curdling scream reverberated round the courtyard.

'What in God's name …' Russell began. 'Who lives up there?' he asked the two men.

'Two actors,' the elder of the two replied.

'*Warmer brüder*,' the other added, using the current slang for homosexuals. 'They've been brazen as hell. Someone must have denounced them.' He didn't sound too upset about it.

No other lights were showing in either block, but Russell could almost feel the silent audience watching from behind the tiers of darkened windows. He thought about calling the police, but knew there was no point.

One of the illuminated windows was suddenly flung open, and a man was silhouetted against the opening, looking out and down. A crying, whimpering sound was now audible, and just as the man disappeared another scream split the night, even more piercing than the last. There was a flurry of movement inside the lighted room, and suddenly a naked body was flying out through the window, dropping, screaming, hitting the floor of the courtyard with a sickening, silencing thud. The body twitched once and lay still, as desperate, sobbing pleas of 'no,please,no' leaked out of the open window. Another flurry, another naked body, this one twisting in flight like an Olympic diver who'd mistaken concrete for water. here was no twitch this time, no last-second adjustment to death.

The two bodies lay a couple of feet apart, in the thin pool of light thrown by the block's entrance lamp. One man was face down, the other face up, with only a glistening mess where his genitals had been.

With a shock, Russell recognised the man's face. He'd seen him – talked to him even – at one of Effi's theatrical gatherings. He had no memory of the man's name, but he'd been nice enough. With a passion for Hollywood movies, Russell remembered. Katherine Hepburn in particular.

'Show's over,' the SA man was saying loudly. 'You saw it. They must have cut each other's pricks off before they jumped.' He laughed. 'You can go in now,' he added.

Russell's two companions looked to be in shock. One started to say something, but no sound emerged, and the other just gave him a gentle push on the shoulder. They walked towards their door, drawing a wide circle around the two corpses.

'And you?' the SA man shouted at Russell.

'I was just passing,' he said automatically.

'Then keep moving,' the SA man ordered.

Russell obediently turned and walked away, his eyes still full of the mutilated bodies. The bile in his stomach wouldn't stay down. Supporting himself against a lamp post he retched his supper into the gutter, then leaned against a wall, brain swirling with the usual useless rage. Another crime that would never be punished, another story that begged to be told.

And would he risk losing his son to tell it? No, he wouldn't.

And was he ashamed of his silence? Yes, he was.

He levered himself off the wall and walked slowly on towards his own courtyard and block. As he reached the entrance he remembered the empty car. It was gone.

As usual, Frau Heidegger seemed to be waiting for him. 'What was all that noise about?' she asked, then noticed his face. 'Herr Russell, you look like you've seen a ghost!'

'The SA came for a couple of homosexuals in the next block,' he said. There seemed no point in giving her the gory details.

'Oh,' she said, shaking her head in involuntary denial. 'I know the men you mean. They … well … it's not our business, is it?' She ducked back inside her door and re-emerged with two envelopes, only one of which was stamped. 'These came for you this morning,' she said. 'A policeman delivered the one in the plain envelope.'

He opened the stamped one first. It was a reply from the Soviet press attaché, reiterating the terms of Shchepkin's original offer.

He opened the other, conscious of Frau Heidegger's interest. The Gestapo wanted to see him. Within three days.

'They just want a chat,' he reassured her. 'Something to do with my accreditation, I expect.'

'Ah,' she said, sounding less than completely convinced.

Russell shared her misgivings. As he climbed the stairs, he told himself there was nothing to worry about. They'd read his letter to the Soviets, and just wanted to clarify his intentions. If it was anything else, they wouldn't be delivering invitations and letting him pick the day – they'd be throwing him out of the window.

A frisson of fear shot across his chest, and his legs felt strangely unsteady. Suddenly the photographic book seemed like a very bad idea.

'Ha ho bloody he,' he muttered to himself.

The Knauer boy

The Gestapo's invitation to dance was still on Russell's desk when he got up the following morning. One Sturmbannführer Kleist was expecting to see John Russell in Room 48, 102 Wilhelmstrasse within the next seventy-two hours. No explanation was offered.

It wasn't actually the Gestapo – 102 Wilhelmstrasse was the headquarters of the Party intelligence organization, the *Sicherheitsdienst*. Though both were run by Reinhard Heydrich with a cheery disregard for legal niceties, the SD had a reputation for more sophisticated thuggery – same pain, cleaner floors.

He read the letter through again, looking for a more sinister message between the lines, and decided there was none. Shchepkin had said they'd want to talk to him, and they did. It was as simple as that. A friendly warning was waiting in Room 48, and nothing more. Sturmbannführer Kleist would turn out to be a Hertha supporter, and they would chat about what had gone wrong this season.

Still, Russell thought as he shaved, there was no reason to hurry down there. He couldn't afford to miss the new Chancellery opening at noon, and there was no telling how long the various ceremonies would take. Tomorrow would do. Or even Wednesday.

Back in his room, he picked up the Leica and took a few imaginary photos. It had no flash, but Zembski had said the lens was good enough for indoor shooting as long as he held the camera steady and used the right film. And he could always ask the Führer for the loan of a shoulder.

Cheered by this thought – feeling, in fact, unreasonably buoyant for someone with an appointment at 102 Wilhelmstrasse – he headed downstairs and out into the grey January morning. As if in response to his mood, a tram glided to a halt at the stop on Friedrichstrasse just as he reached it. Ten minutes later he was ensconced in a Café Kranzler window seat, enjoying a first sip of his breakfast coffee as he examined the morning papers.

Foreign Minister Ribbentrop had been talking to the visiting Polish leader, Colonel Beck – now there were two men who deserved each other. The new battleship *Scharnhorst* had been commissioned at Wilhelmshaven, complete with nine eleven-inch guns, two catapults and four planes. The captain's main claim to fame was his shelling of a Spanish seaside town in 1937, while commanding the pocket battleship *Admiral Scheer*. On the home front, Pastor Martin Niemoller's brother Wilhelm had delivered a sermon attacking government policy towards the churches. He had read a list from the pulpit of all those churchmen – including his brother – currently enjoying the state's hospitality. The newspaper was not sure whether this constituted a crime: 'It has recently been established in certain cases,' the editor wrote, 'that to read the names of persons in custody may itself be an offence.'

On a more positive note, the French were demonstrating their usual sound sense of priorities. Parisian cinemas had been closed for a week in protest against a new tax on receipts, but a compromise had now been agreed: the taxes would remain in force, but would not be collected.

Russell smiled and looked out of the window, just in time to see two young women walk by, their faces shining with pleasure over some shared secret. The sun was struggling to emerge. Hitler had probably ordered it for noon; a few shafts of light would show up the medieval perfection of his new castle. Russell wondered how far Speer and his mentor had gone. Would it be the usual Graeco-Roman monstrosity, or something more ambitious? A Parthenon decked out in runes, perhaps.

Another coffee brought the time to 11.45. He walked to the top of Wilhelmstrasse, and headed down past the Hotel Adlon and serried government buildings to the new Chancellery. After showing his journalist's pass and invitation to a security guard, Russell took a photo of the crowd already gathering behind the cordon. The security guard glared at him, but did nothing else.

Russell joined the knot of privileged journalists and photographers already gathered around the entrance, almost all of whom he recognised. Somewhat to his surprise, Tyler McKinley was among them. 'My editor was keen,' the young American said resentfully, as if nothing else could have persuaded him to bless Hitler's new building with his presence. Russell gave him an 'Oh yeah?' look and walked over to Jack Slaney, one of the longer-serving American correspondents. Russell had been in Slaney's office when the latter's invitation had arrived, complete with an unsolicited – and presumably accidental – extra. Slaney had been good enough to pass it on – he had been a freelance himself in the dim distant past, and knew what this sort of exclusive could be worth.

'A one-man band,' he muttered, looking at Russell's camera.

'I prefer to think of myself as Renaissance Man,' Russell told him, just as the doors swung open.

The fifty or so journalists surged into the lobby, where a shiny-looking toady from the Propaganda Ministry was waiting for them. There would be a short tour of the new building, he announced, during which photographs could be taken. The ceremonial opening would take place in the Great Hall at precisely 1 pm, and would be followed by a workers' lunch for the thousands of people who had worked on the project.

'There might be some meat, then,' one American journalist muttered.

The toady led them back outside, and around the corner into Vosstrasse. Huge square columns framed the double-gated main entrance, which led into a spacious vestibule. Russell hung back to take a couple of photos before following his colleagues up a flight of steps to the reception hall. From there, bronze eagles clutching swastikas guarded fifteen foot doors to a bigger hall clad in grey and gold tiles. The Führer was unavailable, so Russell used Slaney's shoulder to steady the Leica.

More steps led to a circular chamber, another door into a gallery lined with crimson marble pillars. This, their guide told them, was, at 146 metres, twice as long as the Hall of Mirrors in Versailles. 'And my mother told me size didn't matter,' one journalist lamented in English. 'I expect your father had a whopper,' another said, provoking an outburst of laughter. The ministry toady stamped his foot on the marble floor, and then took a quick look down to make sure he hadn't damaged it.

The next hall was big enough to build aircraft in. Several hundred people were already waiting for the official opening, but the space still seemed relatively empty, as if mere people were incapable of filling it. Though released by their Ministry minder, the group of journalists stuck together in one corner, chatting among themselves as they waited for Hitler's entrance.

'We used to have arms races,' Slaney observed. 'Now we have hall races. Hitler had this built because he was so impressed by the size of Mussolini's office. And the moment Benito sees this he'll have to have one in Rome that's even bigger. And they'll both keep outbidding each other until the world runs out of marble.'

'I have a feeling they're building arms too,' Dick Normanton said wryly, his Yorkshire accent sounding almost surreal in this setting. He was one of the veteran English correspondents, much pampered by the Propaganda Ministry. This was hardly his fault: Normanton had an acute understanding of where Nazi Germany was headed, and often said as much in his reporting. Unfortunately for him, his London proprietor admired Hitler, and made sure that his editor edited accordingly.

'If you're interested in a horror show,' he told Russell, 'try the University on Wednesday. Streicher's inaugurating a new Chair of Anti-Jewish Propaganda and giving a speech. There should be some good Mad Hatter material.'

'Sounds suitably gruesome,' Russell agreed.

'What does?' McKinley asked, joining them

Normanton explained reluctantly – McKinley was not noted for his love of irony.

'Why would anyone want to listen to Streicher?' the American asked after Normanton had drifted away. 'It's not as if he's going to say anything interesting, is it?'

'I guess not,' Russell agreed diplomatically, and changed the subject. 'What do you make of the building?' he asked.

McKinley sighed. 'It's gross. In every meaning of the word,' he added, looking round.

Russell found this hard to disagree with – the new Chancellery was indeed gross. But it was also impressive, in a disturbing sort of way. It might be a monument to Hitler's lack of aesthetic imagination, but it was also proof of intention. This was not the sort of building you could ignore. It meant business.

It was Russell's turn to sigh. 'How was your weekend?' he asked McKinley.

'Oh, fine. I caught up on some work, saw a movie. And I went dancing at one of those halls off the Alexanderplatz. With one of the secretaries at the Embassy.' He smiled in reminiscence, and looked about sixteen years old. 'And I saw a couple of people for that story I told you about,' he added quickly, as if he'd caught himself slacking.

'You didn't actually tell me anything about it.'

'Ah. I will. In time. In fact I may need your help with ...'

He was drowned out by an eruption of applause. Right arms shot towards the ceiling, as if some celestial puppeteer had suddenly flicked a finger. His Nibs had arrived.

Russell dutifully lined up the Leica and squeezed off a couple of shots. The Führer was not in uniform, and looked, as usual, like an unlikely candidate for leadership of a master race. One arm was stuck at half-mast to acknowledge the welcome, the mouth set in a self-satisfied smirk. The eyes slowly worked their way round the room, placid as a lizard's. This man will kill us all, Russell thought.

A builder's mate in the traditional top hat of the German artisan – his name, the toady had told them, was Max Hoffman – presented Hitler with the keys to his new home. Flashbulbs popped, hands clapped. The Führer volunteered a few words. He was, he said, the same person he had always been, and wished to be nothing more. 'Which means he's learnt absolutely nothing,' Slaney whispered in Russell's ear.

And that was that. Moving like a formation dancing team, Hitler and his ring of bodyguards began mingling with the guests in the privileged section of the hall, the ring working like a choosy Venus Fly-trap, admitting chosen ones to the Presence and spitting them out again. Much to the interest of the watching journalists, the Soviet Ambassador was given by far the longest audience.

'Fancy a drink?' Slaney asked Russell. Two of the other Americans, Bill Peyton and Hal Manning, were standing behind him. 'We're headed over to that bar on Behrenstrasse.'

'Suits me,' Russell agreed. He looked round for McKinley, but the youngster had disappeared.

The sun was still shining, but the temperature had dropped. The bar was dark, warm and blessed with several empty tables. A huge bear's head, half-hidden in the dense layer of smoke which hung from the ceiling, loomed over the one they chose. Slaney went off to buy the first round.

'It's hard to believe that Hitler got started in places like this,' Manning said, lighting a cigarette and offering the pack around. He was a tall, thin man with greying hair and a cadaverous face, and like Slaney a veteran foreign correspondent, in his case having worked his way up through Asian capitals and more obscure European postings to the eminence of 1939 Berlin. Peyton was younger – somewhere in his mid-thirties, Russell guessed – with clipped blonde hair and a boyish face. He worked full-time for a national weekly and sold stuff to the business monthlies on the side.

Russell found Peyton irritatingly sure of himself, but he had soft spots for both Manning and Slaney. If Americans remained ignorant about Nazi Germany, it wouldn't be their fault.

'So how do we tell this one, boys?' Slaney asked once the beers had been passed round. 'Just another grand building? Or megalomania run riot?'

'NEW LAIR FOR MONSTER?' Manning suggested.

'I like it,' Slaney said, wiping froth off his nose. 'Adolf was getting chummy with Astakhov, wasn't he?'

Manning agreed. 'And Astakhov was lapping it up. Looks as if Stalin's given up on the Brits and the French.'

Russell remembered what Shchepkin had said on the subject. 'You can hardly blame him after Munich.'

'True, but you can hardly blame Chamberlain and Daladier for not trusting Stalin,' Peyton said.

'Bastards all,' Slaney summed up. 'I see Chamberlain's on his way to see the Duce' – he pronounced it 'Dootch' – 'in Rome. On some train called the Silver Bullet.'

Russell laughed. 'It's the Golden Arrow.'

'Whatever. A week with Mussolini. I hope he likes parades.'

'Why's he going?' Peyton asked.

'God knows. You'd think that by now someone in London would have noticed that the Duce is a man of moods. If he's feeling good he'll promise the world, set their Limey minds at rest. If he isn't, he'll try and scare the pants off 'em. Whichever he does, he'll be doing the opposite before the week's out.'

'Pity his German chum isn't a bit more mercurial,' Manning said. 'Once he gets his teeth into something, it stays bitten.'

'Or swallowed, in the Jews' case,' Russell added. 'Why the hell isn't Roosevelt doing more to help the Jews here?'

'He's building up the air force,' Peyton said. 'There was another announcement over the weekend.'

'Yes, but that won't help the Jews.'

'He can't,' Slaney said. 'Too much domestic opposition.'

Russell wasn't convinced. 'The British are doing something. Nothing like enough, I know. But something.'

'Two reasons,' Manning said. 'One, and most important – they just don't get it back in Washington. Or out in the Boonies. When Americans think about German Jews having a hard time, the first thing they think about is what American Jews have to put up with – restricted golf clubs, stuff like that. When they realise that Hitler doesn't play golf, they still find it hard to imagine anything worse than the way we treat our negroes. Sure, the negroes are condemned to segregation and poverty, but lynchings are pretty rare these days, and the vast majority get a life that's just about livable. Americans assume it's the same for the German Jews.'

'But what about the concentration camps?' Russell asked.

'They just think of them as German prisons. A bit harsh, maybe, but lots of Americans think our prisons should be harsher.' He shrugged and took a gulp of beer.

'And the second reason?' Russell prompted.

'That's easy. A lot of Americans just don't like Jews. They think they're getting their comeuppance. If they had any idea just how harsh that comeuppance is, some of them might – *might* – have second thoughts, but they don't.'

'I guess that's down to us.'

'Us and our editors,' Slaney said. 'We've told the story often enough. People just don't want to hear it. And if you keep on and on about it they just turn off.'

'Europe's far away,' Manning said.

'And getting farther,' Slaney said. 'Jesus, let's think about something pleasant for a change.' He turned to Russell. 'John, I'm organizing a poker night for next Tuesday. How about it?'

The foursome emerged into the daylight soon after three, and went their separate ways – Peyton to his mistress, Slaney and Manning to write their copy for the morning editions. Walking south down Wilhelmstrasse, Russell decided on impulse to drop in on Sturmbannführer Kleist. A small voice in his head protested that the *Sicherheitsdienst* was best encountered stone-cold sober, but was promptly drowned out by a louder one insisting that there was nothing to be afraid of. The meeting was just a formality. So why not get it over with?

The fresh-faced blonde receptionist seemed pleased enough to see him, gesturing him through to an ante-room with the sort of friendly smile that could soften up any man. Sunk into one of the leather chairs, Russell found himself staring at the latest creation of the Propaganda Ministry's poster artists, Hitler complete with visionary stare and catchy slogan – '*ein Volk, ein Reich, ein Führer*'. On the opposite wall a more colourful poster showed apple-cheeked youth frolicking in the Alps. That was the thing about these people, he thought: they never surprised you.

The minutes dragged by; the later pints of beer pressed ever more urgently for release. He went back out to the receptionist, who pointed him in the direction of a toilet with the same sunny smile. The toilet was spotless and smelt as if it had just been hosed down with Alpine flowers. One of the cubicles was occupied, and Russell imagined Heydrich sitting with his breeches round his ankles, reading something Jewish.

Back in the ante-room he found company. A man in his sixties, smartly dressed, probably German. They exchanged nods, but nothing more. The man shifted nervously in his seat, causing the leather to squeak. Hitler stared at them both.

After about twenty minutes the sound of clicking heels seeped out of the silence, and another young blonde appeared in the doorway. 'Herr John Russell?' she enquired. 'Follow me, please.'

They went down one long corridor, up some steps, down another corridor. All Russell could hear was the rhythmic click of the blonde's shoes – no sounds escaped through the numerous doors they passed, no talk, no laughter, no typewriters. There was no sense that the building was empty, though, more a feeling of intense concentration, as if everyone was thinking fit to burst. Which, Russell realised, was absurd. Maybe the SD had a half-term break, like British schools.

Through the window on a second flight of stairs he caught a glimpse of a large lawn and the huge swastika flying over Hitler's new home. At the end of the next corridor the heels swung right through an open doorway.

Room 48 was not so much a room as a suite. The secretary led him through her high-ceilinged ante-room, opened the inner door and ushered him in.

Sturmbannführer Gottfried Kleist – as the nameboard on the desk announced – looked up, gestured him to the leather-bound seat on the near side of his leather-bound desk, and carried on writing. He was a stout man in denial, his black uniform just a little too tight for what it had to contain. He had a florid face, thinning hair and rather prominent red lips. He did have blue eyes, though, and his handwriting was exquisite. Russell watched the fountain pen scrape across the page, forming elegant whorls and loops from the dark green ink.

After what seemed like several minutes, Kleist carefully replaced the pen in its holder, almost daintily blotted his work and, after one last admiring look, moved it to the right hand side of his desk. From the left he picked up a folder, opened it, and raised his eyes to Russell's. 'John Russell,' he said. It wasn't a question.

'You asked to see me,' Russell said, with as much bonhomie as he could muster.

The Sturmbannführer ran a hand through his hair, straightening a few rebellious wisps with his fingers. 'You are an English national.'

'With resident status in the Reich.'

'Yes, yes. I know. And a current journalistic accreditation.'

'Yes.'

'Could I see it please?'

Russell removed it from his inside jacket pocket and passed it over.

Kleist noticed the invitation card. 'Ah, the opening,' he said. 'A success, I assume. Were you impressed?'

'Very much so. The building is a credit to the Führer.'

Kleist looked sharply at Russell, as if doubtful of his sincerity.

'So much modern architecture seems insubstantial,' Russell added.

'Indeed,' Kleist agreed, handing back the press pass. Apparently satisfied, he sat back in his seat, both hands grasping the edge of his desk. 'Now, it has come to our attention that the Soviet newspaper *Pravda* has commissioned you to write a series of articles about the Fatherland.' He paused for a moment, as if daring Russell to ask how it had come to their attention. 'This was at your suggestion, I believe.'

'It was.'

'Why did you suggest these articles, Mr Russell?'

Russell shrugged. 'Several reasons. All freelance journalists are always looking to place stories with whoever will buy them. And it occurred to me that the Soviets might be interested in a fresh look at National Socialist Germany, one that concentrates on what the two societies have in common, rather than what divides them. What I ...'

Kleist stopped him with a raised hand. 'Why did you think this would interest the Soviets?'

Russell took his time. 'Soviet propaganda has generally been very hostile towards the Reich,' he began. 'And by taking this course, they have backed themselves into a corner. There's no doubt that Germany is the rising power in Europe, and the Soviets – like everyone else – will sooner or later have to deal with that reality. But as things stand at the moment, their own people would not understand a more ... a more accommodating attitude towards the Reich. The articles I propose would prepare the ground, so to speak. They would help restore the Soviet government's freedom of movement, allow them to act in concert with the Reich if and when the two states' interests coincide.'

Kleist looked thoughtful.

'And I see such articles as a contribution to peace,' Russell went on, hoping he wasn't over-egging the pudding. 'I fought in the last war, and I have no desire to see another. If nations and governments understand each other, there's less chance we'll all blunder into one.'

Kleist smiled. 'I don't think there's much chance of the Führer blundering into anything,' he said. 'But I take your point. And we have no objection to your articles, subject to certain conditions. These are sensitive subjects – I'm sure you'd agree. And while you are English, you are also living in the Reich under our protection. Your views would not be seen as official views, but they would be seen as views we are prepared to tolerate. You understand me? Whatever you write could be construed as having our blessing.'

Russell felt anxious for the first time. 'Yes …' he said hesitantly.

'So, you see, it follows that we cannot permit you to write anything that we violently disagree with. Your articles will have to be pre-submitted for our approval. I am sure,' he added, 'that this will only be a formality.'

Russell thought quickly. Should he at least recognize the implied dismissal of his journalistic integrity, or just play the cynic? He opted for the practical approach. 'This is unusual, but I see your point,' he said. 'And I have no objection, provided that your office can approve – or disapprove – the articles quickly. The first one is due in a couple of weeks, and at fortnightly intervals after that – so, a couple of days …'

'That will not be a problem. Nothing gathers dust here.'

Kleist looked pleased, and Russell had the sudden realisation that the SD were as eager to see these articles as Shchepkin and his people. He decided to go for broke. 'Sturmbannführer, could I make a request? In order to write these articles I shall need to travel a great deal around the Reich, and talk to a lot of people. I shall be asking them questions which they may find suspicious, coming, as they will, from a foreigner. A letter from this office confirming my credentials, and stating that I have permission to ask such questions, would be very useful. It would save a lot of time talking to local officials, and might help me avoid all sorts of time-consuming difficulties.'

Kleist looked momentarily off-balance – this was not in his script – but he soon recovered. He scratched his cheek and rearranged his hair again before answering. 'That seems a reasonable request,' he said, 'but I'll have to consult with my superiors before issuing such a letter.' He looked down at his pen, as if imagining the pleasure of writing it out.

'Is there anything else?' Russell asked.

'Just one thing. Your business with the Soviets – you are conducting it by post, I presume?'

'So far,' Russell agreed, hoping to God that Kleist knew nothing of his meeting with Shchepkin. 'Though of course I may have to use the phone or the wire service at some point.'

'Mm. Let me be frank with you, Mr Russell. If, in the course of your dealings with the Soviets, you learn anything of their intentions, their capabilities, we would expect you to pass such information on.'

'You're asking me to spy for you?'

'No, not as such. Mr Russell, you've lived in Germany for many years ...'

'Almost fourteen.'

'Exactly. Your son is a German boy, a proud member of the Hitler Youth, I believe.'

'He is.'

'So presumably you feel a certain loyalty to the Reich.'

'I feel affection, and gratitude. I am not a great believer in loyalty to countries or governments.'

'Ah, you were a communist once, I believe.'

'Yes, but so was Mussolini. A lot of people were in the early 1920s. Like Mussolini, I got over it. As for my loyalty or lack of it … Sturmbannführer, what would you think of a German who, after a decade spent in England, proclaimed his loyalty to the English King? I suspect you would consider him a traitor to the Fatherland.'

'I …'

'I have a German son,' Russell ploughed on. 'I have an American mother, and I had an English father. I was brought up in England. Insofar as I am able, I am loyal to all three countries.'

'But not to the Soviets?'

'No.'

'So if a Soviet contact told you of a threat to the Reich, you would not keep it to yourself.'

'I would not.'

'Very well. Then I think our business is concluded.' Kleist stood up and offered his hand across the desk. 'If you get the articles to me, either by hand or post, I will guarantee to return them within twenty-four hours. Will that suffice?'

'It will.'

'Then good day to you. Fräulein Lange will see you back to the entrance.'

She did. Russell followed the clicking heels once more, picked up his coat from the smiling receptionist, and found himself out on the Wilhelmstrasse pavement. It was dark. In more ways than one.

Tuesday was clear and cold. Walking down to the U-bahn at Hallesches Tor, Russell was more conscious of the icy wind from the east than any theoretical warmth from the sun. At the studio in Neukölln he waited while Zembski shouted at someone down the phone, and then persuaded the Silesian to develop his film that day. Back at the U-bahn station he bought the *Tageblatt* and *Allgemeine Zeitung* at a kiosk and skimmed through their accounts of the Chancellery opening as he waited for a train. As far as he could tell, he'd seen all there was to see.

The only other items of interest were the imminent departure of Reichsbank President Schacht, the Danzig stamp row – which had finally reached the German nationals – and the unsurprising news that US government spokesmen were less than impressed by the Nazis' latest idea of sending all the Jews to either Manchuria or Alaska.

Back at Neuenburgerstrasse Russell settled down to work. If you had a green light from the SD, he noted cynically, it probably paid to get moving. First off, he needed a list of topics for *Pravda*. What was so great about Nazi Germany if you didn't like flags and blood in the gutter? Full employment, for one. A national sense of well-being. Workers' benefits, up to a point. Cheap organised leisure activities – sport, culture, travel. All these came at a cost, and only, needless to say, to aryans, but there was something there. As an English advertising man had once told him, there had to be *something* in the product that was worth having.

What else? Health care was pretty good for the curable. And transport – the rocket trains, the Autobahns and the people's car, the new flying-boats and aeroplanes. The Nazis loved modernity when it speeded things up or made them simpler, hated it when it complicated things, or made it harder for them to live in their medieval mind-set. Einstein being Jewish was most convenient.

He could write something perceptive about Nazi Germany if he had the mind to, Russell thought. Unfortunately …

He could write these articles in his sleep. Or almost. The Soviets liked lots of statistics – something they shared with the Nazis – and that would involve a little work. But not much. Shchepkin's oral reports on the other hand …

He'd been trying not to think about them. Kleist's question about other contacts had also been intended as a warning – he was sure of that. And the Soviets expected him to meet one of their agents outside Germany once a month. Which would no doubt make things safer for the agent, but how was he supposed to explain this new and oddly regular penchant for foreign travel? Could he refuse this part of the Soviet job? He suspected not. He wasn't sure how the Soviets would make any hard feelings felt, but he was sure they'd manage it somehow.

Nor did he feel that happy about wandering round Germany asking questions, even if Kleist did come up with some sort of protective letter. He supposed he could invent any number of imaginary responses – how, after all, could the Soviets check up on him? Then again, who knew what was left of the communist network in Germany? And in any case, part of him liked the idea of finding out what ordinary Germans were feeling in Year Six of Hitler's thousand.

That was it, he thought. 'Ordinary Germans.' The British and American tabloids liked series: the *Daily Mail* was currently running one on 'European Troublespots' – he'd read Number Four (MEMEL – EUROPE'S NAGGING TOOTH) the previous week. He could do something similar about ordinary Germans. The Worker. The Housewife. The Sailor, the Doctor, the Schoolboy. Whatever, as Slaney would say. Interviewing them would provide the ideal cover for gathering the information Shchepkin wanted.

And the trips abroad? It was obvious – 'Germany's Neighbours'. Another series, this one looking at how people in the neighbouring countries viewed Germany. He could travel all he wanted, talk to all the foreigners he wanted, without arousing suspicion. In Poland, Denmark, Holland, France, what was left of Czechoslovakia. He could take Effi to Paris, visit his cousin Rainer in Budapest. He leaned back in his chair feeling pleased with himself. These two series would make him safer and richer. Things were looking up.

The feeling of well-being lasted until the next day. After posting off his text and photos of the Chancellery opening he travelled across town to the university, where Julius Streicher was inaugurating the new chair. It wasn't, as Normanton had mischievously claimed, actually called the Chair of Anti-Jewish Propaganda, but it might have been. There was no sign of Streicher's famous bullwhip, but his veins bulged just the way Russell remembered. The Nazi angrily denied the claim that National Socialism had put fetters on science or research. Restrictions, he insisted, had only been placed on the unruly. In fact decency and sincerity had only obtained their freedom under National Socialism.

He had been ranting for an hour and a half when Russell left, and looked set for many hours more. Coming away, Russell knew what Normanton had meant about Mad Hatter material but, for once in his life, he felt more emotionally in tune with McKinley's simple disgust. Perhaps it was the fact that his next port of call was the Wiesners.

He picked up a *Daily Mail* while changing trams in Alexander-platz and went through it with the two girls. They pored over the fashion pictures and ads, puzzled over the headline which read MAN WHO SLAPPED WOMAN MAYOR SAYS 'I'M ASTOUNDED', and objected to the one which claimed ALL WOMEN ARE MAGPIES. A photograph of the King of Egypt out duck-shooting reduced

Ruth to such a fit of giggles that her mother came out to see what was happening.

After the lesson she brought out the best coffee and cake Russell had tasted for months, and insisted on thanking him profusely for all he was doing. Her husband was well, she said, but her face clouded over when he asked about Albert. He was 'finding things difficult,' she said. He had the feeling she thought about saying more, but decided against it.

He'd planned a few more hours of work before picking up Effi from the theatre, but after Streicher and the Wiesners he felt more like punching someone. He found another western on the Ku'damm and sank into a world of huge skies, lofty canyons and simple justice. Chewing gum for the heart.

Effi was tired and seemed as subdued as he felt. They walked slowly back to her flat, went to bed, and lay quietly in each other's arms until she went to sleep. Her face grew younger in sleep, and she looked even more like Ruth Wiesner.

Wednesday evening, Russell was listening to dance band music on the BBC when McKinley knocked on his door and suggested a drink. While he collected his shoes from the bedroom the young American scanned his bookshelves. 'Half of these are banned,' he said admiringly, when Russell returned.

'I haven't got round to burning them yet,' he said, reaching for his coat.

Outside it was warmer than it had been, but there were specks of rain in the air. As they turned the corner into Lindenstrasse McKinley took a sudden look over his shoulder, as if he'd heard something.

'What?' Russell asked, seeing nothing.

McKinley shook his head. 'Nothing,' he said.

They walked under the elevated U-bahn tracks at Hallesches Tor, and across Blücherplatz to the bar they used for their infrequent drinks together. It was almost empty, the barman yawning on his stool, two old men in the corner staring morosely at each other. McKinley bought them beers – dark for Russell, light for himself – while Russell commandeered the only bowl with any nuts and carried it across to the table with the fewest standing pools. As he lowered himself into the seat it groaned alarmingly but held together. 'We have to find a new bar,' he murmured.

McKinley tried his beer and smiled in satisfaction. 'OK,' he said. 'Now tell me about Schacht.'

'He's dead in the water.'

'OK, but why? I never understood economics.'

'Schacht does. That's why.'

'What do you mean?'

Russell thought about it. 'Schacht wants to see the economy run according to the laws of economics. He did when he was Finance Minister, and as long as he's in charge of the Reichsbank he'll keep beating the same drum. The trade deficit is soaring, the Reichsbank's holdings of foreign exchange are dwindling, and there's a real possibility of another runaway inflation. The economy's running out of control. Schacht would like to raise taxes and switch production from armaments to something that can be sold abroad. Some hope, eh? If Hitler and Goering have to choose between their armament programme and the laws of economics, which do you think they'll choose?'

'But if the economy is in real trouble?'

'Nothing a war won't fix.'

'Ah.'

'Ah, indeed. Schacht, shall we say, has the narrow view. He's assuming several years of peace, at the very least. Hitler, on the other hand, sees a choice. He can either do what Schacht wants – rein back the war machine, raise taxes and get the real economy moving again – or he can go for broke, and use the army to put things right. He sees all that wealth beyond his borders, just begging to be collected. That's why Schacht has to go. Hitler's not going to risk higher taxes in Germany when he can steal the same money from conquered foreigners.'

McKinley looked at him. 'I never know how serious you are. If this is such a big story – Schacht going, I mean – then why isn't it on the front pages back home? If war's so absolutely certain, how come you're the only one who knows it?'

Russell smiled. 'Just gifted, I guess. Another beer?' When he got back from the bar, McKinley was making notes in his little black book. 'Was your dance night a one-off, or are you going out with that girl from the Embassy?' Russell asked him.

McKinley blushed. 'We've only been out twice. Merle, her name is – you know, like Merle Oberon. Her father's just a storekeeper in Philadelphia but she's determined to really see life. She wants to see Europe while she's working here, and then the rest of the world if she can.'

'Good for her.'

'You've travelled a lot, haven't you?'

'Once upon a time.'

'Have you been to Russia?'

'Yes. I met my wife there – my ex-wife, I should say. At a Comintern youth conference in 1924. Lenin had just died and Trotsky hadn't noticed that the rug was gone from under his feet. It was a strange time, a sort of revolutionary cusp – not the moment it all went wrong, but the moment a lot of Party people realised that it already had. Does that make sense?'

'I suppose. I'm hoping to go in March. The nineteenth Congress is being held in Moscow and I'm trying to persuade the paper to send me.'

'That'll be interesting,' Russell said, though he doubted it would be.

Neither of them wanted another drink, and the nuts were all gone. It was raining outside, and they stood for a moment in the doorway, watching the neon shimmers in the puddles. As they passed under the elevated tracks a Warschauer Brucke train rumbled across, its sides streaming with water.

At the bottom of Lindenstrasse McKinley took a look back across the Belle Alliance Platz. 'I think I'm being followed,' he said, almost guiltily, in response to Russell's enquiring look.

'I can't see anyone,' Russell said, staring into the rain.

'No, neither can I,' McKinley said, as they started up Lindenstrasse. 'It's more of a feeling ... I don't know. If they are following me, they're really good.'

Too many *Thin Man* movies, Russell thought. 'Who's they?' he asked.

'Oh, the Gestapo, I suppose.'

'Moving like wraiths isn't exactly the Gestapo style.'

'No, I suppose not.'

'Why would they be following you?'

McKinley grunted. 'That story I told you about. That story I was going to tell you about,' he corrected himself.

'I'm not sure I want to know any more,' Russell said. 'I don't want them following me.'

It was meant as a joke, but McKinley didn't take it that way. 'Well, OK ...'

Russell was thinking about the car he'd seen outside their block. He couldn't imagine the Gestapo being that patient, but there were other sharks in the Nazi sea. 'Look, Tyler. Whatever it is, if you really are being stalked by the authorities I should just drop it. No story's worth that sort of grief.'

McKinley bristled. 'Would you have said that ten years ago?'

'I don't know. Ten years ago I didn't have the responsibilities I have now.'

'Maybe you should ask yourself whether you can still be an honest journalist with those sort of responsibilities.'

That made Russell angry. 'You haven't cornered the market in honest journalism, for God's sake.'

'Of course not. But I know what matters. That once mattered to you.'

'Truth has a habit of seeping out.' Russell wasn't even convincing himself, which made him angrier still. 'Look, there's seventy-five million people out there keeping their heads down. I'm just one of them.'

'Fine. If you want to keep your head down, wait until it all blows over – fine. But I can't do that.'

'OK.'

They walked the rest of the way in silence.

The conversation with McKinley – or, more precisely, the sense of letting himself down that it engendered – lurked with annoying persistence at the back of Russell's mind over the next few days. He finished his first article for *Pravda* – a paean to organised leisure activities – and delivered it himself to the smiling blonde at 102 Wilhelmstrasse. He received a wire from his US agent bubbling with enthusiasm for the two series. And, by special delivery, he received the letter he had asked Sturmbannführer Kleist for. It was typed rather than written, which was something of a disappointment, but the content left little to be desired – John Russell, it seemed, had full authority from the Propaganda Ministry and Ministry of the Interior to ask such questions 'as would widen the foreign understanding of National Socialism and its achievements'. Those shown the letter were 'asked and expected to offer him all the assistance they could'. All of which would have felt much better if he hadn't seen the disappointment in McKinley's eyes.

The weekend gave him a welcome break from worrying about his journalistic integrity. On Saturday afternoon he and Paul went to the zoo. They had been so many times that they had a routine – first the parrot house, then the elephant walk and the snakes, a break for ice cream, the big cats and, finally, the *pièce de résistance*, the gorilla who spat, with often devastating accuracy, at passers-by. After the zoo, they strolled back down the Ku'damm, looking in shop windows and eventually stopping for cake. Russell still found his son's Hitler Youth uniform slightly off-putting, but he was gradually getting used to it.

Sunday, a rare treat – an outing to the fair at the end of Potsdamerstrasse with both Paul and Effi. Getting them together was always harder than the actual experience of their being together – both worried overmuch that they'd be in the other's way. It was obvious that Paul liked Effi, and equally obvious why. She was willing to try anything at least once, was able to act any age she thought appropriate, and assumed that he could too. She was in fact, most of the things his mother wasn't, and had never been.

After two hours of circling, sliding, dropping and whirling they took a cab to Effi's theatre, where she showed Paul round the stage and back-stage areas. He was particularly impressed by the lift and trapdoor in mid-stage which brought the Valkyries up to heaven each evening. When Russell suggested that they should build one for Goebbels at the Sportspalast, Effi gave him a warning look, but Paul, he noticed delightedly, was unable to suppress his amusement.

The only sad note of the weekend was Paul's news that he would be away for the next weekend at a Hitler Youth adventure camp in the Harz Mountains. He was sorry not to be seeing his dad, and to be missing the next Hertha home game, but Russell could see he was looking forward to the camp. It was particularly annoying because he would be away himself the following weekend, delivering his first oral report to Shchepkin. And on that weekend he would also be missing Effi's end-of-run party – *Barbarossa* had apparently raised all the national consciousness it was going to raise.

Early on Monday morning, he took the train to Dresden for a one-night stay. It was only a two-hour journey, and he had several contacts there: a couple of journalists on the city paper; an old friend of Thomas's, also in the paper business; an old friend of his and Ilse's, once a union activist, now a teacher. Ordinary Germans, if such people existed.

He saw them all over the two days, and talked to several others they recommended. He also spent a few hours in cafés and bars, joining or instigating conversations when he could, just listening when that seemed more appropriate. As his train rattled northwards on Tuesday evening he sat in the buffet car with a schnapps and tried to make sense of what he had heard. Nothing surprising. 'Ordinary Germans' felt utterly powerless, and were resigned to feeling so for the foreseeable future. The government would doubtless translate that resignation as passive support, and to some extent they were right. There was certainly no sense that anyone had a practical alternative to offer.

When it came to Germany's relations with the rest of the world, most people seemed pleasantly surprised that they still had any. The Rhineland, the Anschluss, the Sudetenland – it was as if Hitler had deliberately driven his train across a series of broken points, but

– thanks be to God – the train was still on the track. Surely, soon, he would pull the damn thing to a halt. Once Memel and Danzig were back in the fold, once the Poles had given Germany an extra-territorial corridor across their own corridor, then that would be that. Hitler, having expanded the Reich to fit the Volk, would rest on his laurels, a German hero for centuries to come.

They all said it, and some of them even believed it.

Their own daily lives were getting harder. Not dramatically, but relentlessly. The economic squeeze was on. Most people were working longer hours for the same pay; many ordinary goods were growing slightly harder to find. The relief which had followed the return of full employment had dissipated.

Children seemed to be looming ever-larger in their parents' minds; the demands in time and loyalty of the Hitler Youth, the year-long exile of the *arbeitsdienst*, the prospect of seeing them marched off to war. If Ordinary Germans wanted anything, it was peace. Years of the stuff, years in which they could drive their people's cars down their new Autobahns.

Only one man mentioned the Jews, and then only in a dismissive preamble – 'Now that the Jewish question is nearing solution.' What did he mean? Russell asked. 'Well,' the man replied, 'they'll all be gone soon, won't they? I have nothing against them personally, but a lot of people have, and they'll be happier elsewhere – that's obvious.'

The Wiesners would have agreed with him. The girls seemed subdued when he saw them on Wednesday morning, polite and willing as ever, but less perky, as if more bad news had just descended on the household. One reason became clear when Frau Wiesner asked for a word with him after the lesson.

She wanted to ask him a favour, she said. She didn't want her husband to know, but could he, Russell, have a word with Albert? He was behaving recklessly, just saying whatever came into his mind, associating with ... well, she didn't know who, but ... he wouldn't listen to his father, she knew that, and he wouldn't listen to her, but Russell, well, he was outside it all – he wasn't a Jew, wasn't a Nazi, wasn't even a German. He knew what was happening, how dangerous things were. They were working on getting visas, but it took so long. Albert said they were dreaming, they'd never get them, but he didn't know that, and he was putting the girls' future at risk as well as his own ...

She ran out of words, and just looked at him helplessly.

Russell's heart sank at the prospect, but he agreed to try.

'I'll make sure he's here on Friday, after the lesson,' she said.

That evening, he was getting his Dresden notes in order when Tyler McKinley knocked on his door. 'I've come to apologise,' the American said.

'What for?' Russell said.

'You know. The other night.'

'Oh that. Forget it.'

'OK. How about a drink?'

Russell rubbed his eyes. 'Why not?'

They went to their usual bar, sat at the same table. Russell thought he recognised the stains from the previous week. His companion seemed relieved that he wasn't holding a grudge, and he was drinking dark beer for a change. The bar was more crowded than usual, with a population reaching towards double figures.

McKinley got out his pipe and tin of Balkan mixture.

'What got you started in journalism?' Russell asked.

'Oh, I always wanted to be one. Long as I can remember.' The American smiled in reminiscence. 'When I was a kid I used to spend the summer with my mother's folks in Nugget City – you probably never heard of it – it's a small town in California. Grew up in the Gold Rush days, been shrinking ever since. My granddad ran the local paper in his spare time. Just a weekly. Two pages. Four if something had actually happened. I used to help him with stuff. On print day we'd both come home covered in ink. I loved it.' He picked up the tobacco tin, and put it down again. 'Granddad and grandma both died when I was twelve, so all that stopped. I tried offering my services to the San Francisco papers, but they didn't want kids hanging around in their print rooms. Not surprising really. Anyway, I got involved with my high school paper, and then the college paper, and eventually got a job at the *Examiner*. Three years in sports, three on the city desk, and I finally got myself sent to Europe.' He grinned. 'I still love it.'

'What did your family think?' Russell asked. He meant about coming to Europe, but McKinley, busying loading his pipe, answered a different question.

'My father was furious. He has his own law firm, and I was supposed to sign up, start at the bottom and eventually take over. He thinks journalists are grubby little hacks, you know, like *The Front Page*.' His eyes lit up. 'Did you know they're re-making that, with a woman reporter? Rosalind Russell, I think. And Cary Grant's her editor. I read about it in one of Merle's Hollywood magazines.'

'Your dad still furious?'

'Not so much. I mean, they're happy enough to see me when I come home.' He sounded like he was trying to convince himself. 'It's funny,' he added, 'my sister seems angrier than my father.'

'What does she do?'

'Nothing much, as far as I can tell. She'd make a much better lawyer than I would, but … well, you know … Dad would never take a woman into the firm.' He struck a match, applied it to the bowl, and sucked in. The bowl glowed, and a noxious plume of smoke escaped from his lips.

'That's enough to make anyone resentful,' Russell said. 'Not being offered something you want is bad enough; someone else turning it down just adds salt to the wound.'

McKinley looked at him as if he was a magician. 'You know, that never occurred to me.'

'When did you last go home?' Russell asked.

'Oh, the Thanksgiving before last. But I write quite often.'

Russell thought about his own family. His mother in America, his half-brother in Leeds. Bernard was well over fifty now, the single offspring of his father's brief liaison with the army nurse who treated him – in more ways than one – after the Gordon campaign in the Sudan. Russell hadn't seen him in years, and had no particular desire to. There were a couple of uncles in England, one aunt in America, cousins dotted here and there. He hadn't seen any of them either. It was time he took Paul on a visit to England, he thought.

He looked at McKinley, happily puffing away at his pipe. 'Do you never get homesick?' he asked.

'Sure, sometimes. Days like today I miss the sunshine. I know everyone thinks San Francisco is always shrouded in fog, but it isn't. It's still the loveliest city I've seen.' He smiled. 'But this is where the story is.'

'Unfortunately.'

'Well, yes. I was wondering … I'm arranging this interview next week – I don't know which evening yet – and I wondered if you'd be willing to come along. My German is pretty good, but yours is obviously a lot better, and the only time I met this woman I could hardly understand anything she said. And I really can't afford to misunderstand anything she tells me.'

'Who is she?'

McKinley hesitated. 'She used to work for the Health Ministry.'

'This is the big story?'

McKinley grinned briefly. 'You could say that. You remember that story I did on asylums last year?'

Russell did. It hadn't been at all bad. The American had managed to raise quite a few awkward questions, and it was hardly his fault that no one else had demanded any answers. 'I remember,' he said.

'Well, this woman was one of the people I interviewed. She told me a pack of lies, as far as I could tell. And then last week she contacted me out of the blue, said she was willing to give me some information about some of the other stuff I've heard.'

'About the asylums?'

'Yes and no. Look,' he said, looking round. 'I don't want to talk about it here. Let's go back to the house.'

'OK,' Russell agreed. He was beginning to feel intrigued, despite himself.

As they walked back to Neuenburgerstrasse he kept an eye open for possible shadows, and noticed that McKinley was doing the same. None crept into view, and the street outside their block was empty of cars.

'The Knauer boy,' McKinley said, once they were ensconced in Russell's two armchairs. 'I don't think his parents gave him a Christian name. He was blind, had only one arm, and part of one leg was missing. He was also, supposedly, an idiot. A medical idiot, I mean. Mentally retarded. Anyway, his father wrote to Hitler asking that the boy should be killed. Hitler got one of the doctors employed by the KdF to confirm the facts, which they did. He then gave the child's own doctors permission to carry out a mercy-killing. The boy was put to sleep.' He paused to re-stoke his pipe.

'That's a sad story,' Russell said cautiously.

'There's two things,' McKinley said. 'Hitler has never made any secret of his plan to purify the race by sterilising the mentally handicapped and all the other so-called incurables. And the Nazis are always going on about how much it costs to keep all these people in asylums. They actually use it as an example in one of their school text-books – you know, how many people's cars you could build with what it costs to feed and clothe ten incurables for a year. Put the two things together, and you get one easy answer – kill them. It purifies the race and saves money.'

'Yes, but …'

'I know. But if the Knauer boy is expendable, why not the others? About 100,000 of them, according to the latest figures. Tell the parents they're doing it to cut short the child's suffering, give them an excuse not to have the problem any more. In fact, don't even tell the parents. Spare their suffering by saying that the child died of natural causes.'

'100,000 of them?'

'Perhaps not, but …'

'OK, it sounds feasible. It sounds like the Nazis, for Christ's sake. But are they actually doing it? And if they are, do you have any proof that they're doing it?'

'There are all sorts of indications …'

'Not good enough.'

'Plans then.'

'On paper?'

'Not exactly. Look, will you come and see this woman with me?'

Russell knew what the sensible answer was, but McKinley had

him hooked. 'OK,' he said, checking his watch and realising that he'd be late for Effi.

Once out on Lindenstrasse he decided to spend some of his anticipated earnings on a cab. As it swung around the Belle Alliance Platz and headed up Königgrätzerstrasse towards Potsdamer Bahnhofplatz, he watched the people on the pavements and wondered how many of them would protest the mercy killing of 100,000 children. Would that be one step too far, or just another milestone in the shedding of a nation's scruples?

Russell didn't expect to find many similarities between Tyler McKinley and Albert Wiesner. On the one hand, a boy from a rich family and country with a rewarding job and instant access to a ticket out of Nazi Germany. On the other, a boy without work or prospects of any kind, whose next forwarding address was likely to be a concentration camp. Russell, however, soon realised he'd been wrong. The characters and personalities of both young men had been formed in successful families and, it seemed, in reaction to powerful fathers. And both seemed blessed with enough youthful naivety to render them both irritating and likeable in turn.

Frau Wiesner produced her son at the end of Friday's lesson. For his mother's and sisters' sake the boy made a token effort to mask his sullen resentment at this unnecessary intrusion on his time, but once out of the door he swiftly abandoned any pretence of amiability.

'Let's get some coffee,' Russell said.

'No cafés will serve us,' was Albert's reply.

'Well, then, let's go for a walk in the park.'

Albert said nothing, but kept pace at Russell's side as they strolled down Greifswaldstrasse towards the northern entrance of the Friedrichshain, the park which gave the whole district its name.

Once inside the main gates Russell led them past the Märchen-Brunnen, a series of artificial waterfalls surrounded by sculptured characters from fairytales. He had brought Paul to see it several years ago, when Hansel and Gretel – the figures in the foreground – could still conjure up night-time terrors of wicked witches. As Ilse had bitterly complained on the following day.

Albert had a more topical agenda in mind. 'The witch must have been Jewish,' he said.

'If she wasn't then, she will be now,' Russell agreed.

They walked on into the park, down a wide path through the leafless trees. Albert seemed unconcerned by the silence between them, and made a point of catching the eyes of those walking in the opposite direction.

Russell had mentally rehearsed a few lines of adult wisdom on the U-bahn, but they'd all sounded ridiculous. 'Your mother wanted me to talk to you,' he said at last. 'But I have no idea what to say. You and your family are in a terrible situation. And, well, I guess she's frightened that you'll just make things worse for yourself.'

'And them.'

'Yes, and them.'

'I do realise that.'

'Yes …' This is a waste of time, Russell thought. They were approaching one of the park's outdoor cafés. 'Let's have a coffee here,' he said.

'They won't serve me.'

'Just take a seat. I'll get them.' He walked up to the kiosk window and looked at the cakes. They had *mohrenkopfen*, balls of sponge with custard centres, chocolate coats, and whipped cream hats. 'Two of them and two coffees,' he told the middle-aged man behind the counter.

The man was staring at Albert. 'He's a Jew,' he said finally, as if reaching the end of an exhaustive mental process. 'We don't serve Jews.'

'He's English,' Russell said. 'As am I.' He showed the man his Ministry of Propaganda accreditation.

'He looks Jewish,' the man said, still staring at Albert, who was now staring back. Why don't you just take out your circumcised prick and wave it at him, Russell thought sourly. 'He may be Jewish for all I know,' Russell told the man, 'but there's no law against serving English Jews.'

'There isn't?'

'No, there isn't.'

The man just stared at him.

'Do you need to hear it from a policeman?'

'Not if you say so.' He gave Albert one final glare and concentrated on pouring out the coffee.

God help us, Russell thought. He could understand Albert's reaction, no matter how counter-productive it was. But this man – what was he so outraged about? There were no SS men lounging at his tables, no ordinary citizens on the brink of racial apoplexy. Why did he care so much that a Jew was sitting at one of his rusty tables? Did he really think Jewish germs would rub off on his cups and saucers?

The coffee was slurped in the saucers, but it didn't seem worth complaining. He carried them back to the table, where Albert was now slouched in his chair, legs splayed out in defiance. Russell resisted the temptation to say 'sit up in your chair' and handed him a *mohrenkopf*. His eyes lit up.

They concentrated on eating for a few minutes.

'Do you really think there's any chance we'll get visas?' Albert asked eventually, allowing the merest hint of hope to mar his cynicism.

'Yes,' Russell said, more convincingly than he felt. 'It may take a while, but why not? The Nazis don't want you, so why shouldn't they let you go?'

'Because they're even more interested in hurting us?'

Russell considered that. It had, unfortunately, the ring of truth. 'The way I see it,' he said, 'you don't have many options. You can fight back and most likely end up in a camp. Or dead. Or you can try and work their system.'

Albert gave him a pitying look. 'There are half a million of us,' he said. 'At the current rate it'll take seven years for us all to get visas.'

Russell had no answer.

'And how long before we're at war?' Albert persisted.

'Who knows …'

'A year at most. And that'll put a stop to emigration. What do you think they'll do with us then? They won't let us work for a living now, and that won't change. They'll either leave us to starve or put us in work camps – slave labour. Some of my friends think they'll just kill us. And they may be right. Who's going to stop them?'

He could add Albert to the list of people he'd under-estimated, Russell thought.

'My father's Iron Cross was First Class,' Albert said. 'Unlike our beloved Führer's.'

Russell stared out at the winter trees, and the roof of the old hospital rising above them to the south. 'If you're right – if your friends are right – then all the more reason not to jeopardise your chances – your family's chances – of getting out.'

'I know that,' Albert said. 'But what about the others? One family's success is another family's failure.'

Russell had no answer to that either.

'But thanks for the coffee and cake,' Albert said.

* * *

Lying in bed unable to sleep, Russell thought about Papa Wiesner's Iron Cross First Class. It wasn't a medal given to many – he must have done something pretty special. He supposed he should have realised that a Jew of Wiesner's age would have fought in the war, but it hadn't occurred to him. Goebbels' propaganda was obviously working.

He wondered which front Wiesner had served on. He wondered, as he often did with Germans of his own age, whether they'd been facing him across those hundred yards of churned-up meadow near Merville. He sometimes wondered whether Frau Heidegger's repeated accusation that he might have shot her husband was simply her way of warding off the possibility that he really had.

He had once thought that he was over the war, that time and circumstance had turned the horror into anger, the anger into politics and the politics into cynicism, leaving only the abiding belief that people in authority tended, by and large, to be incompetent, uncaring liars. The war, by this accounting, had been the latest demonstration of a depressingly eternal truth. Nothing more.

He'd been fooling himself. All those who'd been in that particular place at that particular time had been indelibly marked by the experience, and he was no exception. You never shook it off completely – whatever it was it had left you with, whether nerves in tatters, an endless rage or a joy-sapping cynicism. And the memories never seemed to fade. That sudden waft of decomposing flesh, the rats' eyes reflected in the shell-burst, the sight of one's own rotting feet. The unnerving beauty of a flare cracking the night sky open. Splashed with someone else's brain. Slapped in the face by death.

Jimmy Sewell his name was. After helping carry what was left of him back to the medical station, Russell had somehow ended up with the letter he had just written to his girlfriend. Things were looking up, Sewell had told her, now that the Yanks were arriving in force. It had been late June or early July, 1918. One of a string of sunny days in northern France.

He and Razor Wilkinson had hitched a ride to Hazebrouck that evening, and got pissed out of their minds in a dingy back street bar. The more he drank, the more his brain-spattered face seemed to itch, and he had ended up wading into the River Lys and frantically trying to wash himself clean. Razor had stood on the bank laughing at him, until he realised that Russell was crying, and then he'd started crying too.

Twenty-one years ago, but Russell could still feel the current tugging at his legs. He levered himself out of bed and went to the window. Berlin was sleeping, but he could imagine Albert Wiesner lying in bed on his back, hands clenched around the blankets, staring angrily at the ceiling.

With Paul off on his *Jungvolk* adventure weekend, Russell and Effi spent most of Saturday morning in bed. Russell slipped on some clothes to bring back pastries and coffee from the shop around the corner, and slipped them off again when making love seemed more urgent than eating. Half an hour later Effi re-warmed the coffee on her tiny stove, and brought it back to the bedroom.

'Tell me about the film part,' Russell said, once they were propped up against the headboard. Effi had told him about the offer the night before, but had been too tired to go into details.

'They start shooting on the thirteenth,' she said. 'Two weeks on Monday. Marianne Immel had the part, but she's sick – pregnant, probably, though no one's said so. They want me to audition on Tuesday morning, but I'll have to be pretty bad to miss out – they won't have time to find anyone else.'

'What's it called?'

'*Mother*. And that's me. It's a big part.'

'Can I see the script?'

'Of course, but let me tell you the story first.' She licked a pastry crumb from her upper lip and pushed her hair back behind her ears. 'I am Gerta,' she said. 'I have a job in a factory, an important administrative job. I almost run the place for the owner. I like my work and I'm good at it.'

'But only a woman,' Russell murmured.

'Indeed. My husband Hans has a good job on the railways. And needless to say he's active in the SA, very active in fact. Hans earns more than enough money to support the family – we have two children by the way, a sixteen-year-old girl and eleven-year-old boy – and he rather thinks that I should give up work and look after them. But he's too kind-hearted to insist, and I keep on working.'

'I sense tragedy in the offing.'

'Ah, I should add that my boss fancies me no end. I don't fancy him – he looks decidedly Jewish by the way – but Hans is always away on Party business – you know, organizing parades, running youth camps and generally saving the nation – and the boss is kind enough and smooth enough to be good company, so I flirt with him a little and let him buy me pastries. Like you, in fact,' she added, looking at Russell.

'Do you flaunt your beautiful breasts at him?' Russell asked.

'Certainly not,' she said, pulling her nightdress closed. 'Now concentrate.'

'I'll try.'

'One day she and the boss go to visit a factory he's thinking of buying, and on the way back they decide to stop off at a guesthouse with a famous view. On the way down the mountain his car gets a puncture, and she's late home. Meanwhile, son and daughter have arrived home from school, and can't get in. They wait for a while, but it's raining – buckets of the stuff – and son already has a cold.

Daughter notices that one of the upstairs windows is ajar, and decides to climb up and in.'

'Only she doesn't make it.'

'How did you guess?'

'Dead or just paralysed?'

'Oh, dead. Though I suppose having her in a wheelchair would provide a constant reminder of my guilt. Which is, of course, enormous. I give up my job, despite the pleas of my boss. But the guilt is still too much, so I try and kill myself. And guess who saves me?'

'Son?'

'Exactly. He comes home with a couple of *Jungvolk* buddies to find me head down on the kitchen table with a empty bottle of pills. They rush me to the hospital on the cart they've been using to collect old clothes for Winter Relief.'

'And when you come round you realise that you can only atone for daughter's death by becoming the perfect stay-at-home mother.'

'Hans comes to collect me, takes me home, and tells me he can't bear me being so unhappy and that I can go back to work if I want to. Whereupon I give the speech of my life, castigating him for letting me have my own way in the past, and saying that all I really want to be is a wife and mother. He weeps with joy. In fact we both do. The end.'

'It does bring a tear to the eye,' Russell said. 'Is it going to make you famous?'

'Shouldn't think so. But the money's good, and it will involve some acting.'

'But no breast-flaunting.'

'I only do that for you,' she said, pulling the nightdress open.

* * *

After he'd walked Effi to the theatre for the *Barbarossa* matinée, Russell ate a snack lunch at the Zoo station buffet, climbed up to the elevated platforms and sat watching the trains for a while. It was something he and Paul did on occasion, marvelling at the long lines of carriages snaking in across the bridge from Cologne or Paris or the wonderfully named Hook of Holland. Today, though, he waited in vain for a continental express. There were only the neat little electric trains of the Stadtbahn, fussing in and out of the local platforms.

He walked round the northern wall of the zoo and, for want of something better to do, headed home along the Landwehrkanal. It was a long time since he'd spent a Saturday afternoon in Berlin alone, and he felt unexpectedly disoriented by the experience. To make matters worse it was the sort of winter day he hated: grey, damp and almost insultingly warm, so that the canal smelled even worse than usual.

When he reached home Frau Heidegger was lying in wait. Schacht's long-expected dismissal as president of the Reichsbank had been all over the front pages that morning, and she was worried about how this might affect share prices. 'My Jurgen's family gave me some Farben shares after the war,' she explained, after press-ganging him in for coffee. 'Just a few, you understand, but I always thought they might come in handy in my old age.'

Russell reassured her that Schacht's dismissal was unlikely to have any lasting affect. Unlike the coming war, he added to himself. Or her coffee.

'The Führer's angry with the Czechs,' she said from the kitchen, as if following his thoughts.

'What about?' Russell asked.

'Does it matter?' she asked, coming in with the familiar pot.

'No,' he agreed. He was often surprised by Frau Heidegger's perceptiveness, and surprised he could still be surprised.

'I told my brother-in-law what you said about air defences,' she went on. 'He said he hoped you were right.'

'So do I,' Russell agreed.

After climbing the stairs to his apartment he wished he hadn't: the combination of muggy weather and full throttle-heating had turned it into a Turkish bath. He tried opening a window, but there was no welcome hint of cooler air. He tried reading, but nothing seemed to stick.

He went back out again. It was just after four – he had about six hours to kill. He walked south down Belle-Alliance Strasse to Viktoria Park, climbed to the brow of the Kreuzberg and found an empty bench with a view across the city. There was even a slight breeze.

The sky darkened, and his mood seemed to darken with it.

He thought about Effi and the film. They'd had fun that morning, but it was a pretty disgusting piece of work. Did she have any qualms about doing it? She hadn't said so. He couldn't believe she needed the money, and he'd heard her views on the Nazi attitude to women often enough. So why was she doing it? Should he ask her? Was it possible to ask someone a question like that without making it an accusation?

He decided it wasn't, but later that night, halfway down an empty street on their way home from the theatre, he asked it anyway.

'To make a living?' she answered sarcastically.

'But you don't …' he said, and stopped himself. But not soon enough.

'Lots of people think that because my family is rich, I'm rich,' she said coldly. 'I took the flat when they offered it. Ten years ago. And I haven't taken anything since.'

'I know.'

'Then what?'

He sighed. 'It's just so sordid. I hate the idea of you playing in something … of you playing a part that goes against everything you believe.'

'That just makes it more of a challenge.'

'Yes, but the better you do it, the more convincing you are, the more women will think they have to accept all this nonsense.'

She stopped in her tracks. 'Are we talking about my work or yours?' she asked. 'How about your paean to Strength Through Joy cruises? Or your "car for every German worker" piece. You've hardly been cutting the ground from under their feet.'

He bit back the surge of anger. She was right.

They both were.

Next afternoon, he went to the Plumpe. Paul had asked him for a programme, and with Effi visiting her family that seemed a good enough reason for going. He had Thomas and Joachim for company, but he missed Paul, and the game itself was dire – a dull 1–1 draw with Berliner SV. Thomas was subdued – like Frau Heidegger and seventy-five million other Germans, he'd noticed the tell-tale flurry of government antagonism towards the Czechs. Sandwiched between SV supporters on the southbound U-bahn they arranged to have lunch on the following Thursday.

Back at the apartment he found a courier delivery waiting for him: a copy of the previous day's *Pravda*, complete with his first article. His Russian wasn't up to much, but as far as he could tell they hadn't altered anything. 'Approved by the SD, approved by the NKVD,' he thought out loud. 'I should have been a diplomat.' More gratifying still was the accompanying bank draft in Reichsmarks.

There was also the promised list of suggestions for future articles. The last-but-one letters of the words in the opening sentence –

who thought up this stuff? – spelled Cracow. Russell groaned. Two sixteen-hour train journeys, just for a chat with Shchepkin. At least, he hoped it was just for a chat.

Zygmunt's Chapel

'This is it,' McKinley said, with the sort of enthusiasm others reserved for stumbling across El Dorado. The object of his excitement was a short cul-de-sac of decaying tenement blocks wedged between railway arches, small industrial workshops and the Neuköllner-Schiffahrtkanal. One forlorn streetlight threw a faint yellow glow over glistening brickwork and rusty iron. It looked, Russell thought, like the sort of place a particularly sentimental German communist would come to die.

They had been looking for it for almost an hour, ever since playing hide-and-seek with their probably imaginary Gestapo tail in Neukölln's famous Karstadt department store. The object of their quest had, according to McKinley, told them to make sure they were not followed, and he had done his best to oblige, leading Russell into the store by the main entrance and out through the kitchens, pursued only by the shouts of an enraged chef. They had then headed east on foot, turning this way and that down a succession of rapidly darkening and profoundly unwelcoming streets. Russell had expected streams of workers returning home, but they had only come across a few, and McKinley's requests for navigational assistance had been met with either guarded suspicion or outright hostility. There were lights behind the curtains of the residential streets, but they felt far away.

Schönlankerstrasse was no exception. The block they were looking for was the last, pushed up against the elevated tracks of what was probably a freight line. As they reached the entrance another source of light came into view – the red glow of a signal hanging in the darkness.

The limp swastika over the entrance looked like it hadn't been washed since 1933. Entering the dimly lit hall, they found the concierge's door. McKinley tried two taps with the door-knocker – too softly, Russell thought, but the door swung open almost immediately. A middle-aged woman with a rather striking face ushered them inside and quickly closed the door behind them.

'Who is this?' she asked McKinley with an angry gesture towards Russell. She had a thick Rhenish accent, which explained why the American had so much trouble understanding her.

'He's a friend. He speaks better German than I do,' McKinley explained, rather in the manner of someone reassuring a foolish child.

She gave Russell another look, thought for a moment, then shrugged. 'Come through,' she said shortly.

The living room was clean but almost bare. There were no comfortable chairs, only a couple of upright chairs beside a small table and what looked like homemade cushions on the floor. A tattered but once-expensive rug occupied the centre of the wooden floor. A girl of around five or six was sitting on it, leaning forward over a drawing she was doing. She didn't look up when they entered.

'That's Marietta,' the woman said. 'She gets very absorbed in what she's doing,' she added, as if she needed to explain the child's lack of reaction.

Her name, as McKinley had already told Russell, was Theresa Jürissen. She was younger than he'd first thought – around thirty-five, probably – but she looked both exhausted and malnourished. Only the eyes, a penetrating grey, seemed full of energy.

'Please take the chairs,' she said, but McKinley insisted that she took one. He remained standing, his lanky bulk seeming somewhat incongruous in the centre of the room. Apparently realising as much, he retreated to a wall.

'Have you brought the money?' Frau Jürissen asked, almost apologetically. This was not a woman who was used to poverty, Russell thought. 'This is the only work I can do and look after her all day,' she added, as if more explanation was needed.

McKinley produced his wallet, and counted what looked like several hundred Reichsmarks into her hand. She gazed at the pile for a moment, and then abruptly folded the notes over, and placed them in the pocket of her housecoat. 'So, where shall I begin?' she asked.

McKinley wasted no time. 'You said in your letter that you could not keep silent when children's lives were at stake,' he said, pronouncing each word with the utmost care. 'What made you think they were?'

She placed her hands on the table, one covering the other. 'I couldn't believe it at first,' she said, then paused to get her thoughts in order. 'I worked for the Brandenburg Health Ministry for over ten years. In the medical supplies department. I visited hospitals and asylums on a regular basis, checking inventories, anticipating demands – you understand?'

McKinley nodded.

'After the Nazi take-over most of the women in my department were encouraged to resign, but my husband was killed in an accident a few weeks after I had Marietta, and they knew I was the only bread-winner in the family. They wanted me to find another husband of course, but until that happened … well, I was good at my job, so they had no real excuse to fire me.' She looked up. 'I'm sorry. You don't need to know all this.' She looked across at her daughter, who had still shown no sign of recognition that anyone else was in the room. 'I suppose I knew from the start that she wasn't, well, ordinary, but I told myself she was just very shy, very self-absorbed … I mean, some adults are like that – they hardly notice that anyone else exists.' She sighed. 'But I got to the point where I knew I had to do something, take her to see someone. I knew that might mean she'd be sterilised, but … well, if she stayed the way she is now, she'd never notice whether she had any children or not. Anyway, I took her to a clinic in Potsdam, and they examined her and tested her and said they needed to keep her under observation for a few weeks. I didn't want to leave her there, but they told me not to be selfish, that Marietta needed professional care if she was ever to come out of her shell.'

'Did they threaten you?' McKinley asked.

'No, not really. They were just impatient with me. Shocked that I didn't immediately accept that they knew best.'

'Like most doctors,' Russell murmured.

'Perhaps. And maybe they were completely genuine. Maybe Marietta does need whatever it is they have to offer.'

'So you took her away?' McKinley asked.

'I had to. Just two days after I left her in the clinic I was at the Falkenheide asylum – you know it? – it's just outside Fürstenwalde. I was in the staff canteen, checking through their orders over a cup of coffee, when I became aware of the conversation at the next table. I tried to ignore it, but I couldn't. And they were speaking quite normally – there was nothing clandestine about it. In a way that was what was most shocking about it – they assumed that their topic of conversation was common knowledge. As far as the asylum staff were concerned, that is.' She paused, and glanced across at Marietta. 'What they were talking about was a letter which had been sent out by the Ministry of Justice to all directors of asylums. That letter wanted the directors' opinions on how they should change the system to allow the killing of incurable children. Should they announce a new law, or should they issue administrative decrees and keep the public in ignorance? This is what the people at the next table were debating, even joking about. Three of them were doctors I recognised, and the woman looked like a senior nurse.'

'This was all spelled out?' Russell asked incredulously. He instinctively trusted her – could see no reason for her to lie – but her scene in the canteen sounded like one of those stage conversations written to update the audience.

'No,' she said, giving Russell an indignant look. 'They were talking more about how the parents would react, whether they would prefer to hear that their child had simply died of whatever illness they had. It was only when I read the letter that it all made sense.'

'How? Where?' McKinley asked excitedly.

'Like I said, I was in that job a long time. I was on good terms with people in all the asylums. I knew I had to see the letter for myself, and I waited for a chance. A few days later a director was called out early, and I pretended I had to work late. I found the letter in his office.'

'I wish you'd kept it,' McKinley said, more to himself than her.

'I did,' she said simply.

'You did!' McKinley almost shouted, levering himself off the wall he'd been leaning against. 'Where is it? Can we see it?'

'Not now. I don't have it here.'

'How much do you need?' Russell asked.

'Another five hundred Reichsmarks?' The question mark was infinitesimal.

'That's …' McKinley began.

'Good business sense,' Russell completed for him. 'She needs the money,' he added in English.

'Yes, of course,' McKinley agreed. 'I just don't know how … But

I'll get it. Shall I come back here?' he asked her.

'No,' she said. 'It's too risky for me. Send the money to the post restante on Heiligegeiststrasse. When I get it, I'll send you the letter.'

'It'll be there by tomorrow evening,' McKinley said, as he wrote out the Neuenburgerstrasse address.

Russell stood up. 'Did you have any trouble getting Marietta back?' he asked Theresa Jürissen.

'Yes,' she said. 'They wouldn't let me take her. I had to steal my own child. That's why we're here in this place.'

They both looked down at Marietta. Her drawing looked like a forest after a hurricane had hit it. 'I wish you luck,' Russell said.

He and McKinley reached the street as a coal train thundered across the arches, and set about retracing their steps. It was raining now, the streets even emptier, a rare neighbourhood bar offering a faint splash of light and noise. They didn't speak until they reached the tram stop on Berlinerstrasse.

'If you get this story out, it'll be your last one from Germany,' Russell said.

McKinley grinned at him. 'Worth it though, don't you think?'

Russell saw the excitement in the young American's eyes, like an echo of his own younger self. He felt a pang of envy. 'Yes, I do,' he agreed.

Russell's first port of call on the following morning was about ten kilometres, and several worlds, away from the dingy Schönlankerstrasse. The villa, just around the corner from the State Archive in the wealthy suburb of Dahlem, was surrounded by trees full of singing birds, most of whom were probably warbling their gratitude to the Führer. In Schönlankerstrasse it was probably still raining in the dark, but here the sun shone down out of a clear blue sky. The coffee had not been as good since the Jewish cook was 'allowed to leave,' but everyone had to make sacrifices.

His pupil Greta was a sixteen-year-old with no interest in learning English. She did, however, like practising her flirting techniques on him. Today it was a new wide-eyed expression which she seemed to think was appealing. She was, he had to admit, a lesson in the nature of beauty. When he'd first set eyes on her, he'd been struck by how gorgeous she was. But after eighteen months of getting to know her, he found her only marginally more attractive than Hermann Goering. Her grasp of English had hardly improved at all in that time, but that didn't seem to worry anybody. Her father, a doctor of similar age to Wiesner, had not been cursed with the same tainted blood.

An hour later, richer in Reichsmarks but poorer in spirit, Russell retraced his steps down the sunny avenues to the Dahlem Dorf U-bahn station. Changing at Wittenbergplatz, he bought a paper at a platform kiosk and glanced through it on the ride to Alexanderplatz. The Swiss were the latest target – as neutrals, a lead writer announced, they should refrain from expressing opinions about other countries and refuse to take in refugees. The Germans, on the other hand, should get their colonies back. Three reasons were given. The first was 'inalienable right', whatever that was. The second was 'economic need,' which presumably came under the inalienable right to loot. The third, which made Russell laugh out loud, was Germany's 'right to share in the education of backward peoples'. 'Thanks to her racial principles,' the writer announced confidently, 'the Third Reich stands in the front rank of Powers in this respect.' Russell thought about this for a while, and decided it could only mean that Germany was well-placed to educate the backward peoples in how deserving their backwardness was.

At Alexanderplatz he picked up the previous Saturday's *Daily*

Mail for the girls, and discovered that rain was likely to affect the weekend's English cup-ties. Several columns were given over to Schacht's dismissal, though, and he found three other articles on German matters. This, as McKinley had said, was where the story was.

Most interesting to Russell, though, was the picture on the back page of the streamlined steam locomotive *Coronation*, hanging between ship and quay *en route* to America for some celebration or other. He would keep that for Paul.

He thought about his son as the tram ground its way north-west towards Friedrichshain. On the telephone two nights earlier Paul had used all the right words to describe a thrilling weekend with the *Jungvolk*, but there had been a different story in the tone of his voice. Or had there? Maybe it was just that adolescent reticence which psychiatrists were so full of these days. He needed a proper talk with the boy, which made this weekend's summons to Cracow all the more annoying. And to make matters worse, Hertha were at home two Sundays running. Paul could always go with Thomas, but … An away game, he thought suddenly. He could take Paul to an away game the following Sunday. A real trip. He could see no reason why Ilse would object.

And Cracow would be interesting, if nothing else. He had already booked his sleeper tickets and hotel room, and was looking forward to seeing the city for the first time. Both his agents had loved the 'Germany's Neighbours' idea, so there should be some money in it too.

He reached the Wiesners' stop, walked the short distance to their block, and climbed the stairs. Dr Wiesner, who he hadn't seen for a couple of weeks, opened the door. He looked noticeably more careworn, but managed a smile of welcome. 'I wanted to thank you for talking to Albert,' he said without preamble. 'And I'd like to ask you another favour. I feel awkward doing this – and please say no if it's too difficult – but, well, I am just doing what I must. You understand?'

Russell nodded. What now? he wondered.

Wiesner hesitated. He also seemed more unsure of himself, Russell noticed. And who could blame him?

'Is there any way you could check on the rules for taking things out of the country? For Jews, I mean. It's just that they keep changing the rules, and if I ask what they are then they'll just assume I'm trying to get round them.'

'Of course,' Russell said. 'I'll let you know on Friday.'

Wiesner nodded. 'One person I know asked about a miniature which had been in his family for a hundred years, and they simply confiscated it,' he went on, as if Russell still needed convincing.

'I'll let you know,' Russell said again.

'Yes, thank you. I'm told there's a good chance that the girls will be allowed to go, and I'd like to …well, provide for them in England. You understand?'

Russell nodded.

'Very well. Thank you again. I mustn't take up any more learning time.' He stepped to the adjoining door and opened it. 'Girls, come.' He said it gruffly, but the smile he bestowed on them as they trooped in was almost too full of love. Russell remembered the faces on the Danzig station platform, the sound the woman had made.

The two girls fell on the *Daily Mail*.

'You can keep it apart from the back page,' he told them, and explained that he wanted the picture for his son.

'Tell us about your son,' Marthe said. 'In English, of course,' she added.

He spent the next twenty minutes talking and answering

questions about Paul. The girls were sympathetic to the philatelist, indulgent towards the football fan and lover of modern transport, dismissive of the toy soldier collector. They were particularly impressed by the tale of how, around the age of five, he had almost died of whooping cough. Telling the story, Russell felt almost anxious, as if he wasn't sure how it was going to end.

He turned the tables for the second half of the lesson, inviting them to talk about their own histories. He regretted this almost instantly, thinking that, given their situation, this was likely to prove upsetting for them. They didn't see it that way. It wasn't that they thought the family's current difficulties were temporary; it was more a matter of their knowing, even with all their problems, that they had more love in their lives than most other people.

It was one of the nicest hours he had ever spent, and walking back to the tram stop on Neue Königstrasse he reminded himself to thank Doug Conway for the introduction the next time he saw him. The opportunity soon presented itself. Back at the apartment, he found a message from Conway, asking him to call. He did so.

Conway didn't sound like his usual self. 'One of our people would like a word,' he said.

'What about?' Russell asked warily.

'I don't know. I'm just the messenger.'

'Ah.'

'Could you come in, say, tomorrow morning, around eleven?'

'I suppose so.'

'I'd like to see you too. We're leaving, by the way. I've been posted to Washington.'

'When? And why haven't you told me?'

'I'm telling you now. I only heard a couple of days ago. And we're going in a couple of weeks.'

'Well I'm sorry to hear that. From a purely selfish point of view, of course. Is it a promotion?'

'Sort of. Touch of the up, touch of the sideways. Anyway, we're having a dinner for a few people on the third – that's next Friday – and I hoped you and your lady friend could come.'

'Oh, Effi will be ...' Working, he was going to say. But of course she wouldn't – *Barbarossa* would be over, and *Mother* didn't start shooting until the thirteenth. 'I'll ask her,' he said. 'Should be OK, though.'

The Café Kranzler was full of SS officers the next morning, their boots polished to such perfection that any leg movement sent flashes of reflected light from the chandeliers dancing round the walls. Russell hurried his coffee and, with half an hour to burn, ambled down Unter den Linden to the Schloss. The Kaiser's old home was still empty, but the papers that morning were full of his upcoming eightieth birthday party in Holland. 'Come back, all is forgiven,' Russell murmured to himself.

After the Unter den Linden the British Embassy seemed an oasis of languor. The staff drifted to and fro, as if worried they might be caught speeding. Was this the new British plan, Russell wondered. Slow the drift to war by slowing diplomats.

Doug Conway eventually appeared. 'One of our intelligence people wants to talk to you,' he said quietly. 'Nothing formal, just a chat about things.' Russell grunted his disbelief, and Conway had the grace to look embarrassed. 'Not my idea – I'm just the messenger.'

'You said that yesterday.'

'Well, I am. Look, I'll take you up. He's a nice enough chap. His name's Trelawney-Smythe.'

It would be, Russell thought. He had a pretty good idea what was coming.

The office was a small room high at the back of the building, with a compensating view of the Brandenburg Gate. Conway introduced Russell and withdrew. Trelawney-Smythe, a tall dark-haired man in his thirties with a worried-looking face, ushered him to a seat.

'Good of you to come,' he began, rifling through papers on his over-crowded desk. Russell wondered if Sturmbannführer Kleist gave private lessons in desk arrangement. 'Ah,' Trelawney-Smythe said triumphantly, extracting a copy of *Pravda* from the mess. A hand-written sheet was attached with a paper-clip.

'My latest masterpiece,' Russell murmured. Why was it, he wondered, that British officialdom always brought out the schoolboy in him? After reading one of the *Saint* stories Paul had asked him why the Saint was so fond of prodding Chief Inspector Teal in the stomach. He had been unable to offer a coherent explanation, but deep down he knew exactly why. He already wanted to prod Trelawney-Smythe in his.

The other man had unclipped the handwritten sheet from the newspaper, and carefully stowed the paper-clip away in its rightful place. 'This is a translation of your article,' he said.

'May I see it?' Russell asked, holding out a hand.

Somewhat taken aback, Trelawney-Smythe handed it over.

Russell glanced through it. They had printed it more or less verbatim. He handed it back.

'Mr Russell, I'm going to be completely frank with you,' Trelawney-Smythe said, unconsciously echoing Sturmbannführer Kleist.

Don't strain yourself, Russell thought.

'You used to be a member of the British Communist Party, correct?'

'Yes.' He wondered if Trelawney-Smythe and Kleist had ever met.

'Then you know how the communists operate?'

'You think they all operate the same way?'

'I think the Soviets have certain well-practised methods, yes.'

'You're probably right.'

'Well, then. We don't think this will be the end of it. We think they'll ask for more and more.'

'More and more articles? And who is we?'

Trelawney-Smythe smiled. 'Don't play the innocent. You know who "we" are. And you know I'm not talking about your articles, amusing as they are. We think they'll be asking you for other information. The usual method is to keep upping the ante, until you're no longer in a position to refuse. Because they'll shop you to the Germans if you do.'

'As you said, I know how they operate. And it's my lookout, isn't it?'

'Not completely. Do you see this?' Trelawney-Smythe asked, indicating the words at the foot of the article, which identified the name, nationality and credentials of the author.

'Yes.'

'An Englishman currently living in Germany,' Trelawney-Smythe read out, just to be sure.

'That's me.'

Trelawney-Smythe tapped on the paper with an index finger. 'You are English, and your behaviour will reflect on the rest of us. Particularly at a time like this.'

'A "don't-rock-the-boat-for-God's-sake" sort of time?'

'Something like that. Relations between ourselves and the Soviets are, shall we say, difficult at the moment. They don't trust us and we don't trust them. Everybody's looking for signals of intent. The smallest thing – like *Pravda* inviting you to write these articles – could mean something. Or nothing. They could be planning to use you as a channel to us or the Germans, for passing on information or disinformation. We don't know. I assume you don't know.'

'I'm just doing my job.'

'All right. But how would you feel about providing us with advance copies of your articles. Just so we know what's coming.'

Russell laughed. 'You too?' He explained about his arrangement with the SD. 'Why not?' he said. 'I might as well run off a few carbons for Mussolini and Daladier while I'm at it.' He put his hands on the chair-arms, prior to lifting himself up. 'Anything else?'

'We would appreciate being told if this goes beyond a mere commercial arrangement. And obviously we'd be interested in anything you learn which might be of use to your country.'

'I've already learned one thing. The Soviets think the British and French are trying to cut them out. Look how long Hitler gave the Ambassador at the opening last week. Look at the new trade deal talks. If you don't start treating the Soviets as potential allies, they'll do a deal with Hitler.'

'I think London's aware of that.'

'You could have fooled me. But what do I know?' He looked at his watch. 'I have a lunch date.' He extended his hand across the desk. 'I'll bear what you've said in mind.'

'Enjoy your lunch.'

Russell dropped in on Conway on his way out.

'Still talking to me?' the diplomat asked.

'You, yes; the Empire, no.'

'He's just doing his job.'

'I know. Look, thanks for the dinner invitation. I'll let you know soon as I can.' He paused at the door. 'And I'll be sorry to see you go,' he added.

* * *

It was a fast five minute walk to the Russischer Hof on Georgen-strasse, where he and Thomas usually met for lunch. As he hurried east on Unter den Linden Russell replayed the conversation with Trelawney-Smythe over in his mind. Rather to his surprise it had been refreshingly free of threats. If British intelligence wanted to, he imagined that they could make his life a lot more difficult. They could take away his passport, or just make renewal harder. They could probably make it harder for him to sell his work in England, his prime market. A word to a few knighthood-hungry editors – in fact, a mere appeal to their patriotism – and his London agent would be collecting rejections on his behalf. On the plus side it was beginning to look as if every intelligence service in Europe was interested in employing him.

It was a raw day, the wind whipping in from the east, and Russell turned up his collar against it. A tram slid under the railway bridge, bell frantically ringing, as he turned off Friedrichstrasse and into Georgenstrasse. The Russischer Hof was a nineteenth-century establishment once favoured by Bismarck, and sometimes Russell wondered if they were still recycling the same food. The elaborate décor created a nice atmosphere though, and the usual paucity of uniformed clientele was a definite bonus.

Russell's former brother-in-law was seated at a window table, glass of Riesling in hand, looking dourly out at the street. The dark grey suit added to the sober impression, but that was Thomas. When they'd first met in the mid-twenties Russell had thought him the epitome of the humourless German. However, once he got to know him, he had realised that Thomas was anything but. Ilse's brother had a sly, rather anarchic sense of humour, completely lacking in the cruelty which marked much popular German humour. If anything, he was the epitome of the decent German, an endangered species if ever there was one.

The pot roast with cream sauce, red cabbage and mashed potatoes seemed an ideal riposte to the weather, which was now blowing snow flurries past their window. 'How's the business?' Russell asked, as Thomas poured him a glass of wine.

'Good. We've got a lot of work, and exports are looking up. The new printers have made a huge difference. And you know the World's Fair in New York this April? It looked for a moment as if we might have a stand there.'

'What happened?'

'It seems the organisers have decided to include a pavilion celebrating pre-Nazi German Art. And émigré art. If they do, the government will boycott the fair.'

'That's a shame.'

Thomas gave him a wintry smile. 'Given the context, it's hard to be that upset. And there's always the chance that the Ministry would have refused to let us go. Because of our employment policies.'

Only one firm in Berlin employed more Jews than Schade Printing Works.

'You don't have room for one more, I suppose?' Russell asked, thinking of Albert Wiesner.

'Not really. Who do you have in mind?'

Russell explained the Wiesners' situation.

Thomas looked pained. 'I have a waiting list of around two hundred already,' he said. 'Most of them are relatives of people who already work there.'

Russell thought of pressing him but decided not to. He could hear Albert in his head – 'One family's success is another family's failure.' 'I understand,' he said, and was about to change the subject when the waiter arrived with their meals.

Both men noticed that the portions seemed smaller than usual. 'Sign of the times,' Thomas observed.

'Any chance of things getting better?' Russell asked. Thomas had no more inside information than Russell's other friends in Berlin – and considerably less than many – but he'd always had a knack of knowing which way the wind was blowing.

'I don't know,' was his answer. 'Ribbentrop's off to Warsaw again. They seem to be trying.' He shrugged. 'We'll probably find out more on Monday.'

That was the day of Hitler's annual speech to the Reichstag commemorating his own accession to the Chancellorship. 'I'd forgotten about that,' Russell admitted.

'You're probably the only person in Europe who has. I think the whole continent's hanging on it. Will he keep the pressure up, demand more? Or will he take the pressure off? That would be the intelligent move. Act as if he's satisfied, even if he's only pausing for breath. But in the long run it's hard to see him stopping. He's like a spinning coin. Once he stops spinning, he'll fall flat.'

Russell grunted. 'Nice.'

They asked after each other's better halves, both current and former.

'You're asking me?' Thomas said when Russell enquired after Ilse. 'I haven't see her for weeks. Last time we went over there, well …' He didn't continue.

'You didn't have a row?'

'Oh no, nothing like that,' Thomas said, as if rows were something that happened to other people. Which, in his case, they usually were. 'I just find Matthias so … oh, I don't know … complacent? Is that the right word for people who say they fear the worst but live their lives as if there's bound to be a happy ending?'

'It might be,' Russell agreed. He realised he hadn't told Thomas about his trip to Cracow, or asked him to take Paul to the match on Sunday, and did so now.

Thomas was happy to take Paul, but bemused by Russell's choice of Cracow for the 'Germany's Neighbours' series. 'Wouldn't a day trip to Posen have been good enough?' he wanted to know.

Russell had a sudden desire to tell Thomas about Shchepkin – if something went wrong, there would be someone to offer some sort of explanation to Paul and Effi – but he held himself back. He would be compromising Thomas, and to what real end? What could go wrong?

Waiting behind another customer for his Friday morning paper, Russell caught sight of the headline – BARCELONA FALLS. On impulse, he turned away. That was one story he didn't want to read. The Spanish Civil War was over. The good guys had lost. What else was there to say?

As it had gone down so well on his last visit, he bought another ancient *Daily Mail* at the Alexanderplatz kiosk. This had an article on young English girls collecting stamps, which he knew would interest Ruth and Marthe, and a big piece on the recent loss of the Empire flying boat *Cavalier*, complete with map and diagram, which Paul would love. He saved the best, however, for the very end of the girls' lesson – a report of a tongue-twisting competition on the BBC. Trying to say 'should such a shapeless sash such shabby stitches show' soon had Ruth giggling so hard she really was in stitches, and Marthe fared little better with 'the flesh of freshly fried flying fish.'

The doctor was not at home, so Russell handed the copy of the latest rules governing Jewish emigration to Frau Wiesner. He had collected them the previous day from the British Passport Control Office. 'But they ignore their own rules half the time,' the young official had told him bitterly. 'You can count on getting a change of clothes past them, but anything else is as likely to be confiscated as not. If your friends have any other way of getting stuff out, they should use it.'

Russell passed on the advice, and watched her heart sink.

'If you need help, ask me,' he said, surprising himself. 'I don't think I'd have any trouble shipping stuff to my family in England.'

Her eyes glowed. 'Thank you,' she said, and reached up to kiss him on the cheek.

He journeyed home to pack, stopping off in Alexanderplatz for a late lunch. At least he was pleasing some people. He hadn't seen Effi since Sunday and the round of mutual accusations which he had so stupidly instigated. They hadn't had a row – they had even managed two reasonably friendly conversations on the telephone – but he knew she was angry with him, and his non-availability for the *Barbarossa* send-off had made things worse.

Paul didn't seem that much happier with him, despite the promise of a trip the following Sunday to see the cup-tie in Dresden. There was something going on, but Paul wasn't prepared to talk about it, or at least not on the telephone.

Frau Heidegger was glad to see him, and sorry his imminent train prevented him from joining her for coffee. Up in his apartment, he threw a few spare clothes into a suitcase, checked he had his notes for the next article, and headed back down. On the next landing he ran into a smiling McKinley.

'Everything OK?' Russell asked in passing.

'Uh-huh. I'm just waiting for our friend's letter and ... bingo!'

Russell laughed and clattered on down the stairs.

He arrived at the Schlesinger Bahnhof with twenty minutes to spare. The train was already sheltering under the wrought iron canopy, and he walked down the platform in search of his carriage and seat. As he leaned out of the window to watch a train steam in from the east a paper boy thrust an afternoon edition under his nose. The word 'Barcelona' was again prominent, but this time he handed over the pfennigs. As his train gathered speed through Berlin's industrial suburbs he read the article from start to finish, in all its sad and predictable detail.

Three years of sacrifice, all for nothing. Three years of towns won, towns lost. Russell had registered the names, but resisted further knowledge. It was too painful. Thousands of young men and women had gone to fight fascism in Spain, just as thousands had gone to fight for communism in Russia twenty years earlier. According to Marx, history repeated itself first as tragedy and then as farce. But no one was laughing. Except perhaps Stalin.

Russell supposed he should be glad that Spain would soon be at peace, but even that was beyond him. He stared out of the window at the neat fields of the Spree valley, basking in the orange glow of the setting sun, and felt as though he was being lied to. Seconds later, as if in confirmation, the train thundered through a small town station, its fluttering swastika deep blood-red in that self-same glow, a crowd of small boys in uniform milling on the opposite platform.

The food in the restaurant car proved surprisingly good. The menu had a distinctly Polish flavour, although as far as Russell could see there were few Poles on the train. Most of his fellow-passengers were German males – mainly commercial travellers or soldiers on leave. There was only a sprinkling of couples, though the pair at the next table had enough sexual energy for ten. They could hardly keep their hands off each other while eating, and the young man kept checking his watch, as if willing the train on to Breslau, where the sleeping coaches would be attached.

The couple soon disappeared, probably in search of an empty

bathroom. The romance of trains, Russell thought, staring at his own reflection in the window. He remembered the overnight journey to Leningrad with Ilse in 1924, just after they'd met. People had slept in the bathrooms on that train, and anywhere else they could find a space. He and Ilse had had to wait.

Fifteen years. The Soviet Union had come a long way since then, one way or another. Some people came back from visits singing its praises. There was still much to do, but it was the future in embryo, a potential paradise. Other returnees shook their heads in sadness. A dream warped beyond recognition, they said. A nightmare.

Russell guessed the latter was nearer the truth, but sometimes wondered whether that was just his natural pessimism. It had to be a bit of both, but where the balance lay he didn't know.

More to the point, what did Moscow want with him? What they said they wanted? Or something else? Or both? Trelawney-Smythe had been certain they would ask for more, and Kleist had hinted as much. He didn't even know who he was dealing with. Was Shchepkin NKVD or GRU? Or some other acronym he hadn't even heard of? A French correspondent in Berlin had told him that the NKVD was now split between a Georgian faction and the rest, and for all Russell knew the GRU was eaten up by factional rivalry over how much salt they put in the canteen borsht.

And why was he assuming it would be Shchepkin again? The revolution was burning its human fuel at quite a rate these days, and Shchepkin, with his obvious intelligence, seemed highly combustible.

He would have to deal with whoever presented himself. Or herself. But what would he or she want? What could they want? Information about German military strengths and weaknesses? About particular weapons programmes? Political intentions?

Military plans? He had no information – no access to information – about any of that. Thank God.

What did he have that they valued? Freedom to move around Germany. Freedom to ask questions without arousing suspicion. Even more so now, with Kleist's letter in his possession. Maybe one of their agents had gone missing, and they would ask Russell to find out what had happened to him. Or they might want to use him as a courier, carrying stuff to or from their agents. That would explain the meetings outside Germany.

Or they could use him as a conduit. The Soviets knew the Germans would check up on him, and assumed he would be asked for reports on his meetings. And the British too. They would have counted on the British calling him in. They could use him as a human post-box, with Kleist and Trelawney-Smythe as the sorters.

They might be just making it up as they went along. His unusual situation made him potentially useful, and they were still looking for a way to realise that potential. That would explain the articles and oral reports – a sort of halfway house to prepare him for a truly clandestine life. There was no way of knowing. Russell leant back in his chair, remembering the remark of a Middlesex Regiment officer he'd met in 1918. 'Intelligence services,' the man had said, 'were prone to looking up their own arses and wondering why it was dark.'

Soon after ten the train reached Breslau, the destination of most passengers. As they filtered out through the dimly lit exit, many of the remaining passengers took the chance to stretch their legs on the snow-strewn platform. Russell walked to the back of the train and watched a busy little shunter detach four saloons and replace them with three sleepers. It was really cold now, and the orange glow from the engine's firebox made it seem more so.

He walked back up the platform, arms clasped tightly across his chest. 'Cold, eh?' a young soldier said, stamping his feet and taking a deep drag on his cigarette. He was only about eighteen, and seemed to be wearing a summer uniform.

As Russell nodded his agreement a whistle sounded the all aboard.

Walking up the train, he reclaimed his seat in an almost empty carriage. The sleeping car attendants would be rushed off their feet for the next quarter of an hour, and he wasn't ready for sleep in any case. As the train pulled out of the station the ceiling lights were extinguished, allowing him a view through the window of flat meadows stretching north towards a distant line of yellow lights. The Oder river, likely as not.

Hoping for some conversation he revisited the restaurant car, but the only customers were a middle-aged German couple deep in the throes of an argument. The barman sold him a *Goldwasser*, but made it abundantly clear he was through talking for the day. Around eleven-thirty Russell reluctantly worked his way back down the train to the sleeping cars. The attendant showed him to his berth, and generously pointed out that the one above was unoccupied. He could take his pick.

Russell tossed his bag on the upper bunk, used the bathroom, and climbed half-dressed into the lower bunk. He would have a bath when he reached his hotel, he thought. It was an expensive one, so there shouldn't be any problem with hot water.

As usual he had trouble getting to sleep. He lay there, feeling the sway of the train, listening to the click of the wheels on the rail joints, thinking about Effi. She was younger than him – eight years younger. Maybe people's expectations shifted after a certain age, which he'd reached and she hadn't. Was that why they were still living apart? Why had neither of them ever mentioned marriage?

Was he afraid of something? He didn't think so. But then what was the point of turning their lives upside-down when the Führer was about to do it for them?

Shortly after eight in the morning he was standing, yawning, on one of Cracow Plaszów station's snow-covered platforms. After eventually getting to sleep, he had twice been roused for border inspections, and could hardly have felt worse if he'd been awake all night.

He started towards the exit, and almost went over on a patch of ice. Further up the platform a line of young railway employees were working their way towards him, breath pumping, shovelling snow and noisily digging at the ice beneath with their spades. The sky above them seemed heavy with future snowfalls.

His hotel was on the other side of Cracow's old town, some three miles away. He found a taxi outside the station, and a taxi-driver who wanted to practise his English. He had a cousin in Chicago, he said, but he wanted to go to Texas and work in the oil industry. That was where the future was.

As they drove north through the Jewish quarter Russell noticed the Marx Brothers adorning a cinema on Starowislna Street. The name of the film was in Polish, but his driver's English failed him. He asked again at the Hotel Francuski reception, and received a confident answer from a young man in a very shiny suit. The film, which had only just opened, was called *Broth of the Bird*.

His room was on the third floor, looking out on Pijakska Street. This was full of well-insulated, purposeful walkers, presumably on their way to work. A church stood just across the way, the beauty of its rococo façade still visible beneath the clinging snow.

The room itself was large, high-ceilinged and well-furnished. The bed gave without sagging, the two-person sofa was almost luxurious. The small table and upright chair by the window were custom-made for the visiting journalist. There was a spacious wardrobe for hanging his clothes. The lights all worked, both here and in the adjoining bathroom, which seemed almost as big. The water ran hot in the big four-legged bath, and Russell lay soaking until he realised he was falling asleep.

After a shave and change of clothes he ventured out again. As expected it was snowing, large flakes of the stuff floating down in dense profusion. Following the receptionist's directions, Russell turned right outside the door, and right again opposite the church, into Sw Jana Street. Following this south across two intersections he reached the Rynek Główny, Europe's largest market square. The centre of the huge expanse was occupied by a Gothic hall, but Russell's eyes were instantly drawn to his left, and the loveliest church he had ever seen. Two asymmetrical towers soared skyward through the curtain of snow, one climaxing in a flurry of spires, the other, slightly less high, in a small Renaissance dome. Both were stacked with windows, like a medieval skyscraper.

For several minutes he stood there entranced, until the cold in his feet and a hunger for coffee drove him into one of the cafés that lined the square. Two cups and a roll packed with thick slices of bacon later he felt ready to face a day of work. The café might be half-empty, but all the customers were 'Germany's Neighbours'. He introduced himself to one young Polish couple and took it from there. For the next few hours he worked his way round the cafés and bars of the old town, asking questions.

Most of those he approached spoke some English or some German, and he didn't get many refusals. His own Englishness usually got him off to a favourable start, since many of his interviewees chose to believe that he had a personal line to Neville Chamberlain. Would England fight for Poland? they all asked. And when Russell expressed a sliver of doubt as to whether she would, they couldn't believe it. 'But you fought for Belgium!' several of them said indignantly.

There was virtual unanimity about Poland's situation. Germany was a menace, the Soviets were a menace – it was like choosing between cholera and the Black Death. What did they think about the German request for an extra-territorial road across the corridor? They could whistle. Would they fight for German Danzig? Every last stone. Would they win? He must be joking.

He couldn't be certain of course, but the few people who refused him all looked Jewish. A shadow dropped over their eyes when he introduced himself, a hunted look on their faces as they backed away, pleading lack of time or some other excuse. As if he was an advance guard for the Nazis, his very presence in Cracow a harbinger of disaster.

The snow kept falling. He ate an omelette for lunch in one of the Rynek Główny cafés, and then trudged up and down the main shopping streets in search of a present for Effi. He half-expected Shchepkin suddenly to appear at his shoulder, but there was no sign of him or anyone else. As far as Russell could tell, no one was tracking his footsteps in the snow.

After slipping on some icy cobbles and being almost run over by a tram he decided a rest was in order, and retreated to his hotel for a nap. It was seven by the time he woke, and he felt hungry again. A new receptionist recommended a restaurant on Starowislna Street, which turned out to be only a few doors from the cinema showing the Marx Brothers movie. It was too good an opportunity to miss. After partaking of a wonderful *wienerschnitzel* – at least Cracow had something to thank the Hapsburg empire for – he joined the shivering queue for the evening showing.

Inside the cinema it was hot, noisy and packed. Surveying the audience before the lights went down, Russell guessed that at least half of it was Jewish. He felt cheered by the fact that this could still seem normal, even in a country as prone to anti-Semitism as Poland. He wished Ruth and Marthe were there with him. And Albert. He couldn't remember ever seeing Albert laugh.

The newsreel was in Polish, but Russell got the gist. The first item featured a visit to Warsaw by the Hungarian foreign minister, and no doubt claimed that he and Colonel Beck had discussed matters of mutual importance, without spelling out what everyone knew these were – choosing their cuts of Czechoslovakia once the Germans had delivered the carcass. The second item concerned Danzig, with much piling of sandbags round the Polish post office. The third, more entertainingly, featured a man in New York walking a tightrope between skyscrapers.

The movie proved a surreal experience in more ways than one. Since it was subtitled in Polish, the audience felt little need to keep quiet, and Russell had some trouble catching all the wisecracks. And as the subtitling ran a few seconds behind the visuals, he often found himself laughing ahead of everyone else, like some eccentric cackler.

None of it mattered, though. He'd loved the Marx Brothers since seeing *Animal Crackers* during the last days of the Weimar Republic, before Jewish humour followed Jewish music and Jewish physics into exile. By the time *Broth of the Bird* was half an hour old he was literally aching with laughter. The film's subject matter – the approach of an utterly ridiculous war between two Ruritanian countries – was fraught with contemporary relevance, but any dark undertone was utterly overwhelmed by the swirling tide of joyous anarchy. If you wanted something real to worry about, there were cracker crumbs in the bed with a woman expected. The only sane response to rampant patriotism was: 'Take a card!' As the audience streamed out of the cinema, at least half the faces were streaked with tears of laughter.

It had stopped snowing. In fact, the sky seemed to be clearing. As he walked back towards the city centre, Russell had glimpses of the Wawel Castle and Cathedral silhouetted against a starry slice of sky. Following the tram-lines through a gap in the old medieval walls he eventually reached the Rynek Główny, where the cafés and restaurants were humming with conversation and all sorts of music. Standing in mid-square beside the Cloth Hall he could hear pianos playing Mendelssohn, Chopin and American blues.

People were having fun. They did that in Berlin too, but there was something different in the air. In Berlin there was always an edge of caution: looks over the shoulder, a rein on the tongue. Maybe there was one here too – heaven knew, the regime in Warsaw was illiberal enough – but he couldn't feel it. If the Poles were facing the most threatening year of their recent existence, they weren't letting on.

He thought about having a nightcap, but decided not to make things any more difficult for Shchepkin than he needed to. He was only spending one night at the hotel.

There was no sign of him in the lobby, or of anyone else, suspicious or not. There was no message at reception when he collected his key. After ascending in the delightful glass and wrought iron cage, he found his corridor silent, his door locked. The room was empty. Laughing at himself, he checked the wardrobe. No Shchepkin. No Harpo Marx.

It was almost midnight. He stretched out on the sofa with the John Kling detective stories which Paul had loaned him weeks before, one ear cocked for footsteps in the corridor, but all he heard was an occasional drunken shout from the street below. At 12.45 he gave up and went to bed, laughing in the dark about cracker crumbs.

* * *

He was woken by church bells. It was just after eight, a thin line of grey light separating the curtains on the near window. Russell clambered out of bed and pulled them back. The tip of the church spire opposite was lit by an invisible sun, the sky clear. It looked bitterly cold.

He had mixed feelings about Shchepkin's non-appearance. He couldn't help feeling annoyed that he might have come all this way, missing a weekend with Effi and Paul, only to be stood up. On the other hand, he could hardly say the weekend had been wasted – he liked Cracow, had loved *Duck Soup*, and had the makings of a 'Germany's Neighbours' article. If the Soviets were already tired of him he supposed he should feel relieved, but he couldn't help feeling a poignant sense of anti-climax.

Whatever, he told himself. If nothing else, the projected Soviet series had inspired him to generate others. And Shchepkin – he looked at his watch – still had seven hours to make contact before his train left.

He was damned if he was going to stay cooped up in his room, even if the hotel would let him. He decided to pack and take his bag to the left-luggage at the main station, which was only five minutes walk away. He could get a taxi from there to the Plaszów station when the time came.

An hour later, he was enjoying coffee and rolls in an almost empty station buffet. There were no English or German papers for sale, and – it being Sunday morning – little activity to observe. One small shunting engine chugged its way through in apparent search of work, but that was it. Russell was about to leave when a dark-haired young man loomed over his table. 'Have you a pencil I could use?' he asked in German.

Russell handed his over.

The man sat down, wrote out what appeared to be train times on the corner of his newspaper, and handed the pencil back. 'Zygmunt's Chapel,' he said pleasantly as he got to his feet. 'Two o'clock.'

Russell reached the foot of the ramp leading up to the Wawel with time to spare. On the slopes of the hill several bunches of children were throwing snowballs at each other and squealing with delight, while their parents stood and chatted, plumes of breath coalescing in the air between them. Away to the left, the yellow walls and red tile roof of the Royal Palace stood stark against the clear blue sky.

The ramp ended in a gate through the old fortifications, close by the southern end of the cathedral. This – in contrast to the church on the Rynek Główny – was an elegant mess featuring spires and domes in a bewildering variety of styles and sizes, as if the whole thing had been arranged by a playful child.

The Zygmunt Chapel was off the nave to the right. The tombs of two men – kings, Russell assumed – were vertically stacked amidst a feast of Renaissance carving. The accompanying writing was in Polish, but he recognised the name Jagiello from the Danzig stamp wars.

'Beautiful, yes?' said a familiar voice at his shoulder.

'It is,' Russell agreed. Shchepkin was wearing the same crumpled suit, and quite possibly the same shirt, but on this occasion a dark green tie was hanging, somewhat loosely, beneath the collar. A fur hat covered his hair.

'Have you visited Cracow before?' the Russian asked.

'No, never.'

'It's one of my favourite cities.'

'Oh.'

'Have you seen the Holy Cross Chapel?' Shchepkin asked.

'No ...'

'You must. Come.' He led the way back towards the entrance, and the chapel to its left. Russell followed, somewhat amused at being shown the wonders of Christendom by a communist agent.

The chapel was extraordinary. There was another Jagiellonian tomb, carved in marble in the year Columbus stumbled across America, and a series of slightly older Byzantine frescoes. As they emerged, Shchepkin stood looking down the nave, then turned his eyes upwards toward the soaring roof.

'My father was a priest,' he said in reaction to Russell's look. 'One thing more,' he added, gesturing toward the shrine in the centre of the nave. It held a silver coffin of staggering workmanship. 'It was made in Danzig,' Shchepkin pointed out, as if their relationship needed geographical continuity. 'Enough,' he added, seeing Russell's expression, 'we'll save the crypts for another time. Let's go outside.'

Between the cathedral and the walls overlooking the Vistula there was a large open space. Russell and Shchepkin joined the scattering of couples and small groups who were following the freshly cleared circular path, almost blinded for a while by the brightness of sun on snow.

'The article was perfect,' Shchepkin said eventually. 'Just what was required.' He produced an envelope from his pocket and slipped it into Russell's. 'For your research work,' he said.

Russell stole a quick look at it. It was a banker's draft in Reichsmarks. Lots of them.

'What's the next article about?' Shchepkin asked.

'Transport.'

'Excellent. So what are you telling me today?'

Russell went through the results of his visit to Dresden, his impressions and analysis. It all seemed pretty obvious to him, but

Shchepkin seemed satisfied enough, nodding and interjecting the occasional question or comment. Russell had the feeling he could have listed the stations on the Ringbahn.

After one circuit they started another. They were not alone in this, but one man in particular, limping along fifty yards behind them, struck Russell as suspicious. But when he glanced over his shoulder for the third time Shchepkin told him not to worry. 'One of mine,' he said almost affectionately. 'Local help,' he added, rubbing his hands together. 'What did the SD have to say?' he asked.

Russell recounted his meeting with Kleist, and the demand for previews of each article. He also told Shchepkin about the letter Kleist had written for him, and regretted doing so almost instantly – he wanted the Russian worried for his safety, not encouraged to risk it. 'And the British want previews too,' he added quickly, hoping to divert his listener with an unwelcome shock.

Shchepkin, though, just laughed. 'And how are you explaining these trips?' he asked.

Russell explained about 'Germany's Neighbours' and 'Ordinary Germans'.

'Not bad,' Shchepkin said. 'We will make an intelligence officer of you yet.'

'No thanks.'

Shchepkin gave him one of those looks, amused but disappointed. 'Are you planning to take sides in the coming war?' he asked.

'Not if I can help it,' was Russell's instinctive response.

'Have you heard of the poet Yeats?' Shchepkin asked out of the blue.

'Of course.'

Shchepkin grunted. 'One never knows with the English. So many of you look down on anything Irish.'

'Yeats is a wonderful poet.'

'He died yesterday,' Shchepkin said.

'I didn't know.'

'You know that poem – *The Stolen Child*? I always loved that line – "For the world's more full of weeping than you can understand."'

Russell said nothing.

Shchepkin shook his head, as if to clear it. 'We'll meet in Posen next month. Or Poznan as the Poles call it now. And we'd like you to talk to armament workers,' he said. 'In Berlin, the Ruhr – you know where the big factories are. We need to know if there are problems there, if the workers are ready for political action.'

'That'll be difficult,' Russell said.

'Ordinary German workers, caught between their natural desire for peace and patriotic concern for the Fatherland,' Shchepkin suggested. 'I'm sure you can manage it.'

'I'll try,' Russell agreed.

'You must,' Shchepkin said. 'And you really should wear a hat.'

Idiots to spare

Berlin was grey and overcast. As his train drew into Friedrich-strasse station, Russell thought about taking the Stadtbahn another couple of stops and surprising Effi in bed, but decided against. She was rarely at her best this early in the morning.

Having breakfasted on the train, he skipped coffee in the buffet and headed straight for his bank on Behrenstrasse, where he deposited Shchepkin's banker's draft. As he headed for Französ-ischestrasse in search of a tram home Russell felt an almost dizzying sense of solvency. Presents for everybody, he thought. Including himself.

The sense of well-being evaporated the moment he saw Frau Heidegger's face. 'Oh Herr Russell,' she said, grabbing his left arm with both hands. 'Thank God you're back. I …'

'What's happened?'

'Herr McKinley – he's dead. He committed suicide – can you believe it? The poor boy … And he seemed so happy these last few weeks. I can't …'

'How?' Russell asked. He felt cold all over, and slightly nauseous. 'How did he kill himself?' He couldn't believe it. He didn't believe it.

Frau Heidegger mopped up a tear. 'He threw himself in front of a train. At Zoo station. There were lots of witnesses.'

'When?'

'Late on Saturday. The police came just before midnight and locked his room. Then they came back yesterday. They were up there for hours.'

'The Kripo?'

She looked bewildered for a second. 'Yes, yes, I think so. There were so many of them. They must have been looking for a suicide note, I think. Or something to tell them why he did it.'

Or a letter, Russell thought.

'But I don't think they found anything,' Frau Heidegger went on. 'They seemed very frustrated when they went. I suppose they're worried that the Americans won't believe he killed himself.'

'Perhaps,' Russell said. He still felt stunned.

'They left the room very tidy,' Frau Heidegger said inconsequentially. 'And they want to talk to you,' she added. '"As soon as he gets back," they said. And they put a note under your door saying the same thing. I have the telephone number.' She disappeared back into her apartment for a few seconds and re-emerged with what looked like a torn-off page from a police notebook. There was a number and a name – Kriminalinspektor Oehm.

'I'll ring him now,' Russell said.

'Yes, please,' Frau Heidegger said, as if it would take a huge weight off her mind.

The underling who answered knew who Russell was. 'The Kriminalinspektor would like to see you immediately,' he said, with the stress on the last word. 'At the Alex. Room 456.'

'I'm on my way,' Russell said. It seemed the politic thing to do.

'I'll look after your bag,' Frau Heidegger said, picking it up and moving towards her door. 'You can collect it when you get back.'

He started walking towards the U-bahn, thinking it would be quicker, but changed his mind once he reached Lindenstrasse. Why was he hurrying? A tram ride would give him time to think.

He climbed aboard the first Alexanderplatz-bound tram and stared blankly out of the window. If there was one thing he knew, it was that McKinley hadn't killed himself. In fact, he could hardly think of anyone less likely to do so. He supposed it could have been an accident – the platforms got pretty crowded at Zoo station after theatre-closing time – but if so, why the rush to a suicide verdict? Frau Heidegger had mentioned witnesses – lots of them. An apparent suicide, Russell realized, offered stronger grounds for a police investigation than a simple accident. They'd spent most of yesterday in McKinley's room, and they must have been looking for something. Theresa Jürissen's letter was an obvious candidate, but who knew what other pieces of paper McKinley had collected in support of his story? And it looked as though they hadn't found what they were looking for. Russell wasn't sure how reliable a judge of Kripo moods Frau Heidegger was, but the urgency of his summons certainly suggested they were missing something.

If they hadn't found the letter, then where the hell was it? Six days had passed since he and McKinley visited Theresa Jürissen, and McKinley had been in a hurry – it didn't seem likely that he'd taken his time sending her the money. Unless, of course, he'd had trouble raising it. And she might have had trouble getting down to the poste restante to pick the money up. The letter could still be in the post. Or in her possession. He'd have to warn her, for his own sake as well as hers. If she was arrested, his own involvement would come out, and even if the Kripo accepted that he'd only been along as an interpreter, he'd still failed to report a possible crime against the state. At the very least, grounds for deportation. At worst … it didn't bear thinking about.

If McKinley had received the letter and they hadn't found it, then what had he done with it? He might have risked posting it off to the States, but Russell didn't think so. If they'd been watching him – and it seemed likely that they had – then any outgoing mail would have been intercepted. Russell remembered McKinley's reluctant admission that he thought he was being followed, and his own scarcely concealed derision. 'Sorry, Tyler,' he murmured out loud, drawing a stare from a woman opposite.

Of course, McKinley's suspicions would have made him doubly careful. Which meant there was a good chance he had hidden the letter. But where? If he hadn't stashed it in his room, where could he have hidden it? Just about anywhere in Berlin, Russell thought, looking out at the Königstrasse. McKinley had probably stolen an idea from one of the endless detective novels he read.

He got off outside the Alexanderplatz branch of Wertheim and walked under the railway bridge and into the square itself. The station and another department store, Tietz, occupied the northern side, the huge drab mass of the police praesidium – the 'Alex' as all Berliners called it – the southern side. Russell walked past entrances 4, 3 and 2 – the latter housing the morgue where McKinley's body was presumably residing – and in through the doors of 1, the all-purpose entrance.

The whole Berlin detective force, around 1,800 strong, worked out of this building, and Russell imagined some of them were still waiting for their offices to be discovered. He was gestured towards one of several staircases, and then spent about ten minutes pacing down a succession of identical-looking corridors in search of room 456. The windows overlooking the inner courtyard were all barred, suggesting a guests' penchant for self-defenestration which Russell found less than comforting. Eventually he was intercepted by a surprisingly helpful detective, who took him down the right flight of stairs and turned him into the right corridor.

Kriminalinspektor Oehm's office looked like a work in progress. There were files everywhere – piled on the desk, floor, windowsill and filing cabinets. Oehm, a chubby man with florid face, abundant fair hair and sharp-looking blue eyes, seemed unconcerned by the chaos, but his companion, a redhead with unusually pale skin, kept looking round in apparent disbelief. He was not introduced, but even without the tell-tale leather coat Russell would have assumed Gestapo.

Oehm invited him to sit down. 'We've been trying to contact you since yesterday morning,' he said.

'I've been out of town,' Russell said.

'So your fiancée told us.'

Russell said nothing. He hoped Effi had behaved herself.

'Where exactly were you?' the Gestapo man asked.

'Poland. Cracow to be precise. I'm working on a series of articles on Germany's neighbours.'

'You know why we wish to talk to you?' Oehm said.

'I assume it's about Tyler McKinley.'

'Correct. You were surprised by the news?'

'That he committed suicide. Yes, I was.'

Oehm shrugged. 'He must have had his reasons.'

'Perhaps. Are you certain he killed himself?'

'Absolutely. There is no doubt. We have several witnesses. Reliable witnesses. A police officer, for one.'

'Then he must have,' Russell agreed. He still couldn't see why they – whoever, exactly, they were – had needed to kill McKinley, and he didn't suppose he would ever find out. It didn't much matter, really. His knowing certainly wouldn't help McKinley.

'There is one possible reason for his action,' Oehm said. 'I do not wish to speak ill of the dead, but …well, we have good reason to believe that your friend had become involved with political elements hostile to the State, that he may have become part of a plot against the State involving forged official documents – documents, that is to say, which have been fabricated to create a misleading and slanderous impression of activities inside the Reich.'

'What sort of activities?' Russell asked innocently.

'That is not your concern,' the Gestapo man said.

'And he wasn't my friend,' Russell added. 'I liked him, but we hardly ever saw each other for more than a chat on the stairs. A drink every month or so, perhaps. Nothing more.'

'Ah ...'

'And if he was involved in this plot, why would that lead him to kill himself?' Russell asked.

'Perhaps it all got too much for him, and he couldn't think of any other way out,' Oehm suggested.

'He didn't give you anything to keep for him?' the Gestapo man asked.

'No, he didn't.'

'You are sure about that.'

'One hundred per cent.'

The Gestapo man looked sceptical, but said nothing.

'One more thing,' Oehm said. 'Herr McKinley's sister will be arriving in Berlin on Wednesday. To take the body home ...'

'How's she getting here so quickly?' Russell asked.

'She is apparently flying across the Atlantic. The Americans have these new flying-boats – 'Clippers' I believe they're called – and though they're not yet in public service, there are frequent trials. Proving flights, they call them ...'

'Yes, yes,' the Gestapo man murmured, but Oehm ignored him.

'I am a flyer myself,' he told Russell. 'Weekends only, of course.'

'We all need hobbies,' Russell agreed. 'But how has McKinley's sister wangled a flight on one these ...?'

'Clippers. I imagine Senator McKinley used his influence to get his niece a place on one of them.'

'*Senator* McKinley?'

'Tyler McKinley's uncle.' Oehm noticed the surprise in Russell's face. 'You did not know his uncle was a US senator?'

'Like I said, we weren't exactly friends.' He could understand why McKinley had kept quiet about it – the boy would have hated anyone thinking he owed anything to family connections. But he was amazed that none of his fellow American journalists had spilled the beans. They must have assumed Russell knew.

'As I was saying,' Oehm continued. 'His sister will arrange for the body to be sent home and collect her brother's effects. I was hoping you could be here when we talk to her, as an interpreter and someone who knew her brother.'

'I can do that.'

'Her plane from Lisbon arrives around eleven. So, if you could be here at one?'

'I will be. Is that all?'

'Yes, Herr Russell that is all.' Oehm smiled up at him. The Gestapo man gave him the merest of nods.

Russell retraced his steps to the main entrance. As he emerged into the open air he took a deep breath in and blew it out again. One thing was certain – they hadn't found the letter.

He crossed the square and walked into a café underneath the Stadtbahn tracks which he occasionally frequented. After ordering a couple of frankfurters and a *kartoffelsalat* he perched on a stool by the window, cleared a hole in the condensation, and looked out. No one had followed him in, but was anyone loitering outside? He couldn't see anyone obvious, but that didn't mean much. He would have to make sure in Tietz, pull a variation of the same trick he and McKinley had pulled in the Neukölln Karstadt department store. But it would have to look like an accident. He didn't want them thinking he'd lost them on purpose.

The food tasted bad, which was unusual. It was the taste in his mouth, Russell thought. Fear.

He crossed the road and walked into Tietz, heading for the rank of telephone booths that he remembered outside the store's ground floor tea-room. Ensconced in the first booth, he looked back along the aisle he had just walked. No one looked furtive. He dialled Effi's number.

She answered on the second ring. 'You're back. I had the police ...'

'I know. I've just spent twenty minutes in the Alex. I'm sorry you got...'

'Oh, it was no problem. They didn't break anything. I was just worried about you. Are you really upset? You didn't know him that well, did you?'

'No, I didn't. I feel sad, though. He was a nice enough man.'

'Are you coming over?'

'Yes, but it'll be a few hours. Say around six. I have to see someone.'

'OK.'

'I'll see you then.'

'I love you.'

'I love you too.'

He replaced the receiver and scanned the aisle again. Still nothing. A taxi, he decided. From this side of the station, where there were often only two or three waiting.

He was in luck – there was only one. 'Friedrichstrasse station,' he told the driver, and watched through the rear window as they swung round beneath the railway and headed down Kaiser Wilhelmstrasse. There was no sign of pursuit. At Friedrichstrasse he hurried down the steps to the U-bahn platform, reaching it as a Grenzallee train pulled in. He stepped aboard, standing beside the doors until they closed, but no one else emerged through the platform gates.

The train pulled out and he sank into the nearest seat. Should he be waiting for darkness, he wondered. Or would that be even riskier? He had no real idea, and felt shaken by how important such a decision could be.

It took twenty minutes to reach Hermannplatz. Russell climbed up to the street, where the loudspeakers were broadcasting Hitler's long-awaited speech to the Reichstag. A small crowd had gathered around the one outside Karstadt, their faces as overcast as the sky. The Führer's tone was calm and reasonable, which suggested he was still warming up.

Russell walked on, following a trail of street-names familiar from the week before. It was a good thing he recognised these, because the area seemed utterly different by daylight, its workshops and factories bursting with noisy activity, its cobbled streets full of rumbling lorries. Most of the workplaces were broadcasting the speech to their employees, and Hitler's words seeped out through doors and over walls, a promise here, a threat there, a piece of self-congratulation sandwiched in between. Stopping for a moment on a bridge across the Neuköllner Schiffahrtkanal Russell heard fragments of the speech tossed around on the breeze, like the puffs of wind-strewn smoke belching from the myriad chimneys.

Schönlankerstrasse was empty, the block door wide open. He walked in and knocked on Theresa Jürissen's door. There was no answer. He knocked again with the same result, and was wondering what to do when footsteps sounded on the stairs. It was her.

Her face registered alarm, and then anger. Without speaking, she opened her door and gestured him in. Marietta was sitting exactly where she had been on his last visit, still drawing, still oblivious.

'What do you want?' Theresa asked, the moment the door was closed behind her.

'I'm sorry,' he said. 'I know this is dangerous for you, but not coming might have been more dangerous.'

He told her about McKinley's death.

'Could the police connect you?' he asked. 'Did you ever write to him?'

'No,' she said. 'Never.'

'What about the document you told us about?'

'I sent it, but that's all. I gave no name or address.'

Russell sighed in relief. 'When did you send it?'

'Last week. Thursday afternoon.'

McKinley had received it. He must have. Russell explained why he had asked. 'They haven't found it,' he told her. 'He must have hidden it somewhere.'

'There's nothing to connect me,' she said. 'Except you,' she added, the look of alarm back on her face.

'They won't hear about you from me,' Russell promised her, hoping he could live up to such an assurance.

'Thank you,' she said doubtfully, as if she wasn't that sure either. 'And their secret will stay secret,' she added, as much to herself as to him.

'Looks like it.'

She nodded, her view of the world confirmed.

'I'll be going,' he said.

'Let me make sure there's no one about,' she cautioned him. A few moments later she returned. 'It's all clear.'

Russell smiled goodbye to a closing door and began the long walk back to the centre of Neukölln. The Führer was well into his stride now, each torrent of words reinforced by the sound of his fist hammering at the lectern. By the time he reached Karstadt the listening crowd had spilled into the street, all eyes raised to the crackling loudspeaker, as if Hitler would emerge genie-like from the mesh, a head spouting venom on a shimmering tail.

It was dark by the time he reached Effi's flat. She was wearing a dress he hadn't seen before, deep red with a black lace collar. And she wanted to eat out, at a Chinese restaurant which had opened a few weeks earlier at the Halensee end of the Ku'damm.

'I've been learning my lines,' she announced as they walked downstairs. 'Would you hear me later?'

It was a peace offering, Russell realised. 'Love to,' he told her.

They walked through to the Ku'damm and took a westbound tram. The wide pavements were crowded with homegoing workers, the restaurants and cinemas gearing up for the evening as the shops closed down. Alighting at Lehninerplatz they found the Chinese restaurant already filling up. 'Goering eats here,' Effi said, as if in explanation.

'He eats everywhere,' Russell said. 'And this is on me,' he added.

Effi gave him a look.

'I've sold a lot of work lately,' he explained.

They were shown to their table, which stood beneath a huge scroll of dragons. Russell picked up the menu, hoping it was in German, but needn't have bothered.

'Let me order,' Effi said.

'Include beer,' Russell insisted. He was still feeling tense, he realised. And maybe still a little in shock. Sitting there, half-listening as Effi questioned the waiter, he found himself imagining McKinley's death – the moment of falling, of realisation. Of terror. 'How was your weekend?' he asked.

'Miserable. You know I hate going to parties on my own. All

the women I know were queuing up to ask if you'd left me – none of them asked whether I'd left you – and all the men were trying to work out how available I was, without actually asking. Every conversation was fraught with significance. Every dance was a means to an end. I couldn't just *be* for a single moment. When I go to something like that with you, I can just enjoy myself.' She sighed. 'Anyway, the party went on to about six, so I got to bed about seven, and the Kripo started hammering on the door at about nine. So I wasn't in a good mood. And I was upset for you too. I know you liked him, even if he was a bit Rin Tin Tin-like. And I could just see it too. Zoo station gets so crowded on a Saturday evening.' She watched a tray of food go by, and sniffed at the passing aroma. 'And my dear sister Zarah's such a misery as well. She's convinced there's something wrong with Lothar. I tell her she's jumping to conclusions, that he's probably just a slow learner. She was herself, according to Mama. But she's convinced there's something wrong. She's made an appointment with a specialist.'

'When for?' Russell asked.

'Oh, I don't know. Next week sometime. I think she said Monday. Why?'

'Just wondered.' The arrival of their drinks gave Russell a few seconds to think. He couldn't say anything, he realised. And probably didn't need to. Zarah's husband Jens was a Party official, and Russell couldn't believe the Nazis would start killing their own children. And if he did say anything to Effi, and she said something to Zarah, then he might end up in a Gestapo cellar trying to explain where he'd got his information from.

'You look worried,' Effi said.

'I've heard a few rumours, that's all. Just journalist talk probably. The word is that the government's thinking of tightening up the

Law on the Prevention of Hereditary Diseases. Sanctioning mercy killing when the parents agree.'

She gave him an angry look. 'There's nothing wrong with Lothar,' she said. 'And even if there was, Zarah would never agree to... I can't believe you think...'

'I don't. But Jens is a Nazi, after all. He believes in all this purification of the race nonsense.'

Effi snorted. 'Maybe he does. But if he tried to take Lothar away from Zarah she'd never forgive him. And he knows it.'

'OK.'

'And there's nothing wrong with Lothar,' she insisted once more.

He read the Führer's speech next morning on his way home for a change of clothes. The editorials were calling it 'a major contribution to world peace', and the speech certainly seemed accommodating by Hitler's standards. There were friendly references to Poland and the non-aggression pact between the two countries. There was a marked absence of attacks on the Soviet Union. But one passage chilled Russell to the bone, and that concerned the Jews, who were only likely to start a war in Hitler's frenzied imagination. If they did, 'the result would not be the Bolshevisation of the earth and victory for the Jews but the annihilation of the Jewish race in Europe.' Russell wondered how the Wiesners felt reading that, even if Hitler was not speaking about physical annihilation. At least he hoped he wasn't. He remembered Albert's words in the Friedrichshain park: 'They'll just kill us. Who's going to stop them?'

Frau Heidegger had listened to the speech and found only grounds for optimism. 'There'll be an agreement with the Poles,' she said. 'Like the one with the Czechs at Munich. And then there'll be nothing more to fight over.'

Russell said he hoped she was right.

'The police were back yesterday,' she went on. 'Herr McKinley's sister will be here on Wednesday or Thursday to collect his things.'

'I know,' Russell told her. 'They want me to interpret for them.'

'That's nice,' Frau Heidegger said.

Once upstairs, Russell bathed, changed and worked for a couple of hours planning his transport piece for *Pravda*. Autobahns and the People's Car, streamlined trains and new U-bahn lines, the latest Dornier flying-boats. Perhaps a hint of regret for the passing of the Zeppelins, he thought, but absolutely no mention of the *Hindenburg*.

He fried up a potato omelette for lunch, found a dusty bottle of beer to accompany it, and reluctantly considered the prospect of interviewing Hitler's armament workers for Stalin. It could be done, he supposed, but he'd have to be damn careful. Start off by talking to the Party people in the factory, the managers and Labour Front officials. Only move out onto the metaphorical lake if the ice feels really solid. Don't do a McKinley.

He thought about the missing letter. If he was going to take a look around the American's room it had to be today.

He walked down to the ground floor, and tapped on Frau Heidegger's open door. 'Have you still got a spare key for Tyler's room?' he asked. 'I loaned him some books, and it would be awkward searching for them when his sister's here, so I thought I could slip in and get them today. You don't need to come up,' he added quickly, hoping that Frau Heidegger's bad knees would triumph over her curiosity.

They did. 'Make sure you bring it back,' she told him.

McKinley's room was still suffused with the faint odour of his Balkan tobacco. As Frau Heidegger had intimated, the room was almost preternaturally tidy, and now he knew why the Kripo had refrained from leaving their usual mess. A senator's nephew! No wonder they were on their best behaviour.

The clothes were neatly put away – shirts, jacket and suit in the wardrobe, socks and underwear in drawers. There was a thin pile of papers on the desk – left for show, Russell guessed – he remembered two great towers of paper on his last visit. The desk, too, had been mostly emptied. One drawer contained a single eraser, another, three pencils. It was as if the Kripo had decided to spread things out.

There was no obvious reduction in the number of books, but the lines on the shelves seemed anything but neat. Each had been taken out and checked for insertions, Russell assumed. Well at least that meant he didn't have to.

The same applied to the floorboards. The Kripo weren't amateurs. Far from it.

He sat on McKinley's bed, wondering why he'd imagined he could find something which they couldn't. The shelf above the headboard was full of crime novels, all in English. More than fifty, Russell guessed: Dashiell Hammett, Edgar Wallace, Dorothy L. Sayers, several authors he hadn't heard of. There were around a dozen Agatha Christies, and a similar number of 'Saint' books. Russell's earlier notion that McKinley had stolen an idea from one of these stories still seemed a good one, but the only way of finding out for certain was to go through them all, and that would take forever.

And what would he do with the letter if he found it? He had no proof of its authenticity, and without such proof there was little chance of anonymously arranging its publication outside Germany. He would have to guarantee it with what was left of his own reputation, either risking arrest by doing so inside Germany or forfeiting his residence by doing so from the safety of England. Neither course appealed. 'And their secret will stay secret,' he murmured to himself. He took one last look round the room and took the key back to Frau Heidegger.

Early that evening he telephoned Paul. The conversation seemed oddly awkward at first – his son seemed happy to talk, but there was something in his voice that worried Russell, some faint edge of resentment which was quite possibly unconscious. His *Jungvolk* group had spent much of Saturday making model gliders out of balsa wood and glue, something which Paul had obviously enjoyed, and on the coming Saturday they were visiting an airfield to examine the real thing. At school a new music teacher had given them a talk on the different types of music, and how some of them – jazz for example – were fatally tainted by their racial origins. He had even played several pieces on the school gramophone, pointing out what he called 'animal rhythms'. 'I suppose he's right,' Paul said. 'I mean, jazz was invented by negroes, wasn't it? But most of my friends thought the records he played were really good,' he admitted.

Russell looked in vain for an adequate response.

'What are you doing?' Paul asked, somewhat unusually.

'This and that,' Russell said. Paul was probably too old to have nightmares about falling under trains, but it wasn't worth the risk. 'Actually I'm looking for something that someone hid,' he said. 'If the Saint wants to hide something, how does he do it?' he asked, not really expecting an answer.

'What sort of thing?'

'Oh, money, a letter…'

'That's easy. He sends it to himself. At a – what do you call it?'

'Poste restante.'

'That's it. He sends diamonds to himself in *Getaway* and *The High*

Fence. And he does it in another story, I think. I can't remember which, though…'

Russell was no longer listening. Of course. If McKinley had forgotten the Saint's trick, then Theresa's use of the poste restante would have reminded him. He sighed inwardly. There was no way of collecting anything from a poste restante without identification. McKinley's sister could probably get access, but only by asking permission from the police.

'Dad, are you listening?'

'Yes, sorry – I think you've solved it for me.'

'Oh.'

'And I'm reading the book you loaned me,' he added, eager to please his son.

'Isn't it great?'

'It's pretty good,' Russell agreed, though he'd only read thirty pages. 'I haven't got far,' he admitted, hoping to ward off a cross-examination. 'I'll talk to you about it on Saturday.'

'OK. On Sunday are we getting the train from Anhalter Bahnhof?'

'I expect so. I'll let you know.' Actually, a different means of transport was suggesting itself.

The first day of February was as grey as nature intended. His Wednesday morning lesson with Ruth and Marthe was enjoyable as ever, but there was no sign of their brother or parents. Arriving back at Alexanderplatz with twenty minutes to spare he stopped for a coffee in Wertheim and ran into Doug Conway. They chatted for a few minutes, until Russell realised he was late for his appointment. The search for Oehm's office made him even later, and McKinley's sister was looking none too happy when he finally arrived.

'We were talking about Fräulein McKinley's flying boat,' Oehm said, which further explained her look of irritation.

She was almost as tall as her brother – about five foot eleven, he guessed – and even thinner. Severely cut brunette hair framed a face that might have been pretty if the already-thin lips had not been half-pursed in disapproval, but Russell sensed that her current expression was the one she most usually presented to the world. She was wearing a cream blouse and smart, deep blue suit. There was no hint of black and no obvious sign of grief in her face. He told himself that she'd had several days to take it all in.

He introduced himself and offered his condolences.

'Eleanor McKinley,' she responded. 'Tyler never mentioned you.'

'We weren't close friends – just neighbours. I'm here because the police thought an interpreter would make things easier for everyone. Have they told you what happened?'

'Oh, we got all the details from the German Embassy in Washington. A man came out to the house and explained everything.'

Russell wondered what to say next. He found it hard to credit that the family believed Tyler had committed suicide. But it was hardly his place to question it, particularly with Oehm trying to follow their conversation.

The German interrupted. 'There are papers to sign.' He passed them to Russell. 'If you could…'

Russell looked through them, and then explained the gist to Eleanor McKinley. 'There's two things here. One is an account of the investigation, complete with witness statements and the police conclusion that Tyler committed suicide. They need your signature to sign off on the case. The other form waives your family's right to an inquest. This is because you're taking him home with you.'

'I understand,' she said.

'I'll read it through then.'

'No, no, don't bother,' she said, extracting a pack of Chesterfields from her handbag. 'You won't mind if I smoke?' she asked Oehm, holding up a cigarette in explanation.

Russell felt taken aback. 'You understand that you're accepting their version of events, that this exempts them from any further investigation?' he asked.

'Are there any other versions?' she asked.

'No. I just wanted to be sure you knew that this puts an end to any...'

'Good,' she interrupted. She made a writing mime at Oehm, who handed her his pen.

'Here and here,' Russell said, placing the papers in front of her. She signed both, writing 'Eleanor V. Tyler' in a large looping hand.

'Is that it?' she asked.

'That's it.'

'What about Tyler's... what about the body?'

Russell asked Oehm. It was still in the morgue, he thought, but phoned to check.

It was. 'They need her for a formal identification before they can release it,' Oehm told Russell in German. 'But not now – they're still trying to repair his face. If she comes at eleven in the morning they'll have plenty of time to seal it for transport and get it across to Lehrter.'

Russell relayed the salient points.

'Can't we do it now?' she asked.

'No, I'm afraid not.'

She made a face, but didn't press the issue. 'All right. Well, let's get out of this dreadful place.' She offered Oehm her hand and the briefest of smiles, and headed for the door. 'I suppose I can get Tyler's apartment over with instead,' she said as they walked back to the entrance. 'You'll come with me,' she added. It was more of an assumption than a question.

They took a taxi. She said nothing as they drove through the old city, just stared out of the window. As they swung through Spittelmarkt towards Dönhoffplatz and the bottom of Lindenstrasse she murmured something to herself, then turned to Russell and said: 'I've never seen such a grey city.'

'The weather doesn't help,' he said.

She was even less impressed with Neuenburgerstrasse. Frau Heidegger climbed the stairs to let them in, and insisted that Russell pass on her deepest condolences. 'And tell Fräulein McKinley how much I liked her brother,' she added. 'How much we all did.'

Russell did as he was bid, and McKinley's sister flashed another of her brief smiles in Frau Heidegger's direction. 'Tell her we'd like to be alone,' she said in English.

Russell passed on the message. Frau Heidegger looked slightly hurt, but disappeared down the stairs.

Eleanor sat down on the bed looking, for the first time, as if her brother's death meant something to her.

Now was the moment, Russell thought. He had to say something. 'I find it hard to believe that your brother killed himself,' he said tentatively.

She sighed. 'Well, he did. One way or another.'

'I'm sorry…'

She got up and walked to the window. 'I don't know how much you knew about Tyler's work…'

'I knew he was working on something important.'

'Exposing some terrible Nazi plot?' she asked.

'Maybe.' She was angry, he realised. Furious. 'Well, that was a pretty effective way of committing suicide, wouldn't you say?'

Russell bit back an answer. He'd said much the same thing to McKinley himself.

'Look at this,' she said, surveying the room. 'The life he chose,' she said bitterly.

That you couldn't, Russell thought. He relucantly abandoned the idea of asking for her help in checking out the poste restante.

She picked up McKinley's pipe, looked round, and took one of his socks to wrap it in. 'I'll take this,' she said. 'Can you get rid of the rest?'

'Yes, but...'

'I can't imagine it would be much use to anyone else.'

'OK.'

He accompanied her downstairs and out to the waiting taxi.

'Thank you for your help,' she said. 'I don't suppose you're free tomorrow morning? I could use some help at the morgue. My train leaves at three and I can't afford any hold-ups. And some moral support would be nice,' she added, as if it had just occurred to her that identifying her brother might involve an emotional toll. 'I'll buy you lunch.'

Russell felt like refusing, but he had no other appointments. Be generous, he told himself. 'It's a deal,' he said.

'Pick me up at the Adlon,' she told him. 'Around ten-thirty.'

He watched the cab turn the corner into Lindenstrasse and disappear. He felt sorry for McKinley, and perhaps even sorrier for his sister.

He arrived at the Adlon just before ten, and found Jack Slaney sitting behind a newspaper in the tea-room. 'I've got something for you,' Russell said, sitting down and counting out the ninety Reichsmarks he owed from the last poker game.

'A sudden inheritance?' Slaney asked.

'Something like that.'

'What are you doing here?' the American said, as he gestured the waiter over to order coffees.

Russell told him.

'He was a nice kid,' Slaney said. 'Shame about his family.'

'The uncle's not one of your favourite senators?'

Slaney laughed. 'He's a big friend of the Nazis, anti-Semitic through and through. The usual broken record – on the one hand, we should be leaving Europe well alone, on the other, we should be realising that Britain and France are on their last legs and Germany's a progressive powerhouse, our natural ally. Bottom line – it's just business as usual. The Senator's brother – McKinley's dad – has a lot of money invested here. One plant in Düsseldorf, another in Stuttgart. They'll do well out of a war, as long as we stay out of it.'

'The daughter's not exactly soft and cuddly,' Russell admitted.

'I know. Hey!' Slaney interrupted himself. 'Have you heard the latest? Over the weekend some Swedish member of parliament nominated Hitler for the Nobel Peace Prize. Wrote a letter of recommendation and everything.' Slaney flipped back the pages on his notebook. 'He praised "Hitler's glowing love of peace, heretofore best documented in his famous book *Mein Kampf*."'

'A spoof, right?'

'Of course. But at least one German paper missed that bit. They printed the whole thing as if it was completely kosher.' He threw back his head and laughed out loud, drawing stares from across the room.

At 10.30 Russell asked the receptionist to let Eleanor know he was in the lobby. She appeared a couple of minutes later. The suit was a deep crimson this time, the silk scarf a shimmering gold. The heels were higher, the seams of her stockings straight as arrows. The fur coat looked expensive. 'It doesn't look like they're getting ready for a war,' she said, as their cab motored down Unter Den Linden.

The morgue was ready for them. McKinley's body was laid out on a trolley in the middle of the spacious cold-store. She marched confidently forward, heels clicking on the polished floor, then suddenly faltered and looked back at Russell. He came forward, took her arm, and together they advanced on the trolley.

A white sheet concealed whatever injuries her brother had suffered below the neck. The familiar shock of dark hair had been burnt away at the front, and the entire left side of his face looked blackened beneath the mortician's make-up. The eyes looked as though they'd been re-inserted in their sockets; one was not quite closed, and presumably never would be again. The bottom lip had been sewn back on, probably after McKinley had bitten clean through it. An angry red-brown wound extended round the American's neck above the uppermost edge of sheet, causing Russell to wonder whether he had been decapitated.

'It's him,' Eleanor said in a voice quivering with control. She signed the necessary documentation on the small table by the door and left the room without a backward glance. During the first part of their ride back to the Adlon she sat in silence, staring out of the window, an angry expression on her face. As they crossed over Friedrichstrasse she asked Russell how long he'd lived in Berlin, but hardly listened to his answer.

'Come up,' she said when they reached the lobby, and gave him a quick glance to make sure he hadn't read anything into the invitation.

Her suite was modest, but a suite just the same. An open suitcase sat on the bed, half-filled with clothes, surrounded by bits and pieces. 'I'll only be a minute,' she said, and disappeared into the bathroom.

An item on the bed had already caught Russell's eye – one of the small grey canvas bags that the Kripo used for storing personal effects.

There was no sound from the bathroom. Now or never, he told himself.

He took one stride to the bed, loosened the string, and looked inside the bag. It was almost empty. He poured the contents onto the bed and sorted through them with his fingers. A reporter's notebook – almost empty. German notes – almost 300 Reichsmarks' worth. McKinley's press accreditation. His passport.

The toilet flushed in the bathroom.

Russell slipped the passport into his pocket, rammed the rest back into the bag, tightened the string and stepped hastily away from the bed.

She came out of the bathroom, looked at the mess on the bed, staring, or so it seemed to Russell, straight at the bag. She reached down, picked it up... and placed it in the suitcase. 'I thought we'd eat here,' she said.

Five minutes later, they were being seated in the hotel restaurant. Having locked her brother away in some sort of emotional box, she chatted happily about America, her dog, the casting of Vivien Leigh as Scarlett O'Hara in the new film of *Gone with the Wind*. It was all very brittle, but brittle was what she was.

After they had eaten he watched her look round the room, and tried to see it through her eyes – a crowd of smart people, most of the women fashionably dressed, many of the men in perfectly tailored uniforms. Eating good food, drinking fine wines. Just like home.

'Do you think there'll be a war?' she asked abruptly.

'Probably,' he said.

'But what could they gain from one?' she asked, genuinely puzzled. 'I mean, you can see how prosperous the country is, how content. Why risk all that?'

Russell had no wish to talk politics with her. He shrugged agreement with her bewilderment and asked how the flight across the Atlantic had been.

'Awful,' she said. 'So noisy, though I got used to that after a while. But it's a horrible feeling, being over the middle of the ocean and knowing that there's no help for thousands of miles.'

'Are you going back the same way?'

'Oh no. It was Daddy who insisted I came that way. He thought it was important that I got here quickly, though I can't imagine why. No, I'm going back by ship. From Hamburg. My train leaves at three,' she added, checking her watch. 'Will you take me to the station?'

'Of course.'

Upstairs he watched her cram her remaining possessions into the suitcase, and breathed a silent sigh of relief when she asked him to close it for her. A taxi took them to the Lehrter Bahnhof, where the *D-Zug* express was already waiting in its platform, car attendants hovering at each door.

'Thank you for your help,' she said, holding out a hand.

'I'm sorry about the circumstances,' Russell said.

'Yes,' she agreed, but more in exasperation than sadness. As he turned away she was reaching for her cigarettes.

Near the front of the train three porters were manhandling a coffin into the baggage car. Russell paused in his stride, and watched as they set it down with a thump by the far wall. Show some respect, he felt like saying, but what was the point? He walked on, climbing the steps to the Stadtbahn platforms which hung above the mainline station's throat. A train rattled in almost instantly, and three minutes later he was burrowing down to the U-bahn platforms at Friedrichstrasse. He read an abandoned *Volkischer Beobachter* on the journey to Neukölln, but the only item of interest concerned the Party student leader in Heidelberg. He had forbidden his students to dance the Lambeth Walk, on the grounds that it was foreign to the German way of life, and incompatible with National Socialist behaviour.

How many Germans, Russell wondered, were itching to dance the Lambeth Walk?

Not the family in Zembski's studio, that was certain. They were there to have their portrait taken, the father in SA uniform, the wife in her church best, the three blonde daughters all in pigtails, wearing freshly ironed BDM uniforms. Nazi heaven.

Russell watched as the big Silesian lumbered around, checking the lighting and the arrangement of the fake living-room setting. Finally he was satisfied. 'Smile,' he said, and clicked the shutter. 'One more,' he said, 'and smile this time.' The wife did, the girls tried, but the father was committed to looking stern.

Russell wondered what was going through Zembski's mind at moments like this. He had only known the Silesian for a few years, but he'd heard of him long before that. In the German communist circles which he and Ilse had once frequented, Zembski had been known as a reliable source for all sorts of photographic services, and strongly rumoured to be a key member of the Pass-Apparat, the Berlin-based Comintern factory for forged passports and other documents. Russell had never revealed his knowledge of Zembski's past. But it was one of the reasons for his using him for his photographic needs. That and the fact that he liked the man. And his low prices.

He watched as Zembski ushered the family out into the street with promises of prints by the weekend. Closing the door behind them he rolled his eyes toward the ceiling. 'Is smiling so hard?' he asked rhetorically. 'But of course he'll love it. I only hope the wife doesn't get beaten to a pulp for looking happy.' He walked across to the arc-lights and turned them off. 'And what can I do for you, Mister Russell?'

Russell nodded towards the small office which adjoined the studio.

Zembski looked at him, shrugged, and gestured him in. Two chairs were squeezed in either side of a desk. 'I hope it's pornography rather than politics,' he said once they were inside. 'Though these days it's hard to tell the difference.'

Russell showed him McKinley's passport. 'I need my photograph in this. I was hoping you'd either do it for me, or teach me how to do it myself.'

Zembski looked less than happy. 'What makes you think I'd know?'

'I was in the Party myself once.'

Zembski's eyebrows shot up. 'Ah. A lot's changed since then, my friend.'

'Yes, but they're probably still using the same glue on passports. And you probably remember which remover to use.'

Zembski nodded. 'Not the sort of thing you forget.' He studied McKinley's passport. 'Who is he?'

'Was. He's the American journalist who jumped in front of a train at Zoo station last weekend. Allegedly jumped.'

'Better and better,' the Silesian said dryly. He opened a drawer, pulled out a magnifying glass, and studied the photograph. 'Looks simple enough.'

'You'll do it?'

Zembski leaned back in his chair, causing it to squeak with apprehension. 'Why not?'

'How much?'

'Ah. That depends. What's it for? I don't want details,' he added hurriedly, 'just some assurance that it won't end up on a Gestapo desk.'

'I need it to recover some papers. For a story.'

'Not a Führer-friendly story?'

'No.'

'Then I'll give you a discount for meaning well. But it'll still cost you a hundred Reichsmarks.'

'Fair enough.'

'Cash.'

'Right.'

'I'll take the picture now then,' Zembski said, manoeuvring his bulk out of the confined space and through the door into the studio. 'A plain background,' he muttered out loud as he studied the original photograph. 'This'll do,' he said, pushing a screen against a wall and placing a stool in front of it.

Russell sat on it.

Zembski lifted his camera, tripod and all, and placed it in position. After feeding in a new film, he squinted through the lens. 'Try and look like an American,' he ordered.

'How the hell do I do that?' Russell asked.

'Look optimistic.'

'I'll try.'

'I said optimistic, not doe-eyed.'

Russell grinned, and the shutter clicked.

'Let's try a serious one,' Zembski ordered.

Russell pursed his lips.

The shutter clicked again. And again. And several more times. 'That'll do,' the Silesian said at last. 'I'll have it for you on Monday.'

'Thanks.' Russell stood up. 'One other thing. You don't by any chance know of a good place to pick up a second-hand car?'

Zembski did – a cousin in Wedding owned a garage which often had cars to sell on. 'Tell him I sent you,' he said, after giving Russell directions, 'and you may get another discount. We Silesians are all heart,' he added, chins wobbling with merriment.

Russell walked the short distance back to the U-bahn, then changed his mind and took a seat in the shelter by the tram stop. Gazing back down the brightly lit Berlinerstrasse towards Zembski's studio, he wondered whether he'd just crossed a very dangerous line. No, he reassured himself, all he'd done was commission a false passport. He would cross the line when he made use of it.

After teaching the Wiesner girls next morning, Russell headed across town in search of Zembski's cousin. He found the garage on one of Wedding's back streets, sandwiched between a brewery and the back wall of a locomotive depot, about half a kilometre from the Lehrter station. Zembski's cousin Hunder was also a large man, but looked a lot fitter than Zembski. He seemed to have half a dozen young men working for him, most of them barely beyond school age.

The cars for sale were lined up round the back. There were four of them: a Hanomag, an Opel, a Hansa-Lloyd, another Opel. 'Any colour you want as long as it's black,' Russell murmured.

'We can re-spray,' Hunder told him.

'No, black's good,' Russell said. The more anonymous the better, he thought. 'How much are they?' he asked.

Hunder listed the prices. 'Plus a ten per cent discount for a friend of my cousin,' he added. 'And a full tank. And a month's guarantee.'

166

The larger Hansa-Lloyd looked elegant, but was way out of Russell's monetary reach. And he had never liked the look of Opels.

'Can I take the Hanomag out for a drive?' he asked.

'You do know how?' Hunder enquired.

'Yes.' He had driven lorries in the War, and much later he and Ilse had actually owned a car, an early Ford, which had died ignominiously on the road to Potsdam soon after their marriage had gone the same way.

He climbed into the driving-seat, waved the nervous-looking Hunder a cheerful goodbye, and turned out of the garage yard. It felt strange after all those years, but straightforward enough. He drove up past the sprawling Lehrter goods yards, back through the centre of Moabit and up Invalidenstrasse. The car was a bit shabby inside, but it handled well, and the engine sounded smooth enough.

He stopped by the side of the Humboldt canal basin and wormed his way under the chassis. There was a bit of rust, but not too much. No sign of leakages, and nothing seemed about to fall off. Brushing himself down, he walked round the vehicle. The engine compartment looked efficient enough. The tyres would need replacing, but not immediately. The lights worked. It wasn't exactly an Austro-Daimler, but it would have to do.

He drove back to the garage and told Hunder he'd take it. As he wrote out the cheque, he reminded himself how much he'd be saving on tram and train tickets.

It was still early afternoon as he drove home, and the streets, with the exception of Potsdamerplatz, were relatively quiet. He parked in the courtyard, and borrowed a bucket, sponge and brush from an excited Frau Heidegger. She watched from the step as he washed the outside and cleaned the inside, her face full of anticipation.

'A quick drive?' he offered, and she needed no second bidding. He took them through Hallesches Tor and up to Viktoria Park, listening carefully for any sign that the engine was bothered by the gradient. There was none. 'I haven't been up here for years!' Frau Heidegger exclaimed, peering through the windscreen at the Berlin panorama as they coasted back down the hill.

Effi was just as excited a couple of hours later. Her anger at his late arrival evaporated the moment she saw the car. 'Teach me to drive,' she insisted.

Russell knew that both her father and former husband had refused to teach her, the first because he feared for his car, the second because he feared for his social reputation. Women were not encouraged to drive in the new Germany. 'OK,' he agreed. 'But not tonight,' he added, as she made for the driver's seat.

It was a ten minute drive to the Conways' modern apartment block in Wilmersdorf, and the Hanomag looked somewhat overawed by the other cars parked outside. 'Don't worry,' Effi said, patting its bonnet. 'We need a name,' she told Russell. 'Something old and reliable. How about Hindenburg?'

'He's dead,' Russell objected.

'I suppose so. How about Mother?'

'Mine isn't reliable.'

'Oh all right. I'll think about it.'

They were the last to arrive. Phyllis Conway was still putting the children to bed, leaving Doug to dispense the drinks. He introduced Russell and Effi to the other three couples, two of whom – the Neumaiers and the Auers – were German. Hans Neumaier worked in banking, and his wife looked after their children. Rolf and Freya Auer owned an art gallery. The third couple was Conway's replacement Martin Unsworth and his wife Fay. Everyone present, Russell reckoned, was either approaching, enjoying or had recently departed, their thirties. Hans Neumaier was probably the oldest, Fay Unsworth the youngest.

Effi disappeared to read the children a bedtime story, leaving Russell and Doug Conway alone by the drinks table. 'I asked the Wiesners,' Conway told him. 'I went out to see them.' He shook his head. 'They were pleased to be asked, I think, but they wouldn't come. Don't want to risk drawing attention to themselves while they're waiting for their visas, I suppose. They talk highly of you, by the way.'

'Is there nothing you can do to speed up their visas?'

'Nothing. I've tried, believe me. I'm beginning to think that someone in the system doesn't like them.'

'Why, for God's sake?'

'I don't know. I'll keep trying, but…' He let the word hang. 'Oh,' he said, reaching into his jacket pocket and pulling out two tickets. 'I was given these today. Brahms and something else, at the Philharmonie, tomorrow evening. Would you like them? We can't go.'

'Thanks. Effi'll be pleased.'

'What's she doing now? *Barbarossa* has finished, hasn't it?'

'Yes. But you'd better ask her about the next project.'

Conway grinned. 'I will. Come on, we'd better join the others.'

The evening went well. The conversation flowed through dinner and beyond, almost wholly in German, the Conways taking turns at providing translation for Fay Unsworth. The two German men were of a type: scions of upper-middle-class families who still prospered under the Nazis but who, in foreign company especially, were eager to demonstrate how embarrassed they were by their government. They and Freya Auer lapped up Effi's account of the *Mother* story-line, bursting into ironic applause when she described the hospital bed denouement. Only Ute Neumaier looked uncomfortable.

Among her fellow-housewives in Grunewald she would probably give the story a very different slant.

Rolf Auer was encouraged to recount some news he'd heard that afternoon. Five of Germany's most famous radio comedians – Werner Finck, Peter Sachse, and the Three Rulands – had been expelled from the Reich Cultural Chamber by Goebbels. They wouldn't be able to work in Germany again.

'When was this announced?' Russell asked.

'It hasn't been yet. Goebbels has a big piece in the *Beobachter* tomorrow morning. It's in there.'

'Last time I saw Finck at the Kabarett,' Russell said, 'he announced that the old German fairytale section had been removed from the programme, but that there'd be a political lecture later.'

Everyone laughed.

'It'll be hard for any of them to get work elsewhere,' Effi said. 'Their sort of comedy's all about language.'

'They'll have to go into hibernation until it's all over,' Phyllis said.

'Like so much else,' her husband agreed.

'Where has all the art gone?' Effi asked the Auers. 'Six years ago there must have been thousands of modern paintings in Germany – the Blau Reiter group, the Expressionists before them, the Cubists. Where are they all?'

'A lot of them are boxed up in cellars,' Rolf Auer admitted. 'A lot were taken abroad in the first year or so, but since then... A lot were owned by Jews, and most of those have been sold, usually at knock-down prices. Bought mostly by people who think they'll make a good profit one day, sometimes by people who really care about them as art, and want to preserve them for the future.'

It sounded as if the Auers had a few in their cellar. 'I've heard Hermann's building up his collection,' Russell said.

'He has good taste,' Auer replied, with only the faintest hint of sarcasm.

The conversation moved on to architecture, and Speer's plans for the new Berlin. Russell watched and listened. It was a civilised conversation, he thought. But the civilisation concerned was treading water. There was an implied acceptance that things had slipped out of joint, that some sort of correction was needed, and that until that correction came along, and normal service was resumed, they were stuck in a state of suspended animation. The Conways, he saw, were only too glad to be out of it – America would be a paradise after this. The Unsworths hadn't got a clue what they were getting into and, unless they were much more perceptive than they seemed, would draw all the wrong conclusions from gatherings like this one. But the three German couples – he included himself and Effi – were just waiting for the world to move on, waiting at the Führer's pleasure.

'What'll happen to you if there's a war?' Unsworth was asking him.

'I'll be on the same train as you, I expect,' Russell told him. Across the table, Effi made a face.

'That'll be hard, after living here for so long.'

'It will. I have a son here too.' Russell shrugged. 'But it'll be that or internment.'

On the way home, sitting in a line of traffic at the eastern end of the Ku'damm, Effi suddenly turned to him and said: 'I don't want to lose you.'

'I don't want to lose you either.'

She slipped an arm through his. 'How long do you think a war will last?'

'I've no idea. Years, at least.'

'Maybe we should think about leaving. I know,' she added

quickly, 'that you don't want to leave Paul. But if there's a war and they lock you up you'll be leaving him anyway. And we... Oh I don't know. It's all so ridiculous.'

Russell moved the car forward a few metres. 'It's something to think about.' And it was. She was right – he'd lose Paul anyway. And he couldn't spend the rest of his life clinging to the boy. It wasn't fair on her. It probably wasn't fair on Paul.

'I don't want to go either, but...'

'I know. I think we've got a few months at least.' He leaned over and kissed her, which drew an angry blow of the horn from the car behind them. 'And I can't let Paul run my whole life,' he said, testing the thought out loud as he released the clutch.

'Not for ever, anyway. Has he seen the car yet?'

'No. Tomorrow.'

There was sunshine on Saturday, the first for a week. He arrived at the Gehrts' house soon after two, and felt somewhat deflated by the sight of Matthias's almost new Horch. How had he expected Paul to get excited by a 1928 Hanomag?

He needn't have worried. His son, happily changed out of his *Jungvolk* uniform, was thrilled by the car, and thrilled by their exhilarating 100 kph dash down the new Avus Speedway, which took them from the eastern end of the Ku'damm to the first completed stretch of the Berlin orbital outside Potsdam. On their way back they stopped for ice cream at a café overlooking the Wannsee, and Russell allowed his son to work the petrol pump at the adjoining garage. 'Father – I mean Matthias – wouldn't let me do this,' Paul said, anxiously scanning Russell's face for signs of hurt or anger at his slip.

'It's OK. You can call him Father,' Russell said. 'Short for Stepfather.'

'All right,' Paul agreed.

During their four hours together, his son showed none of the reticence he'd displayed on the phone. Just a passing something, Russell hoped. He had a wonderful afternoon.

The evening wasn't bad either. Effi looked stunning in another new dress – *Mother* was certainly paying well – and three members of the Philharmonie audience came up and asked for her autograph, which pleased her no end. Unlike Russell, she had been brought up on a diet of classical music, and sat in rapt attention while his wandered. Looking round the auditorium, it occurred to him that this was one of the places where nothing much had changed. The music was *judenfrei*, of course, and Hitler's picture dominated the lobby, but the same stiff-necked, over-dressed people were filling the seats, wafting their fans and rustling their programmes. It could have been 1928. Or even 1908. All across Germany there were people living in time bubbles like this one. That was the way it was, and would be, until Hitler marched across one border too many and burst them all.

Russell couldn't complain about the effect the music had on Effi – she insisted on their going straight home to make love. Afterwards, lying in an exhausted heap among the tangled sheets, they laughed at the trail of clothes disappearing into the living room. 'Like our first time, remember?' Effi said.

Russell couldn't remember a better day, and hated to spoil it. 'I've got something to tell you,' he said, propping himself up against the headboard. 'You know I said I'd heard rumours that they were planning to change the Law on the Prevention of Hereditary Diseases?'

'Yes.' She sat up too.

'I didn't.'

'Then why …?'

'Tyler McKinley was working on a story about it. He got me to go with him when he interviewed this woman in Neukölln.' Russell told her about Theresa Jürissen, about Marietta, about the KdF letter to clinic heads and what she had claimed was in it.

'Why didn't you tell me?' Effi asked, more surprised than angry.

'Because you'd have to tell Zarah, and Zarah would have to tell Jens, and I'd have to explain where I got the information from.' He looked her in the face. 'McKinley's dead, Effi. And he didn't commit suicide. He was murdered.'

She took that in, looking, Russell thought, extraordinarily beautiful.

'So why are you telling me now?' she asked calmly.

He sighed. 'Because I hate keeping things from you. Because I owe it to Zarah. I don't know. Could you swear Zarah to secrecy, do you think?'

'Maybe. But in any case I don't think Jens would turn you in. Zarah would certainly kill him if he did. For my sake, of course, not yours.'

'Of course.'

'But – and I hate to say this – given how Zarah feels about you, she'll want more than your word. So will he. They'll want some sort of proof.'

'I don't blame them. When's that appointment you mentioned?'

'Monday.'

'She should put it off.'

'How will that help?'

He explained his hunch about the poste restante, about McKinley's passport and Zembski's commission. 'On Tuesday, if I've guessed correctly, I can pick up the letter and whatever else McKinley had.'

'You're going to claim it using a bogus passport? Isn't that risky? What if they remember McKinley from when he handed it in?'

'He won't have handed it in – he'll have posted it. It'll be OK.'

'Are you sure?'

He laughed. 'No, of course not.'

Sunday was another cold bright day. Russell picked his son up in Grunewald soon after ten, and headed for Potsdam on the Avus Speedway. From there they took the Leipzig road, driving south-west through Treuenbrietzen and over the hills to Wittenberg, stopping for an early lunch by the bridge across the Elbe. They reached Leipzig ninety minutes ahead of kick-off, and did a quick spin round the town centre. Paul, though, was eager to reach the ground, and seemed somewhat lacking in faith that his father would find it in time.

He found it with twenty minutes to spare. They followed another father-son couple wearing Hertha favours through the turnstiles, and worked their way round to where the hundred or so others who'd made the trip from Berlin were standing, behind one of the goals. The stadium was bigger than the Plumpe, and seemed almost full for this cup-tie. Standing there waiting for the teams to come out, watching the flicker of matches being struck in the shadowed grandstand, Russell felt a sudden surge of sadness. Another time bubble, he thought.

The home crowd greeted their team with a hearty roar, but that was almost the last thing they had to cheer. The home team had one of those afternoons, doing everything but score on numerous occasions, before making one fatal mistake at the back. Paul was ecstatic, and quite unwilling to admit there was anything undeserved in Hertha's victory. 'It's about goals, Dad,' he said trenchantly, before Russell could suggest anything to the contrary. On the way out, Paul scanned the ground for a discarded programme and finally found one. 'For Joachim,' he said triumphantly.

Russell had thought about inviting Thomas and Joachim to join them, but had decided he wanted the time alone with his son. If Paul wanted to get something off his chest, he wouldn't do it with Thomas and Joachim in the car.

The decision bore fruit, though hardly in the way Russell had expected. It was dark by the time they left Leipzig, the road lit only by their own lights and the occasional passage of a vehicle in the opposite direction. On either side the darkness was relieved only by the dim lights of an occasional farm.

They had been driving about ten minutes when Paul broke the silence. 'Dad, I think you should move to England,' he blurted out, as if he couldn't hold the thought in any longer.

'Why?' Russell asked, though he could guess the answer.

'Well, you can't help being English, can you?'

'No, I can't.'

'But that won't help. I mean it doesn't help the Jews, does it?'

'No,' Russell agreed. 'What made you think about this?' he asked. 'Has something happened? Has someone said something?' He half expected to find that Paul had overheard a conversation between his mother and stepfather.

'Not exactly,' Paul replied. 'At the *Jungvolk* ... no one has actually said anything, but they know I'm half-English, and when they look at me it's like they're not sure whose side I'm on. I'm not saying it's bad being half-English – it's not like being half-Jewish or half-Polish or anything like that – and if there's a war with England I can tell everyone I'm loyal to the Führer, but you won't be able to do that. I don't think you'll be safe in Germany. You'll be much safer in England.'

'Maybe,' Russell said, for want of something better.

'Wouldn't Effi go with you?'

'She might.'

'I really like her, you know.'

'I know you do. And I'm glad.'

'I don't want you to go. I just…'

'What?'

'I just don't want you to stay for my sake. I mean, I'm twelve next month. It's not like I'll be a child for much longer.'

'I think you have a few more years yet.'

'OK, but …'

'I understand what you're saying. And I appreciate it. But I don't want you to worry about this. If a war comes I'll probably have to leave – there won't be any choice. But until then, well, I can't leave while we're still in the Cup, can I?'

After dropping Paul off, Russell found a bar off Hochmeisterplatz and sat for almost an hour nursing an expensive double whisky. His life seemed to be breaking up in slow-motion, with no clear indication of where any of the pieces might land. Moving to England might seem like a sensible move, but it was sensible moves that had landed him in his current predicament. The peculiarity of his situation, he thought, might be a double-edged sword. It could be the death of him, or at least the death of those relationships which had made his life worth living these last few years. There was no doubt about that. But was there also a chance that he could exploit that situation to save himself, and those relationships? Shchepkin, Kleist and Trelawney-Smythe had no compunction about making use of him, and he felt none about making use of them. But could he pull it off? Was he still quick enough on his feet? And was he brave enough to find out?

Driving east along the Ku'damm towards Effi's, he realised he didn't know. But that, he told himself, the Wiesners uppermost in his mind, was another sign of the times. When the time bubbles burst, you got to find out all sorts of things about yourself that you probably didn't want to know. And maybe, if you were lucky, a few that you did.

Arriving at Effi's flat, he was almost bundled into the kitchen by Effi herself. 'Zarah's here,' she whispered. 'I've told her about the letter to the asylum directors, but nothing about you knowing where it is now. Or the passport. OK?'

'OK,' Russell agreed.

Lothar was there too, sitting with his mother and a picture book on the sofa.

'You remember Uncle John?' Effi asked him.

'No,' he said authoritatively, looking up briefly and deciding that Russell was less interesting than his book. If there was anything wrong with him, it wasn't the same thing as afflicted Marietta.

Russell leant down to kiss Zarah's upturned cheek. Effi's older sister was an attractive woman of thirty-five, taller and bigger-boned than Effi, with larger breasts and wider hips. Her wavy chestnut hair, which usually fell to her shoulders, was constrained in a tight bun, and there were dark circles of either tiredness or sadness around her brown eyes. Russell had never actually disliked Zarah, but he had never felt any real connection either. She had none of her younger sister's fearless appetite for life: Zarah was the careful, responsible one, the one who had always sought safety in conventionality, whether of ideas or husbands. Her positive feature, as far as Russell was concerned, was her obvious devotion to Effi.

'Effi told me what you told her,' she said, 'but I want to hear it from you.'

Russell retold the story of his and McKinley's visit to Theresa Jürissen, omitting her name.

'She stole this letter?' Zarah asked, as if she couldn't believe people did things like that.

'She was desperate.'

'That I can understand,' Zarah said, glancing sideways at the happily engaged Lothar. 'But are you sure she was telling the truth?'

'As sure as I can be.'

'But you don't know any of the details of this new law those doctors were talking about? What it will say? Who it will affect?'

'No. But whatever it says, the first thing they'll need is a register of all those suffering from the various conditions. All the institutions and doctors will be asked to submit lists, so that they know exactly what they're dealing with. And any child on that list will be subject to the new law, whatever it is. That's why I think you should cancel your appointment. Wait until I can tell you more.'

'But when will that be?'

'Soon, I hope.'

'But what if it isn't?' She was, Russell realised, on the edge of tears. 'I have to talk to someone about him.'

Russell had an idea. 'How about abroad? Go to Holland or France. Or England even. See a specialist there. No one here will know.'

He watched her eyes harden as she remembered the aborted abortion, then soften again as the idea impressed itself. 'I could, couldn't I?' she said, half to herself, half to Effi. 'Thank you, John,' she said to him.

'Will Jens agree to that?' Effi asked.

'Yes, I think so.'

'You do understand how dangerous this will be for John if anyone finds out he knows about this law?' Effi insisted.

'Oh yes.'

'And you'll make sure Jens understands it too.'

'Yes, yes. I know you disagree about politics,' she told Russell, 'but Jens is as crazy about Lothar as I am. Believe me, even the Führer comes a long way second. Jens will do anything for his son.'

Russell hoped she was right. After driving Zarah and Lothar home to Grunewald he watched Jens in the lighted doorway, picking up his son with every sign of fatherly devotion, and felt somewhat reassured. In the seat next to him, Effi sighed. 'Did you see anything wrong with Lothar?' she asked.

'No,' Russell said, 'but Zarah sees more of him than anyone else.'

'I hope she's wrong.'

'Of course.'

'How was your day with Paul?'

'Good. He's away again next weekend.'

'Then let's go away,' Effi said. 'I start filming on the Monday after, and I'll hardly see you for two weeks after that. Let's go somewhere.'

'How about Rügen Island?'

'That'd be lovely.'

'We can drive up on Friday afternoon, come back Sunday. I'll teach you to drive.'

Russell woke early, with an empty feeling in his stomach which toast and coffee did nothing to dispel. 'Are you going to get the passport today?' Effi asked, brushing hair out of her eyes before sipping the coffee he'd brought her in bed.

'I hope so.'

'Do you want me to come with you? As cover or something?'

'No thanks. You'd make me even more anxious.' He kissed her, promised to ring the moment he had something to tell, and walked out to the car. There was no sign of the weekend sunshine – a thick blanket of almost motionless cloud hung over the city, low enough to brush the spires of the Memorial Church. As he drove on down Tauenzienstrasse, Russell decided to leave the car at home – the U-bahn seemed more anonymous. On arrival, he steeled himself to refuse a coffee from Frau Heidegger, but for once she wasn't at home. He put on fresh clothes and was soon on the train to Neukölln.

Zembski had the passport waiting in a desk drawer. 'A nice job, if I say so myself,' he muttered, using a photographer's black cotton bag to pick it up and hand it over. 'You should keep your own fingerprints off it,' he advised. 'And please – burn it the moment you're finished with it. I've already burned the negatives.'

'I will,' Russell said, examining the photograph inside. It looked as though it had always been there.

He walked back to the U-bahn station, hyper-conscious of the passport in his pocket. Pretending to be McKinley might get him through a spot check, but anything more rigorous and he'd be in real, real trouble. The passport was far too big to eat, though he supposed he could just tear the picture out and eat that. Explaining why he'd done so might prove difficult, though.

He reminded himself that he was only guessing about the poste restante, but it didn't feel like guessing – he knew it was there. Once on a train, he decided on another change of plan. The U-bahn might be anonymous, but he would be needing somewhere to read whatever it was McKinley had accumulated. He couldn't take it to his own flat or Effi's, and he had no desire to sit in a park or on a train with a pile of stolen documents on his knee. In the car, on the other hand, he could drive himself somewhere secluded and take his time. This seemed like such a good idea that he wondered why it hadn't occurred to him earlier. How many other obvious possibilities had he failed to notice?

Frau Heidegger was still out. He backed the Hanomag out of the courtyard, accelerated down Neuenburgerstrasse, and almost broad-sided a tram turning into Lindenstrasse. Calm down, he told himself.

On the way to the old town his head raced with ideas for foiling discovery and capture. If he checked who was on normal duty in the poste restante, and then waited till whoever it was went to lunch, he'd probably be seen by someone less liable to go over the passport with a magnifying glass. Or would the lunchtime stand-in, being less used to the work, be more careful? A crowded post-office would give more people the chance of remembering him, an empty one would make him stand out.

He parked the car on Heiligegeiststrasse, a hundred metres north of the block which housed the huge post office, and walked down to the main entrance. The poste restante section was on the second floor, a large high-ceilinged room with high windows. A line of upright chairs for waiting customers faced the two service windows. One of these was occupied, the other not.

Heart thumping, Russell walked up to the available clerk and placed McKinley's passport on the counter. 'Anything for McKinley?' he asked, in a voice which seemed to belong to someone else.

The clerk took the briefest of looks at the passport and disappeared without a word. Would he come back with a sheaf of papers or a squad of Gestapo? Russell wondered. He stole a look at the other customer, a woman in her thirties who was just signing for a parcel. The clerk serving her was now looking at Russell. He looked away, and wondered whether to put the passport back in his pocket. He could feel the man still looking at him. Don't do anything memorable, he told himself.

His own clerk returned, quicker than Russell had dared hope, with a thick manila envelope. Letting this drop onto the counter with a thump, he reached underneath for a form. A couple of indecipherable squiggles later he pushed the form across for signing. Russell searched in vain for his pen, accepted the one offered with a superior smirk, and almost signed his own name. A cold sweat seemed to wash across his chest and down his legs as he scrawled an approximation of McKinley's signature, accepted his copy of the receipt and picked up the proffered envelope. The five yards to the door seemed endless, the stairs an echo chamber of Wagnerian proportions.

On the street outside a tram disgorging passengers was holding up traffic. Fighting the ludicrous temptation to run, Russell walked back towards his car, scanning the pavement opposite for possible watchers. As he waited to cross Kaiser Wilhelmstrasse he snuck a look back. There was no one there. If there had been, he told himself, they'd have seen the envelope and arrested him by now. He'd got away with it. For the moment, anyway.

Much to his relief the car started straight away. He turned onto Königstrasse by the post office and headed up towards the railway bridge, chafing at the slowness of the tram in front of him. As he rounded Alexanderplatz he decided, at the last moment, that Landsbergerstrasse offered the quickest route out of the city, and almost collided with another car. Away to his right the grey bulk of the Alex leered down at him.

He slowed the Hanomag and concentrated on driving the three kilometres to the city's ragged edge without getting arrested. As he swung round Büschingplatz he thought for one dreadful moment that a traffic cop was flagging him down, and the beads of sweat were still clinging to his brow as he drove past the huge state hospital on the southern edge of the Friedrichshain. Another kilometre and he could smell the vast complex of cattle markets and slaughter houses that sprawled alongside the Ringbahn. As he reached the top of the bridge that carried the road over the railway by Landsbergerallee station he had a brief panoramic view of the countryside to the east: the two small hills rising, almost apologetically, from the vast expanse of the Prussian plains.

Mentally searching, earlier that day, for a safe place to study McKinley's material, he had recalled a picnic with Thomas's family on one of those hills. As he remembered it, a road ran south from Marzahn between them, and a winding access road led up to a picnic area on the hill nearest the city.

His memory was correct. The road wound up through dark, dripping trees to the bald brow of the hill, where picnic tables had been arranged to take advantage of the view across the city. There was no one there. Russell parked in the allotted space behind the tables and gazed out through the windscreen at the distant city. The nearest clump of large buildings, which Thomas had pointed out on their previous visit, made up Berlin's principal home for the mentally ill, the Herzberge Asylum. Which was highly apt, given the probable content of the reading matter on the seat beside him.

He reached for the envelope and carefully prised it open. There were about fifty sheets of paper in all, a few in McKinley's writing, most of them typed or printed. Russell skipped through them in search of Theresa Jürissen's letter. He found it at the bottom of the pile, with a date – the date it had been written – scrawled in pencil across the right-hand corner. Going back through the other papers, Russell found other dates: McKinley had arranged his story in chronological order.

The first document was a 1934 article from the *Münchner Zeitung*, a journalist's eye-witness report of life in an asylum entitled ALIVE YET DEAD. McKinley had underlined two sentences – 'They vegetate in twilight throughout the day and night. What do time and space mean to them?' – and added in the margin: 'Or life and death?' The second document was a story from the SS journal *Das Schwarze Korps*, about a farmer who had shot his mentally handicapped son and the 'sensitive' judges who had all but let him off. A reader's letter from the same magazine begged the authorities to find a legal and humane way of killing 'defective' infants.

Russell skipped through several other letters in the same vein and numerous pages of unattributed statistics which demonstrated a marked decline in the space and resources devoted to each mental patient since 1933. So far, so predictable, Russell thought.

The next item was an article by Karl Knab in the *Psychiatrisch-Neurologische Wochenschrift* journal. Again, McKinley had underlined one passage: 'We have before us in these asylums, spiritual ruins, whose number is not insignificant, notwithstanding all our therapeutic endeavours, in addition to idiots on the lowest level, patient material which, as simply cost-occasioning ballast, should be eradicated by being killed in a painless fashion, which is justifiable in terms of the self-preservatory finance policy of a nation fighting for its existence, without shaking the cultural foundations of its cultural values.' This was chilling enough, Russell thought, but who was Knab? He was obviously far from a lone voice in the wilderness, but that didn't make him a spokesman for government.

There was a lot of stuff on the Knauer boy, but most of it was in McKinley's writing – guesses, suppositions, holes to be filled.

It was the last few sheets of paper which really caught Russell's attention. Most were from a memorandum by Doctor Theodore Morell, best known to the foreign press community as 'Hitler's Quack'. He had been given the task of gathering together everything written in favour of euthanasia over the last fifty years, with a view to formulating a draft law on 'The Destruction of Life Unworthy of Life'. Those eligible included anyone suffering from mental or physical 'malformation', anyone requiring long-term care, anyone arousing 'horror' in other people or anyone situated on 'the lowest animal level'. The Nazis qualified on at least two counts, Russell thought.

As Theresa Jürissen had said, the main area of controversy among those who favoured such a law was the openness or otherwise of its administration. In this memorandum Morell concluded that secrecy was best, that parents would be much happier thinking that their child had simply succumbed to some illness or other. He hadn't yet decided whether doctors should be involved in the actual killing of their patients, but he insisted on their compulsory registration of all congenitally ill patients.

The final item was the letter, and Russell now realised why McKinley had been so excited by it. Theodore Morell might be Hitler's doctor, but he was a private citizen, entitled to his own ideas, no matter how psychopathic they might be. The letter, though, was something else. It confirmed the gist of Morell's memorandum under the imprint of the KdF, the *Kanzlei des Führers*. It tied Hitler to child-killing.

Russell shook the papers together and stuffed them back into the envelope. After sliding the whole package under the passenger seat, he got out of the car and walked across the damp grass to the lip of the slope. A small convoy of military trucks was driving east down Landsbergerallee, a solitary car headed in the opposite direction. A dense layer of cloud still hung over the city.

McKinley had had his story, Russell thought. The sort of story that young journalists dreamt of – one that saved lives *and* made you famous.

But what was *he*, John Russell, going to do with it? Get rid of it, was the obvious answer. Along with the passport.

He watched a distant Ringbahn train slide slowly out of sight near the slaughter houses. It might be the obvious answer, but something more courageous was required. He owed it to McKinley, and probably to himself. He owed it to all those thousands of children – tens of thousands, for all he knew – that a creep like Morell found 'unworthy of life'.

McKinley had probably thought his story would save them all. Russell had rather less faith in the power of the press, but having everything out in the open would at least make it more difficult for the bastards.

How could he get the stuff to McKinley's paper? Not by post, that was for sure. He'd have to carry it out himself, and that would be no fun whatever.

How had McKinley planned to file the story? Or had he been just as stuck as he now was? That would explain why he'd put it in the poste restante.

Which had been a good idea. And still was, Russell decided. Under his own name this time. The passport would have to go.

But how could he get rid of it? Burning it made sense, but flames tended to be conspicuous, particularly on a day as dark as this one, and in any case he had no means of creating any. He could burn the damn thing in his apartment, but he felt reluctant to carry it a moment longer than he had to, and particularly reluctant to bring it home, where the Gestapo might be waiting on his sofa. Somewhere on the open road, he thought, with a good view in either direction. Back in the car, he slid it under his seat. Driving back down the hill he felt a strange urge to sing. Hysteria, he told himself.

At the post office in Marzahn he bought a book of matches and – since it seemed less suspicious – a packet of cigarettes to go with them. He also purchased a large envelope which he addressed to himself, care of the poste restante in Potsdam – he had no desire to revisit the counter at Heiligegeiststrasse under a different name. He then used the public telephone to call Effi.

'Is everything all right?' she asked anxiously.

'Too wonderful to talk about,' he said pointedly. 'What are you doing?'

'Trying to memorise my part.'

'Can you meet me in the Zoo station buffet?' he asked. 'At four o'clock,' he added, checking his watch.

'I'll be there.'

Once back on the Landsberg road Russell started looking for a suitable place to burn the passport. A mile or so short of the Ringbahn bridge he found a wide entrance-way to a farm track and pulled over. Retrieving the passport from under his seat he ripped it into separate pages and set light to the first one, holding it down between his knees until it was too hot to hold, then shifting it to and fro with his feet until all that remained were black flakes. With his other hand he wafted the resulting smoke out through the open windows.

In the time it took him to burn the remaining five sheets only two lorries went by, and their drivers showed no interest in Russell's slightly smoking car. He gathered the blackened remains in his handkerchief, which he knotted and placed in his pocket before resuming his journey. Twenty minutes later he consigned both handkerchief and contents to a lonely stretch of the scum-covered Luisenstrassekanal. The final remains of Zembski's handiwork disappeared with a dull plop, leaving Russell with several burnt fingers to remember them by.

It was almost 3.15. He got back in the Hanomag, and drove west towards Potsdamerplatz. The traffic round the southern edge of the Tiergarten was busy for the time of day, but he reached his destination – a street halfway between Effi's flat and Zoo station

– with five minutes to spare. He parked facing the direction she would come from, assuming she hadn't picked this day of all days to change her usual route.

Ten minutes later she came into view, walking quickly in her high heels, a few wisps of dark hair floating free of the scarf and hat.

She didn't see him, and jumped with surprise when he told her to get in. 'You said Zoo station,' she said angrily, as he moved the car down the road. As far as he could see no one had been following her.

'That was for the benefit of anyone listening. I've got something to show you. In private.'

'Why didn't you just come to the flat then?'

'Because,' he explained, 'anyone caught with this lot in their flat is likely to end up like McKinley.'

'Oh.' She was taken aback, but only for a second. 'So where are we going?'

'Along the canal, I thought, opposite the zoo restaurant. There's always people parked there.'

'Mostly kissing and cuddling.'

'We can always pretend.'

Once they were there, Russell reached down for the manila envelope under Effi's seat. Even with the assistance of the nearby streetlamp, reading was difficult, but he didn't dare turn on the car's internal light. 'Look,' he said, 'you don't need to read all of this. These last few pages – he handed her Morell's memo and Theresa's letter – should be enough to convince Zarah.'

'You want me to show them to her?'

'God, no. I want you to tell her what they are and what's in them. She'll believe you. If you tell her, she won't need to see them.'

'OK.' Effi started to read, her face increasingly frozen in an expression of utter disgust. Russell stared out of the window, watching the last of the daylight fade. A coal barge puttered by on the canal, the owner's dog howling his response to an unknown animal's cry emanating from deep within the zoo. 'My country,' Effi murmured, as she moved on to the next sheet.

She read the whole memorandum, and then the KdF letter. 'You were right,' she said. 'If she'd kept that appointment, Lothar would be on a list by now.'

'And it won't be an easy list to get off,' Russell said.

They sat there in silence as another barge went by. In the zoo restaurant across the water someone was stacking dishes.

'What can we do?' Effi wanted to know.

'I don't know. But you can tell Zarah you're convinced. And tell her I'm destroying the papers.'

'You're not going to?'

'I don't know. Not yet, anyway. I'm going to put them somewhere safe for a while.'

She gave him a searching look, as if she wanted to reassure herself of who he was. 'All those children,' she said.

'Achievements of the Third Reich'

After the excitement of the previous day, Russell spent Tuesday trying to work. The third article for *Pravda* was due by the end of the week, and one of the Fleet Street heavies wanted a second 'Ordinary Germans' piece before committing themselves to a series. It was write-by-numbers stuff, but he kept finding his mind drifting away from the subjects at hand, usually in the direction of potential threats to his liberty.

If the SD had the same bright idea about the poste restante that he had had, and checked through the records, they'd discover that McKinley had collected something nine days after his death. Everyone knew that Himmler was prone to strange flights of dark fantasy – rumour had it that SS agents were searching for the elixir of eternal life in Tibet – but he'd probably draw the line at mail-collecting ghosts. A light bulb would go on over his head, complete with the word-bubble: 'It must have been someone else!' And who would he and his minions think of first?

There'd be no point in denying it – they'd just drag him down to Heiligegeist and have him identified. He'd have to blame Eleanor McKinley, who was now beyond their reach. She'd given him the passport, he'd say. Asked him to pick up the papers, and he'd sent them on to her. Simple as that. What was in the envelope? He hadn't opened it. A different photograph in the passport? The clerk must have imagined it. The passport? He'd sent that on as well.

It was about as convincing as one of Goering's economic forecasts. And if some bright spark of Heydrich's decided to find out if there was anything under his name in any German poste restante, he'd be left without a prayer. He'd just have to hope that no one in the SD had read *Getaway* or *The High Fence*, which was at least possible – the Saint seemed far too irreverent a hero for Nazis.

Such hopes notwithstanding, every sound of a car in the street, every ring of footsteps in the courtyard below, produced a momentary sinking of the stomach, and later that evening, over at Effi's, a sharp rat-a-tat on the door almost sent it through the floor. When Effi ushered a man in uniform through the door, it took him several seconds to realise it was only Zarah's husband.

Jens Biesinger worked for some government inspectorate or other – Russell had never bothered to find out exactly which – and was on his way home. He accepted Effi's offer of coffee, shook Russell's hand, and took a seat, boots and belt creaking as he leaned back with a tired sigh. 'How is your work?' he asked Russell politely.

Russell made appropriate noises, his mind working furiously on what the man could want. His only real conversation with Jens, almost three years earlier, had escalated into a serious argument almost immediately, and Effi of all people had been forced to adopt the role of peacemaker. They had rarely been in the same room since, and on those occasions had treated each other with the sort of icy politeness reserved for loathed relations.

Jens waited until Effi was with them before he stated the object of his visit. 'John,' he began, 'I have a large favour I would like to ask you. Zarah wishes to take Lothar to England, for reasons that you are aware of. I cannot go with her, for reasons that I'm sure you will understand. And Effi starts work on her film on Monday. Zarah doesn't want to wait, so ... would you escort them? Someone has to, and as an English-speaker – and, of course, someone who is almost part of the family – you would be the ideal person. Naturally, I would pay all the expenses – the flights, the hotel, whatever else is necessary.'

Recovering from his surprise, Russell considered the idea. And had another.

'I'd feel happier if you went with them, John,' Effi interjected.

'When are you thinking of?' Russell asked Jens. 'We're going away this weekend, and I'll be in Hamburg on Monday and Tuesday – the *Bismarck* launch. So it couldn't be until the middle of next week – Thursday perhaps?'

'That sounds reasonable.'

Russell brought up his other idea. 'I'd like to take my son too. I'll pay for him, naturally, but if you could arrange the trip for four ... I'll need his mother's agreement, of course,' he added.

Jens smiled. 'An excellent plan – it will look more ... natural. I'll arrange things for four. If your son can't go we can always amend the reservations.' He placed the cup of coffee on the side table and got up, looking pleased with himself. 'Zarah will be relieved,' he said. 'She was not looking forward to making such a journey alone.'

'I'm sure she'd have managed,' Effi said with a slight edge, 'but this will be better.'

'This is my number at the ministry,' Jens said, handing Russell a card.

'This is mine at home,' Russell replied, tearing a sheet from his notebook and pencilling out the Neuenburgerstrasse number. England with Paul, he thought, and he was still revelling in the notion when Effi returned from seeing Jens out. 'You're not to fall in love with my sister,' she told him.

He phoned Ilse from Effi's flat early next morning and arranged to have coffee at a café in Halensee which they knew from their earlier life together. Russell wanted to ask her in person rather than over the phone, and she sounded more than willing – eager, in fact – to get out of the house for a couple of hours.

The café looked more run-down than Russell remembered, a

consequence, perhaps, of the fact that a large proportion of its former clientele had been Jewish. Ilse was already there, looking less severe than usual. Her shoulder-length blonde hair, which over the last few years had invariably been tied back in a knot, hung loose, softening the stretched lines of her face. She still seemed painfully thin to Russell, and her blue eyes never seemed to soften as they had once, but she seemed genuinely pleased to see him.

He told her what he wanted, at worst expecting a flat refusal, at best a painful argument.

'I think it's a wonderful idea,' she said. 'We'll have to inform the school of course, and his *Jungvolk* leader, but I don't see how either of them could object. It'll be an educational experience, won't it?'

'I hope so. Matthias won't object?'

'Why should he?'

'No reason at all. Well, that's good. I expected more of an argument,' he admitted.

'Why, for heaven's sake? When have I ever tried to come between you and Paul?'

He smiled. 'You haven't.'

She smiled back. 'You must be getting lots of work,' she said. 'Paul's very impressed with the car.'

They talked about Paul, his interests and anxieties, for more than half an hour. Afterwards, driving back across the city for his Wednesday appointment at the Wiesners, Russell found it hard to remember a warmer conversation with his ex-wife. He was still bathing in its glow when he rapped on the door of the apartment in Friedrichshain.

There was no answer for several moments, then an anxious voice called out, 'Who is it?'

'It's John Russell,' he shouted back.

The door opened to reveal a haggard-looking Frau Wiesner.

'I'm sorry,' she said, looking down the stairs behind him. 'Come in, please.'

There was no sign of the girls.

'I'm afraid there will be no lesson today,' she said. 'And perhaps no more lessons for a while. My husband has been arrested. They have taken him to a camp. Sachsenhausen, we think. A friend of a friend saw him there.'

'When? When was he arrested? What was he arrested for?'

'They came here on Monday. The middle of the night, so it was really Tuesday.' She sat down abruptly, as if she needed all her strength to tell the story. 'They kept hitting him,' she almost whispered, a solitary tear running down her right cheek. 'He wasn't resisting. He kept saying, "I'm coming with you – why are you hitting me?" They just laughed, called him names. Called the children names. I only thank God that Albert wasn't here when they came.'

Russell sat down on the settee beside her and put an arm round her shoulder. 'Frau ...' he started to say. 'I should know your name by now.'

'Eva.'

'Did they give a reason for his arrest?'

'Not to me. Our friends are trying to find out whether there was a reason ... not a real reason, of course ... but surely they have to say something, write something down in their record books.' She looked at him almost imploringly, as if their having a reason would make a difference.

'Where are the girls?' he asked. 'And where's Albert?'

'The girls are with friends down the road. They love your lessons, but today ... they couldn't ...'

'Of course not.'

'And Albert ... He came back on Tuesday morning, heard what

had happened, and ran straight out again. I haven't seen him since.'

'The Gestapo haven't been back?'

'No. If they came back, I could ask them about Felix. I don't know what to do. Some friends say kick up a fuss, or you'll never be told anything. Others say that if you do it makes matters worse, and that Felix will be released eventually, like Albert was. And I wouldn't know where to go if I wanted to make a fuss. The Alex? If I go there and demand to know where Felix is and why they've arrested him they might arrest me, and then who'll look after Albert and the girls?'

'That wouldn't be a good idea,' Russell agreed. He wondered what would be.

'Have the Conways gone?' she asked.

'I'm afraid they have.' They'd been at sea for at least thirty-six hours. 'But I can try talking to someone at the Embassy. I doubt whether they'll be able to do anything, but it's worth a try.'

'They're not allowed visitors in Sachsenhausen,' she said. 'We found that out when Albert was there. Not family or friends that is. But perhaps they'd let you visit him. You could say he owed you money for the girls' lessons, and you need his signature for something – a cheque on a foreign bank account or something like that.'

'You don't have a foreign bank account?'

'No, of course not, but they think we have – they think we all have them.'

Russell winced. What could he do? The Embassy certainly, but how much would a Jewish doctor's kindness to a now-departed colleague count for in the grand scheme of things? Not much. He could go to the Alex – or, more worryingly, the Gestapo HQ on Prinz Albrechtstrasse – and make some polite enquiries. Not as a journalist, of course. In fact, Eva Wiesner's suggestion was a good one. He could say that Wiesner owed him for the girls' lessons, and that the Jewish swine wasn't going to get out of it by running away to a Kz. That should give the bastards a good laugh.

And then there was Jens, who now owed him a favour. A last resort, Russell decided. That was one favour he wanted to keep in reserve.

'I'll make some enquiries,' he told her. 'Tactfully. I won't stir up any resentment. I'll try and find out where he is and why he's been arrested. And if there's any chance of arranging a visit.'

She gave him a despairing look. 'Why is it that you can see how wrong this is, and so many people can't?'

'I like to think most people can,' he said. 'And that they're just too afraid to speak up. But lately …' He spread his hands. 'If I find out anything definite, I'll be back to let you know. Otherwise I'll come on Friday at the usual time.'

'Thank you, Mr Russell. You are a real friend.' Another solitary tear crawled down her cheek, as if her body was conserving its supply for future contingencies.

As he walked back to the car, Russell found himself hoping he was the friend she thought he was. He had considered giving her his address, but there was no way he could keep one or more of the Wiesners in his apartment. If Frau Heidegger didn't report it, one of his neighbours would.

Driving down Neue Königstrasse he decided on visiting the Gestapo first. Another voluntary encounter with the Nazi authorities, he told himself, would weaken any suspicions they might hold with regard to McKinley's missing papers. He knew, deep down, that was wishful thinking, but the idea helped to strengthen his nerve.

He parked behind a shiny, swastika-embossed limousine on Prinz Albrecht Strasse, and approached the impressive portals of the State Police HQ. Taking a deep breath, he walked up the steps and in through the revolving door. As usual, the Führer was up there in his frame, beady eyes tracking you round the room like some scary inversion of the Mona Lisa – you *knew* what *he* was thinking.

Russell explained his plight to the receptionist: the Jew, the debt, the joke about Wiesner running away to a Kz. She laughed, and directed him to the appropriate office for Ongoing Cases. Another receptionist, another laugh, and he was on his way to Completed Cases, which sounded bad for Felix Wiesner.

The officer in charge was in a good mood. It took him less than a minute to find the file for Dr Wiesner, and less than that to read it. 'You're out of luck,' he said. 'The kike's in Sachsenhausen, and he won't be back. Your money's gone.'

'What did the bastard do?' Russell asked.

'Gave a German girl an abortion. That's twenty-five years, if he lasts that long.'

Russell felt his heart sink, but managed not to show it. 'Win some, lose some,' he said. 'Thanks for your help.'

He made his way back to the entrance, half-expecting to hear muffled screams from the rumoured torture chambers in the basement, but, as in the SD HQ round the corner, there was only the whisper of typewriters to break the silence.

He left the car where it was, walked up Wilhelmstrasse to the British Embassy and sat beneath the latest King's picture – the third in two years – while he waited for Martin Unsworth to see him. It proved a waste of time. Unsworth had heard about the Wiesners from Doug Conway, but felt no dramatic compulsion to risk his career on their behalf. He pointed out, reasonably enough, that a British Embassy could hardly involve itself in the domestic criminal matters of a host nation. He added, just as reasonably, that the host nation would, at best, ignore any request in such a matter and, at worst, make use of it for propaganda purposes. Russell hid his fury, elicited a promise from Unsworth to investigate the Wiesners' visa applications, and then thumped the wooden banister so hard on his way down that he feared for a moment he'd broken his hand. Walking back down Wilhelmstrasse, surrounded by billowing swastikas, he simmered with useless rage.

Back at Effi's – he seemed to be living there at the moment – he told her what had happened. She advised him to ring Jens – 'There's a human being in there somewhere,' she said. 'Though you have to dig a bit.'

Why not, he told himself. Cash in the favour owed while it was still fresh in the memory.

After talking his way past two secretaries, Russell was finally put through to Jens. 'I haven't managed to arrange anything yet,' Zarah's husband said, trying and failing to conceal his irritation.

'This is about something else,' Russell told him. 'I need a favour from you this time.'

Something between a groan and a grunt greeted this statement.

Russell ploughed on. 'Someone I know has been arrested and taken to a camp. A Jew.'

'I ...'

'Please, hear me out. This is nothing to do with politics – it's a matter of honour. This man's a doctor and back in 1933, before the Jews were forbidden to practice, he saved the life of my friend's child.' He went on to explain who Conway was, how he'd involved Russell in teaching Wiesner's daughters, and his current unreachability in mid-Atlantic. 'This is not about helping the Jews, it's about repaying a debt.'

'I understand what you …' Jens began, his tone now mixing sympathy with the reluctance.

'I don't want you to do anything,' Russell insisted, somewhat disingenuously. 'I just need to know the details of why he's been arrested, and what the chances of a visit are. A visit from me, I mean – I know there's no chance of a family visit. At the moment, his wife and children are in limbo – they can't do anything but wait. I think the wife needs his blessing to do what's best for the children.'

There was a moment's silence at the other end. 'I'll find out what I can,' Jens said eventually.

'Thank you,' Russell said. He put down the phone. 'I'll drive over to the Wiesners and tell them,' he told Effi.

She went with him. Frau Wiesner seemed calmer, or perhaps just more resigned. When Russell reported the Gestapo claim about an abortion she seemed torn between derision and despair. 'Felix would never – never – do anything so foolish,' she said.

At first, she looked somewhat askance at Russell's glamorous-looking companion, but Effi's obvious empathy quickly won her over. The girls were there, and both insisted on getting the visiting film star's autograph. Marthe produced her movie scrapbook and the three of them took over the sofa. Watching their dark heads together, poring over the neatly arranged photographs of German and Hollywood stars, Russell found he was fighting back tears.

He spent Thursday immersed in work, his apartment door open to catch the sound of the ground floor telephone. It was late afternoon when Frau Heidegger shouted up the stairs that the call was for him.

'I have the tickets and reservations,' Jens told him. 'We were lucky – there were four seats left on next Thursday's London flight.

It leaves at two, but you should be there half an hour earlier. The return flight is on Sunday, at eleven. I have booked two rooms at the Savoy hotel – have you heard of it? – on a road called Strand. And a car to take you from the airport in Croydon to the hotel and back again. And of course the appointment. I hope that covers everything.'

Russell almost asked where the appointment was, but presumed Jens was being cagey for a reason. 'It sounds perfect,' he said. The Savoy! he thought.

'Good. Now, this other business.' He paused for a moment and Russell could imagine him checking that his office door was shut. 'Your friend's Jewish doctor has been arrested for conducting an abortion on a girl of seventeen. Her name is Erna Marohn, from a good German family. Her father is an officer in the Kriegsmarine.'

'Who made the complaint?'

'The mother. The father is away at sea. There is no doubt the girl had an abortion – she was examined by a police doctor. And there is little doubt that Wiesner carried it out – she was seen entering the clinic he runs in Friedrichshain for other Jews.'

'That sounds bad.'

'It is. A German doctor caught performing an abortion can expect a lengthy term of imprisonment. A Jewish doctor caught performing one on a German girl, well …'

'Yes.'

'But there is some good news. I have managed to arrange a pass for you to visit him in Sachsenhausen. Next Wednesday, the day before you go to England. A courier will bring the pass to your house. You should be at the camp by 11 a.m. But you will not be able to take anything in or out. And you must not report anything you see or hear. They are letting you in as a favour to me, but not as a journalist. You do understand that?'

'Absolutely.'

'If anything appears in print, in England or anywhere else, describing the conditions there, they will assume that you have broken your word, and, at the very least, you will lose your journalistic accreditation. I was asked to tell you this.'

'I understand. And thank you, Jens.'

'You are welcome.'

Friday was clear and cold. Russell packed a bag for the weekend, and headed towards Friedrichshain, stopping for a newspaper and coffee at Alexanderplatz station. The only interesting piece of news concerned a train: in Westphalia a thirty-seven ton excavating machine had run amok on a night freight. Whatever it was that pinioned the steel arms in an upright position had come undone, dropping them into their working position over one side of the wagon. A mile's worth of telegraph poles, signals and huts had been demolished, and a station reduced to rubble when the canopy supports were swept away. The train had only been stopped when a witness phoned ahead to a signal box. The guard hadn't noticed anything was amiss. Hitler's Germany in microcosm – flailing away in the darkness, ruins piling up behind.

At the apartment in Friedrichshain he told Frau Wiesner what Jens had told him. 'I don't believe it,' she said. 'Felix will tell you what really happened.' He gave the two girls an English lesson, and promised to come by on the following Tuesday when he returned from Hamburg. Driving back across town to pick up Effi, he wondered how to dispel the sense of gloom that seemed to be enveloping him.

He needn't have worried. It was about two hundred kilometres to Stralsund, and by the time they reached it Effi's defiant mood of romantic adventure had taken him over. After crossing the narrow sound on the steam ferry, they drove the last forty kilometres to Sassnitz in gathering darkness, their headlights catching nothing on the road except two deer hurrying each other across.

As Russell had expected, the small resort was virtually empty, and they had their pick of those hotels not closed for the winter break. They chose the Am Meer, right on the promenade, and were given a room with views across the darkened Baltic. With the dining room closed for refurbishing, dinner was served in the lounge, in front of a dancing fire, by a girl of about fourteen. Happy and full, they walked out across the promenade and listened to the comforting caress of the tide. Above the sea the sky was bursting with stars, and over the hills behind them a thin crescent moon was rising. As they clung together for warmth, and kissed on the stony beach, it crossed Russell's mind that this was as perfect as life ever got.

Back in their room they discovered, much to Effi's amusement, that the bed squeaked and creaked at their slightest movement, and midway through making love she got the giggles so badly that they had to take a break before resuming.

The good weather continued, sunlight advancing across their bed the following morning. After wrapping up warmly they set out for the famous Stubbenkammer cliffs, a ten kilometre drive through the Stubnitz beech woods. After gingerly looking over the hundred and forty metre precipice, Russell gave Effi her first driving lesson on the large expanse of tarmac laid out for the summer charabancs. Clanking the gears atrociously, she jerked her way through several circuits before pronouncing: 'This is easy!'

They had lunch in a restaurant they had noticed on the drive up, a sprawling wooden building with intricately carved façades which nestled among the beeches, and then spent a couple of hours walking along the well-tended paths of the sun-dappled forest. The only other humans were several fragments of a Hitler Youth group on a weekend trip from Rostock: groups of two or three boys, their eyes flickering from compass to path and back again. Their leaders, who brought up the rear, claimed to have seen a bear, but the beer on their breath suggested otherwise.

It got dark too early, but there was always the creaking bed. Afterwards, they drank, ate and sat in front of the same fire, hardly speaking, and not needing to. The bed was uncomfortable as well as noisy, but Russell slept better than he had for weeks.

On their final morning he drove them north-west towards the long sandspit that connected the Jasmund and Wittow peninsulas. Seeing that the road along the spit was empty he gave the wheel to Effi, and she drove the next twenty kilometres, far too fast, with a huge smile lighting up her face. At the end of the spit they walked on the sandy beach, a kilometre or more and back again, watching the wind raising whitecaps on the water, and the clouds scudding eastwards across the blue-grey Baltic. No cars went by, no walkers. No ships appeared on the horizon. The earth was theirs.

But not for long. Effi's train back to Berlin left Stralsund at three, and as they made their way back across the island the sunshine became increasingly intermittent, finally disappearing beneath a wall of cloud. The short ferry ride was choppy, the railway carriages clanking ominously in their chains, and rain was falling by the time they reached the Hauptbahnhof.

'This is really sad,' Effi said. 'You'll only be back for a day or so, and you'll be gone to London again. And I've no idea what the filming schedule's going to be.'

'It's only a couple of weeks,' he told her.

'Of course,' she smiled, but he knew he'd said the wrong thing.

'Let's do this again,' he said. 'Soon.'

'Please.' A whistle sounded, and she leaned out of the window to kiss him. 'Are you sure we have this the right way round?' she asked.

'You should be on a train to Hamburg and I should be driving back to Berlin.'

'Sometimes other people want to use the road,' he told her as the train jerked into motion.

She made a face, and blew him a kiss. He stood there watching the train's red tail light recede into the distance, then strode back down the platform and out of the station. The car seemed colder without her.

The road across the damp northern heathland was mostly empty, the rain persistent and occasionally heavy. He drove west at a steady fifty kilometres an hour, half-hypnotised by the steady slap of the windscreen wiper as his eyes struggled to pierce the gloom ahead. Darkness had fallen by the time he left Lübeck, and on the last stretch across southern Holstein a stream of lorries did their best to blind him with their headlights. The dimly lit suburbs of eastern Hamburg came as a blessed relief.

He had already booked himself a room with bath at the Hotel Kronprinz on Kirchen-Allee. This was one of the Hamburg establishments favoured by journalists on an expense account. It was expensive, but not that expensive – the journalists concerned could always produce proof that other hotels were more so. The receptionist confirmed what he already expected, that he was a day ahead of the crowd. With the launch set for lunchtime Tuesday, most of the press would be arriving late on Monday.

After examining his room and eating dinner in the hotel restaurant he went out. The Kronprinz was just across from the main station, which lay at the eastern end of the old town. Russell walked through the station and down Mönckebergstrasse towards the looming tower of the Rathaus, turning right before he reached it, and headed for the Alster-Bassin, the large square of water which lay at the city's heart. He had visited Hamburg many times over the last fifteen years, and walking the mile-long, tree-lined perimeter of the Alster-Bassin had become almost a ritual.

Despite the damp cold, many others were doing the same. On summer days the water was usually busy with rowing, sailing and steam-boats, but on this winter evening the seagulls had it to themselves. Russell stopped for a beer at a café on one of the quays, and thought about Effi. She was wonderful with children, but he couldn't remember her ever saying she wanted them. Did he want another one, with her? Despite the fact that the world was about to collapse around them, he rather thought he did. Far across the water a seagull squawked in derision.

He slept well, ate a large breakfast, and drove across the city to St Pauli, the suburb between Hamburg and Altona which housed a high proportion of the city's seafaring population. His British agent had particularly liked the idea of including sailors among his 'Ordinary Germans', and this was an obvious place to find them. Interviewing men past active service seemed like a good way of deflecting any suspicion that he was collecting intelligence rather than human interest news, and his first port of call was one of several homes for retired seamen close to the waterfront.

Over the next couple of hours he talked to several delightful pensioners, all eager to share the sources of alcohol concealed on their persons. They had all fought in the war: one was a rare survivor from the Battle of the Falklands; two others had been participants in the Battle of Jutland. Both of the latter offered broad hints that they'd taken part in the High Seas Mutiny of 1918, but they clearly hadn't suffered for it, either then or under the Nazis. Their retirement home seemed comfortable, efficient and friendly.

All the residents he talked to admired the new ships, but none was impressed by the current standards of gunnery. Not, they admitted, that this mattered that much. Ships like the new *Bismarck* looked good – and were good – but the money and labour would be better spent on U-boats. That, unfortunately, was where future naval wars would be won or lost.

Russell had less success with working sailors. Trawling the waterfront bars he found some amiable seamen, but rather more who treated his questions with suspicion verging on hostility. Some were clearly supporters of the regime: one young officer, pacified by a brief perusal of Sturmbannführer Kleist's letter, was particularly optimistic about Germany's naval prospects: he saw the *Bismarck*, in particular, as symbolic of a burgeoning renaissance. 'In five years' time,' he promised, 'we'll have the British hiding in their harbours.' Others, Russell guessed, would once have been open opponents of the regime – Hamburg, after all, had been a KPD stronghold, and a key centre of the Comintern's maritime organization. As far as these men were concerned he was, at best, a naïve English journalist, at worst, an agent provocateur.

That afternoon Russell spent a few marks on the circular tour of Hamburg harbour, an hour and a half of channels, shipyards, quays and towering cranes. Coloured bunting was going up everywhere, and the Blohm and Voss slipway which housed the future *Bismarck* was a ferocious hive of activity, as last-minute preparations were made for the launching ceremony. The ship itself was disappointing. Still lacking a superstructure, it looked more like a gigantic canoe than the future of naval warfare. The overall impression Russell carried back to the hotel, however, was of power and energy, of a nation with a long and lengthening reach.

He ate dinner at a small restaurant on the Jungfernstieg which he'd been to before – the oysters were as good as he remembered – and made his way back across town to the Klosterburg, the beer restaurant near his hotel where journalists usually gathered.

Hal Manning and Jack Slaney were sitting at the bar, staring across the room at a boisterous table of SA men. One man, beer slopping from a raised glass, was outlining what he'd do to Marlene Dietrich if she ever dared set foot in Germany again. His proposal made up in violence what it lacked in imagination.

Russell hoisted himself onto the vacant stool next to Slaney's and bought a round of drinks.

'She's making a film with Jimmy Stewart at the moment,' Slaney said. 'And her character's called Frenchie. I guess that shows which side she's on.' He carried on staring at the SA table, whisky chaser poised in his hand. 'We should think up a new collective noun for these people – you know, like a gaggle of geese. A crassness of storm-troopers. No, that's much too kind.' He threw his head back and tipped in the chaser.

'A void,' Manning suggested.

'Too intellectual.'

'A deposit,' Russell said.

'Mmm, not bad. A passing, perhaps.' He reached for his beer. 'If only they would,' he added sourly.

At eleven the next morning, two buses sent by the Ministry of Propaganda arrived at the forecourt of the Reichshof, just up the road from the Kronprinz, to collect the assembled foreign press corps. 'We'll be hanging around for hours,' Slaney complained, as their bus headed south towards a bridge across the Norder Elbe, but he had reckoned without the traffic. There was only one road through the docks to the Blohm and Voss shipyard, and forward movement was soon reduced to a crawl.

'Adolf won't like sitting in a jam,' Russell said.

'He's coming by yacht,' Manning told him. 'The *Grille*. A little journalistic detail for you.'

'Thanks, Dad.'

They reached Slipway 9 at quarter-past twelve, and were dragooned, rather like schoolboys, into an enclosed area behind, and slightly to the right, of the ship's towering bow. From here a flight of steps led up to a platform around ten metres square, and from that a smaller flight of steps to the actual launching platform, right up against the bow.

It wasn't 'Hitler weather', but at least it was dry, with a few desultory streaks of blue amidst the grey. Several thousand people were present, lining the sides of the slipway and the area behind the platforms. Some shipyard workers were leaning over the ship's rail, others perched precariously on the vast scaffolding of girders which rose above the ship. The larger platform was full of city and state officials, naval brass and Party hacks.

The first of several loud booms silenced the crowd.

'Naval salutes,' Slaney murmured. 'Unless they're firing on Hitler's yacht.'

'No such luck,' Russell said, indicating the man in question, who had just appeared at the bottom of the steps leading to the first platform. Bismarck's elderly grand-daughter was climbing the steps ahead of him, and Hitler was visibly chafing at the delay, casting frequent glances at her progress as he talked to the portly Goering.

Once the Führer, Dorothea von Bismarck and the three service chiefs were all gathered on the higher platform, the former gave, by his own standards, a remarkably brief speech extolling the virtues of Germany's last navy – scuttled to spite the British in 1919 – and of the Iron Chancellor himself, 'a true knight without fear or reproach'. Bismarck's grand-daughter then named the ship – her quavering voice barely audible above the raucous shouts of the seagulls – and broke the traditional bottle of champagne on the bow.

There was a sound of blocks being knocked away, and then ... nothing. The ship failed to move. Hitler continued staring at the bow, like a cat facing a door which refused to open. One of the service chiefs looked round, as if he was asking himself, 'What do we do now?' A couple of seagulls hovered above the upper platform, as though intent on mischief.

'If this goes on much longer,' Slaney said, watching them, 'the Limeys will be running a book on who gets crapped on first.'

There were more knocking noises from below, but still no sign of movement. Russell looked at his watch – two minutes and counting. Hitler was still staring rigidly ahead, but what else could he do? It was hardly the place for a major tantrum.

One of the service chiefs leaned over to say something, and stiffened as if he'd been slapped. And then a cheer burst forth from those lining the slipway – at last the ship was inching forward. The figures on the platform visibly relaxed, and as the stern slid into the river, Hitler, turning slightly to one side, smiled and brought a clenched fist sharply down on the railing.

'They must have sent Goering down to give it a push,' Slaney said. 'Anyway,' he added, 'the good news is that it won't be ready for sea until 1941.'

Slaney's train wasn't until nine that evening, and he jumped at the offer of a lift back to Berlin in the car. There was little conversation – Slaney slept for most of the journey, despite snorting himself awake on several occasions – and Russell was left to brood on his visit to Sachsenhausen the following day. At least he'd have no trouble getting there. Come to think of it, that was what made car ownership in Germany special – the concentration camps became so accessible.

After dropping Slaney off in the city centre he drove up Neue Königstrasse to see if the Wiesners had any news, or any last-minute instructions for his visit. There was none of the former, but Frau Wiesner had written a short letter to her husband.

'They won't allow ...' Russell started to say, but then relented. 'I'll try,' he promised.

'Please read it,' she said, 'and if they take it then you can tell him what's in it.'

'Tell Daddy we love him,' Ruth said, her head suddenly appearing round the door to the other room. The voice was brittle, the smile almost unbearable.

'I will.'

He motored back down Neue Königstrasse, and stopped at the Alexanderplatz station to call Effi. The phone just rang, so he drove home to Neuenburgerstrasse. Frau Heidegger's skat evening was in boisterous swing, but she'd pinned a message for him beside the phone: 'Herr Russell! Your fiancée is working late tonight and early tomorrow morning. She finishes work at six tomorrow evening!'

Russell went upstairs and ran a bath. The water was almost scalding, the pain of immersion almost pleasurable.

Wednesday was a nice day for any drive but this one. Berlin looked its best under a pale sun: the Spree sparkled, the windows glittered, the brightly coloured trams shone in the grey stone streets. While walkers huddled against the brisk cold wind, mouths and ears swathed in wool, the Hanomag proved remarkably draught-proof for a ten-year-old car. As he drove up Brunnenstrasse towards Gesundbrunnen he murmured a prayer of thanks for the Zembski cousins. More than a thousand kilometres in twelve days, and no sign of a problem.

As he drove over the Ringbahn bridge he could see the Hertha flag flying from the Plumpe grandstand. This was the way he and Effi had come on the previous Friday, but the feeling on that day was one of leaving Hitler's world behind. Today he was journeying into its heart, or the space where a heart might have been.

Sachsenhausen was only an hour's drive from Berlin, a reasonable commute for the Gestapo interrogators who had previously plied their trade in the modern dungeons of Columbia Haus. According to Slaney, the new camp was a lot bigger, but neither he nor any other member of the foreign press corps had ever visited it. They had been shown round a sanitised Dachau in the early days, but that was that.

Ten kilometres short of his destination, Russell pulled into a small town garage for petrol and used the stop to read Eva Wiesner's letter to her husband. It was simple, touching, to the point. Heartbreaking.

Back on the Stralsund road, a neat sign announced the turn-off to Sachsenhausen Concentration Camp and Re-Educational Facility. Two or three kilometres of newly laid road led through a flat land of pastures and small woods to the gates of the camp. Parallel wire fences ran off to both left and right, one of which was clearly electrified. The gates themselves were flanked by a concrete watchtower and gatehouse.

Russell pulled up beside the latter, as a man in *Totenkopfverbände* uniform emerged with palm raised and a sub-machine gun cradled in his other arm. Russell wound down the window and handed over his documents. The guard read through them twice, told him to wait, and walked back inside the gatehouse. Russell heard him talking, presumably on the telephone, and a few moments later he re-emerged with another guard. 'Get out,' he said.

Russell obliged.

'Raise your arms.'

He did as he was told. As one guard checked his clothes and body for weapons, the other went over the car.

'What is this?' the first guard asked, taking the letter from Russell's coat pocket.

'It's a letter for the man I've come to see. From his wife.'

'Not permitted,' the guard said, without apparent emotion. He crumpled the letter in his fist.

Russell opened his mouth to protest but thought better of it.

'The car's clean,' the other guard reported.

'Turn left inside the gate, and report to the *Kommandantura*,' the first guard said. 'It's the second building on the left.' He handed back the documents and gestured to the guard who had now appeared inside the gates to open them. Russell thanked him with a smile – which was not returned – and drove carefully through the opened gates, conscious that they would soon be closing behind him. Turning left, he could see, in a wide space some distance ahead, several hundred prisoners standing in formation. Most had bare arms and heads, and must have been freezing in the cold wind. Two *Totenkopfverbände* officers were ambling along the front rank, shouting something indecipherable. One had a muzzled Alsatian on a lead.

He stopped outside the two-storey concrete building which bore the label *Kommandantura*, took one last look at the apparent roll-call, and headed for the door. On either side of the entrance two large pots held the withered remains of what might have been geraniums.

Inside, a middle-aged Gestapo officer looked up from his desk, wordlessly extended a hand for Russell's documentation, and gestured him to a chair. As he examined the pass and accompanying letter he repeatedly ran his right hand through his thinning hair, as if intent on wearing out what little remained. Picking up the phone with that hand, he switched to using the other on his head. 'You are needed here,' he told someone, and hung up.

A minute later the someone – a younger man with a remarkably unintelligent face – arrived. 'Hauptscharführer Gründel will take you to your meeting,' the adjutant announced.

Russell stood up. 'This way,' the Hauptscharführer barked, leading him through a door, down a short corridor and out through another door into the open air. A short walk down a gravel path brought them to another, larger two-storey building, and a small windowless room on the ground floor. Several chairs and a table were arranged round the walls, leaving the centre of the room empty. The floor had a thin covering of sawdust.

'Why are you so interested in this Jew?' the Hauptscharführer asked, sounding almost bewildered beneath the bluster.

'He helped a friend of mine – years ago,' Russell said shortly.

The Hauptscharführer thought about that, and shook his head. 'Wait here,' he said.

Russell waited, pacing too and fro across the room. There was a dark residue in the centre of the floor which could have been dried blood. He squatted on his haunches for a better look, but admitted to himself that he didn't really know what dried blood in quantity looked like. It was the sort of thing you needed to know in Hitler's realm, he thought. If the Eskimos had fifty words for snow, the Nazis probably had fifty for dried blood.

The minutes stretched out. At one point a frenzied burst of barking erupted in the distance, and died out with equal abruptness. Almost twenty minutes had gone by when the door opened and Felix Wiesner was pushed inside, the Hauptscharführer close behind him. Russell had expected cuts and bruises, and there were lots of them – one of Wiesner's eyes was swollen shut, there were dark bruises on his neck, throat and cheeks, and blood in his hair. But that was just the superficial damage. His right hand was encased in a bloody bandage, concealing God knew what injuries, and the doctor was hunched over, apparently unable to walk upright. He looked, Russell thought, like a man who'd just been kicked in the genitals. Many, many times.

He was obviously surprised to see someone he knew. 'Come,' Russell said, helping Wiesner into a chair and feeling the pain it cost him.

The Hauptscharführer, who had taken a chair by the door, watched with contempt.

'Can we speak in private?' Russell asked, knowing what the answer would be.

'No. This bastard has forfeited any right to privacy. You have ten minutes,' he added, looking at his watch.

Russell turned to Wiesner. 'Your wife wrote you a letter, but they confiscated it. She told me to read it in case that happened. She wrote that she and the children love you and are dreaming of the day when you come home.'

Wiesner sighed, then made a visible effort to gather himself. 'Thank you,' he said quietly, moving his mouth with obvious difficulty. 'Why are you here?' he asked, as if there had to be more.

'To help, if I can,' Russell said. 'You know what they accuse you of?'

'Yes.'

'Did you see this girl?'

Wiesner shifted his body in a vain search for comfort. 'She came to the clinic. Wanted an abortion. Abused me when I said no.'

'You don't know who gave her the abortion?'

'No. But look,' he said, speaking slowly, making sure the words came out right, 'that doesn't matter. That's over. We are all guilty here.' He reached out his good hand and laid it on Russell's arm. 'You must tell my wife to go if she can. To save the girls. And

Albert if he's willing to be saved. And herself. She mustn't count on my getting out of here. In fact, she must act as if I were already dead. Do you understand? Can you tell her that? Can you make her believe it?'

'I can tell her.'

'She knows where my stamp collection' – he used the English words – 'is. It would be worth a lot to Stanley Gibbons. And I would be greatly in your debt.'

'No you wouldn't,' Russell said, glancing across at the Hauptscharführer, who was looking at his watch.

'I am ashamed to say it,' Wiesner continued, still struggling with every word, 'but I thought Albert was exaggerating about this place – that he had been less than a *mensch*. Tell him I am sorry, that now I know.'

'One minute,' the Hauptscharführer said.

'Don't tell my wife how bad it is,' Wiesner said. 'Tell her I'm all right. There's nothing she can do.'

Russell looked at him. 'I feel like I want to apologise,' he said.

'Why – you have done nothing.'

Russell grimaced. 'Maybe that's why. I don't know if there's anything I can do to help you, but I'll move heaven and earth to get your family out. I promise you that.'

Wiesner nodded, as if that were a deal worth having. 'Thank you,' he whispered as the Hauptscharführer got to his feet.

'Time,' the man shouted with evident satisfaction. 'You wait here,' he told Russell, shoving Wiesner in the direction of the door. Russell watched the doctor shuffle painfully out, arms folded against the wind, the Hauptscharführer demanding greater speed. The door slammed shut behind them.

Russell sat and waited, staring numbly into space, until the Hauptscharführer returned. Back at the *Kommandantura* he insisted on asking the Gestapo officer whether the doctor's account of events had been checked out. The man hesitated, as if wondering whether the offer of an answer could be justified, and decided it could. 'Our interrogations are not yet complete,' he said dismissively.

'You mean he's not dead yet,' Russell said.

The Gestapo man gave him a thin smile. 'What happens here is no concern of foreigners,' he said.

Several retorts sprang to mind, but silence seemed wiser. 'I can leave?' he asked.

'You can leave.'

Russell walked outside to the car. The prisoners were still lined up in the distance, the icy wind still blowing. He reversed the car, drove back to the gates, and waited for them to be opened. As he motored out past the gatehouse he saw the crumpled ball of Eva Wiesner's letter lying where the wind had blown it, up against the concrete wall. A kilometre or so down the access road he pulled to a stop, slumped forward with his head against the wheel, and let the waves of rage wash over him.

A little over an hour later he was pulling up outside the Wiesners' apartment block in Friedrichshain. He sat in the car for a while, reluctant to go up, as if bringing the bad news would make it real. Many of the people walking by looked Jewish, and most of them looked as if they'd seen better times. Did the faces look haunted, or was he just thinking that they should? Could they see the fist coming? The coshes, the belts, the whips?

Russell wearily climbed the stairs and knocked on the familiar door. It opened immediately, as if Frau Wiesner had been waiting behind it. 'He's all right,' Russell said, the lie sour on his tongue.

The girls' faces filled with hope, but Frau Wiesner searched his face, and saw a different truth. 'They are not treating him badly?' she asked, almost incredulously.

'Not too badly,' Russell said, glancing pointedly at the girls.

Her face sank with the knowledge that he needed to talk to her alone, but she managed a smile as she shooed the girls back into the other room. 'Tell me how bad it is,' she asked, once the door had closed behind them.

'He's been beaten. But not too badly,' Russell lied. 'He has cuts and bruises. What you'd expect from those animals.'

'God save us,' she said, her legs buckling.

Russell helped her into a seat, and steeled himself to pass on her husband's words. 'He gave me a message for you,' he began. 'You must leave the country if you can, you and the children. He hopes he will be released eventually, but for the moment – for the moment,' he emphasised – 'he says you must act as if he were dead.'

He expected tears, but she gave him a look full of defiance. 'The children, yes,' she said. 'But I will not go.'

'The children will need you,' Russell said. And your husband will not be coming back, he thought.

'They will be all right,' she said firmly, as if trying to convince herself. 'In a decent country, they will be all right. Albert is old enough to look after the girls.'

'Where is Albert?'

'Out somewhere. But I will make sure that he looks after the girls.'

'Your husband sent him a message too,' Russell said. 'He says he understands now what Albert must have been through in the camp. He wants Albert to know he's sorry for doubting him.'

'Oh, God,' she said, burying her face in her hands.

Russell pulled her to him, feeling her silent, racking sobs through his shoulder. 'One other thing,' he said when she was finally still. 'I am going to England tomorrow. For a few days, taking Effi's sister to see an English doctor. Your husband asked if I could get his stamps out of Germany, and this seems like an ideal opportunity. If you agree, I can put them in a safety deposit box in London, and leave the key with my agent. He's trustworthy.'

'You are sure?'

'That he's trustworthy? Yes. That I can get them past customs? Not completely, but I'm travelling with the wife of a Nazi and two children. It seems like the best chance we're likely to get.'

She got up and disappeared into the other room, returning a few moments later with a large, soft-covered book called *Achievements of the Third Reich: The First Five Years*. 'Collect all fifty full-colour stickers!' a splash in the corner announced, and Felix Wiesner obviously had. Stickers displaying busy factories, the People's car, Strength Through Joy cruise ships and forty-seven other bounties of Hitler's reign were neatly affixed to their appropriate squares.

'The pictures are only stuck around the edges,' she explained. 'There's a stamp behind each one.'

Effi seemed happy enough to see him, but was, in her mind, it seemed to him, still on the film-set. Russell could have shocked her out of her absorption with an account of his visit to Sachsenhausen, but there didn't seem any point. He gave her a sanitised version of the visit, more sanitised indeed than the one he'd given Frau Wiesner. They made love that night in a friendly, somewhat desultory fashion, rather in the way, Russell imagined, that 'Mother' made love to her over-sensitive SA husband.

The dawn was only breaking over the mist-shrouded Havelsee location when he dropped her off, and he arrived outside the British

Embassy almost an hour before it opened. The queue of Jews seeking visas was already stretching round the corner into Pariserplatz.

Coffee and hot rolls in the Café Kranzler restored his body, but the morning's *Beobachter* further sank his spirits. An editorial congratulated the British on their obvious willingness to give up their empire – sarcasm was the *highest* form of wit in Goebbelsland – before condemning that same willingness as a clear sign of weakness and decadence. The British had succumbed to *humanitätsduselei*, humanitarian nonsense. This was not something the Reich would ever countenance.

The queue of people eager to escape Hitler's paradise was receding round another corner when Russell got back to the Embassy. Martin Unsworth was in a meeting, and had nothing good to tell him when he eventually came out of it. Someone had stuck a 'to be refused' note on Frau Wiesner's file, but he didn't know when or why. He was still working on it but, as Russell could see, they were pretty busy. Russell's graphic account of his visit to Sachsenhausen elicited sympathy but little else. He had telegraphed the Washington Embassy with a message for Conway, Unsworth said, but had not had a reply. For all he knew, Conway was taking a few days' holiday in New York. And in any case, he didn't see what Conway or anyone else could do about one Jew in a concentration camp, no matter how innocent he was, or how badly he was being treated.

More resigned than raging, Russell left without hitting the banister and drove home to Neuenburgerstrasse. Frau Heidegger's door was open, his Sudeten neighbour sitting helplessly in the chair she reserved for the sacrificial coffee-drinker. Russell flashed him a sympathetic smile and ran upstairs to pack the larger of his two worn-out suitcases with three changes of clothes, a toothbrush and several books. The latter included *Achievements of the Third Reich* and the 1937 Coronation edition of the *A1 Guide and Atlas of*

London, which he'd discovered the previous year in a second-hand bookshop on the Ku'damm. Miniatures of their majesties sat side by side over a scrolled 'Long May They Reign'.

The aerodrome at Tempelhof field was on the other side of the Kreuzberg, about three kilometres away. As they lived fairly close together, Jens had agreed to pick up Paul for a noon arrival at the aerodrome, and Russell arrived with some twenty minutes to spare. The car park was small, but the quality of cars – his Hanomag excepted – made up for the lack of quantity. Flying was not for the poor.

The others arrived five minutes later, Paul with a *Jungvolk* rucksack on his back, his face a study in repressed excitement. The fur-coated Zarah looked anxious, Lothar like a normal four-year-old. Jens ushered them into the one-storey terminal building, clearly intent on smoothing their path. As Zarah disappeared in the direction of the ladies' room, he took Russell aside.

'It went well yesterday?' he asked.

Russell nodded.

'And you understand that you must not talk or write about your visit?'

Russell nodded again.

'For everyone's sake,' Jens added pointedly.

'Look!' Paul called out from a window. 'It's our aeroplane.'

Russell joined him.

'It's a Ju-52/3m,' Paul said knowledgeably, pointing at the plane being fuelled out on the tarmac. 'It has a cruising ceiling of 5,000 metres. It can go 264 kilometres an hour.'

Russell looked up. The sky was clearer than it had been. 'We should see a lot,' he said.

'We'll be over the Reich for two hours,' Paul said, as if nothing else was worth seeing.

Zarah had returned. 'Time to go through customs,' Russell told his son, feeling a flutter of nerves run down his spine.

Jens led the way, chatting and laughing with the officials as if they were old friends. Zarah's large suitcase was waved through unopened, as was Paul's rucksack. Russell's suitcase, however, they wanted to inspect.

He opened it up and watched, heart in mouth, while the customs official ran his hands through the clothes and came to the books. He looked at these one by one, ignoring those in English and settling on *Achievements of the Third Reich*. He skipped through a few pages, and gave its owner a quizzical look.

'It's for a nephew in England,' Russell explained, suddenly conscious that Paul was looking at the book with some surprise. Don't say anything, he silently pleaded, and Paul, catching his eye, seemed to understand.

The man put it back with the others and closed the suitcase. 'Enjoy your journey,' he said.

Once Jens and Zarah had said their goodbyes, the four of them walked out across the tarmac to the silver aeroplane. It had a stubby nose, three engines – one at the front, one on either wing – and windows like rectangular portholes. LUFTHANSA was stencilled on the side, a large swastika painted on the tailfin. A short flight of steps took them up to the door, and into a vestibule behind the passenger cabin, where their cases were stowed. In the cabin itself there were ten leather-covered seats, five on each side of the carpeted aisle, each with a high head-rest. Theirs were the four at the rear, Russell sitting behind Paul, Zarah behind Lothar.

The other passengers came aboard: a youngish English couple whom Russell had never seen before and four single men, all of whom looked like wealthy businessmen of one sort or another.

Judging from their clothes one of these was English, the rest German.

A mail lorry drew up beside the aeroplane. The driver jumped down, opened the rear door and dragged three sacks marked *Deutschespost* to the bottom of the steps. A man in a Lufthansa uniform carried them aboard.

'We used these against the communists in Spain,' Paul said, leaning across the gangway to make himself heard above the rising roar of the engines. 'They were one of the reasons we won.'

Russell nodded. A discussion with his son about the Spanish Civil War seemed overdue, but this was hardly the place. He wondered if Paul had forgotten that his parents had both been communists, or just assumed that they'd seen the errors of their ways.

The pilot and co-pilot appeared, introducing themselves with bows and handshakes as they walked down the aisle to their cabin. The stewardess followed in their tracks, making sure that everyone had fastened their leather safety belts. She was a tall, handsome-looking blonde of about nineteen with a marked Bavarian accent. A predictable ambassador for Hitler's Germany.

Out on the tarmac a man began waving the plane forward, and the pilot set them in motion, bumping across the concrete surface towards the end of the runway. There was no pause when they reached it, just a surge of the engines and a swift acceleration. Through the gap between seat and wall, Russell could see Paul's ecstatic face pressed to the window. On the other side of the aisle, Zarah's eyes were closed in fright.

Seconds later, Berlin was spreading out below them – the tangle of lines leading south from Anhalter and Potsdamer stations, the suburbs of Schonefeld, Wilmersdorf, Grunewald. 'There's my school!' Paul almost shouted. 'And there's the Funkturm, and the Olympic Stadium!'

Soon the wide sheet of the Havelsee was receding behind them, the villages, fields and forests of the northern plain laid out below. They were about a mile up, Russell reckoned, high enough to make anything look beautiful. From this sort of height a *Judenfrei* village looked much like one that wasn't.

They flew west, over the wide traffic-filled Elbe and the sprawling city of Hanover, crossing into Dutch air space soon after three o'clock. Rotterdam appeared beneath the starboard wing, the channels of the sea-bound Rhine – or whatever the Dutch called it – beneath the other. As they crossed the North Sea coast the plane was rocked by turbulence, causing Zarah to clutch the handrests and Paul to give his father a worried look. Russell gave him a reassuring smile. Lothar, he noticed, seemed unconcerned.

The turbulence lasted through most of the sea crossing, and the serene sea below them seemed almost an insult. Looking down at one Hook of Holland-bound steamer Russell felt a hint of regret that they'd travelled by air – not for the lack of comfort, but the lack of romance. He remembered his first peacetime trip to Europe – the first few had been on troopships during the war – the train journey through Kent's greenery, the Ostend ferry with its bright red funnels, the strange train waiting in the foreign station, the sense of striking out into the unknown. He hadn't been on a plane for the better part of ten years, and he hadn't missed them.

But Paul was having the time of his life. 'Can you see England yet?' he asked his father.

'Yes,' Russell realised. The Thanet coast was below him. A large town. Margate probably, or Ramsgate. Places he'd never been. And within minutes, or so it seemed, the south-eastern suburbs of London were stretching beneath them in the afternoon sun, mile upon mile of neat little houses in a random mesh of roads and railways.

The pilot brought the plane down on the Croydon runway with only the slightest of jolts. The entry formalities were just that, and the car Jens had ordered was waiting at the terminal doors. They drove up the Brighton Road, slowed by the busy late-afternoon traffic. Paul marvelled at the double-decker buses, but was more astonished by the paucity of buildings reaching above two storeys. It was only after Brixton that third, fourth and fifth floors were grudgingly added.

Russell asked the driver to take them across Westminster Bridge, and was rewarded by the singular sight of Big Ben and the Houses of Parliament aglow in the light of the setting sun. As they drove up Whitehall he pointed out Downing Street and the Horseguards; as they swung round Trafalgar Square, Nelson on his lonely column. The Strand seemed choked with buses, but they finally arrived at the Savoy to find that their fifth-floor rooms overlooked the Thames.

These must have cost a fortune, Russell thought. He and Paul looked out of the window at the barges on the tide-swollen river, the electric trains of the Southern Railway moving in and out of Charing Cross station. Away to their left the piles of the new Waterloo Bridge stuck out of the water like temple remains. 'This is good,' Paul said, with the air of someone truly satisfied.

Russell got an outside line and phoned his London agent Solly Bernstein, hoping to catch him before he went home. 'I'm just on my way out of the door,' Bernstein told him. 'What the hell are you doing in London?'

'Hoping to see you. Can you squeeze me in tomorrow afternoon?'

'Well, all right. Just this once. Four o'clock?'

'Fine.'

Russell hung up and explained the call to Paul. 'I'm hungry,' was the response.

They ate with Zarah and Lothar in the hotel restaurant. The food was excellent, but Zarah, clearly anxious about the next morning, just picked at it. When she and Lothar wished them goodnight and retired to their room, Russell and his son took a stroll down to the river, and along the Embankment towards the Houses of Parliament. Opposite County Hall they stopped and leaned against the parapet, the high tide slurping against the wall below. Pedestrians and buses were still crowding Westminster Bridge, and long chains of lighted carriages rumbled out of Charing Cross. A line of laden coal barges headed downstream, dark silhouettes against the glittering water. Some lines of Eliot slipped across his brain:

The barges wash
Drifting logs
Down Greenwich reach
Past the Isle of Dogs

He had hated 'The Wasteland' when it came out – its elegant despair had felt like defeatism. But the words had stuck. Or some of them at least.

'It's been a long day,' he told Paul. 'Time for bed.'

Zarah looked exhausted over breakfast next morning, as if she'd hardly slept. Lothar, by contrast, seemed more animated than usual. Paul, asked by his father for an opinion of Zarah's son, had shrugged and said, 'He's just a bit quiet, that's all.'

Reception suggested a bank on the Strand which offered currency exchange and probably a safety deposit service, and Russell left Paul examining the huge model of the *Queen Mary* in the hotel lobby while he swapped his and Zarah's Reichsmarks for pounds. Safety deposit boxes were available, the cashier informed him proudly. The bank was open until three.

Their appointment in Harley Street was at eleven, and Zarah had booked a taxi for ten. Trafalgar Square was busy, but the cab then raced round Piccadilly Circus and up Regent Street, delivering them to the doctor's door with forty-five minutes to spare. A stern-looking receptionist showed them into the waiting room, which was full of highly polished wooden chairs. Paul found a few children's comics among the society magazines, and went through one with Lothar, pointing out what was happening in the various pictures.

'How did you find this doctor?' Russell asked.

'A friend of Jens' at the Embassy here,' she replied. 'He said this man was highly thought of. And he speaks a little German.'

'Little', as they eventually discovered, was the operative word, and Russell had to function as a full-time interpreter. Doctor Gordon McAllister was a tall ginger-haired man in his forties, with a rather gaunt face, a slight Scottish accent and an almost apologetic smile. He seemed a nice man, and one who clearly liked children. Effi always claimed that doctors who specialised in women's problems were usually women-haters, but apparently the same logic did not apply to paediatricians.

His office was a bright, spacious room with windows over-looking the street. In addition to his desk, there were several comfortable chairs and a large wooden box full of children's toys and books. 'So tell me about Lothar,' he asked Zarah through Russell.

She started off nervously but grew more confident as she went on, thanks in large part to the doctor's obvious involvement. She said that Lothar sometimes seemed uninterested in everything, that he didn't respond when people talked to him, that at other times he would suddenly seem to lose interest in whatever it was he was doing, and just stop. 'He'll be in the middle of eating,' she said, 'and just leave the table and go and do something else. And he doesn't always seem to understand what I'm telling him to do,' she added.

'He's four, yes?' the doctor asked.

'And three months.'

'Can he recognise different animals?' He walked over to the box and took out a tiger and a rabbit. 'Lothar, what's this?' he asked holding out the tiger.

'A tiger.'

'And this?'

'A rabbit.'

'No problems there, then. How about colours? Can he recognise them?'

He could. A red balloon, a blue sky, a yellow canary. Having done so, without warning he walked across to the window and looked out.

The doctor asked Zarah about the birth, about Lothar's eating habits, whether there was any history of problems in her or her husband's family. She answered each question, and, in a halting voice, volunteered the information that she had considered aborting Lothar before he was born. 'I can't help thinking there's a connection,' she said, clearly close to tears.

'You're completely wrong about that,' the doctor insisted, the moment Russell had translated her words. 'There is no possible connection.'

'Then what is it?' she asked, wiping a tear away.

'Does he get tired easily? Does he seem weak – physically weak, I mean? Can he lift things?'

She thought about that. 'Jens – my husband – he sometimes says that Lothar lacks strength in his fingers. He doesn't like carrying things. And yes, he does get tired.'

The doctor leaned forward on his desk, fingers intertwined beneath his chin. 'I don't think there is anything seriously wrong with Lothar,' he said. 'Or at least, nothing that cannot be corrected. There is no name for this, but it isn't uncommon. Essentially, he has a weaker link with the rest of the world than most people do, but everyone is different in this respect – he's just a bit more different than the norm. And his link can be strengthened. What Lothar needs,' – he ticked them off on his fingers – 'is fresh air and exercise, really good, nutrient-rich, food – fresh eggs, fresh fruit, fresh everything – and physical stimulation. Regular massage would help. Give and take games – the sort that involve instant physical reactions. And music. All these things stimulate the body, make it more responsive.'

'But there's nothing seriously wrong?' Zarah asked.

'Not in my judgement. No.'

'And he doesn't need any tests?'

'No.'

She took a deep breath. 'Thank you, doctor.' She reached inside her handbag for the neat package of pound notes.

'You pay the receptionist,' he said with a smile.

But not usually with cash, Russell thought, as they waited for the taxi which the receptionist had ordered. Zarah, who looked as if a huge weight had been lifted off her shoulders, was eager to get back to the Savoy, where she could telephone Jens. 'It's wonderful news,' Russell told her, and received the warmest of smiles in return.

Once back at the hotel, they agreed to meet for lunch in an hour. Leaving Paul exploring the lobby, Russell retrieved *Achievements of the Third Reich* from their room, and came back down.

'Here's the room key,' he told Paul. 'I'll be back in half an hour or so.'

Paul was looking at the book. 'Where are you taking that?' he wanted to know. 'I didn't know you had a nephew in England,' he added suspiciously.

'I don't,' Russell admitted. 'I'll explain it all this afternoon.'

He walked down to the Continental bank, paid a year's rent in cash for the safety deposit box, and was shown into a small room with a single upright chair and table. A clerk brought him a rectangular metal box and two keys, and told him to press the buzzer when he was finished. 'I already am,' Russell said, placing *Achievements of the Third Reich* inside and locking the box shut. If the clerk was surprised by the nature of the deposit he didn't show it.

'There's more to the Nazis than meets the eye,' Russell said.

'I don't doubt it,' the clerk replied gloomily.

Lunch was an altogether more cheerful affair than breakfast or the previous night's dinner, but twenty-four largely sleepless hours had taken their toll on Zarah. 'I'm going to take a nap,' she said. 'We'll see you this evening.'

Asked if there was anything he wanted to do, Paul suggested a walk down to Big Ben. 'I didn't see it properly in the dark,' he explained.

They set off down the Strand, stopping in at Charing Cross to see the Southern trains and admire the cross itself. After circling the Trafalgar Square ponds and climbing on a lion they marched down the Mall towards Buckingham Palace. 'The King's out,' Russell said, pointing out the lowered flag. 'Kings are out-dated,' Paul told him.

They cut through to Parliament Square and walked out onto Westminster Bridge, stopping in the middle to turn and admire Big Ben. 'You were going to tell me about that book,' Paul said rather hesitantly, as if unsure how much he wanted to know.

A small voice in Russell's head reminded him how many children had already denounced their parents to the authorities in Germany, and a whole host of other voices laughed out loud. And if he was so wrong about his own son, he told himself, then he probably deserved to be denounced.

He told Paul about the Wiesners. The family's need to emigrate, the father's arrest, the certain confiscation of their savings – the savings they would need to start a new life somewhere else.

'The savings are in that book?' Paul asked incredulously.

'Valuable stamps,' Russell told him. 'Hidden behind the stickers.'

Paul looked surprised, impressed, and finally dubious. 'They collected the stamps? Like ordinary Germans?'

'They *are* ordinary Germans, Paul. Or they were. How else do you imagine they would get hold of them?'

Paul opened his mouth, then obviously thought better of whatever it was he was going to say. 'They paid you to bring them?' he asked, as if he couldn't quite believe it.

'No. I did it because I like them. They're nice people.'

'I see,' Paul said, though clearly he didn't.

It was almost 3.30. Back in Parliament Square they joined the queue for a 24 bus, and managed to find seats upstairs for the short ride up Whitehall and Charing Cross Road. Solly Bernstein's office was two storeys above a steam laundry in Shaftesbury Avenue and its owner was accustomed, as he frequently observed, to hot air. A bulky, middle-aged man with gold-rimmed glasses, a notable nose and longish black hair, Russell's agent seemed unchanged by the last three years.

'This is my son, Solly,' Russell said.

'My, he's bigger than I imagined. Welcome to England, young man.'

'Thank you,' Paul said in English.

'Ah, a linguist. I have just the book for him.' He searched through the piles on the floor and extracted a large picture book of world aeroplanes. 'Have a look at that and tell me what you think,' he said, handing it over. 'Throw those books on the floor,' he added, indicating a loaded seat in the corner.

He turned back to Russell's grinning face. 'It's good to see you in the flesh. Three years, isn't it? A long time in today's world.'

'Something like that,' Russell agreed, taking a seat.

'You haven't come to tell me you've found a better agent?'

'Good God, no.'

'Well then, I can tell you we've sold the "Germany's Neighbours" series in both Canada and Australia. And here' – he rummaged in a drawer – 'is a cheque to prove it.'

Russell took it, and passed a sheaf of papers in the opposite direction. 'One for each series,' he said. 'I thought I'd save the postage.'

'An expensive way to do it. You came by train, I take it?'

'Nope. We flew.'

Bernstein's eyebrows rose. 'Even more expensive. My percentage is obviously too low.'

'I came for another reason. Two, actually. And one was to ask you a favour.' Russell outlined the Wiesners' circumstances, his hope that at least some members of the family would be given exit visas before a war broke out. Paul, he noticed, was listening with great interest to his recital. 'I've just put the family wealth in a safety deposit box,' he told the unusually sober Bernstein. 'There are two keys, and I was hoping you'd hang on to one of them. They'll have the other, but there's a good chance it would be confiscated at the border.'

'Why, in heaven's name?'

'Simple spite. If Jews are caught carrying a key out, the Nazis will guess it's for something like this.'

'I'd be happy to keep one of them.'

'Thanks,' Russell said, handing the key over. 'That's a weight off my mind.' He stole a glance at Paul, who looked more confused than anything else.

'How long are you here for?' Bernstein asked.

'Oh, only till Sunday. I came with my girlfriend's sister – that was the other reason – she wanted to have her son examined by an English doctor. A long story. But if there's a war, well, I guess I'll be back for the duration.'

'Without him?' Bernstein said, nodding in Paul's direction.

'Without him.'

Bernstein made a sympathetic face. 'Anyway, at least you've got a lot of work at the moment. No other ideas you want to talk about?'

'Not at the moment,' He looked at his watch. 'We'd better go. Paul?'

His son closed the book and brought it over. 'You can keep it,' Bernstein said. 'Practise your English on the captions.'

'Thank you,' Paul said. 'Very much,' he added carefully.

'It's working already.' He smiled and offered Paul his hand, then did the same to Russell.

'He was a nice man,' Paul said, as they made their way down the steamy stairwell.

'He is,' Russell agreed, as they reached the pavement. 'And he's Jewish,' he added, hoping that Paul was not going to wipe the handshake off on his coat.

He didn't, but he did look upset.

'They're wrong about the Jews,' Russell said firmly. 'They may be right about many things, but they're wrong about the Jews.'

'But everyone says …'

'Not everyone. I don't. Your mother doesn't. Your Uncle Thomas doesn't. Effi doesn't.'

'But the government says …'

'Governments can be wrong. They're just people. Like you and me. Look what foreign governments did to Germany in 1918. They were wrong. It happens, Paul. They get things wrong.'

Paul looked torn between anger and tears.

'Look. Let's not spoil the trip arguing about politics. We're in London – let's enjoy it.' They were walking down Charing Cross Road by this time. 'I know where we can get a cup of tea and a cake,' he said, steering Paul off to the left. A few minutes later they were on the edge of Covent Garden market, dodging lorries piled high with crates of fruit and vegetables. Russell led Paul into one of the cafés.

It was full of men sawing at rashers of bacon and dribbling egg down their chins. Fried grease in its gaseous, liquid and solid forms filled the air, lay congealing on the tables and covered the walls. England, Russell thought. He had a sudden memory of a similar café just outside Victoria station, where he'd eaten his last meal before service in France. Twenty-one years ago.

Russell bought two large cups of tea and two aptly named rock cakes. Paul nibbled at the edges of his, rightfully fearing for his teeth, but liked the tea once he'd added four teaspoons of sugar. 'The cake is terrible,' he told his father in German, causing several sets of less-than-friendly eyes to swivel their way.

'Do you know anything about football?' Russell asked the nearest man in English.

'Maybe.'

'Are there any games on in London tomorrow?'

'Arsenal are playing Chelsea,' another man volunteered.

'At Highbury?'

'Of course.'

'And the games still kick off at three? I've been working abroad for a while,' he added in explanation.

'So we see,' the first man said with a leer. 'Yeah, they still kick off at three.'

'Thanks. Would you like to see a game tomorrow?' he asked Paul. 'Arsenal are playing Chelsea.'

His son's eyes lit up. 'Arsenal are the best!'

'Well I'm sure Zarah and Lothar can look after themselves.'

They finished their teas, abandoned the half-excavated rock cakes, and picked their way through the vegetable market, taking particular care outside the skin-strewn frontage of a banana wholesalers. It was getting dark now, and Russell wasn't sure where he was. Looking for a street sign they found one for Bow Street.

'Bow Street,' Paul echoed. 'This is where Chief Inspector Teal brings the men he's arrested.'

Away to their left a blue light was shining. They walked up the street and stood across from the forbidding-looking police station, half-expecting the fictional inspector to emerge through the double doors, busily chewing on a wodge of Wrigley's as he adjusted his bowler hat.

Back on the Strand they found the Stanley Gibbons stamp shop was still open, and Paul spent a happy twenty minutes deciding which packets of cheap assorted he most wanted. Russell looked in the catalogue for the ones Wiesner had given him in payment and was surprised to find how valuable they were. He wondered how many pounds-worth were nestling behind the stickers in their safety deposit box.

Zarah was more talkative at dinner than he ever remembered, and seemed newly determined to encourage the idea of his marrying her sister. She and Lothar accompanied them on their after-dinner walk this time, and Lothar, like Paul, seemed enthralled by the huge glittering river and its never-ending procession of barges and other boats. Russell and Zarah agreed their plans for Saturday: shopping in the morning, football for him and Paul in the afternoon, dinner with Jens' Embassy friend for her and Lothar in the evening. When they said goodnight outside her and Lothar's room, she thanked him warmly for his help. They'd almost become friends, Russell thought. Effi would be amazed.

Paul was yawning, but Russell felt far too restless for sleep. 'Bedtime for you,' he told his son. 'I'm going back downstairs for a drink. I won't be long.'

'You're just going downstairs?'

'Yes. No stamp-smuggling tonight. Just a drink.'

Paul grinned. 'All right.'

For a Friday night, the cocktail lounge seemed unusually empty. Russell bought a pint of bitter, parked himself on a stool at the end of the bar, and played with a beer mat. The taste of the English beer made him feel nostalgic. He had thought about taking Paul out to Guildford, to show him the house where he'd spent most of his own boyhood, but there wouldn't be time. The next trip perhaps, if there was one.

He pictured the house, the large garden, the steeply sloping street he'd walked to school each day. He couldn't say he'd had a happy childhood, but it hadn't been particularly unhappy either. He hadn't really appreciated it at the time, but his mother had never really settled in England, despite almost thirty years of trying. His father's inability or unwillingness to recognise that fact had undermined everything else. There had been a lot of silence in that house. He should write to her, he thought.

A quick trip to reception provided him with a few sheets of beautifully embossed Savoy writing paper, and he ordered another pint. But after telling her where he was and why, and sketching out the plot of Effi's new film, he could think of nothing else to say.

She hadn't seen Paul since he was four, and it would need a book to explain his son and their relationship.

He comforted himself with the knowledge that her letters to him were equally inadequate. On those rare occasions when, as adults, they'd been together, they had both enjoyed the experience – he was sure of that – but even then they'd hardly said anything to each other. His mother wasn't much of a talker or a thinker, which was why she had never liked Ilse. She and Effi, on the other hand, would probably become bosom friends. They were both do-ers.

A shadow crossed the paper as a man slid onto the stool next to his. He had short dark, brilliantined hair, a sharpish face with a small moustache and skin that looked unusually pink. He looked about twenty, but was probably older.

'John Russell?' he asked.

Oh God, Russell thought. Here we go again. 'I think you're mistaking me for someone else,' he said. 'I'm Douglas Fairbanks Jr.'

'Very good,' the man said admiringly. 'Can I get you another drink?'

'No thanks.'

'Well, I think I'll have one,' he said, raising a finger to the distant barman.

'Are you old enough?' Russell asked.

His new companion looked hurt. 'Look, there's no need to be offensive. I'm just …' He paused to order a Manhattan. 'Look, I think you know Trelawney-Smythe in Berlin.'

'We've met.'

'Well, he passed your name onto us, and …'

'Who might you be?'

'War Office. A department of the War Office. My name's Simpson. Arnold Simpson.'

'Right,' Russell said.

Simpson took an appreciative sip of his Manhattan. 'We checked up on you – we have to do that, you understand – and it looks as if Trelawney-Smythe was right. You are a perfect fit. You speak German like a native, you have family and friends there, you even have Nazi connections. You're ideally placed to work for us.'

Russell smiled. 'You may be right about means and opportunity, but where's the motive? Why would I want to work for you?'

Simpson looked taken aback. 'How about patriotism?' he asked.

'I'm as patriotic as the next businessman,' Russell said wryly.

'Ah. Very good. But seriously.'

'I *was* being serious.'

Simpson took a larger sip of the Manhattan. 'Mr Russell, we know your political history. We know you've been badgering the Berlin Embassy about a Jewish family. Whatever you write for the Soviets, we know you don't like the Nazis. And there's a war coming, for God's sake. Don't you want to do your bit to defeat them?'

'Mr Simpson, can't you people take no for an answer?'

Now the young man looked affronted. 'Of course,' he said. 'But …'

'Goodnight, Mr Simpson.'

They spent the first part of Saturday morning following Zarah in and out of clothes stores on Bond Street, the second scouring Hamleys for the stimulating toys which Dr McAllister had recommended. They found nothing which Zarah considered suitable in either. 'German toys are much better,' she announced with a satisfied air on the Regent Street pavement, and Paul agreed with her. There had been no dead soldiers, and those still breathing had been markedly inferior to the ones back home.

They parted at midday, Russell and Paul cutting through the streets beyond Oxford Street to the trolleybus terminus at Howland Street. The 627 took them up the Hampstead, Camden and Seven Sisters Roads to Finsbury Park, where the pubs were already overflowing with men *en route* to the match. It was a cold afternoon, the would-be spectators exhaling clouds of breath and clapping their gloved hands together as they threaded their way down the back streets to the ground. A rosette seller offered red and white for Arsenal, blue and white for Chelsea, and Paul wanted both. 'Covering the field, eh?' the man asked with a grin. He had a red and white scarf wrapped around his head, and a flat cap rammed on top of it.

The match itself was a disappointment – another point in Germany's column as far as Paul was concerned. It was hard to argue with him – if this was the best football in the world, then the world of football was in trouble. There was none of the magic England had shown in Berlin nine months earlier. In fact, both teams seemed markedly less endowed with basic skills than poor old Hertha.

What Paul did find fascinating was the crowd. He had no way of appreciating the wit, but he revelled in the sheer volume of noise, and the swirling currents of emotion which rose and fell all around him. 'It's so …' he began, as they crunched their way out across the carpet of roasted peanut shells, but an end to the sentence eluded him.

At the Arsenal station they shared a seemingly endless tunnel to the platform with several thousand others, and their Piccadilly Line train was full to bursting until it reached King's Cross. After the relative spaciousness of the U-bahn, the train itself seemed ancient, airless and claustrophobic – another point in the German column.

They walked back to the Strand through Covent Garden market, and ate another delicious dinner in the Savoy restaurant. Paul was quiet, as if busy absorbing his impressions of the last two days. He seemed, Russell thought, more German somehow. But that, he supposed, was only to be expected in England. He hadn't anticipated it though.

On the way to breakfast next morning he stopped off at reception to consult the hotel's *ABC Railway Guide*, and after they'd eaten he told Paul there was something he wanted to show him. They took a bus up Kingsway and Southampton Row to Euston, and walked through the giant archway to the platforms. The object of their visit was already sitting in Platform 12 – the blue and silver *Coronation Scot*. They bought platform tickets and walked up to where a dozen youngsters were paying court to the gleaming, hissing, streamlined 'Princess Alice'.

'It's beautiful,' Paul said, and Russell felt a ridiculous surge of pride in his native country. Paul was right. The German stream-liners reeked of speed and power, but this train had a grace they lacked. One mark at least for England.

Back at the Savoy they packed, took a last look at the Thames, and joined Zarah and Lothar in the lobby. The car was on time, the Sunday roads empty, and they arrived at Croydon airfield almost two hours early. While Paul stood transfixed by the planes outside the window, Russell scanned the *News of the World* for a clue to British concerns. He discovered that a vicar had been assaulted by a young woman in a village street, and that now was the time to protect your crocuses from sparrows. A half-page ad for constipation relief featured a wonderful photograph – somehow, the man really did look constipated. And much to Russell's relief, the game they'd seen the previous afternoon got a highly critical write-up – so at least it wasn't the norm.

It was the same aeroplane and crew that had brought them over. This time though, the clouds were lower, the flight rockier, the view more restricted. Jens, waiting for them at Tempelhof, hugged Zarah and Lothar as if they'd been away for weeks and thanked Russell profusely. He also offered to take Paul home, but Russell demurred, unwilling to sacrifice half an hour of his son's company.

As it was, Paul sat mostly in silence, as they drove west, gazing out of the window at his home city. 'It seems … well, strange,' he said, as they turned into his road. 'After being there, the idea of a war against England seems … it seems silly.'

'It is,' Russell agreed. But coming nevertheless. And, in one way, the sooner the better. Say it lasted four years, like the last one. Assuming they stuck to the current call-up at eighteen, Paul would be drafted in March 1945. For the war to be over by then, it had to get started early in 1941.

No need to worry, Russell told himself. Hitler wouldn't be able to wait that long.

Blue scarf

After spending the night with Effi he drove her out to the studio for an early start. She was pleased but not surprised by Dr McAllister's diagnosis – 'I said there was nothing wrong with him!' – but despondent about *Mother*. The director was a mechanic; her co-stars all thought, wrongly, that they were God's gift to acting; the on-set adviser from the Propaganda Ministry kept trying to clarify the film's 'social role' by inserting lines that even a baboon would have trouble misunderstanding. 'I suppose I should be grateful,' she said, as they drove in through the studio gates. 'I'll probably go down in history as one of Germany's great *comédiennes*.'

Russell drove back to Zoo station, where he bought breakfast and a paper. Nothing unusual seemed to have happened during his time in England. The widening of the Kiel Canal had been decreed – it obviously wasn't big enough for the *Bismarck*. Hitler had opened the International Motor Show just down the road, and unveiled a model of the new People's Car. For 950 marks – about fifty British pounds – the average German would get a small five-seater, with deliveries to begin in about fifteen months' time. Having been in at this birth, the Führer had proceeded to the funeral of some obscure Carinthian Gauleiter – the man had probably held his hand when the bullets started flying in 1923. He'd certainly been given all the Nazi trimmings – swastikas everywhere, black banners with runic emblems, lines of flaming pylons to light his way across the Hesperus.

Back at Neuenburgerstrasse, Frau Heidegger was waiting to ply him with coffee. She was elated by his impression of British unreadiness for war, which she thought, rather perceptively, both lessened the chance of war and increased the chance of German success if there was one. Before retiring upstairs to work, Russell phoned Unsworth at the British Embassy. He was told that Conway had been in touch, and that representations were being made in the appropriate quarters. Russell thought about visiting the Wiesners but decided against. He had nothing really to tell them, and instinctively felt that it was safer to limit his visits to the scheduled lessons.

He spent most of the next forty-eight hours working in his room, writing the fourth *Pravda* article, which he hoped to deliver in Posen that weekend, and sketching out a piece on artists and entertainers for the 'Ordinary Germans' series. His only trip out was to the Greiner works in Wedding, one of the Reich's major production centres for military vehicles. Expecting suspicion and probable refusals, he went straight to the Labour Front office, and was almost laughably surprised by the warm welcome he received. Yes, of course the German worker was torn between his love of peace and his desire to arm the Fatherland against its foes. What human being would not be? And of course Herr Russell could talk to the workers about their feelings. The rest of the world should be given every chance to understand both the German hunger for peace and the nation's determination to defend its rights and its people.

After this, talking to several groups of workers in the canteen proved something of an anti-climax. Most were understandably reticent, and those prepared to speak their minds had nothing surprising to say. It was a job, that was all. As usual, the pay was bad, the hours too long, management more of a hindrance than a help. The Labour Front at least listened, if only to ward off potential trouble. Open discussions were infinitely preferable to either non-cooperation – slow working, mostly – or the sort of covert resistance that could lead to sabotage. Reading between the lines and facial expressions of the men he spoke to, Russell decided that the level of non-cooperation was probably significant without seriously affecting production levels or quality, and that the amount of real resistance was negligible. And when war came, he guessed, both would decrease.

Wednesday morning, he called in at the Embassy on his way to the Wiesners. The moment he saw Unsworth's face he knew what had happened. 'He's dead, isn't he?'

'The official line is that he hanged himself,' Unsworth said. 'I'm sorry.'

Russell sat down. A wave of sadness – of utterly useless sadness – seemed to flow through him. 'When?' he asked. 'Has the family been told?'

Unsworth shrugged. 'We received this note from the Foreign Ministry this morning.' He passed it over. 'A reply to our representations on Friday.'

The message comprised one sentence: 'In response to your enquiries of 18 February, we regret to inform you that the prisoner Wiesner has taken his own life, presumably out of guilt for his crime.'

Wiesner had been dead within two days of his visit, Russell thought. Beaten to death, most probably. A blessed release, perhaps. But not for his family.

'We assume the family has been informed,' Unsworth was saying.

'Why?' Russell asked, handing back the note. 'Because it's the decent thing to do?'

Unsworth nodded, as if taking the point.

'What about the visa situation?' Russell wanted to know. 'There's nothing to keep them here now. And surely …'

'I'm told the decisions on the next batch are being taken tomorrow afternoon. If you come back Friday morning I hope I'll have some good news for you.'

Russell walked down the stairs and out past the line of visa-seekers on Unter den Linden. Once behind the Hanomag's driving wheel, he just sat there, staring down towards the Brandenburg Gate and the distant trees of the Tiergarten.

Eventually, almost somnambulantly, he put the car into gear and moved off, circling Pariserplatz and heading back up Unter den Linden towards Alexanderplatz and Neue Königstrasse. What did you say to someone whose husband or father has just been murdered for the sin of being born into a particular race? What could you say? All around him the people of Berlin were going about their usual business, walking and driving and shopping and talking, laughing at jokes and smiling in friendship. If they'd heard of Sachsenhausen, they no doubt imagined neat rows of barracks, and some well-merited hard labour for the criminals and perverts residing there at the State's pleasure. They hadn't seen a man they knew and liked twisted and torn out of human shape for the pleasure of others.

He couldn't even tell the story, not without Jens suffering for it. And even if he could, he had no evidence to back up his suppositions. The Nazis would claim that a crime like Wiesner's was bound to provoke an angry reaction from his aryan guards, and that the wretched Jew had simply taken the easy way out when he received a few well-deserved bruises. What, they would say, was the problem? Everyone had behaved in a racially appropriate manner, and the world had one less Jew to worry about.

On the Wiesners' street he sat in the car, putting off the moment of truth. There was another car parked on the other side of the road, its windows open, with two bored-looking men smoking in the front seat. They looked like Kripo, Russell thought, and they were probably on loan to the Gestapo, which was notorious for believing itself above the more mundane aspects of police work.

Well, there was no law against teaching Jewish children English. He got out, walked up the familiar steps, rapped on the familiar door. An unfamiliar face appeared in the opening. A rather attractive woman, with a mass of curly brown hair and suspicious eyes. In her late thirties, Russell guessed.

He introduced himself, and her face changed. 'Come in,' she said. 'You've heard?' she added.

'About Dr Wiesner's death? Yes. Half an hour ago, at the British Embassy.'

As he spoke, Marthe Wiesner emerged from the other room, closing the door behind her. 'Herr Russell ...' she began.

'I can't tell you how sorry I am to hear about your father,' he said. There were two broken table lamps on the wooden chest, he noticed, and the curtain rail was hanging at an awkward angle.

'Thank you,' she said stiffly. She seemed calm – almost overly so – but for the moment at least the light in her eyes had gone out. 'This is Sarah Grostein,' she said, introducing the other woman. 'She's an old friend of the family. Mother is ... well, you can imagine. The shock was terrible. For all of us, of course. Mother and Ruth are sleeping at the moment.'

'Please give her my condolences,' Russell said, the hollow words tripping off his tongue. He wondered whether to leave the safety deposit box key with Marthe, especially in the presence of a stranger. He decided against. 'I need to talk to your mother,' he said. 'Not now, of course,' he added quickly. 'I'll come at the usual time on Friday.'

Marthe nodded, just as the sound of wailing erupted in the other room. A few seconds later Eva Wiesner called her elder daughter's name. 'I must go,' she said.

'Of course.' He waited till the door had closed before asking Sarah Grostein when the family had heard of Felix Wiesner's death.

'Saturday evening,' she said. 'I wasn't here of course, but the police behaved abominably. I can understand why Albert lost his head.'

Russell's heart sank. 'What did he do?'

'Oh, don't you know? He attacked the Gestapo bastard, hit him with one of these table lamps. The man's in hospital. They said he might die, but Marthe says it didn't look that bad. I think they were just trying to scare Eva.'

'Where have they taken Albert?' he asked. The wailing was quieter, but just as insistent.

She gave a bitter laugh. 'They haven't. He got away. Pushed the other bastard over the sofa and ran for it. He got out the back – there's a maze of alleys out there – and the conscious one knew better than to follow him. He wouldn't have found Albert, and he knew damn well he might not come out again.'

'Where's Albert now?'

'No one knows,' she said, leaving Russell with the distinct impression that she was lying. 'They came back yesterday,' she went on. 'Shouted at Eva to tell them where he was, which she couldn't have told them if she'd wanted to. But they didn't arrest her. Maybe they realised that there was no one else to look after the girls, that they'd be up to their eyes in paperwork if they tried to send them away somewhere.'

'Maybe,' Russell agreed. He thought it more likely that the British expression of interest in Wiesner's fate had kept the Gestapo in check. 'Can you pass on a message to Frau Wiesner? Tell her …' He paused. 'I was going to say that it looks like the children will get

British visas in the next week or so, but it doesn't seem as though Albert will have any use for his. If he goes to the Germans for an exit visa, they'll just arrest him. Still, the girls should be able to go. And maybe their mother too.'

'She won't leave Albert.'

'Perhaps he can persuade her.'

'Perhaps. But the Gestapo are parked outside, which makes arranging meetings rather difficult.'

He looked at her, standing there with arms crossed and anger simmering behind her eyes. 'Are you trying to get out?' he asked.

'Not at present,' she said, in a tone that didn't invite questioning.

'I'll get going,' he said. 'I'll be back on Friday morning.'

She nodded, opened the door, and closed it behind him. He walked out to the car, ignoring the watching police, and drove it slowly down Neue Königstrasse towards the city centre. He knew there was nothing more he could do, but that knowledge did nothing to diminish the sense of anger and helplessness that dogged him through the rest of that day and the next. By the time he entered the British Embassy on Friday morning he felt ready to explode, but was equally certain that murdering anyone other than Hitler would only make matters worse.

British entry visas for the three Wiesner children were waiting on Unsworth's desk, but Unsworth had the decency not to be too pleased with himself. 'I've found out why the mother's been refused,' he told Russell. 'Our intelligence people have quite a dossier on her. She was a Spartacist – you know what they were? Of course you do. Apparently they grade communists out of ten, and anyone scoring over seven is refused immigration. Eva Wiesner's an eight.'

Russell was astonished. 'How recent is this information?'

'It isn't. The dossier has nothing later than 1919, so she probably gave up politics when she got married. But that won't help her. An eight's an eight – that's what their man told me ...'

'Trelawney-Smythe?'

'You've met him? No exceptions, he said.'

Russell didn't know whether to laugh or cry. 'I don't suppose it matters,' he said, before explaining about Albert.

Half an hour later he was back in Friedrichshain. This time Frau Wiesner opened the door, and managed a slight smile as she let him in. After brushing aside his condolences, she sat him down and made them both coffee. 'He was a wonderful man,' she said. 'And nothing can take that away from him, or from me.'

He gave her the British entry visas for the three children, and explained why she was being refused.

She smiled sadly at that. 'I thought that must be the reason,' she said, 'but it doesn't matter now. Take this back,' she added, handing over Albert's visa – 'Someone else can take his place.'

He also gave her the safety deposit box key, and a piece of paper containing two names and addresses. 'This is the bank where the box is, and this is my agent in London, Solly Bernstein. Get the girls to memorize it all, and then burn it,' he said. 'And I think it would probably be safer for you to keep the key yourself. Solly has another one, and they can use that when they get to London.'

She stared at the writing, as if it was in a foreign language.

'Have you seen Albert?' he asked.

She shook her head. 'But he's all right.'

After leaving Effi at the studio early the next morning, he took the car back to her street and walked to Zoo tation. With an hour to wait for the Warsaw train, he had breakfast in the buffet before climbing up to the eastbound platforms. It was the first time, he realised, that he'd been up there since McKinley's death. He had no idea where the American had gone under his train, and a morbid search for tell-tale signs came up empty. If there was one thing the Germans were good at, it was cleaning up after themselves.

He put five pfennigs in a burnt almond machine, and walked down the platform feeding from his cupped hand. It was a misty morning, the trees in the Tiergarten fading by stages into nothing. Some geese flew across the glass dome of the station, squawking noisily, heading God-knew-where considering it was late February. There were few finer sights, Russell thought, as their V-formation curled and furled like a banner in the wind. He remembered the seagulls at the *Bismarck* launching, and laughed out loud.

The Warsaw train arrived, empty save for the few who had boarded at Charlottenburg. Russell found his seat by the time it reached Friedrichstrasse, and dropped off to sleep as the last of the south-eastern suburbs slid past his window. Dimly aware of the stop at Frankfurt-am-Oder, he was roused by officialdom for the customs stops on either side of the Polish border, and spent the rest of the journey staring out of the restaurant car window. A wintry sun had finally burnt off the mists, and the rye and potato fields of Prussia's lost province stretched away into the distance, interrupted only by the occasional dirt-track or farm, the odd meandering stream.

The train rolled into Posen – or Poznan, as the plethora of signs proclaimed – a few minutes early. Russell took a taxi from the forecourt to the Bazar hotel, where he'd booked a room. 'Just the one night?' the receptionist asked incredulously, as if the charms of Posen required weeks to appreciate. 'Just the one,' Russell agreed, and was shown rather begrudgingly to an adequate first floor room. There were only a few hours of light remaining, so he went straight back out again, pausing only to examine the display in the lobby, which documented the hotel's pre-war role as a hotbed of Polish nationalism.

The town, though pleasant enough, suffered by comparison to Cracow. Its churches were not quite as beautiful, its streets not quite as charming, its square – the Stary Rynek – not quite as grand. As he wandered somewhat aimlessly around the city centre he noticed several faded German names on streets and buildings, but the German language was still audible on those same streets, along with Polish and Yiddish. It would take another war, Russell thought, before the winners could take it all.

He dined in the hotel restaurant. The veal escalopes – *zrazikis* – were excellent, the wine surprisingly good, but neither could dispel his deepening depression. It wasn't just McKinley and Wiesner – he had hardly spent two waking hours with Effi since Rügen Island, and his contact with Paul since returning from England had consisted of two friendly, but brief, telephone conversations. And here he was in the gloom of Posen, waiting for Shchepkin to go through one of his cloak-and-dagger mating rituals.

He went back to his room, hoping against hope for a simple knock on the door. An hour or so later he got one, but it wasn't Shchepkin. A short woman in a long skirt and blouse brushed past him and into the room before he could say anything.

'Close the door, Mr Russell,' she said. The language was definitely German, but not a sort that Russell had ever heard before.

The woman had roughly parted blonde hair which just failed to reach her shoulders, blue-eyes, thin lips and heavily accented cheekbones. In another life she might have been attractive, Russell thought, but in this one she wasn't really trying. She wore no make-up, and her cream-coloured blouse badly needed a wash. He now remembered seeing her on the other side of the dining-room, arguing with one of the waiters.

'John Russell,' she said, as much to herself as him. 'I am your new contact.'

'Contact with whom?' he asked. It was hard to imagine her as a Gestapo agent provocateur, but how would he know?

'My name is Irina Borskaya,' she said patiently. 'I am here in place of Comrade Shchepkin,' she added, glancing round the room and finding a chair.

'Has something happened to Comrade Shchepkin?' Russell asked.

'He has been re-assigned. Now, please sit down Mr Russell. And let us get down to business.'

Russell did as he was told, feeling a pang of sorrow for Shchepkin. He could see him on the Cracow citadel – 'You really should wear a hat!' But why assume the worst? Perhaps he really had been re-assigned. Stalin couldn't kill everyone who'd ever worked for him.

He pulled the latest article out of his briefcase and handed it over. She took a cursory glance at the first page and placed it in her lap. 'You were asked to talk to armament workers.'

He recounted his visit to the Greiner works, the conversations he had had with Labour Front officials and ordinary workers. She listened intently but took no notes. 'Is that all?' she said when he was finished.

'For the moment,' Russell said. 'Where is your accent from?' he asked, partly out of curiosity, partly to take her mind off his skimpy research.

'I was born in Saratov,' she said. 'In the Volga region. Now, we have another job for you …'

Here it comes, Russell thought – the point of the whole exercise.

'We need you to collect some papers from one of our people and bring them out of Germany.'

Not a chance, Russell thought. But refuse nicely, he told himself. 'What sort of papers?' he asked.

'That doesn't concern you.'

'It does if you expect me to bring them out.'

'They are naval plans,' she said grudgingly.

Russell burst out laughing.

'What is so amusing?' she asked angrily.

He told her about Shchepkin's comment in Danzig – 'None of those naval plans Sherlock Holmes is always having to recover.'

She wasn't amused. 'This is not a Sherlock Holmes story – the comrade in Kiel has risked his life to get a copy of the German fleet dispositions for the Baltic.'

'Then why not risk it again to bring them out?' Russell argued.

'His life is worth something,' she said tartly, and quickly realised that she had gone too far. 'He is too valuable to risk,' she amended, as if he might have mistaken her meaning.

'Then why not send someone else in to get them?'

'Because we have you,' she said. 'And we have already established that you can come and go without arousing suspicion. Were you searched on your way here, or on your way to Cracow?'

'No, but I wasn't carrying anything.'

She put the article on the carpet beside her chair, crossed her legs and smoothed out the skirt on her thigh with her left hand. 'Mr Russell, are you refusing to help us with this?'

'I'm a journalist, Comrade Borskaya. Not a secret agent.'

She gave him an exasperated look, delved into her skirt pocket and brought out a rather crumpled black and white photograph. It was of him and Shchepkin, emerging from the Wawel Cathedral.

Russell looked at it and laughed.

'You are easily amused,' she said.

'So they tell me. If you send that to the Gestapo I might get thrown out of Germany. If I get caught with your naval plans it'll be the axe. Which do you think worries me more?'

'If we send this to the Gestapo you are certain to be deported, certain to lose your son and your beautiful bourgeois girlfriend. If you do this job for us, the chances of your being caught are almost non-existent. You will be well-paid, and you will have the satisfaction of supporting world socialism in its struggle against fascism. According to Comrade Shchepkin, that was once important to you.'

'Once.' The clumsiness of the approach angered him more than the blackmail itself. He got up off the bed and walked across to the window, telling himself to calm down. As he did so, an idea came to him. An idea that seemed both crazy and compelling.

He turned to her. 'Let me sleep on this,' he said. 'Think about it overnight,' he explained, in response to her blank expression.

She nodded. 'Two p.m. in the Stary Rynek,' she said, as if she'd had the time and place in reserve.

'It's a big square,' Russell said.

'I'll find you.'

Sunday was overcast but dry. Russell had coffee in one of the many Stary Rynek cafés, walked up past the Garbary station to the Citadel, and found a bench overlooking the city. For several minutes he just sat there enjoying the view: the multiplicity of spires, the Warta River and its receding bridges, the smoke rising from several thousand chimneys. 'See how much peace the earth can give,' he murmured to himself. A comforting thought, provided you ignored the source. It was a line from Mayakovsky's suicide note.

Was his own plan a roundabout way of committing suicide?

Paul and Effi would miss him. In fact, he liked to think they'd both be heartbroken, at least for a while. But he was neither indispensable nor irreplaceable. Paul had other people who loved him, and so did Effi.

All of which would only matter if he got caught. The odds, he thought, were probably on his side. The Soviets would have no compunction about risking him, but their precious naval plans were another matter – they wouldn't risk those on a no-hope adventure. They had to believe it would work.

But what did he know? There could be ruses within ruses; this could be some ludicrously Machiavellian plot the NKVD had thought up on some drunken weekend and set in motion before they sobered up. Or everyone concerned could be an incompetent. Or just having a bad day.

'Shit,' he muttered to himself. He liked the idea of the Soviets having the German fleet dispositions for the Baltic. He liked the idea of doing something, no matter how small, to put a spoke in the bastards' wheels. And he really wanted the favours he intended asking in return.

But was he fooling himself? Falling for all the usual nonsense, playing boys' games with real ammunition. When did self-sacrifice become a warped form of selfishness?

There were no answers to any of this, he realised. It was like jumping through an open window with a fuzzy memory of which floor you were on. If it turned out to be the ground floor, you bounced to your feet with an heroic grin. The fifth, and you were jam on the pavement. Or, more likely, a Gestapo courtyard.

A life concerned only with survival was a thin life. He needed to jump. For all sorts of reasons, he needed to jump.

He took a long last look at the view and started back down the slope, imagining the details of his plan as he did so. A restaurant close to the Stary Rynek provided him with a plate of meat turnovers, a large glass of Silesian beer, and ample time to imagine the worst. By two o'clock he was slowly circling the large and well-populated square, and manfully repressing the periodic impulse simply to disappear into one of the adjoining streets.

She appeared at his shoulder halfway through his second circuit, her ankle-length coat unbuttoned to reveal the same skirt and blouse. This time, he thought, there was worry in the eyes.

She managed to leave the question unspoken for about thirty metres, and then asked it with almost angry abruptness – 'So, will you do this job for us?'

'With one condition,' Russell told her. 'I have a friend, a Jewish friend, in Berlin. The police are looking for him, and he needs to get out of the country. You get him across the border, and I will do the job for you.'

'And how are we supposed to get him across the border?' she asked, suspicion in her tone.

'The same way you always have,' Russell said. 'I was in the Party myself once – remember? I knew people in the Pass-Apparat,' he added, stretching the truth somewhat. 'Everyone knew about the escape routes into Belgium and Czechoslovakia.'

'That was many years ago.'

'Not according to my information,' Russell bluffed.

She was silent for about fifty metres. 'There are a few such routes,' she admitted. 'But they are not safe. If they were, we would not be asking you to bring out these papers. Maybe one person in three gets caught.'

'In Berlin it's more like three out of three.'

She sighed. 'I can't give you an answer now.'

'I understand that. Someone will have to contact me in Berlin to make the arrangements for my friend's journey, and to give me the details of the job you want me to do. Tell your bosses that the moment my friend calls me from outside the Reich, I will collect your papers from wherever they are and bring them out.'

'Very well,' she said after a moment's thought. 'You had better choose a point of contact in Berlin.'

'The buffet at Zoo station. I shall be there every morning this week. Between nine and ten.'

She nodded approvingly. 'And a mark of identification. A book works well.'

'*Storms of Steel*? No, half the customers could be reading that. Something English.' He mentally pictured his bookshelves at Neuenburgerstrasse. 'Dickens. *Martin Chuzzlewit*.'

'A good choice,' she agreed, though whether for literary or other reasons she didn't say. 'Your contact will say that he's been meaning to read it, and will ask you if it's any good.'

'He?' Russell asked.

'Or she,' she conceded.

Nine o'clock on Monday morning found him in the Zoo station buffet, his dog-eared copy of *Martin Chuzzlewit* prominently displayed on the counter beside his cup of mocha. He wasn't expecting the Soviets to respond that quickly, and he wasn't disappointed – ten o'clock came and went with no sign of any contact. He collected the car from outside the zoo and drove across town to the Wiesners. There was no obvious police presence outside, which probably meant that they'd recruited some local busybody for their observation chores. A curtain twitched as he walked up the outside steps, but that could have been coincidence.

The sense of raw pain had gone from the Wiesners' flat – replaced by a grim busyness, a determination to do whatever needed doing. There was grief to spare, the faces seemed to say – no need to spend it all at once.

And there was good news, Frau Wiesner told him. They had old friends in England, she said, in Manchester. The Doctor had written to them several weeks ago, and a reply had finally arrived, offering a temporary home for the girls. They had tickets to travel a week from Thursday.

'I may have more good news,' Russell told her. 'I have friends who may be willing to smuggle Albert across the border.'

Mother and daughters all stared at him in amazement. 'What friends?' Frau Wiesner asked.

'The comrades,' he said simply. The comrades they had both abandoned, he thought.

'But I had no idea you were ...'

'Like you, I left a long time ago. And I can't go into details about the arrangements. But if I can fix things, can you get in touch with Albert at short notice?'

'Yes.' The hope in her eyes was painful to see.

'And will he trust me, do you think?

She smiled at that. 'Yes, he likes you.'

'And if we can get him out, there is nothing to keep you here?'

'The lack of a visa. Nothing else.'

'I'm still working on that.'

He tried to write that afternoon, but the words refused to matter. As evening fell he took himself off to the Alhambra and sat through an overblown Hollywood musical, murmuring sour asides to himself in the dark. The film had been made on the sort of budget which would feed a small country, but was mercifully devoid of consciousness-raising pretensions. The consciousness-lowering effect was presumably accidental.

As he emerged the Ku'damm was gearing up for the night, thick with human and motorised traffic. He walked slowly westwards with no real destination in mind, looking in windows, studying faces, wondering if the Soviets would agree to his terms. People queued outside the theatres and cinemas, streamed in and out of the restaurants, most of them laughing or happily talking, living the moment as best they could. A police car careened up the centre of the wide road, its siren parting the traffic like waves, but the visible signs of a police state were thin on the ground. In fact, Russell thought, it was the absence of violence which told the real story. The blood and the broken glass, the groups of men on corners, clutching their razors and itching for a brawl – they were all gone. The only violent law-breakers left on the streets of Berlin were the authorities.

He walked back down the opposite pavement, picked up the car and drove home.

Tuesday offered more of the same: waiting in vain at the buffet counter, working with words like a juggler in mittens. Frau Heidegger seemed irritating rather than quirky, Paul almost provokingly gung-ho in his description of the previous Saturday's *Jungvolk* outing. Even the weather was bad: a cold rain fell throughout the day and into the evening, creating lake-size puddles in many of the streets. The Hanomag, as Russell discovered on his way to collect Effi, had a less than waterproof floor.

At least her film was finished. 'I have seen the error of my ways, and a good wife is all I want to be!' she exclaimed as they left the studio. 'But only,' she added as they reached the car, 'after I've slept for at least a week. In the meantime you may wait on me hand and foot.'

Later, he was still working up to telling her about his weekend in Posen when he realised she'd fallen asleep. Which was all for the best, he decided. There'd be time enough for explanations if and when the Soviets said yes. As he looked down at her sleeping face, the familiar lips ever-so-slightly curled in a sleeper's smile, the whole business seemed utterly absurd.

* * *

Contact was made on Thursday. The buffet clock was reaching towards ten when a man loomed over Russell's shoulder and almost whispered the pre-arranged sentence. 'Let's walk,' he added, before Russell had time to declaim on the virtues or otherwise of *Martin Chuzzlewit*.

The man made for the door with what seemed unnecessary haste, leaving Russell floundering in his wake. He seemed very young, Russell thought, but he looked anonymous enough: average height and build, tidy hair and a typical German face. His suit was wearing at the elbows, his shoes at the heels.

At the station exit he turned towards the nearest Tiergarten entrance, pausing for a nervous look back as they reached it. Russell glanced back himself – the street was empty. Ahead of them, a few solitary walkers were visible among the leafless trees.

'It's not a bad day,' the young man said, looking up at the mostly grey sky. 'We will walk to Bellevue station, like friends enjoying a morning stroll in the park.'

They set off through the trees.

'I am Gert,' the young man said. 'And it is agreed. We will take your friend across the Czech border, and you will bring the papers to us in Prague.' He fell silent, as a steady stream of walkers passed them in the opposite direction – a middle-aged couple and their poodles, a younger couple arm in arm, an older man with a muzzled Doberman – and paused to offer Russell a cigarette on the Lichtenstein Bridge across the Landwehrkanal. The young man's hand, Russell noticed reluctantly, was shaking slightly.

The paths around the Neuersee were mostly deserted, just a couple of women with small children happily feeding the ducks. 'You must memorise the arrangements,' Gert said, with the air of someone reading from a script. 'Your friend must be in the station buffet at Görlitz at five o'clock on Monday afternoon.

He must wear workingmen's clothes, with a blue scarf around his neck. He must not have a suitcase or bag of any kind. When a man asks him if he knows where the left luggage is he should say, "Yes, but it's easier to show you than explain," and walk out with that man. Understood?'

'Yes.'

'Then repeat what I've just told you.'

Russell did so.

'Good. Now for your part. Your contact is in Kiel. Or in Gaarden, to be precise. You must be in the Germania Bar – it's on the tram route to Wellingdorf, just outside the main entrance to the Deutsche Werke shipyards – at 8 p.m. on Friday the 10th. With your *Martin Chuzzlewit*.'

'I made it clear to the comrade in Posen that I wouldn't collect your papers until I knew my friend was safe.'

Gert gave an exasperated sigh. 'He will be in Czechoslovakia by Tuesday morning, Prague by the afternoon. You should hear from him that day. Either that, or some of our people have been captured or killed with him. And if that happens, we hope you will honour their memory by honouring the bargain.'

Russell gave him a look. 'Let's hope it doesn't come to that.'

'Of course. Now, you will bring the papers back to Berlin, and then take them on to Prague as quickly as possible …'

'I have to be in Berlin on that Sunday,' Russell said.

'It would better if you travelled before that. The border guards tend to be less vigilant on a Saturday night.'

'Sorry, it'll have to be Monday,' Russell said. The Sunday was Paul's birthday.

Gert controlled himself with a visible effort. 'Very well,' he agreed, as if he'd made a huge concession.

'And how do you suggest I carry them?'

This was clearly in the script. 'We do not know how many papers there are. If it is a matter of a few sheets, they can be sewn into a lining, of your coat or your jacket. If there are a lot, then that will not be possible. If they search you and your luggage, they will probably find them. The best thing is not to be searched.'

'And how do I manage that?'

'You probably won't have to. They only search about one in ten, and foreigners very rarely. As long as you don't draw attention to yourself, everything should be fine. Now, once you reach Prague, you must check in to the Grand Hotel on Wenceslas Square. You will be contacted there. Is that clear? Now please repeat the details of your *treff* in Kiel.'

Russell repeated them. 'What if no one approaches me on that day?' he asked.

'Then you return to Berlin. Any other questions?' Gert's hands seemed to be writhing in his coat pockets.

He had none, or none that could be answered. At Bellevue station they went their separate ways, Gert bounding up the stairs to the eastbound Stadtbahn platform, Russell ambling along the bank of the Spree to the kiosk beneath the Bellevue Schloss. He bought a cup of hot chocolate, took it to a riverside table, and watched a long train rumbling across the bridge to his left. 'Everything should be fine,' he told himself in Gert's Bavarian accent. It was the 'should' which worried him.

His next stop was the British Embassy. Rather than return for the car, he walked down the river to Kurfürstenplatz, and then along Zellen Allee to the Brandenburg Gate and the western end of Unter den Linden. The queue outside the Embassy seemed longer than ever, the atmosphere inside the usual mix of irritation and self-righteousness. He asked to see Unsworth, and was shown up to his office. Once there, he admitted it was Trelawney-Smythe that he really wanted to see. 'But I didn't want to announce that in reception,' he explained to Unsworth. 'I wouldn't put it past the Nazis to include an informer or two among the Jews.'

Unsworth looked slightly shocked at the thought, but agreed to escort Russell to the MI6 man's door. Trelawney-Smythe looked startled to see him, and somewhat put out. 'I know why you're here, and the answer is no. We cannot make exceptions.'

Russell sat himself down. 'I take it this room's secure,' he said.

'We went over the whole building with a fine toothcomb a few months ago,' Trelawney-Smythe said proudly.

Russell looked up, half expecting to see a microphone hanging from the ceiling. 'How interested would the Admiralty be in the German navy's Baltic fleet dispositions?' he asked.

To his credit, Trelawney-Smythe didn't jump out of his seat. Instead, he reached for his pipe. 'Very, I should imagine. After all, if a ship's in the Baltic it won't be in the North Sea.'

'That's the conclusion I came to,' Russell said. He smiled at the other man. 'Don't ask me how, but at some point in the next two weeks I should have my hands on those dispositions. Not to keep, mind you, and not for long. But long enough to copy them out.'

Trelawney-Smythe lit his pipe, puffing vigorously out of the corner of his mouth.

A technique learned in spy school, Russell thought.

'You would be doing a tremendous service to your country,' the other man said in an almost torpid tone.

'But not only for my country. There's a price.'

'Ah.' Trelawney-Smythe's eyes narrowed. 'You want money,' he said, with the air of a disappointed vicar.

'I want you to make an exception, and come up with a visa for Eva Wiesner. And while you're at it, I'd like an American passport.'

That surprised the MI6 man. 'How on earth do you expect us to get you one of those?'

'I'm sure you'll have no trouble if you set your mind to it. I do have an American mother, you know, so it's hardly a huge stretch.'

'Why do you want one?'

'I'd have thought that was obvious. If there's a war in Europe, anyone with a British passport will be sent home. With an American passport I can stay.'

Trelawney-Smythe puffed at his pipe, digesting the idea, and Russell watched the slight widening of the eyes as he appreciated the possibilities – MI6 would have a man in Germany once the war started!

Not that Russell had any intention of doing anything more for them, but they weren't to know that.

'In the next two weeks, you said.'

'Yes. But I want the visa for Eva Wiesner by Monday. That should give her time to arrange her exit visa, and she can travel with her daughters on Thursday. There's no hurry about the passport,' he added. 'So long as I have it before a war breaks out.'

'You must like this family,' Trelawney-Smythe said, sounding almost human.

'I do. The girls have only just lost their father, and there's no good reason why they should lose their mother as well. She left the communists twenty years ago, for God's sake. She's not going to start a revolution in Golders Green.'

'I hope not,' Trelawney-Smythe said wryly. 'All right. I can get her a visa by Monday. The passport … I can't promise anything – the Yanks dig their heels in about the silliest things – but we'll do our best. You weren't born in America, were you?'

'I was born in mid-Atlantic, if that helps. But on a British ship.'

'Probably not, then.' He was sounding almost chummy now.

'I'll see you then,' Russell said, resisting the temptation to be churlish. On his way out he noticed that the reading room was empty, and took time to consult the Embassy atlas. Görlitz was about two hundred kilometres south-east of Berlin, and about twenty from the Czech border. There were direct trains from Berlin, but they took most of the day and were probably checked as they neared the border area. If Albert got safely through the ticket barrier at this end he'd probably be picked up at the other. Russell was going to have to take him in the car.

There were two obvious routes: he could stick to the old road or take the Silesian Autobahn to just south of Cottbus, and join it there. He liked the idea of escaping Hitler's Germany by Autobahn, but the old road, for reasons he couldn't explain, felt safer.

So, two hundred kilometres – say, three hours. Stick in an extra half-hour in case he had a puncture. If the car broke down they were sunk, but spending more than a few minutes in Görlitz, with Albert eye-wrestling anyone in uniform, seemed like an excellent way of committing suicide. When it came down to it, the car seemed worthier of trust than Albert's temperament.

Russell walked out to Unter den Linden, climbed into the Hanomag and headed east. If only Albert didn't look so damned Jewish! The boy could hardly wear a mask, though the lifelike Goebbels mask which one of the American correspondents had made for last year's Halloween party would have been entertaining. How could he hide the boy's face? A cap over the eyes, perhaps. Collar turned up and the required blue scarf. A pair of glasses? None of it would help if Albert insisted on visibly seething with rage.

And where was he going to pick him up? Not at the flat, that was for sure. Somewhere crowded? Only if it was somewhere a Jew didn't stick out like a sore thumb, and places like that were thin on the ground. And the police would be looking for him – a Jew who knocked down a Gestapo officer with a table lamp was going to be high on their wanted list. They'd probably taken his picture in Sachsenhausen, and now all the Orpo stations would have copies hanging on their walls.

He parked the car in the Wiesners' street and went up. The girls were out – starting to say their 'goodbyes' – and their mother seemed exhausted by grief and worry. Russell told her about Albert's Monday appointment in Görlitz, and his own role as chauffeur. 'Tell him to join the visa queue outside the British Embassy between twelve and one – as one Jew among several hundred he should be invisible. I'll walk by and collect him soon after one. He should be wearing workingmen's clothes, nothing too smart. But a decent coat on top of them for the queue. People try to look their best for the Embassy.'

'I will tell him.'

'He must be there,' Russell insisted. 'If he's not, that's it. We won't be given a second chance.'

'He'll be there.'

'And I think I've got you a visa. You should be able to go with the girls next Thursday.'

She looked as though she was having trouble believing it all. 'We'll know by then? About Albert?'

'We should,' he said. One way or the other.

Russell's weekend followed the familiar pattern, but thoughts of the week ahead kept spinning around his head, sending his stomach into momentary freefall. It wasn't every week he delivered a fugitive from the Gestapo to the communist underground, went looking for military secrets in a dockside bar, and played some lethal form of hunt-the-parcel with the border police. In fact, it wasn't any week, and he was scared. The only time he could remember feeling like this was in the trenches, on those few occasions when he'd been ordered over the top. What had he let himself in for?

Paul was too distracted himself to notice his father's distraction. On Saturday they did the rounds of Berlin's best toy-shops, so that Paul could provide Russell with some useful hints on which birthday presents to surprise him with. On Sunday they went to another away game, at Viktoria Berlin's stadium in Steglitz, and came away delighted with a fortunate draw. Paul was still full of the trip to London, and eager to know when they could visit his grandmother in New York. 'Maybe this summer,' Russell said, surprising himself. But why not? The money was there.

Effi did notice. On Saturday evening they went to a Comedy Theatre revue involving friends of hers, and he twice needed prodding to join in the applause. An hour's dancing in one of the halls off Alexanderplatz took his mind off everything else, but on the drive home he almost drove through a red light at Potsdamerplatz.

'What's eating you?' she asked.

As they drove along the southern edge of the Tiergarten he gave her the whole story of his dealings with Shchepkin and Borskaya, ending with the request to take out the documents, and his realisation that he could use the situation to help the Wiesners. 'Seduced by my own cleverness,' he admitted. 'And now I feel like digging myself a very deep hole and hiding in it.'

'Like a fox?'

'More like a rabbit.'

She took his right hand and squeezed it.

Glancing to his right, he could see the worry in her face. 'I can't back out now,' he said.

'Of course not. Why don't we stop here?' she added.

He pulled up under the trees, and turned to face her.

'You couldn't go on the way you were,' she said.

'What do you mean?'

She took his hand again. 'You know what I mean,' she insisted. And he did.

Monday was a rush. Effi insisted on coming to the Embassy with him – 'Everyone says I look Jewish, so they'll think I'm his sister' – and then displayed her usual inability to be ready on time. Once Russell had finally got her to the car, he suddenly remembered, with another downward lurch of his stomach, that he'd forgotten to tell Eva Wiesner about the blue scarf. A ten-minute search for something suitable in the Ka-De-We on Wittenbergerplatz made them five minutes late, a derailed tram in Potsdamerplatz five minutes more. Russell had a mental picture of a Gestapo officer walking along beside the queue, then suddenly stopping and pointing at Albert.

They left the car on Dorotheenstrasse and walked the single block to the Unter de Linden. Across the wide, now *lindenfrei* avenue, they could see the queue stretching up Wilhelmstrasse past the side of the Adlon. There were no uniforms in sight, no pointing finger, no scuffle in progress.

They crossed Unter den Linden and walked towards the end of the queue. Albert was about ten from the back, standing close to the stone building on his right, but making no effort to conceal himself. When he saw Russell he simply walked out of the queue. 'This is hopeless,' he said to no one in particular. 'I'll come back tomorrow.'

'We were looking for you,' Russell said. 'The car's this way,' he added, thinking that he'd seen pantomimes with more convincing scripts. Several facial expressions in the queue offered unwelcome confirmation of this opinion.

But there was no sign of the audience that mattered. The three of them walked back to Dorotheenstrasse.

'In the back,' Russell told Albert, indicating the tight space behind the seats. He drove three blocks down Dorotheenstrasse, turned right onto the much busier Friedrichstrasse and headed south towards Hallesches Tor. He dropped Effi off by the elevated station.

'Be careful,' she said, as she kissed him goodbye through the driver's window. 'I'll see you tonight.'

I hope so, Russell thought. He glanced across at Albert, who was now sitting beside him. The boy looked about sixteen.

'How old are you?' he asked.

'I was eighteen last month.'

The age I was when I went to war, Russell thought. A tram swung in front of him, causing him to brake sharply. Concentrate, he told himself. An accident now really would be fatal.

They drove past Tempelhof as a small plane took off, then under the Ringbahn and on towards Mariendorf, the city growing thinner with each mile. A police car went past in the opposite direction, two plain-clothes Kripo men chatting in the front seats, but that was all. Twenty minutes after leaving Dorotheenstrasse they were out on the lake-strewn Mittelmark, passing under a completed section of the orbital Autobahn.

So far, so good, Russell thought.

'My mother gave me the message from my father,' Albert said, breaking the silence. 'What exactly did he say?'

Russell repeated what he remembered.

'They beat him badly, didn't they?' Albert asked.

'Yes, they did.'

Albert fell silent again. They passed through Zossen, where a surfeit of signs pointed would-be visitors in the direction of

General Staff HQ. The complex of buildings came into view, and Russell found himself wondering which maps the planners had on the tables that day. Poland, most likely, and all points east.

He wondered if the Soviets would put up a fight. Their German operation was hardly impressive – a boy with shaky hands and a man in Kiel they couldn't risk. Where had all the communists gone? Seven years ago they'd been slugging it out with the Nazis – millions of them. Some would still be lying in wait for the right moment, but most, he suspected, had simply turned their backs on politics. He hoped that whoever was waiting in Görlitz knew what the hell he was doing.

'Where have you been staying?' he asked Albert, once they were back in open country.

'It's better you don't know,' the boy said.

'It probably is,' Russell agreed.

Silence descended again. Albert seemed calm enough, Russell thought. Calmer, in fact, than he felt himself. At least the car was behaving, its engine purring smoothly as they cruised along the mostly deserted road at 65 kph. Everyone else had chosen the Autobahn.

The sky to the south seemed clearer, which suggested a cold, clear night. Did that augur well or badly for an illicit border crossing? Visibility would be better for everyone – pursuers and pursued. He tried to remember what phase the moon was in, and couldn't.

Albert had rescued the *Beobachter* from the floor between them. 'Why do you read this rubbish?' he asked, scanning the front page.

'To know what they're doing,' Russell said.

Albert grunted disapproval.

'Which reminds me,' Russell went on. 'There's a piece in there about the crisis in Ruthenia …'

'Ruthenia? Where's that?'

'It's part of Czechoslovakia. Look, you need to know this stuff. Czechoslovakia is more than Czechs and Slovaks. There's Moravians and Hungarians and God knows who else. And Ruthenians. The Germans are encouraging all these groups to rebel against the Czechoslovak government, in the hope that they'll provoke a major crackdown. Once that happens, they'll march in themselves, saying that they're the only ones who can restore order and protect these poor victimised minorities.'

'All right.'

'And the Czech government has started taking action against the Ruthenians. Read the piece. See how pleased the Germans are. "This is not the sort of behaviour that any government could tolerate in a neighbouring state," etc – you can practically see them rubbing their hands with glee. They're preparing the ground. So keep an eye on the news. Don't hang around in Prague any longer than you have to, or you'll find Hitler's caught up with you.'

'I have the names of people in Prague,' Albert insisted. 'They will tell me.'

'Good. But remember *Kristallnacht* – and what a surprise that was, even after five years of persecution. If I were you, I'd head for Hungary as soon as I could. Once you're there you can work out the best way to England.'

'I don't think I will be going to England. My plan is to go to Palestine.'

'Oh,' Russell said, taken by surprise. 'Does your mother know?'

'Of course. I am a man now. I must do what is best for the whole family. When I get work and somewhere to live, I can send for them.'

'Immigration is restricted.'

'I know that. But we will find a way.'

'If there's a war, they'll stop it altogether.'

'Then we will wait.'

They were entering Cottbus now, and Russell concentrated on not drawing attention to his driving. But the market town seemed caught in its afternoon nap, and they were soon back in open country. A few kilometres more, and they passed under the Silesian Autobahn. Their road grew suddenly busier, and a sign announced that they were ninety-three kilometres from Görlitz.

It was not yet three o'clock. At this rate they would arrive far too early. They needed one of those stopping places with a view which the Germans loved so much.

The Germans, Russell repeated to himself. After fifteen years of living there, of feeling a little more German each year, the process seemed to have slipped into reverse. Lately, he seemed to be feeling a little less German each day. But not more English. So what did that make him?

'Why are you doing this?' Albert asked him.

Russell just shrugged. 'Who knows?'

'The reason I ask – a year ago, before *Kristallnacht*, I used to wonder how people could be so cruel, but I never questioned why someone was kind. Now it's the opposite. I can see all sorts of reasons why people are cruel, but kindness is becoming a mystery.'

He was six years older than Paul, Russell thought. Just six years. He tried to think of an adequate answer to Albert's question.

'Whatever the reason, I thank you anyway,' Albert said. 'My family thanks you.'

'I think there are many reasons,' Russell said. 'Some good, some not so good. Some I don't understand myself. I like your family. Maybe it's as simple as that.' And maybe, he thought, any half-decent family in the Wiesners' situation would have been enough to push him off his fence.

The phrase 'I used to be a good journalist,' passed through his mind, leaving him wondering where it had come from. This had nothing to do with journalism. He thought about McKinley's papers, uselessly hidden in the poste restante, and came, with a sudden lift of the heart, to a realisation so obvious that he couldn't believe he had missed it. If he was going to risk his life and liberty for a few military secrets, then why not take out McKinley's papers as well? He had only one head to cut off.

The road was climbing now, and the sky was almost cloudless. Around ten kilometres from Görlitz Russell found the stopping place he had been looking for, a wide gravelled ledge overlooking a pretty river. Eager to stretch, they both got out, and Russell ran through the arranged script for the Görlitz buffet. 'Once you are in Prague, the first thing you must do – the first thing – is to telephone me. Your mother won't leave Germany until she knows you're safe.'

'You haven't given me the number,' Albert said sensibly.

Russell made him repeat it several times, wondering as he did so how long the boy would resist a Gestapo interrogation.

Albert seemed to know what he was thinking. 'I won't give you up,' he said simply.

'None of us know what we'll do in a situation like that.'

'I won't get into a situation like that,' Albert said, pulling a grubby-looking Luger from his coat pocket.

Oh shit, Russell thought, glancing left and right in search of approaching traffic and barking: 'Put it away!' The road was blissfully empty. 'That's ...' he started to say, and stopped himself. What right did he have to give the boy advice? Albert had been in Sachsenhausen once, and his father had died there. It wasn't hard to see why going out in a blaze of gunfire seemed preferable to going back.

He breathed out slowly. 'You have to leave the coat with me,' he said. 'Won't the gun be obvious in your jacket pocket?'

'I'll put it in my belt,' Albert said, and did so. He then took the coat off and offered Russell a 360-degree turn, like a model at a fashion show. The gun didn't show.

Back in the car, Albert pulled a workingmen's cap from a pocket of the discarded coat, and Russell reached into the Ka-De-We bag for the blue scarf. 'The recognition signal,' he explained, and Albert wrapped it around his neck, reminding Russell of Paul on a skating trip.

They drove on, the sky a deepening blue as dusk approached, the mountains slowly creeping above the southern horizon. As they reached the outskirts of Görlitz it occurred to Russell that anyone with a brain would have studied a plan of the town – the last thing he wanted to do was ask directions to the station. Go to the town centre and look for signs, he told himself. The Germans were good at signs.

He picked up some tram tracks and followed them in what seemed the obvious direction. After passing several large industrial concerns, the road narrowed through a handsome arch and arrived in a wide street full of old buildings. There were theatres, statues, a large water fountain – in any other circumstances, Görlitz would be worth an afternoon stroll.

'There!' Albert said, indicating a sign to the station.

They drove down a long straight street, towards what looked like a station. It was. The station building was about a hundred metres long, the entrance to the booking hall right in the centre. There were lighted windows to the left of this entrance, and steam billowing out of two large vents.

Russell pulled the car to a halt behind a Reichsbahn parcels lorry. 'The buffet,' he said, pointing it out. 'There'll be an entrance from the booking hall.'

It was ten to five.

Albert just sat there for a few seconds, then turned to shake

Russell's hand. The boy looked nervous now, Russell thought. 'Safe journey,' he said.

Albert climbed out and, without a backward look, headed towards the entrance. There was nothing furtive about his stride – if anything it was too upright. He leapt up the two steps and in through the doorway.

Start driving, Russell told himself, but he didn't. He sat there watching as the minutes passed. Two men in SA uniform emerged, laughing at something. A man ran in, presumably late for a train. Only seconds later a spasm of chuffs settled into the accelerating rhythm of a departing engine.

He imagined Albert sitting there, and wondered whether he'd tried to buy a coffee. If he had, he might have been refused; if he hadn't, some power-mad waiter might have tried to move him on. He imagined a challenge, the gun pulled out, the sound of shots and a frantic Albert flying out through the doorway. Russell wondered what would he do. Pick him up? Race out of Görlitz with the police in hot pursuit? What else could he do? His mouth seemed suddenly dry.

And then Albert did come out. There was another man with him, a shortish man in his forties with greying hair and a very red nose, who shifted his head from side to side like an animal sniffing for danger. The two of them walked across to the small open lorry with a timber load which Russell had already noticed, and swung themselves up into their respective cab seats. The engine burst into life and the lorry set off down the street, leaving a bright tail of exhaust hanging in the cold evening air.

Left luggage

After leaving Görlitz, Russell took the next available chance to telephone Effi. A brass band was practising in the first bar he tried, but with receiver and hand clamped tight against his ears he could just about hear the relief in her voice. 'I'll be waiting,' she said.

He chose the Autobahn north from Cottbus, hoping to speed the journey, but an overturned vehicle in a military convoy had the opposite effect. By the time he reached Friedrichshain it was almost nine o'clock. Frau Wiesner could hardly have opened the door any faster if she'd been waiting with her hand on the knob.

'He was collected,' Russell said, and her lips formed a defiant little smile.

'Sit down, sit down,' she said, eyes shining. 'I must just tell the girls.'

Russell did as he was told, noticing the bags of clothing piled against one wall. To be given away, he supposed – there was no way they would be allowed to take that much with them. He wondered if the Wiesners had any more valuables to take out, or whether the bulk of the family assets had been concealed behind the stickers in *Achievements of the Third Reich*. It occurred to him that Germany's Jews had several years' experience in the art of slipping things across the German border.

'And my visa has arrived,' Frau Wiesner said, coming back into the room. 'By special courier from the British Embassy this afternoon. You must have some influential friends.'

'I think you do,' Russell told her. 'I'm sure Doug Conway had a hand in it,' he explained, somewhat untruthfully. There seemed no reason for her to know about his deals with Irina Borskaya and Trelawney-Smythe. 'But there is something you might be able to do for me,' he added, and told her what he wanted. She said she would ask around.

He left her with a promise of driving over the moment Albert phoned, and a plea not to worry if the wait lasted more than a day. If they still hadn't heard anything by Thursday he knew she'd be reluctant to leave, even though they both knew that in this context no news was almost certain to be bad news.

On the other side of the city, Effi welcomed him with an intense embrace, and insisted on hearing every detail. Later, as they were going to bed, Russell noticed a new film script on the dressing table and asked her about it. It was a comedy, she told him. 'Twenty-three lines, four come-on smiles, and no jokes. The men got those.' But at least it was pointless, a quality which *Mother* had taught her to admire.

Next morning, Russell left her propped up in bed happily declaiming her lines to an empty room, and drove home to Neuenburgerstrasse. There was no sign of Frau Heidegger, and no messages on the board, from either Albert or the Gestapo. He went up to his room and read the newspaper, his door propped open in case the phone rang. The paper revealed that Jews had been forbidden to use either sleeping or restaurant cars on the Reichsbahn, on the grounds, no doubt, that they would appreciate their hunger more if they were kept awake.

He heard Frau Heidegger come in, and the clink of bottles as she set them beside her door. It was Tuesday, Russell realised – skat night. With Effi not working, and his own weekends given over to espionage, he was beginning to lose track of the days. He went down to warn her about his expected call, and paid the price in coffee.

Back upstairs, the hours ticked by with agonising slowness, and the only calls were for Dagmar, the plump little waitress from Pomerania who had taken McKinley's room. She, not unusually, was out. According to Frau Heidegger she sometimes came in at three in the morning with beer on her breath.

Russell nipped out to buy some eggs while Frau Heidegger kept guard, and cooked himself an omelette for dinner. Most of the other tenants returned home from work, and the concierges arrived, one by one, bottles in hand, to play skat. The waves of merriment reached higher up the stairs as the evening went on, but the telephone refused to ring, and Russell felt his anxiety grow. Where was Albert? Sitting in some border lock-up waiting to be picked up by the Gestapo? Or lying dead in some frozen mountain meadow? If so, he hoped the boy had managed to take some of the bastards with him.

The skat party broke up soon after 10.30, and once the other concierges had passed noisily into the street Frau Heidegger took the phone off the hook. Russell went to bed and started reading the John Kling novel which Paul had leant him. Next thing he knew, it was morning. He walked briskly down to Hallesches Tor for a paper, skipping through it on the way back for news of spies or criminals apprehended on the border. As he replaced the phone a red-eyed Frau Heidegger emerged with an invitation to coffee, and they both listened to the morning news on her People's Radio. The Führer had recovered from the slight illness which had caused the cancellation of several school visits on the previous day, but no young Jews named Albert had been picked up trying to cross into Czechoslovakia.

The morning passed at a snail's pace, bringing two more calls for Dagmar and one from Effi, wanting to know what was happening. Russell had no sooner put the phone down on her than it rung again. 'Forgot something?' he asked, but it was Albert's voice, indistinct but unmistakably triumphant, which came over the line. 'I'm in Prague,' it said, as if the Czech capital was as close to heaven as its owner had ever been.

'Thank God,' Russell shouted back. 'What took you so long?'

'We only came across last night. You'll tell my mother?'

'I'm on my way. And they'll be on the train tomorrow.'

'Thank you.'

'You're welcome. And good luck.'

Russell hung up the phone and stood beside it, blissfully conscious of the relief spreading out through his limbs. One down, three to go. He called Effi back with the good news and then set off for the Wiesners.

Frau Wiesner looked as if she hadn't slept since he left her on Monday, and when Russell told her Albert was in Prague she burst into tears. The two girls rushed to embrace her and started crying too.

After a minute or so she wiped her eyes and embraced Russell. 'A last coffee in Berlin,' she said, and sent the two girls out to buy cakes at a small shop on a nearby street which still sold to Jews. Once they were out of the door, she told Russell she had one last favour to ask. Disappearing into the other room, she re-emerged with a large framed photograph of her husband and a small suitcase. 'Would you keep this for me?' she asked, handing him the photograph. 'It is the best one I have, and I'm afraid they will take it away from me at the border. Next time you come to England …'

'Of course. Where is he, your husband? Did they bury him at Sachsenhausen?'

'I do not know,' she said. 'I did not tell you this, but on Monday, after the visa came, I gathered my courage, and I went to the Gestapo building on Prinz Albrechtstrasse. I asked if his body could be returned to me, or if they could just tell me where he is buried. A man was called for, and he came down to see me. He said that my son could claim my husband's body, but I could not. He said that was the legal position, but I knew he was lying. They were using my husband's body as bait to catch my son.'

Sometimes the Nazis could still take your breath away.

'And this,' she continued, picking up the suitcase, 'is what you asked for on Monday.' She put it on the table, clicked it open, and clicked again, revealing the false bottom. 'Before the Nazis, the man who made this was a famous leather craftsman in Wilmersdorf, and he has made over a hundred of these since coming to Friedrichshain.'

'And none have been detected?'

'He doesn't know. Once Jews have left they don't come back. A few have written to say that everything went well, but if it hadn't ...'

'They would be in no position to write.'

'Exactly.'

Russell sighed. 'Well, thank you anyway,' he said, just as the girls came back with a box of assorted cream cakes. They insisted on Russell having the first pick, then sat round the table happily licking the excess cream from their lips. When he suggested driving them to the station the next day, he could see how relieved Frau Wiesner was, and cursed himself for not putting her mind at rest sooner. How else could they have got there? Jews were not allowed to drive, and most cab-drivers wouldn't carry them. Which left public transport, and a fair likelihood of public abuse from their fellow passengers. Not the nicest way to say goodbye.

The train, she said, was at eleven, so he was back the next morning at half-past nine. The girls squeezed into the back with their small bags, Frau Wiesner in the front with a suitcase on her lap, and as they drove down Neue Königstrasse towards the city centre Russell watched the three of them craning their necks and filling their memories with the sights of their disappearing home.

Effi was waiting at the Zoo station entrance, and all five of them walked up to the westbound express platform. A pale sun was shining, and they stood in a little knot waiting for the train to arrive.

'You didn't tell me Albert was going to Palestine,' Russell said to Eva Wiesner.

'I should have,' she admitted. 'Distrust becomes a habit, I'm afraid.'

'And you?' he asked.

'I don't know. The girls prefer England. The clothes are better. And the movie stars.'

'You come see us in England?' Marthe asked him in English.

'I certainly will.'

'And you as well,' Marthe told Effi in German.

'I'd love to.'

The Hook of Holland train steamed in, hissing and squealing its way to a stop on the crowded platform. Russell carried Eva Wiesner's suitcase onto the train, and found their assigned seats. Much to his relief, there were no Stars of David scrawled on the girls' seatbacks. Once the three of them were settled he went in search of the car attendant, and found him in the vestibule. 'Look after those three,' he said, pointing them out and wedging a five hundred Reichsmark note in the man's outside pocket.

The attendant looked at the Wiesners again, probably to reassure himself that they weren't Jews. Fortunately, Eva Wiesner looked as aryan as anyone on the train.

Russell rejoined Effi on the platform. The signals were off, the train almost ready to go. A piercing shriek from the locomotive's whistle brought an answering scream from an animal in the adjoining zoo, and the train jerked into motion. The girls waved,

Eva Wiesner smiled, and they were gone. Russell and Effi stood arm in arm, watching the long train as it rumbled across the iron bridge and leant into the long curve beyond. Remember this moment, Russell told himself. This was what it was for.

After a quick lunch with Effi in the Café Uhlandeck he set off for Kiel. The Berlin–Hamburg Autobahn was still under construction, which left him with the old road through Schwerin and Lübeck, around 350 kilometres of two-lane highway across the gently undulating landscape of the North German plain. After three hours of this he began to wonder whether the train would have been better. The car had seemed a safer bet, but only, he realised, because he had fallen for the juvenile notion that it made escape seem more feasible. In reality, he had about as much chance of outrunning the Gestapo in the Hanomag as an aryan sprinter had of outrunning Jesse Owens.

He arrived in Kiel soon after dark, stopped at the railway station to buy a town guide at one of the kiosks, and studied it over a beer in the station buffet. Kiel itself stretched north along the western shore of a widening bay which eventually opened into the Baltic. Gaarden was on the other side of the bay, accessible by steam ferry or a tram ride around its southern end.

Russell decided on a hotel near the station – nothing too posh, nothing too seedy, and full of single businessmen leading relatively innocent lives. The Europaischer Hof, on the road which ran alongside the station, met the first two requirements, and on a busy day might have met the third. As it was, several lines of hopeful keys suggested the hotel was half empty, and when Russell asked for a room the receptionist seemed almost bemused by the scope for choice. They settled on a second floor room at the front, which looked out across the glass roof of the station, and the seagull colony which had been founded on it.

The hotel restaurant showed no signs of opening, so Russell walked north down the impressive Holstenstrasse and found an establishment with a decent selection of seafood. After eating he walked east in the general direction of the harbour, and found himself at the embarkation point for the Gaarden ferry. The ferry itself had left a few seconds earlier and was churning across the dark waters towards the line of lights on the far side, some half a kilometre away. Looking left, up the rapidly widening bay, Russell saw what looked like a large warship anchored in midstream.

He stood there for several minutes enjoying the view, until the icy wind became too much for his coat to cope with. Back at the hotel he had a nightcap in an otherwise deserted bar, went to bed, and fell asleep with surprising ease.

He woke early, though, and found that the Europaischer Hof considered breakfast an unnecessary luxury. There were, however, plenty of workingmen's cafés selling hot rolls and coffee around the station. By eight he was driving through the town centre, heading for the northern suburb of Wik, where the main harbour for merchant ships was situated. He had already finished his article on German sailors, but the Gestapo weren't to know that, and he needed an honest reason for being in Kiel. Over the next couple of hours he talked to sailors in the cafés on the Wik waterfront, before moving on to the eastern end of the Kiel Canal, which lay just beyond. There he watched a Swedish freighter pass through the double locks which protected the canal from tidal changes, chatting all the while with an old man who used to work there, and who still came to watch. Driving back along the western shore of the haven Russell got a better view of the warship he'd seen the night before. It was the recently commissioned *Scharnhorst*, and its guns were lowered towards the deck, as if apologising for their existence. Two U-boats were tied up alongside.

He wasn't hungry but had lunch anyway, along with a couple of beers to calm his nerves, before following the tracks of the Wellingdorf tram through Gaarden. The Germania Bar wasn't hard to spot – as Gert had said, it was almost opposite the main gate of the Deutsche Werke shipyard – and there was no shortage of places to leave the car. The bar itself was on the ground floor of a four-storey building, and seemed remarkably quiet for a lunch hour. He drove another few hundred metres towards Wellingdorf before turning and retracing the route back to Kiel.

With Paul's birthday in mind, he spent the rest of the afternoon looking round the shops in the town centre. The two toy emporiums he found were uninspiring, and he'd almost given up when he came across a small nautical shop in one of the narrower side streets. Pride of place in the window display had been given to a model of the *Preussen* which, as Paul had once told him, was the only sailing ship ever built with square sails on five masts. The price made him wince, but the model, on closer inspection, looked even better than it had in the window. Paul would love it.

Russell carefully carried the glass case back to the car, did his best to immobilise it in the back, and covered it with the small rug he'd bought for Effi's use on Rugen Island. He checked his watch – another five hours until his appointment at the Germania Bar – and went back to the Europaischer Hof, hoping to while the time away with a nap. Despite the unexpected bonus of a hot bath, he found sleep impossible, and just lay on the bed watching the room grow darker. Around five o'clock he turned on the lights and expanded the notes he'd made that morning.

At seven he walked across to the station for something to eat and another beer, eschewing a second with some difficulty. The concourse was full of boisterous sailors in *Scharnhorst* caps, presumably going on leave.

Back at the hotel, he collected his suitcase, handed in his key, and walked out to the Hanomag. As he headed for Gaarden the road seemed empty, but Gaarden itself was getting ready for Friday night, the open doorways of numerous bars and restaurants spilling light across the cobbled streets and tramlines. There were a lot of sailors in evidence, a lot of women awaiting their pleasure, but no sign of the police.

He parked up against the shipyard wall and sat for a minute, examining the Germania Bar. Conversation and laughter drifted out through the open door, along with a smell of fried onions. Light edged the closed curtains in all but one of the upstairs windows; in the darkened exception a man could be seen leaning out, a cigarette bobbing between his lips. It was a brothel, Russell realised. And it was three minutes to eight.

He could feel his heart beating as he climbed out of the Hanomag, checked it was locked, and waited for a tram to pass before crossing the road. The bar was bigger inside than the outside suggested, with two walls of booths, a few tables and a small area for dancing should anyone feel the need. It was plusher than he'd expected, and cleaner. The booths were bound in leather, the bar itself highly polished. There were several young sailors to be seen, but most of the men, like Russell, were either entering or enjoying middle age inside their respectable overcoats. He took his off, seated himself in one of the two remaining empty booths, and laid *Martin Chuzzlewit* face up on the table.

'Good book?' the waitress asked him. 'Chuzzlewit,' she said with a laugh, 'what sort of name is that?'

'English,' he told her.

'That explains it. What would you like?'

He ordered a *Goldwasser*, and looked round the room. A few faces had looked his way when he entered, but no one had shown any obvious interest since. One of the sailors stood up, playfully pulled his female companion to her feet, and headed for a door in the back wall. As it opened, the bottom of a staircase came into view.

The *Goldwasser* arrived, and a female companion shortly thereafter. She was about his age, thin verging on scrawny, with dark-circled eyes and a tired smile. 'Buy me a drink, Herr Russell,' she suggested in a low voice, before he could say he was waiting for someone else. She leaned across the table, put a hand over his, and whispered: 'After we've had a drink we'll go upstairs, and you'll get what you came for.'

He ordered her drink, a sweet martini.

'I am Geli,' she said, stroking his hand with an absent-minded air. 'And what are you doing in Kiel?'

'I'm a journalist,' he said, joining the charade. 'I'm writing a story about the widening of the Kiel Canal.'

'Extra width is always good,' she said wryly. 'Let's go up. I can see you're impatient.'

He followed her up two flights of stairs, watching the hem of her red dress swish against her black-stockinged calves. There were four rooms on the second floor, and pleasure was being noisily taken in at least one of them. Through the open door of a bathroom he caught sight of a plump blonde wearing only black stockings and a suspender belt, drying herself with a towel.

'In here,' Geli said, opening a door and gesturing him in. 'I'll be back in a few minutes,' she added, closing it behind him.

There was a window that overlooked an alley, and a threadbare carpet that covered half the wooden floor. A bare light bulb illuminated a large unmade bed which was supported in one corner by a pile of books. On the bed's wooden headboard someone had written 'Goebbels was here', and someone else had added 'So that's how I got this disease'. Enough to put anyone off, Russell thought.

The door opened and a man came in, closely followed by Geli. He was younger than her, but not by much. He had fair hair, blue eyes and skin which had seen too much sun and wind. He was wearing a sailor's greatcoat.

He shook Russell's hand, and sat down heavily on the bed, causing it to creak alarmingly. Geli stood with her back to the window, half-sitting on the sill, watching the man unpick the seam of his coat lining with a penknife. It only took a few seconds. Reaching inside he pulled out a small sheaf of papers and handed them over to Russell.

It looked like a small sheaf, but there were more than thirty sheets of text and diagrams, all copied out onto the thinnest available paper. 'These are not the originals,' Russell thought out loud.

'If they were, the navy would know they were gone,' the man said wearily, as if he was explaining matters to a particularly obtuse child.

'Are there other copies?' Russell asked.

'One. For your successor, should you fail.'

'And then you'll need another one for his successor.'

The man offered him a grudging smile. 'Something like that.'

'Can I ask you a question?'

'Go ahead.'

'Why not send this out by radio?

The man nodded at the papers. 'Look at it. By the time we got that lot out every direction-finding squad in Germany would be banging on our door. And you can't convey maps by radio, not with any ease.' He offered a fleeting smile. 'We used to post stuff to the Soviet Embassy in Berlin, but they got wise. They open everything now. Everything.'

Russell folded the papers in two and stuffed them into his inside pocket. 'I have a better hiding place in my car,' he explained.

'Thank God for that. Look, I must go before …'

There was a sudden roar from below. 'The storm-troopers have arrived,' Geli said. 'Don't worry,' she told Russell, 'they're not here for you.'

'They fuck our women, fuck our country, and soon they'll be fucking Europe,' the man said. 'But we'll have them in the end.' He shook Russell's hand again and wished him good luck. 'I'll see you later,' he told Geli, and slipped out of the door.

'Just wait a few minutes,' she told Russell, 'and I'll take you down.'

They were long minutes, but they eventually passed. As they went down, a storm-trooper was coming up, almost dragging a girl in his wake. 'Slow down, Klaus,' Geli pleaded with him – 'she'll be no use to you unconscious.' He grinned at her, as if consciousness was neither here nor there.

The noise from the bar had grown deafening. 'The back door might be better,' Geli said, and led him out through a bright but empty kitchen. 'Just right and right again,' she said, and closed the door behind him, removing most of the light. Russell felt his way along the back wall to the building's corner, from where he could make out the dimly lit road. As he started down the side of the building a silhouette loomed in the mouth of the alley, a man in high boots, with a cap on his head.

Russell froze, heart thumping in his chest. The man was moving towards him, reaching for something with his hand …

His trouser buttons. A couple of metres into the alley he turned, pulled out his penis and, with a loud exhalation, arced a fierce stream of dull golden piss against the wall. Russell stood there, petrified of making any movement, wondering whether it would ever end. A ship in the bay sounded a long and mournful blow on its horn, but still the piss streamed out, forcing the man to shift his feet away from the spreading lake.

The arc finally collapsed. The storm-trooper gave a few pumps for luck, stuffed himself into his trousers and headed for the alley entrance. And then he was gone.

Russell hurried forward, hoping to escape before someone else had the same idea. He almost stepped in the prodigious puddle, but reached the entrance without mishap. His car was sitting across the road, hopelessly sandwiched between the two open lorries which had brought the storm-troopers.

He hurried across, climbed in and started the engine. Five or six manoeuvres later, he was still only halfway out. The temptation to ram the lorries was almost overwhelming, but he doubted whether the Hanomag had the weight to move them if he did. Fighting back desperation, he shifted the car, inch by inch, further into the road. He was almost there when several storm-troopers emerged from the door across the road and started shouting at him. He was about to try a final, metal-scraping, lunge for freedom when he realised they were killing themselves with laughter. They had hemmed him in as a practical joke.

He opened the window and made a wry face, acknowledging their brilliant sense of humour. Three more manoeuvres and he was free, U-turning the Hanomag in front of them with a triumphant raise of the hand. As he headed south towards the centre of Gaarden he could see them happily waving goodbye in his rear-view mirror.

His hotel bed was waiting for him, but it didn't seem far enough away. He wanted, he realised, to get out of Kiel, and as quickly as possible. It was still only nine – time enough to find a small guesthouse in a small town, somewhere between here and Lübeck.

He took the more northerly of the Lübeck roads, and once in open country found a wide verge on which to pull over. With ears alert for approaching traffic he turned on the car light, opened up the false bottom of the suitcase, and placed the papers inside. He had planned to copy them for the British that night, but he'd need a whole weekend to copy this lot. He would have to be selective. They'd be none the wiser.

About ten kilometres further on, he found the town and guesthouse he was looking for. It wasn't much more than a village bar, but the woman who ran it was happy to provide him with a room. 'It was my son's,' she said, without explaining where he'd gone. The sundry toys and books suggested he was expected back.

Once locked in, Russell retrieved the papers from the false bottom and skip-read through them. They were what Irina Borskaya had claimed they were – a detailed rundown of the German navy's current and contingency disposition in the Baltic. Most of the key information seemed to be included in the three maps which accompanied the text, and Russell set out to copy these. The British, he thought, should be thankful for whatever he could give them.

The maps were highly detailed, and it took him almost four hours to finish his work. He felt as if he had only just got to sleep when the landlady knocked on his door suggesting breakfast, and it was indeed only seven o'clock. Still, breakfast was good, and the sun was already above the horizon. Her son, it transpired, had joined the navy.

Russell set out for Berlin soon after nine, papers and copies hidden in the false bottom, the suitcase itself wedged under the eye-catching model of the *Preussen*. There was no need, of course – no roadblock, no spot-checks, no officious small-town policemen eager to find fault with a car bearing a Berlin licence plate. Soon after one, he parked the Hanomag outside Zoo ztation, pulled out the suitcase and nervously carried it in to the left luggage.

'Nice day,' the clerk said, taking the case and handing over a numbered ticket.

'So far,' Russell agreed. He rang Effi from the telephone stand along the hall and told her things had gone to plan. She sounded as relieved as he felt. 'I'm going home to collect some clean clothes, and do a bit more shopping for Paul,' he told her. 'I'll see you about six.'

She told him they had tickets for a revue at one of the smaller theatres near Alexanderplatz, and he tried, in vain, to sound enthusiastic. 'I'm just tired,' he explained. 'I'll be fine by then.'

He certainly felt safer with the suitcase squirrelled away in Zoo station's cavernous left luggage. There was always the ticket of course, but if the worst came to the worst that was small enough to eat. Back at the car, he examined the model ship for the first time in daylight, and congratulated himself on his choice – it really was beautiful.

Frau Heidegger thought so too, and conjured up a bright red ribbon which she'd been saving for such an eventuality. There were messages from both his agents: Jake Brandon had sent a sarcastic wire from New York demanding copy, and Solly Bernstein had phoned to tell Russell that 'his friends' had arrived in London. He was still smiling when he reached his third floor room.

After a much-needed bath and change of clothes, he piled several more changes into his usual suitcase and carried it out to the car. Lunch at Wertheim was followed by a leisurely stroll round the toy department, and the acquisition of two other gifts which Paul had expressed an interest in. A book shop further down Leipzigstrasse supplied a third. He was probably spending too much, but he might never get another chance.

He managed to stay awake through the revue, but was unable to conceal his dismay when Effi suggested dancing. She took pity on him. 'I know what'll wake you up,' she said as they climbed the stairs to her flat, and she was right. Afterwards, she showed him what she had bought for Paul – the gorgeous encyclopaedia of animals which he had admired on their last visit to the zoo shop.

Next morning they joined several hundred other Berliners on the pavement of the Ku'damm, well-wrapped against the cold at their outside table, rustling newspapers, sipping coffee and nibbling cake. This was how it used to be, Russell thought – ordinary Germans doing ordinary things, enjoying their simple civilised pleasures.

His newspaper, though, told a different story. While he'd been slinking round Kiel, the Czechs had lost patience with the German-backed Slovaks, sacking their provincial government and arresting their prime minister. The *Beobachter* was apoplectic – what nation could countenance such a level of disturbance just beyond its borders? Some sort of German intervention seemed inevitable, but then it always had. If the separatists won then Czechoslovakia would disintegrate; if denied, their campaign would simply continue. Either set of circumstances would generate enough turmoil for Hitler's purposes.

Looking up from his paper, the pavement café-dwellers no longer seemed content in their simple pleasures. They looked tense, weary, anxious. They looked as though a war was hanging over their heads.

After lunch with Effi he drove over to Grunewald, dropped off his presents, collected his son and gave him a birthday hug. Twenty minutes later they were picking up Thomas in Lutzow and heading for the Plumpe. Thomas's son Joachim had started his *arbeitsdienst* the previous week, and was repairing roads in the Moselle valley.

The weather was fine, but the team proved incapable of providing Paul with a birthday present. They lost 2–0, and were lucky not to lose by more. Paul's despondency didn't last long – by the time they were halfway to his home he was full of the party in prospect, and forgetful of Hertha's dark betrayal.

Effi was already there when they arrived, talking happily to Thomas's fourteen-year-old daughter Lotte. Over the next hour around a dozen of Paul's friends – all of them male – were delivered by their parents, some in their Sunday best, some, for reasons best known to their parents, in their *Jungvolk* uniforms. The games they played seem surprisingly violent, but that, Russell supposed, was part of the same depressing mind-set. At least they hadn't replaced 'pin the tail on the donkey' with 'pin the nose on the Jew'. Yet. He would write a piece on children for the 'Ordinary Germans' series, he decided. When he got back from Prague.

Still, Paul seemed happy and popular, which was something to celebrate. The adults – Ilse and Matthias, Thomas and his wife Hanna, Russell and Effi – sat together in the huge kitchen, drinking Matthias's excellent wine. They smiled and laughed and toasted each other, but the talk was of happier times in the past, of how things used to be. At one point, watching Ilse as she listened to somebody else, Russell had a mental picture of her in Moscow fifteen years earlier, eyes alive with hopes of a better world. Now all of them were backing into the future, frightened to look ahead. They had their own bubble, but for how long?

The evening ended, bringing tomorrow that much closer. After congratulating each other on how well their presents had been received, both he and Effi lapsed into silence for most of the journey home. They were turning into her street when she suddenly suggested accompanying him to Prague.

'No,' he said. 'There's no point in us both taking the risk.' He switched off the car. 'And you're a German – they'd try you for treason. They'd have more options with me.'

'Like what?'

'Oh, I don't know. Swapping me for one of their spies, maybe.'

'Or just shooting you.'

'I doubt it. But I think having you there would make me more nervous. And more likely to give myself away.'

She searched his face, and seemed satisfied with what she found. 'All right,' she said. 'It's no fun just waiting by the phone, you know.'

'I know.'

Upstairs, he noticed the script on her dressing table and had an idea. 'Can you get another copy for yourself?' he asked.

'I don't see why not. I could say I burnt the first one in a fit of despair. But why?'

'I thought I'd take it with me in the suitcase. Camouflage. And one of your publicity shots would be good.'

She went and got one, a head and shoulders shot taken a couple of years earlier.

'Your face would distract anyone,' he said.

It was still dark when Russell woke and he lay there for a while, listening to Effi's breathing and enjoying the warmth of her body. At seven-thirty he forced himself out of bed, washed and dressed in the bathroom, and finally woke her to say goodbye as she had insisted he must. She enfolded him in a sleepy embrace, then swung her legs out of bed and arched her back in a huge stretch. As he descended the stairs she stood in her nightdress by the half-open door, blowing him a farewell kiss.

Berlin was already waking to another working week. The Avus Speedway was busy, but only in the other direction, and he reached

Potsdam well before nine. After parking the Hanomag near the main post office in Wilhelmplatz, he lingered over breakfast in the coffee shop next door. The newspapers, as expected, were revelling in the misery of the Czechs.

At ten past nine he presented himself at the poste restante desk, and signed for the familiar envelope. Walking back to the Hanomag, he felt like a man who'd just been handed a ticking bomb. Not to worry, he thought – he'd soon have two.

The drive back was slower, and it was gone ten when he turned off the Ku'damm and saw the glass roof of Zoo station framed by the buildings on either side of Joachimsthaler-strasse. He parked the Hanomag near the Tiergarten gate which he and Gert had used, inserted the folded envelope in his inside coat pocket, picked up the suitcase, and walked back to the nearest station entrance.

There was a queue for the left luggage, but no sign of the police, or of anyone loitering suspiciously. When his turn came Russell handed over his ticket, watched the clerk disappear, and waited for a thousand sirens to go off. A child in the queue behind him suddenly screeched, making him jump. A train rumbled overhead, but the roof didn't fall. The clerk returned with the suitcase, took Russell's money, and handed it over.

Next stop was the men's toilet. The cubicles were small, and entering one with two suitcases required a level of planning which was almost beyond him. He clattered his way in, locked the door behind him, and sat on the seat for a few moments to recover what fragments of equanimity he still retained. The walls didn't reach to the ceiling, but the adjoining cubicles were both empty, at least for the moment.

He stood up, put the smaller suitcase on the toilet seat, and opened it up. After unclicking the false bottom, he removed the three maps he had copied, replaced them with McKinley's papers, and closed the false bottom again. A brief struggle then ensued, as he fought to open the other suitcase in what little remaining space the cubicle had to offer. Half its contents ended up on the floor, but all were eventually transferred to the smaller suitcase, which was now satisfyingly full. After checking that the three maps were in his coat pocket, he closed both suitcases, pulled the chain, and fought his way out of the cubicle.

The man at the left luggage looked surprised to see him again, but accepted the empty suitcase without comment, and handed him a new ticket. On the platform above he waited for a westbound Stadtbahn, thinking that this was where McKinley had died and where the Wiesners had left Hitler behind. On the far platform a man was angrily shaking a burnt almond machine, just as another man had been doing at Friedrichstrasse on the morning he returned from Danzig.

His train arrived and set off again, skirting the northern edge of the Tiergarten, crossing and re-crossing the Spree on its three-stop journey to Friedrichstrasse. Russell went out through the less frequented car park entrance and walked briskly towards the Embassy. His steps on the pavements sounded unusually loud, and every car that didn't stop seemed like a gift from God. Halfway across the Unter den Linden he decided that if anyone challenged him now, he would sprint through the Embassy doors and never come out again.

But no one did. As before, he asked the receptionist for Unsworth and Unsworth for Trelawney-Smythe. The latter looked at the three maps as if he couldn't believe his luck. 'Where did you get them?' he demanded.

'A comrade in Kiel,' was all Russell would tell him. 'A one-off,' he added. 'There won't be any more.'

'But how do I know these are genuine?'

'I guess you don't. But they are. And your people must have ways of confirming at least some of it.'

'Perhaps.'

Russell took a meaningful look at his watch. 'I have a train to catch.'

'And where are you off to this time?' Trelawney-Smythe asked, sounding almost friendly.

'Prague.'

'Ah, joining Adolf's reception committee.'

'I hope not.'

Dropping in on Unsworth to say goodbye, he was told much the same. 'And the British guarantee of Czechoslovakia?' Russell asked sarcastically.

'Without Slovakia there is no Czechoslovakia,' Unsworth said. 'And therefore no guarantee.'

'Neat,' Russell said.

'Very,' Unsworth agreed.

Out on the street, Russell hailed a passing taxi. 'Anhalter Bahnhof,' he told the driver. It seemed that he and Hitler were heading in the same direction.

The train to Prague left at noon, and was scheduled to arrive in the Czech capital shortly before seven. Russell boarded it with a sinking sensation in his stomach, and an alcohol-rich lunch in the dining car did nothing to improve matters.

The lunchtime editions carried the news that the Slovak premier Monsignor Tiso had been 'invited' to Berlin. He had, over the past couple of days, seemed surprisingly reluctant to tip over the Czech applecart, and the Führer was doubtless anxious to offer him some kindly advice. Their trains would cross at some point, Russell guessed. He would watch the passing windows for a prelate with a death wish.

Speaking of which ... he reminded himself that the Wiesners were in London, that foreigners were hardly ever searched, that the next life was bound to be better than this one. He fought off a momentary impulse to quit the train at Dresden, the only stop before the frontier. If he did, the Soviets would probably come looking for him with murder in mind. And he could hardly blame them – a deal was a deal.

As the train wound its way up the upper Elbe valley towards the frontier he compiled a compendium of possible explanations for the material in his false-bottomed suitcase that a reefer-smoking Neville Chamberlain would have found impossible to believe. As Gert had said, the important thing was not to be searched.

As the train slowed for the border inspection his heart speeded up. They came to a halt in a wide ravine, shared by double tracks and the loud, foaming river. The snow-speckled walls of the valley rose steeply on either side, and the long, low building which housed the emigration and customs services was partly suspended over the rushing waters. The river ruled out escape in one direction, and the tall electrified fence beyond the tracks precluded any hope of flight in the other. Like rats in a maze, Russell thought – only one way to go.

The loudspeakers suspended from the searchlight pylons crackled into life. All passengers were requested to leave the train and form a queue on the narrow strip of tarmac alongside the tracks.

There were about two hundred people in the queue, Russell reckoned, and they were filing into the building at a gratifying rate. Just a quick look at documents, he thought, and on we go. Beside him the train lurched forward, ready to pick up its passengers on the other side. Without its comforting presence Russell felt suddenly vulnerable.

Finally, he could see through the doorway. Uniformed officers sat behind two desks, while others hovered in the background, sizing up potential prey. Further on, two pairs of officers stood behind tables, searching through bags and suitcases. The first hurdle presented itself. The officer looked at his passport, and then at his face. 'Your name?' he asked, and for a split second Russell's mind was a terrifying blank.

'John Russell,' he said, as if he hadn't been concentrating.

'Birth date?'

That was easier. '8 August 1899.'

'Thank you,' the official said, and handed him back his passport. Russell moved on, carefully avoiding all eye contact. Ignore me, he silently pleaded with the customs officials behind the tables.

In vain. 'You,' the nearest said. 'Open your case, please.'

Russell placed it on the table, willing his hands not to shake as he clicked the case open. The man and his blond partner stared for a second at the top layer of clothes, and the partner started digging around with his hands. 'What's this?' he asked, pulling out Effi's script. *A Girl from the Mountains*?

'It's a film script,' Russell said. 'My girlfriend's an actress,' he added. 'Her photograph's inside.'

The partner extracted it and both men took a good look. 'I've seen her in something,' the first man said.

His partner rubbed his chin with forefinger and thumb. 'I have too.'

'I remember,' the first man said. 'She was the wife of that guy who got killed by the Reds ...'

'*The Necessary Sacrifice*,' Russell suggested helpfully.

'That's the one. And she's your girlfriend?'

'Uh-huh.'

'You're a lucky man,' the partner said, replacing the photograph and closing the suitcase.

Russell had never heard a more beautiful click. 'I know it,' he said with a grateful smile. Suitcase in hand, he walked out through the open doorway, repressing the urge to skip and dance.

The train pulled into Prague's Masaryk station at twenty past seven. On the streets it felt more like midnight – they were dark and mostly deserted, as if the city's people were all at home, hunched over their radio sets. He had never seen Wenceslas Square so empty, even at four in the morning.

The Grand was fully operational though, its multi-lingual staff and art nouveau fittings a match for any barbarian invasion. Russell had stayed there twice before, once in the late twenties and once, the previous September, when Chamberlain and Daladier were licking Hitler's boots in Munich. He asked the receptionist if anything crucial had happened in the last seven hours, and was told that it hadn't. Monsignor Tiso, he supposed, was still *en route* to Berlin.

Russell's room was on the first floor, at the back. Apart from the lack of a view it seemed thoroughly adequate. But then, after those few moments at the frontier, a pigsty would have seemed adequate, provided it was in Czechoslovakia. He dumped the unopened suitcase on the bed and went back down in search of dinner.

The hotel restaurant also seemed a lot emptier than usual, but the baked carp, fruit dumplings and South Moravian white wine were all delicious. A walk seemed in order, but he reluctantly decided against one – his train left at 11.40 on the following morning and he was anxious for the Soviets to collect their papers. The thought of having to dump them in the Vltava was more than he could bear.

He didn't have long to wait. Shortly before ten he answered a familiar-sounding tap on his door, and found Irina Borskaya anxiously glancing up the corridor. 'Come in,' he said superfluously – she had already dodged under his arm. She was wearing the same long, charcoal grey skirt, but a different blouse. Her hair seemed a shade lighter, and this time there was a hint of bright red lipstick on her thin lips.

'The papers,' she said, sitting down on the upright chair.

'It's nice to see you too,' Russell said, opening the suitcase. After dumping his possessions onto the bed, he clicked the false bottom open, removed the sheaf of papers he'd picked up in Gaarden, and handed it over.

'What are those?' she asked, as he placed the envelope containing McKinley's papers on the bedside table.

'A story I'm working on.'

She gave him a disbelieving look, but said nothing. After flicking through the naval dispositions, she reached inside her blouse and brought out a money clip containing Swiss franc notes. High denomination Swiss franc notes. 'We promised to pay you well,' she said, as if reprimanding him for any possible doubts he might have had on that score.

'Thank you,' he said. 'It's been a pleasure doing business with you.'

'There is no need for the pleasure to end,' she said. 'We have other work …'

'No,' Russell said firmly. 'We had a simple deal – you helped my friend out of Germany, I brought your papers to Prague. We're quits. I wish the Soviet Union well, but not well enough to die for it.'

'Very well,' she said, rising from the chair and cradling the papers in one arm. The fact that she had no obvious place to conceal them led Russell to the conclusion that her room was close to his own. 'If that is how you feel,' she told him, 'then we understand. And we thank you for what you have done.'

Somewhat astonished by the ease with which his resignation had been accepted, Russell opened the door for her.

'When are you leaving?' she asked.

'Tomorrow morning.'

'Then have a good journey.' She put her head out, glanced to left and right, and walked off down the corridor in the direction of the stairs. The whole encounter had taken less than five minutes.

Before going downstairs next morning Russell wrote a short covering letter to McKinley's editor in San Francisco, explaining how he had come by the papers and offering his own brief summary of their significance. After breakfast in the hotel restaurant he walked around the corner to the main post office on Jindrisská, bought and addressed a large envelope, and asked for the quickest possible delivery. 'It'll be gone before he gets here,' the clerk observed, reading Russell's mind. 'On the afternoon plane to Paris,' he added in explanation.

Satisfied, Russell walked back to the Grand, collected his suitcase and checked out. He was early for the train but he liked Masaryk station, and he liked the idea of being closer to home.

As it turned out, it didn't matter, because he no longer had a seat or even standing room on the train. Two carriages, including his own, had been commandeered by President Hacha and his swollen entourage. The Czech president, Russell gathered from discussions with sundry railway officials, had also been 'invited' to Berlin, and a heart condition prohibited him from flying. Russell was assured that two extra carriages would be added to the night train, but no one seemed capable of explaining why they couldn't be added to this one.

Oh well, Russell thought, there were many worse places to spend a day than Prague. As President Hacha and his dicey heart were about to find out.

He left the suitcase in the left luggage, took a tram back to the town centre, and spent the next couple of hours ambling down the east bank of the river. The Czech flag was still flying from the ramparts of the famous castle, but for how long? A few days at most, Russell thought, and the city's residents seemed to agree with him. As he walked back through the old town in search of a late lunch, he noticed rapidly lengthening queues at one baker after another. News of Hacha's trip had obviously spread.

This was it, Russell thought – the end of any lingering hopes for peace. There was no way of presenting this as part of some grand scheme to bring Germans home to the Reich. Hitler had thrown off the cloak. It was no longer if, but when.

The sight of an Orthodox Jew on Národní Street reminded him of Albert. Long gone, he hoped, but what of Czechoslovakia's 100,000 Jews? What were they doing this afternoon? Crowding the stations, loading their cars – or just sitting tight and hoping for the best, as so many German Jews had done? This Orthodox Jew had a bagful of groceries, and seemed in no hurry to go anywhere.

He thought about what Albert had said during the drive to Görlitz, that kindness had become more worthy of note, and more interesting to fathom, than cruelty. It was certainly harder to find.

With darkness falling he sought out a bar, and sampled several different Bohemian beers. Each tasted better than the last. He raised a toast to McKinley's papers, now hopefully resting in some Parisian sorting-office, and another to McKinley himself. From time to time, over the last six weeks, he had found himself wondering why they had killed the young American. It was the wrong question to ask, he realised. It was like asking why they had killed Felix

Wiesner. They might have had, or thought they had, particular motives, but the real reason was much simpler – they were killers. It was what they were. It was, in truth, all that they were.

The cold air streaming through his cab's broken window kept him awake on his way back to the station, but once ensconced in the overheated train he soon found himself falling asleep. The jerk of departure woke him for long enough to recline his seat, and the last thing he remembered was that he should have phoned Effi.

The next thing he knew he was waking with a sudden feeling of panic. He looked at his watch. Almost three hours had passed – they had to be nearing the frontier. But that didn't matter any more, he told himself. His subconscious was obviously stuck on the outward journey.

And then it occurred to him. He had never closed the false bottom. After Borskaya had gone he had just shifted the suitcase onto the floor, and this morning he had simply shovelled all the clothes back in.

The thought of another wrestle with a suitcase in a toilet made him groan, but it had to be done. He took it down from the overhead rack, and carried it out to the vestibule at the end of the car. Shading his eyes with his hands, and sticking his face up against the window, he could just make out the river running beside the tracks.

Inside the toilet he opened the suitcase, threw all the clothes on the floor, and went to close the false bottom.

It was already closed.

He stood there for a few moments, thinking back. When had he done it?

He hadn't.

Clicking it open, he found several sheets of paper hidden inside.

Holding the first one up to the dim light of the cubicle, he found that it contained a list of names and addresses – six under Ruhr, three under Hamburg. The other sheets – there were nine of them – followed a similar pattern. There were almost a hundred people listed, from all the different parts of Germany.

Who were they? No indication was given, none at all. But one thing was certain – the Soviets meant them to be discovered. That was why Borskaya had asked him when he was leaving, Russell thought – they had been inserted while he was downstairs at breakfast or out posting McKinley's papers. That was why she'd accepted his resignation so easily. And the money – that worked both ways. Such generosity might keep him working for them, but if it didn't, it could be turned into a threat – possession of so much foreign currency would be hard to explain.

The names, he realised, had to be German communists – real or imaginary. Were these men and women whom Stalin wanted culled, but who were beyond his reach? Or was the list a work of fiction, something to keep the Gestapo busy while the real communists got on with their work? A bit of both, Russell guessed. A few real communists to keep the Gestapo believing, and then the wild goose chase.

He shivered at the nearness of his escape, and realised that the train was slowing down. He shoved the suitcase to the floor, yanked up the lid of the toilet, and started tearing the sheets of paper into smaller and smaller pieces. Once these were all in the bowl he reached for the lever, filled with the sudden dread that it wouldn't work.

It didn't. As beads of cold sweat multiplied on his forehead, Russell worked the lever again. It coughed up some water, but nowhere near enough.

There was a heavy knock on the door. 'We are approaching the frontier,' a German voice said.

'Right,' Russell shouted back. What should he do? Try and swallow all the bits of paper, along with whatever international germs the toilet bowl had been saving for him? Anything but that.

The train was still decelerating. He looked for some access to the toilet's workings, but everything was screwed down. He tried the lever one more time, more out of habit than hope, and for reasons known only to God it flushed. He stood there, revelling in the sight of empty water, until sweet relief gave way to a nightmare vision of Gestapo officers combing the tracks for all the pieces and painstakingly gluing them back together.

'Get a grip,' he murmured to himself. He picked up the suitcase, clicked the false bottom shut, and covered it with clothing retrieved from the floor. As he left the toilet he caught a glimpse of his face in the mirror, and wished he hadn't. He looked deranged.

The train was still moving, the lighted platform of the Czech border point unrolling past the window. It was snowing now, thick flakes drifting down through the cones of light. 'We are not stopping at the Czech crossing point tonight,' the German railway official was saying to a female passenger. No Czechoslovakia, no border, Russell thought. Did that mean they were not stopping at the German border either?

No such luck.

The passengers climbed down onto the platform, a long strip of spotlit tarmac in a sea of darkness. As Russell joined the queue, a new and highly unwelcome thought occurred to him. If the sheets were meant to be found, there had to have been a tip-off. The false bottom might be empty, but it was still a false bottom.

One explanation seemed workable, but only if the officials on duty were different from the ones he had encountered the day before. As the queue sucked him out of the snow and into the building, he anxiously examined the faces, but there were none he recognised.

The immigration official took one look at his passport and gestured to a man in plain clothes behind him. Gestapo. 'This way, Herr Russell,' the man said, without looking at his passport. He walked across to a large table, where another man in plain clothes was waiting.

'Put your suitcase on the table,' the first man said. He had long hair for the Gestapo, and an almost likable face. As he opened the suitcase, Russell noticed that his fingernails badly needed trimming.

'Could I have your name and rank?' Russell asked.

'Ascherl, *Kriminalassistent*,' he said without looking up.

He carefully took out the clothes, and piled them on the other end of the table. Effi's script was placed on the top. Then he ran his hands round the inside of the suitcase, obviously looking for a way of accessing the false bottom. Borskaya had been behind him when he opened it in the hotel room, Russell remembered.

'How do you open it?' Ascherl asked him.

Russell looked perplexed. 'It's open.'

'The hidden compartment,' the Gestapo officer said patiently.

Russell tried to look even more perplexed. 'What are you talking about?'

Ascherl turned to his subordinate. 'Your knife, Schneider.'

Schneider pulled out a large pocket-knife. Ascherl looked at the suitcase for a moment, ran his hand along inside it, then abruptly turned it upside down, pressed in the knife, and patiently sawed from one side of the bottom to the other. 'This hidden compartment,' he said, reaching in a hand.

His look of triumph faded as his scrabbling hand failed to find anything in it. Two more cuts and he was able to wrench back a section of the reinforced leather bottom and shine a torch inside.

'Where is it?' he asked patiently.

'Where is what?' Russell replied, trying to sound bewildered. Most of the others in the room were watching them now, eager to see how the situation played out.

'Let me put it another way,' the Gestapo officer said. 'What reason do you have for carrying a suitcase with a hidden compartment?'

'That's simple. I didn't know it had one. I only bought it yesterday, from a Jew in Prague.' He smiled, as if the answer had just occurred to him. 'The bastard probably used it to smuggle valuables out of the Reich.'

'Undoubtedly,' Ascherl said.

Russell was still thanking heaven for his inspiration when he noticed a new face in the room – one of the customs officials from the day before. The man was looking straight at him, with an expression on his face that seemed part indignation, part amusement.

'But you are from Berlin,' Ascherl continued. 'Did you travel to Prague without a suitcase?'

'It fell apart when I was there. I needed a new one.' Russell braced himself for an intervention by the customs official, but there was none.

'And this Jew just happened along?'

'No, there's a market, like the ones they used to have in Berlin.' The customs official was still looking at him, still saying nothing. Was it possible that he didn't remember this suitcase from the day before?

'You wallet, please,' the Gestapo officer said.

Russell handed it over, and watched him remove the currency – a few Czech notes, some Reichsmarks, the clip of Swiss francs.

'Where did these come from?' Ascherl asked.

'I wrote an article for a Soviet paper, and they paid me in Swiss francs. Several months ago now. I thought they might be useful in

Prague. The SD knows all about this,' he added. 'Look,' he said, indicating the wallet, 'can I show you something?'

Ascherl handed it back, and Russell pulled out the folded sheet of Sturmbannführer Kleist's letter.

As the Gestapo man read it, Russell watched his face. If the list had been found in the hidden compartment then the letter could have been ignored. As it was, all Ascherl had was a story full of holes that he couldn't fill in. Would he keep on trying, and risk falling foul of the big boys on Wilhelmstrasse?

'I see,' he said finally, and looked up at Russell. 'It seems we are all victims of the same plot. We received information … well, I won't go into that. It looks as though the Reds have tried to set you up.'

'The suitcase was suspiciously cheap,' Russell admitted. Across the room the customs official was still watching, still doing his Mona Lisa impersonation.

'It's not worth much now,' Ascherl said, surveying his knife-work.

Russell smiled. 'You were doing your duty, as any friend of the Reich would wish.'

Ascherl smiled back. 'We have others. Confiscated from Jews. Perhaps we can find you another one with a hidden compartment. Schneider?'

Ascherl's assistant disappeared into an adjoining room and re-emerged almost immediately with two suitcases. Russell chose the smaller of the two, and packed it with his clothes and Effi's script. The customs official had disappeared.

But not for long. As Russell came out of the building the man fell into step beside him. 'Nice suitcase,' he said.

Russell stopped.

'I'm getting married next month,' the man said, carefully

positioning himself between Russell and any watchers in the building they had just left.

Russell took out his wallet, removed the clip of Swiss francs, and handed it over. 'A wedding present?'

The man smiled, gave him an ironic click of the heels, and strode away.

Russell walked on towards the train. The snow was heavier now, tumbling down through the pools of light, flakes clinging to the glistening wire. He could feel the sweat on his body slowly turning to ice.

The train, it seemed, was waiting only for him – the whistle shrilled as he stepped aboard. He made his way forward through the swaying cars, slumped into the reclining seat, and listened to the rhythmic clatter of the wheels, rolling him into the Reich.